Diving Ravens & Flying Dolphins

Mahesh Das

BLUEROSE PUBLISHERS
India | U.K.

Copyright © Mahesh Das 2025

All rights reserved by author. No part of this publication may be reproduced, stored in a retrieval system or transmitted in any form or by any means, electronic, mechanical, photocopying, recording or otherwise, without the prior permission of the author. Although every precaution has been taken to verify the accuracy of the information contained herein, the publisher assumes no responsibility for any errors or omissions. No liability is assumed for damages that may result from the use of information contained within.

BlueRose Publishers takes no responsibility for any damages, losses, or liabilities that may arise from the use or misuse of the information, products, or services provided in this publication.

For permissions requests or inquiries regarding this publication, please contact:

BLUEROSE PUBLISHERS
www.BlueRoseONE.com
info@bluerosepublishers.com
+91 8882 898 898
+4407342408967

ISBN: 978-93-7018-689-7

Cover Design: Aman Sharma
Typesetting: Pooja Sharma

First Edition: March 2025

Deep Blue Sea

Once upon a time on Earth, a magical dust of ash danced playfully with a drop of acid. Together, they formed an enchanting magnet that joyfully attracted vibrant fragments from across the galaxies. As these alien fragments united, the magnet transformed into lively avatars of an acid dwarf fish and an ash fire moth, embodying the beauty of diversity. This evolution brought a spark of excitement to the earth, and the sky chimed in with a joyful rain. Storms swirled with vibrant energy, and the tears of the sky turned into a vast saline universe, teeming with life and possibility. The currents playfully collided in a joyous chaos, creating a mesmerizing vortex. Then a dazzling lightning bolt kissed the swirling water, sending forth shock waves that birthed a radiant soul for the saline universe. In that electrifying moment of wonder, joy and adventure, the deep blue sea was born.

Blind Stone Civilization

In an age dominated by the sea, there thrived an ageless amphibious community known as the Ajna tribe, a unique lineage of humans cradled within the shells of turtles. These protective carapaces restricted their agility in comparison to their fellow humans. Yet, nature devised a means to pierce their encasement, presenting them with a poignant choice: to embrace full humanity at the expense of their immortality.

Human transformation happens when the Ajnas awaits the resurrection under the healing sun, guided by a mystical blind stone. This blind stone, a precious gem unearthed from the ocean's deepest abyss, was visible only to the blind. The restless souls of the Ajna who longed to shed their shells were compelled to gaze into the water's mirror while grasping the blind stone. As the journey toward self-acceptance unfolded beneath the sun's gentle embrace, their shells would gradually shatter, clearing the path for their metamorphosis into genuine humans. With the passage of time, the Ajna tribe flourished and evolved, save for Maya, a blind girl left behind. The tribe, unable to change Maya's fate used her for the sake of blind stone and abandoned her to the sea's embrace. There she stayed, isolated in her underwater realm, while the others advanced in their society anchored in the enigmatic blind stone civilization.

Contents

Deep Blue Sea 3

Blind Stone Civilization 4

The Sound of the Silence 1

The Light of the Dark 7

The Kiss of the Rain 23

The Echo of the Swans 38

A Cradle Over the Clouds 50

The Scent of the River 69

The Sweet of the Sea 85

The Flower of the Winter 105

The Wither of the Winter 125

The Frog Under the Mushroom 136

The Tears of The Romance 153

A Skeleton with Golden Fags 162

The Pleasure of the Pain 176

The Glitch of the Moon 191

The Vortex of the Aqua 206

The Key into the Self 222

The Quicksand of the Marshland 241

A Mirage of the Underwater 264

The Tail of the Truth 277

The Hex of the Turtle 299

A Cat with the Aerial Ears 307
The Nightmare of the Blind 323
The Diving Ravens and The Flying Dolphins 334

Chapter 1
The Sound of the Silence

Winter Vibe,

1993.

In a mystical land named Eerht, there lies an ancient town made from gold, nestled beside a mysterious brackish water mangrove known as Spooky Marsh. This enchanted town is surrounded by the tranquil waters of the Scent River, which meanders its way to meet the salty embrace of the Sweet Sea. And standing proudly by the sea is a majestic hill, known as Sleepy Slope, which is adorned with veins of glittering gold.

Eerht is divided by a majestic sight - the natural treasure on one side and the shimmering golden town on the other. The Ajna tribe crafted this opulent town using gold mined from the sleepy slope, blending architecture and wealth into one. The silent bridge serves as a pathway between the allure of nature and the splendor of civilization, spanning a quiet pathway where the river's fragrance mingles with the sea's sweetness below. This flyover which was constructed with a mix of blind stones and vio light has a silencing effect when a person or vehicle enters it. Vio light; a luminescent gum cream formed by lightning striking mercury-infused mangrove mud. By day, the bridge shimmers with a matte violet hue, while by night, it glows with solar-charged UV light, ensuring no one misses its blind & silent presence even in the darkest hours.

As the sun prepares to slip beneath the horizon, a delicate crescent moon stands ready to cast its glow across the firmament. But this is no mere lunar arc; it embodies the cry of the crescent moon which manifests as salt rain. The masses herald this night as a night of jubilation, chasing away the shadows that once cloaked the earth. Meanwhile, a minority known as the Dark Folks, believed to be the direct descendants of Ajnas in the enigmatic realm of Eerht, perceive the shimmering salt rain as a cry of Maya for liberation. Dark folks invoke visions of two fantastical beings from the depths of their imagination: the acid dwarf fish and the ash fire moth. The lifeblood of the acid dwarf fish bestows the extraordinary gift of underwater breathing for a fleeting 33 minutes, while the ash fire moth's dust grants the ability to glide across 33 miles of sky. Legends whisper that only three beings—dolphins, humans, and ravens—are graced with the power of these mystical creatures. Still, these marvels dwell in the realm of myth, their magic still unseen by the living.

Let's see and meet the present reality. Everything crafted by humans and nature on Eerħt holds a touch of magic. The sweet sea is not just a perfect sunset spot, but its salty water transforms into a sweet nectar which is a once in a lifetime experience. Legend says that one can taste the sweetness when they find their true love. Many have attested to this claim for the same reason. The stories of the sweet sea are abundant. The deeper the dive, the deeper the connection to the divine.

Exploring her soul's sweetness can be endless, so let us save that adventure for another lifetime.

For now, let's immerse ourselves in the Scent River. The river carries the fragrance of Champa flowers, with its surface reflecting an orange hue during daylight. Scent River may deceive on the surface and bewilder on a profound level.

Let's plunge into the depths. As one delves down, the orange skin fades, and green flesh appears, surrounded by river weed and aquatic life. Parasitic creatures roam aimlessly while a chorus of voices echoes in the distance. A group of acid dwarf fishes' protests human interference, chanting for freedom.

'Free us from fear, free us from fear, free us from fear.'

Daddy dwarf and mummy dwarf are leading the acid babies demanding an end to industrial fishing and their existential crisis. Amidst the underwater commotion, a frog couple were having some stoner time on river weed in their tiny mud bathtub. The protest even hit the surface and disrupted their peace. Stoners dived into the river and screamed swear words at the top of their lungs in amateur fishy language. The anger was conveyed successfully, but the message out of the broken bubbles were vague. For the fishes, those were two metal heads growling in support of the protest. The shoal lifted their tails fin up and showed them the rock symbol of respect. Protest continued leaving the pot heads on a bad trip.

From the land, a white shirt descended into the midst of the demonstrators. Have you ever pondered what it's like to be struck by a tsunami amid a flood? Just ask the acid dwarf fish. The shirt slowly enveloped the school of fish and floated swiftly to shore. They banded together and escaped the snare except for their beloved father. As the acid offspring cried out in shock from the surprise attack, the teenage frogs awkwardly chuckled, displaying their flexible tongues. Coming to their senses, the stoners saw the lady fish, devoid of any emotion, in shock. Peering up to the surface with hope of rescuing their father, they bore witness to a dreadful spectacle. Daddy fish is making the leaps of faith on the shore with no hope to get back to his shoal. A human child watched his prey perform the dance of death. The fish's body finally settled, but its lips continued to pucker for a drop of water. The eerie display culminated with a motionless daddy fish with its mouth agape, thoroughly unsettling the frogs. They took a deep breath to settle their terrified hearts and dove back into the river. Lady fish remained in the same dark, empty state. The stoners struggled to communicate the news in fishy language, but their actions spoke volumes. It was time for mummy to come to terms with the fact that life is the only true divider between birth and death. The widow fish accepted the reality and mourned. A silent melancholy enveloped the stoners as well. Their hearts were too fragile to face tragedies, so they hastily devised an escape plan. Inviting the weeping lady to join, the stoners offered her the weed as a form of solace. The results were mixed, as each being's brain functions differently across different dimensions. Regardless, they decided to try it. After preparing a weed ball from fresh plants, the girl frog presented the tiny river weed roll to mummy. 'Only a woman can underwear another woman,' she said in amateur fishy, meaning 'understand'. Wiping away her tears, mummy accepted the care without awareness, simply seeking an escape from her agony. Imbibing the weed, she felt a calm placebo effect take over. Her eyes closed tranquilly and entered a realm of three dimensions in the empty river. Swimming about, searching for an exit, she suddenly met a glitch. Her husband reincarnated in his halo acid form. Locking eyes with him, she felt a sense of wakefulness and life. A live earthworm dangled from his lips, evoking memories of their romantic noodle dinners. Racing towards him, she delicately consumed the other end of the worm. Their lips drew closer, but before they could connect, the river darkened. The trip was over, and acid lady were back again in her world of agony. She became frantic to start the trip from where it ended. Watching the extreme signs of a substance addict, psyched out frog boy shared his girlfriend the story of a swan who got kidnapped and killed after a careless overdose of weed. 'The stoned swan was leaving the land post-trip when a giant human in a biker helmet appeared from a car and seized her by the neck. She even regurgitated the acid fish she had eaten during the abduction.' Frog boy recounted in amateur fishy. Unfortunately, every detail of the tale was clear this time, unsettling mummy fish. In the silence of her broken heart, she chose the tumult of her mind. She started sauntering around the pond to clear her mind, but it was futile. Instead, she spiraled further into chaos and turned to more weed, intensifying her madness. In that moment of despair, her deceased husband appeared. Bathed in the fading sunlight, he floated across the water like an empty vessel. With her sanity slipping away, the lady fish swam towards her dead love to bid farewell. Yet fate intervened in the form of a swan descending from the sky, snatching both the living and the deceased. The tragic love saga of the acid fishes concluded inside the swan's belly, leaving the frogs in an existential crisis.

'Ma,,Maakhr,,,Ma,Maakhr' 'Holy Raven' cried the frog boy in an elastic tongue.

'Ma,,Maakhd,,,Ma,Maakhd' 'Holy Dolphin' echoed the frog girl in elastic tongue.

Both tried to bridge the gap between the aquatic and terrestrial realms through their fishy communication. Concluding their peace mission, they embraced the pain as part of their karma. Now, the star turtle appeared as their savior. The turtle imparted a nugget of wisdom derived from his meditative shell existence.

'There is no darkness without light, there is no light without darkness. You are the light, you are the dark, I am the light, and I am the dark.'

Tired stoners tried their best to concentrate throughout the rap, but they were losing it.

'Darkness is the light, light is the Darkness.'

Their eyes flickered dark and light over the drowsy teaching. They paid their teacher a froggy yawn by showing off their elastic tongues as an honorarium. As the protesters ventured elsewhere, the teens delved deeper into their hallucinatory realm, indulging in a potent dose of weed. Amidst their euphoric state, turtle was wasting his precious energy by playing drums to the deaf. Turning to the bald monk-like figure, they grinned with elastic tongues protruding, fixated on the star patterns adorning the turtle's shell. Losing his patience, the turtle unleashed a fishy curse, sprinkling bubbles and a hint of urine over their extended tongues, making them blind. With a golden shower curse, the thunderous turtle bid them farewell and resumed his journey, leaving the trippy frogs stranded at the edge of madness.

In a final attempt to find solace, they surrendered to underwater meditation, quieting the chaos in their minds. As the noise subsided, their vision returned. Just as a sense of peace settled in, a group of another acid dwarf protestors disrupted their tranquility. 'First life is fish, first God is fish', a fight to make fish the official God. The ensuing tumult threw the frogs into a dark night of the soul, torn between inner and outer conflicts. Appearing from the depths, they found clarity under the waning sun, resolving their confusion and alleviating their pain. However, a final trial awaited them in the form of an elderly man casting a fishing net over the river. Amphibious duo saw the web approaching them like a tsunami and luckily got time to dive into their burrow. They missed the trap and watched the rest of the story sitting by their mud lounge. The net plunged deep into the riverbed and laid there for a moment. They floated back with extreme caution. Electric turtle who was meditating got entangled in the net along with some protest fishes and a lot of weeds. Bald head peeped out of the shell feeling the turbulence and he is taking off to the terrestrial world in a web flight. The creed is gone, and so is the weed. The frogs gracefully embarked on a journey of conscious living, embracing a new dimension with grateful elastic tongue kisses.

The sun gracefully began its descent, marking the shift from day to night. As the light waned, a swimming ring drifted onto the river's surface. Used by humans for leisure or relaxation, it seemed almost comical that only they needed lessons in swimming. Approaching the abandoned ring was a young boy, the same who had caused the demise of the acid fish earlier. His attempts to reach the ring were futile, his movements in the water creating a sense of urgency. With each stroke forward, the ring slipped two strokes back, leaving him disheartened. Exhausted and defeated, the boy succumbed to the depths of the river, a moment where he longed to be like the fish. Drifting into a near-death experience, he surrendered to the tranquility of the water, finding solace in the embrace of the liquid abyss. His eyes closed slowly as he peacefully released his final breath, the bubble bursting under the last rays of sunlight.

Meanwhile, as one life found peace beneath the river's surface, another ascended from the depths of the river. An elderly man, familiar with the river's ways, returned to the chaos from which he once appeared. Weightless and ethereal, his body ascended towards the crescent moon, devoid of past or future, emotion or thought. In a state of ultimate liberation, he achieved moksha, free from constraints of the material world. Amidst the chaos of the aquatic realm, a single vibration echoed through the river - the sound of the silence.

Chapter 2
The Light of the Dark

Monsoon Color,
1993.

Amongst the eerie beauty of Spooky Marsh, where the mangroves crack and resonate with mysterious echoes, the summer sun has drained the moisture from the land, leaving it parched and thirsty. But as evening falls and the rainy season begins, the marsh prepares to come alive once more. The mangrove trees stand sentinel over the brackish water, a delicate balance between life and the threat of sinking into the treacherous mud. Spooky can be shallow on the surface but can swallow off the face of the earth.

Across from the marsh sits a quaint cottage, surrounded by blooming plants and fruit trees on a sprawling acre of land. A young boy with grass-green eyes and a curious demeanor gaze is watching the dry soil with a weapon in hand. He sat down in monkey pose and began grinding the ground with a small hoe. As he digs into the ground, the soil transforms from arid to moist, revealing the break-dancing earthworms beneath the surface.

A woman approached the young boy bearing a sizable circular clay vessel filled with mango essence. With precision, she positioned the jar on the ground and sealed it with a wooden lid.

"Are you finished, Christy?" "In progress, mom," he replied with muddy hand and hoe.

She adorned the jar with a silk cloth, securing it tightly with a cork rope. The boy excavated a hole matching the jar's dimension and beckoned her over.

"Mr. Aleena, the grave is prepared."

"Dig a deeper pit. I know what is on your mind." He dug deeper grinning foolishly. The casket of mango extract was buried, and she tapped the surface leaving no trace behind.

"Mom, we need a landmark."

Behind them is the freshwater spring and right in front is the mango tree.

"So, the tree is the head, and the spring is the tail." "Mango wine is the belly button."

He pierced a dot on the ground and got up stretching the legs.

"Mom let us fashion an al fresco dining arrangement. Place a clay oven here and a stone table there. It will be marvelous." He illustrated his vision on air.

"Indeed, I pondered on the idea of expanding the garden. Didn't dad tell you?"

"What?" "He is bidding farewell to sleepy slope."

"And what will become of the coffee farm?"

"He has entrusted his plant workers to oversee it. You could potentially take over after college."

"Absolutely not. Business is not my forte, mom. You see, I am a right brainer."

"I knew you had the wrong brain."

"Haha. Funny. Why not ask Charlie? He is a nature freak."

"Let's wait for the freak to finish high school first."

"Has he departed already?"

"Planning to leave before the harvest."

"Speaking of harvest, when will the mango wine be ready?" He licked his lips and inquired.

"Let it mature. The older it gets, the younger it gets." "A week would be sufficiently young?" He received a knock on the head. "Just forget about it down there. There's beauty in letting the drink remind you of the perfect day." He swallowed in anticipation of that perfect day.

"I'm off to grandma's estate." "Why?" "To watch cartoons. Dad promised a TV this time." He hurriedly washed the mud off his hands from the spring. "Tomorrow you're starting college and still running behind cartoons." "Imagination is also like wine. The older it gets, the younger it gets." He playfully poked at mom's soft belly fat before heading to the neighbor's house.

The sun was setting, casting a sleepy shadow over the marsh. Crickets played their chirping tunes as frogs sang loudly. A cool breeze rustled through the mangrove trees, signaling the approaching monsoon rain. Christy hurried down the eerie pathway, making it to the neighboring property before darkness enveloped him. An ancient mansion stood before him, painted regal white with teak and rosewood doors and windows. Christy kicked off his sandals and dashed through the grand hallway, leaving one sandal neatly on the steps and the other upside down. The TV signal faded as he entered the living room.

"May you always bring luck & prosperity." A brown-eyed teenager with long hair blessed him for the bad omen. "It's just the wind, asshole. Adjusting the aerial might do the trick." Both looked outside and noticed the wind had calmed. "I'll adjust it." The long-haired boy ran out. "Kishan, wait." Christy followed closely behind. Kishan secured his unruly hair and climbed up and got hold of the side roof. He sneaked up to the antenna which was standing in the corner with the shadow as a scarecrow. Christy gaped up as he approached the aerial.

"Shut that mouth and focus on the screen." Christy closed the mouth soon he heard his shout from the top and peeped in through the open lounge window.

"Are the colors on?" He did his first turn. "No." He tried with a different angle.

"Are the colors on?" "No."

The loop of tuning and turning continued. Christy transmits the terrestrial news to space while Kishan transmutes the aerial network.

The longue television remained static with loud white noise.

"Can someone please turn this off? It's giving me a headache." A grandmother in her nineties, clad in white saree and blouse, screamed at the top of her lungs from her rocking chair.

The oldie is accompanied by a masculine batch beneath on the marble floor. Two kids among the group started playing touch me and began running around the screaming television. A young man with eyes black as a raven and dimple cheek covered in trimmed beard crawled on butt towards the screaming screen. He pressed the volume button down and peace spread across.

"My dear Nandhu (Anand), You saved my head." He accepted her gratitude with a dimple smile. Kids are running around the longue surrounded by fragile objects.

"Please, no breaking or falling." Grandma frowned but they didn't give an ass. They took an outdoor turn drifting out of the longue.

"Summer has passed," she mused, watching the cloudy sky. "Vacation is over. Bishan starts school tomorrow and Kishan is off to college. I do not like the kids being home all the time, you know."

"Right, the mood might cloud their minds. How is Shiva?"

"Confined to his bed. Merely a lifeless body consumed by despair. He now rejects even the idea of taking medicine." "Perhaps he is ready to depart. Maybe we should not prolong his suffering." "He speaks of the end approaching, as if his life is engaged in a dialogue with death. Truth be told, we all pray for a peaceful passing. There are no miracles left to hope for." "He must be listening. We understand our part of the divine master plan only when the body rests and listens to the reckless mind. I often wonder why those who seek truth bear the deepest scars. Yes, the court has silenced gold mining on account of his courageous exposes and yet look at the horrors wrought upon his being."

"The authorities mentioned that the assailants were masked."

"But the identity of the culprits is glaringly clear. Justice could easily be served to your family if the law chose to act."

"Ah, but in the face of such treachery, silence may be the wiser course. These fiends are capable of unspeakable harm; losing another family member is a risk far too great. The law cannot shield us indefinitely."

"You speak wisely, Nandhu. Protect your family, no matter the cost—even if it means sacrificing your own dignity." She paused with a somber expression and began to rock back and forth.

"Grandma, are you okay?" "It's Varsha's birthday today and?" Her voice sang a silent lament. "Tomorrow marks 17 years since her luminous presence faded from this world."

He did not know the words that could console a mother mourning her departed daughter, so he simply grasped grandma's weathered arm in silence.

"The first rain of 1944. That day will always stay with me." She tightly held onto his arm with both hands as she reminisced. "Francis supported me through every single moment of pain just like this until she was born. The joy the three of us felt during that moment, words can't capture it." A smile touched her lips. "All I remember is the overwhelming feeling of rain and love." Anand could almost feel the warmth. "Francis wanted us to get on a ship and leave this land, but I convinced him to stay. And that's when our life in society began. Varsha started school. She faced difficulties with people, much like her father. Everyone at school saw her as an oddball. Eventually, she dropped out and we switched to homeschooling. But those were truly the best times of our lives, just the three of us in our own little world. Until that fateful day." Regret filled her voice.

"We faced an inheritance issue. My father's family was trying to claim everything after his passing, so we hired a lawyer to resolve it. That's how Devachan came into our lives, but for Varsha, he was a source of comfort outside of our close-knit family. Their love blossomed over time. All I wanted was my daughter's happiness, but Francis never approved of him. Back then, doctors, engineers, and lawyers were considered prestigious professions. Having a lawyer was a moment of pride for any family, and he even helped us with our legal issue. For Varsha, expressing her love for Devachan was a turning point, and Francis had no choice but to accept. And so, they got married." She let out a sigh of guilt. "Francis was right. He was always right. Devachan was a grave mistake. Our girl, she only knew how to love." Grace began to weep. Anand chose not to offer false comfort and let her grieve in her own way. "I have lived a full life, but Kanya and Maria? My girls have not had the chance to savor it." "Don't worry about them, grandma. They will find their own paths."

"Nandhu, life presents us with two choices: to fear death or to cherish life. What really happened to our girl? Why did she take her own life? I refuse to believe it was suicide. I just can't." She began to struggle for breath. "Grandma, are you feeling, okay?" Grace clung tightly to his arm before he became alarmed. "I'm fine." She regained her composure after a few slow breaths. "The haunting memories leave me breathless. No matter how happy our past may have been, one dark memory can taint it all." "You scared me, grandma. Just relax, all right. Let's not dwell on the past." Anand soothingly patted her wrinkled arms. "Devachan, he knows how to turn your strengths against you. Our girl suffered so much, but she knew how precious life was. She won't take her own life; she won't." A somber silence filled the room, accompanied by a melancholic breeze as Grace leaned back and began to rock in her chair. The children returned from their aimless running, breaking the heavy atmosphere. "Bishan, Charlie. Come here." Anand called out, and both boys obediently approached. "Teach grandma the 'smiling crow' game," he devised a plan to cheer up Grace. Unfamiliar with the game, Grace eagerly asked, "What's next?" With joined palms in a vertical line, they began chanting "Croo Www" like crows. Laughter filled the air as they covered Grace with tickles, driving away her dark thoughts. Reluctant for another round, Grace breathed in the moment of joy. "Wanna play another round?" "No thank you." Kids continued their aimless running.

"Ah, how is Francis pa fairing?" "He's immersed in crafting something enchanting and mystical." "Mystical? What might that be, Grandma?" Grace replied with an enigmatic grin, leaning in closer. "An eye-opening mirror for the blind." "And what does that entail?" They both were aware of its purpose. "For Maya. Francis' great-great-grandmother was blind, and it was her vision that instigated this endeavor. They've been tirelessly perfecting it through the ages. After 333 years of refinement, it's nearly complete."

"Are they made using blind stone?" "Precisely. A magnifying glass for the sighted and a mirror for the visually impaired. He dedicates most of the hours underwater polishing the lens."

"Why does he have to do that?"

"The magnifying glass unveils its secret mirror to our eyes only underwater. So, the water shows him when the lens is primed for revelation."

"Incredible. That's a stunning work of art. Grandma, is all this real or are we, as dark folks, simply lost in illusions?" "Never entertain such thoughts. You dream?" "Every night." "Those visions we see are simply realities waiting to materialize."

"What was the tale of Francis pa being saved by a swan from a tsunami?" "Yes, Francis's family was tragically lost to the tsunami of 1913. It was a night of surreal experiences for a nine-year-old boy. Living by the serene sea, he was startled by a cry. Leaving his home, he met a swan. Enthralled by the call, he followed the graceful bird into the heart of the mangrove."

"That sounds eerie. And then?"

"Suddenly, the call ceased, and he snapped out of his trance, finding himself on a treacherous mud pit." "Goodness, that's terrifying. What did he do?"

"Instead of panicking, he maintained composure, breathing deeply, convincing himself it was just a nightmare." "And then?" Anand shivered with anticipation.

"He remained calm, not allowing the mud to engulf him in the darkness. Patience brought the dawn, revealing a dangling root under the light. Escaping, he hurried back home, only to find the sea had claimed everything but his life." "So, the call was a call for self-rescue." "Sometimes miracles can take on an eerie guise." "Could our realities just be illusions of Maya?" "We will only be liberated once she is unshackled. The recurrent tsunamis are not just a result of gold mining; it's Maya's plea for assistance." "Hopefully, this mirror will free her."

"Nothing is chained forever, not even a heart." "Marvelous words, grandma." "Taken from my latest novel." "Truly?" Anand could barely have his excitement.

"Yes. I am on the cusp of completing it. The climax is within reach." "Exciting. I have already reserved a copy. What's the title, grandma?"

"I give my stories title only once its completed." "How much of your life is there in the story?" "My novels are a mélange of reality and imagination. I cannot divulge all. It includes Francis's mud pit scenario, albeit in a different context."

"I greatly miss your written work. Your narratives have ignited countless imaginations, including mine." "Thank you, Nandhu. I have never attended school or received formal writing lessons." Anand grasped her aged arm and saw the lines on her palm.

"So, you don't create the characters and stories yourself." "No, I narrate them, and Francis transcribes them." "Oh, your fans are unaware of that." "I am aware. I never felt a sense of purpose until I met him. The novels aren't solely mine; they are a collective creation of our imagination." "He doesn't seek credit for his contributions. That's why they are published under the name Grace Francis." "Indeed. Most women take their husband's surname." "Those names are permanent. However, in my case, it's only for the cover. The rest of the time, I am just myself, rooted in my identity. That's what Francis also prefers."

"Behold! Two magnificent masterpieces are currently unfolding. This evening is already drenched in a cascade of thrilling revelations. You two are quite the unconventional lovers, I must say." "Nandhu, have you ever gazed upon those lightning-struck trees?" He nodded after a moment of pondering. "Bereft of their crown, standing tall with unwavering roots. Home to birds and insects, subject to animal activity, yet resilient without complaint. It appears the tree serves its inhabitants, yet in truth, they exploit it. Similarly, humans falter when guided by emotion over reason. Without Francis, I would have been a mere tree stump. Love is a mystifying force." The old woman reminisced about her youth.

"In my adolescence, my solace lay by the river. I conversed, laughed with her. Until one day, I embraced insanity and flung myself into the river, seeking unity with the water droplets. And there he was." Anand envisioned the moment. "Lost in a dream, until I began to suffocate. With a life-saving kiss, he revived me. At that instant, I understood without him, I was a lifeless being."

"Oh, the first kiss of grandma." Blushing, she playfully pinched his cheek. "Our subsequent kisses were even better." "And?"

"Too young for marriage, we yearned to be together. The arrival of a palm reader offered a practical excuse. Viewing us as strangers, he captivated my mother's favor and impressed with his exact readings. A regular visitor, he had permission to linger, to envelop me in his arms." Grace giggled. "Oh, you sly one. What happened next?" "Our love blossomed until my pregnancy. Francis stepped forward, ready to wed me. While my mother approved, my father unleashed his fury. Eventually, he relented, accepting the orphaned suitor." "Grandma, is that the same magnifying glass he employed for deciphering palms?" Grace shot him a playful look, urging him to quiet down as he spoke. With an enigmatic smile, she sank back into her chair, her rocking motion weaving an air of mystery around her. A playful whirlwind of monsoon breeze danced through the space, making the white drapers in the dining hall swirl and sway like enchanted ghosts.

A girl drifted towards the chamber; her presence shrouded in the whispering fabrics of the drapes. Anand could only see her silhouette. He peered intently through the curtains, longing to catch a glimpse of her. As he turned back, Grace was watching him. She raised her eyebrows with a mischievous smile, to which he responded with a bashful dimpled smile.

"So, you are a full-time diver?" "Yes, grandma."

"But are you adequately compensated for your skills?" "Well, it nourishes my soul. However, as you rightly pointed out, there aren't many opportunities for skilled swimmers. I am contemplating a move to Indigo Island. Last winter, I met a research group from there. We engaged in a stimulating intellectual discussion, and they invited me to collaborate on their latest project. Sea pollution. We need to act before it's too late." "Indeed. Go for it, young man. Humans don't realize how easy it is to destroy but creating takes dedication." "But before I dive in, I need to discover some truth." He shared with a dimpled smile. "So, how is Deepa? It's been a while since I saw Prasad and Deepa. Can you take me to visit them tomorrow." "Of course, grandma. They are preoccupied with treatment and other matters." "Who is running Satya newspaper now?" "Ah, brother-in-law."

"Oh, Prasad. It's good that he has taken over. The legacy lives on." on."

"He seems burdened by the newspaper and its demands. He's merely following his dying father's wishes." "Can't blame him. Speaking the truth drains us of our energy. He's the one hosting the FM music show, right?" "Yes, he has joined as an RJ at Dwani radio."

"I had a hunch. His voice is so smooth." "For him, it's currently more about inner cleansing than a part-time gig." "Good for him. Nandhu, truth always finds a way to surface, no matter how long it takes."

"Hmm." Both paused and let silence fill the room. The running children finally settled down and began engaging in deep conversations. Anand and Grace overheard them and decided to join in.

"I'm going to outer space." Bishan declared. "I'm heading deep into the ocean." Charlie announced. "Grandma, where would you like to go? Up or down." Anand inquired. "I'll be joining Charlie. Down into the depths of the ocean."

"I want to see dolphins flying." Bishan interjected. "You'll see flying ass." "You'll see dolphins shitting their ass out."

"You are afraid of water, that's why you chose space, I understand." Bishan groaned and looked at Anand. "Don't look at me. I keep telling you to learn how to swim. Otherwise, people will mock you. The monsoon is starting, and the river will be full and fresh. I'll teach you." Bishan pondered over his decision.

"You know, I am also afraid?" Grace offered some encouragement. "Of what? Water?" Bishan sought companionship.

"Not water, I fear the darkness." "And do you still fear it?" "Yes. Once fear takes root, it's difficult to uproot it." "So, how do you overcome your fear?"

"I don't overcome it, I confront it. That's the only way to move past it." Every gaze in the room shifted towards Bishan, expecting his response.

"If you fear water, how will you swim with the dolphins?" Anand challenged. Bishan hesitated, his young mind contemplating the adventure.

"I will start learning in the winter and swim before the tears of the crescent moon." "Why wait for winter? The monsoon waters are better for practice," Anand urged.

"I need time to mentally prepare."

"Acting like you're diving into the deep sea, huh?" mocked Charlie, resulting in a playful scuffle among the kids. Anand intervened before things escalated, calming the situation. "Grandma has a trick to conquer fear," Anand shared. "What is it?" Bishan was intrigued. "Take deep breaths until the mind falls silent, then listen to your heart. Take more breaths until your heart quiets down, and listen to your soul," Grace explained. "That's your gut instinct. Listen to it, but choose wisely," Anand added. "How do we know which voice to follow?" questioned Bishan. Bishan. "Now that's a journey you must discover," Grace hinted, tapping her belly as the second brain. "That information is privy only to your inner vision." The ideology proved too complex for the young minds to understand, and they simply nodded in agreement. "Listen to your inner truth, whether it calls you to plunge into the depths of the ocean or soar through the vast expanse of space, understand? Speaking of space, it's been ages since those mischievous monkeys took flight? Nandhu, why don't you go and check if they've unfurled the umbrella?" Bishan and Charlie burst into laughter, fully engaged once more. Anand ventured out to seek clarity in the courtyard.

"Are the colors visible?" "No." "Are the colors on?" "No." Outside, the auction continued.

"Kishan, get down from there." Anand shouted to the sky, but his plea went unanswered. The harmonizing persisted.

"Hey monkey, could you kindly tell him to come down?"

"Nandhu uncle, I am Chris. The youngsters call me that."

"Then stop with the uncle nonsense?"

"My dear Nandhu uncle, biologically you are the uncle of that monkey twisting the aerial, and I am his closest companion, thus making you my somewhat peculiar uncle. Perhaps I could refer to you as brother, but uncle sounds smoother."

"Nandhu uncle, are the colors visible?" Kishan's voice echoed from the heavens.

"Are we on the same page now, Nandhu uncle?" Chrisy quipped with a grin.

"Call me whatever absurdity pleases you, and I'll shorten your name to 'monk'."

"Sounds more divine, doesn't it?"

"How do we coax that long-haired monk down?"

"Should we throw a coconut at him?"

Suddenly, a blinding flash of lightning followed by a deafening clap of thunder filled the void.

The earth shook, and all ages trembled.

"You fool, just come down. The antenna attracts lightning." Anand's voice pierced through.

"Let me make one final adjustment." He turned the antenna in an imaginary line from the Northeast to the Southwest. "Are the colors visible now?"

Christy glanced at the screen. With a slight glitch, the Vidhooradarshan Channel came into view. A small figure crawled towards the television and cranked up the volume.

'Spooky marsh is murmuring♪♪♪♪, murmuring about the lady with the golden hair ♪♪♪ ♪♪♪Maya, Maya♪♪♪♪♪♪...Sweet sea is whispering♪♪♪♪, whispering about the lady who sheds sweet tears♪♪♪♪♪ Maya, Maya♪♪♪♪♪......Sleepy slope is screaming, ♪♪♪♪ screaming about the lady who sound like waves♪♪♪♪, Maya, Maya♪♪♪♪♪ Scent river is singing♪♪♪♪, singing about the lady inside a turtle shell ♪♪♪♪♪,Maya, Maya♪♪♪♪♪.'

Christy delivered the news.

As they say, the older she gets, the younger she gets, and Grace sang along too. Kishan meticulously pulled arms out of the antenna. His descent was much quicker than his ascent. Anand was prepared to catch him if he fell, hanging on to the platform with a nonchalant attitude. Kishan landed on the ground with a thud, dusting himself off.

"Nandu uncle, what happens if a person is struck by lightning."

"Let's strap you to the antenna and find out." Kishan playfully jabbed his friend and dashed into the grand estate. Christy followed in hot pursuit, while Anand trailed behind with a charming smile. As he ascended the staircase, a gust of wind chilled him to the bone. The curtains of the window billowed open, revealing a mysterious figure standing behind. In a language known only to his mind, the moon peeked out from behind the clouds.

A young woman with eyes as white as dolphins and juicy cupid bow lips, her face partially shrouded by cascading curls. As the curtains danced in the breeze, he found himself captivated by her presence. But she shot him a fleeting glance before turning away, her expression icy. The sky rumbled and his smile faded. His bare feet stepped back to moist soil again and walked towards spooky marsh. He pulled out a packet of cigarette from his pocket and lit a roll retreating to the green void, each puff seeming to cloud his mind rather than his lungs.

The woman who stole his smile was occupied in the kitchen. Overwhelmed by guilt, she abandoned her tasks and made her way to the living room. The moment she entered, chaos erupted. The boys on the floor greeted her as if she were their teacher.

"Good morning miss." "What nonsense is this? Save the teacher-student dynamic for school." Grandma nearly had a heart attack. "You imbecile, it's evening." "You fool, can't you see it's dark? It should be good night then." "Then go to bed." Bishan and Charlie sparred once more, while Kishan and Christy laughed at their silly siblings. The teacher silenced the commotion with a stern command. "Quiet down and watch your cartoons, little imps." The boys fell silent, but one was conspicuously absent.

A giggle emanated from the mansion's hall, capturing everyone's attention. "Maria, come and join us," Grandma called out. "Sorry, Grandma, I'm busy," came the response. Kishan peered through the sheer curtains with curiosity, but the identity of the voice remained elusive. The woman's eyes scanned the room as if searching for something forever lost. All eyes turned to her in anticipation. "What's the matter?" "I'm just looking for your book." "What book?" "The sound of the silence." "It's under my pillow." "Okay, grandma." Grandma."

After a fleeting exchange, she entered and peered out through the curtains. Anand stood in the distance, cloaked in a cloud of smoke. Snuffing out his cigarette, he made his way back toward the mansion. A voice whispered his name.

"Nandhu." His dark eyes sought out the speaker, revealed by the curtains. A name slipped from his lips like a gentle breeze. "Kanya." With little time to spare, she conveyed her message. message.

"We need to talk. Meet me by the spring." And with that, she disappeared behind the drapes. Though the sky was overcast, a hint of gray still lit the way. Anand scanned his surroundings, then stealthily crept towards the spring. "Why are you staring at me?" A voice broke the silence, appearing from the shadows of the kitchen. Slowly, a figure stepped into view, shrouded in gray. Caught off guard by the question, Anand hesitated.

"Sorry for staring. I didn't mean to. Do you even notice me?" She hesitated at his question. "Let's set our feelings aside and have a chat." She glanced at his feet covered in dirt. "Where is your sandal?" "It's up front. My mind forgets when my heart is hurting." She walked to the spring, lowered the steel bucket tied to a cork rope into the water. The sound of the fall in the distance as the metal dipped into the spring. The wooden wheel turned as she pulled the rope, the technology bringing up a bucket of fresh water.

"Want to wash your legs?" He accepted and poured the water over his dirty legs. The chilly water relaxed the mind and washed away the dirt stains. "Let's just be friends like before." He paused, then placed the bucket on the spring wall. "Don't you like me?" "Any girl would." "I'm not interested in the feelings of a stranger." "I can't defy my father's views on relationships outside of our community." "I didn't realize you still followed patriarchal traditions?" "Can we really live freely?" "Come with me. Home is where our hearts lie, not where we were born." "Do you believe we can find peace in this land?" "Together, true love will lead us to peace." "When the world opens up for us, I'll join you. Until then, I choose to still be where I am. You deserve better, don't limit yourself for me. This is the path I've chosen." "No other world awaits us." "You shouldn't say that, coming from dark folk?" "Enough of crazy stories. I'm following my crazy heart now." "I don't want to be the one to hurt you. Please move on, Nandhu."

Anand gazed at his shadow in the deep spring, tears welling up like a storm. "What do you prefer, Kanya? Beaches or mountains?" He waited for her response. "Beaches." "Me too." He smiled faintly. Her confusion grew. "You're right. I shouldn't have said that as a dark folk." He quoted her. "I'm fine. Please don't feel burdened." He tried to reassure her with a forced smile, but she felt the emotional strain. "There's a wound, it'll heal. Don't fret over me. Are we still friends?" He reached for another cigarette. "That's how wounds are cured, right?" He lit it up. "Nandhu, do you know what a diver needs most?" Anand exhaled, "Breath. Your breath can heal so many wounds. I won't hinder your journey." He dropped the cigarette. "There's one last piece in the box. I'll break it if you say." "It's not just about me." She raised her voice uneasily. "Think about the real loss." She turned away angrily. "Kanya." She paused. "I'll wait until the world opens." "No, I can't watch you lose yourself. You need to let go of me for now." "So? I can't have you, can't hate you." "Keep me hidden, let time reveal." A loud thunderstorm ensued and took away the power. "Kanya, grab the candle." Grandma called out. Kanya rushed to the kitchen, looking for a candle but unable to find matches. "Nandhu, can you light this?" He handed her the box of matches, their skins brushed ever so slightly. A flicker of flame from a struck match ignited the candle's wick. Those blazing eyes, reminiscent of playful dolphins, turned his way once more. Draping a veil of hope over his aching heart, he bid her farewell with a grin that dimpled his cheeks. As she disappeared into the distance, the light seemed to follow suit. Left with only the remnants of a cigarette, but lacking a flame to ignite it, he found himself under a somber shroud of gray, peering into the depths of his own reflection in the murky well. His inner self cried out for answers, but all that met him was a deafening silence. The scenery blurred as tears welled up in his eyes, his shadow elongating slowly as raindrops began to fall, merging with the salty taste of his lips. His vision obscured by the deluge, he gazed up at the inky sky, shrouded in darkness both within and without. However, as his sight cleared, his black eyes caught sight of a bright blue lightning bolt streaking across the heavens. The beacon of blue color amid darkness - the light of the dark.

Chapter 3
The Kiss of the Rain

Monsoon Touch,

1993.

A shadow leisurely gliding along an extended pathway trailed by a silhouette. Kanya, with her intense white gaze, strolling through the vast mansion. The raindrops of the monsoon descend, ushering in a dim light. A gentle breeze tried to extinguish the candle's flame, but she kept the light guarded. As she turned towards the dining hall, her shadow transformed. The fire illuminating the grand room as she entered, vanquishing her own shadow. Pausing by a picture hanging on the wall, she ignited the candle placed in front. The wick illuminated the faded visage, evoking memories of the past. Her fiery white eyes engage in an internal dialogue with those lifeless eyes.

"Nandhu uncle is a good person? You disapprove of him?" a teenage girl with chocolate-hued eyes and bow-shaped lips inquired from the darkness. "Maria, the lights are out yet you play," Kanya smoothly shifted the conversation. "Profound life lessons commence in obscurity." "Really now. And this is how you delve in," she advanced towards the sound of clinking stones with the flickering light. Maria was engrossed in a game of five stones—a nimble and skillful task. Five tiny stones tossed into the air simultaneously, captured on the back of the hand. One stone needed to still be still, serving as the power stone. The challenge was to fling that stone into the air and swiftly retrieve the remaining four without losing the power stone. She released a deep breath and launched the power stone into the air. The other stones were caught in a flash with lightning speed, leaving the power stone hovering. Snatching it effortlessly and capturing all five stones in her hand. "Baby, do you recall mom?" Kanya inquired, gently tousling her hair. Maria hummed a lullaby, gazing at the flicker of fire.

'OH, my sleepy bloom, don't worry about the gloom if there is moon;

OH, my sleepy dolphin, don't worry about the rain if there is sea;

OH, my sleepy shroom, don't worry about the storm if there is tree;

OH, my sleepy raven, don't worry about the wind if there is wild;

OH, my sleepy child, don't worry about the fun if there is sun.

She concluded the lullaby and saw her sister.

"I believed those were tunes from my mind until you revealed they were mother's creations."

"Regardless of her state, joy or sorrow, that lullaby resounded within these walls. Now, my sleepy child, cast some light into that darkness."

"Mom left a gentle spark here." Maria playfully spanked her as she rose. "Kanya................?" Grandma's voice echoed from the living room. "Simply pass on the light, you rascal." "Why can't you do it yourself?" "I have duties in the kitchen, you idle bum." "Do you assume everyone who doesn't budge is idle?"

"My beloved moonbeam, kindly relay the light. I have tasks awaiting me in the culinary realm."

"Oh, that's my pacifist darling. I don't respond well to commands, you see." She sprang to her feet and retrieved the light. "And violence is not my cup of tea." Maria concluded her theatrical exchange, and Kanya playfully pinched her soft behind. Recoiling from the unexpected pinch, she made her way into the dimly lit lounge with the candle and a burning sensation. The moment her fiery chocolate eyes entered the room, the chaotic space transformed into a tranquil haven. Fidgeting for a spot to set down the candle in the awkward silence, Maria found herself face-to-face with Kishan. A tiny spark of fire flickered between their brown eyes as raindrops muffled the sounds around them. A sudden downpour outside broke their gaze, prompting Maria to hastily wax the candle right where she stood. Kishan saw her silently, Christy closing his mouth to safeguard against any invading insects. With a giggle, Maria accidentally spilled wax on her hand, causing the candle to topple over and extinguish, returning the room to its wild state. Taking her arm, Kishan guided her towards the rain-drenched window as the monsoon raged outside.

"Quickly soothe the burn before it blisters," he advised.

As Maria extended her arms to the rain, she felt the icy sensation of relief, a contrast to the eternal flame that still burned. Tilting her head slightly, she found Kishan gazing intently at her silhouette. A sudden gust of wind caused the drapes to billow and envelop them in a cocoon of fabric, intensifying their intimacy. The scent of rain mingled with their desires, prompting an unspoken yearning for closeness. Splashing raindrops on his face, Maria darted back to her mother's image with the candle.

"Mom, is this love or mere desire?" The deceased figure saw the naive teenager's musings with a gentle smile.

"Maria...." "Mom, your lingering presence is unsettling. It is time for you to depart."

She ignited the wick and placed it on a candelabrum, revealing a captivating and illuminating fire head with multiple arms. Safeguarding the light on a sturdy wooden table from the gusts of wind, Maria sat beneath her grandmother with a bashful demeanor. Despite her efforts to avoid glancing at Kishan, the fiery rays from the furniture beckoned Maria to face him, as if the universe had already ordained their connection. Touching her shadow to sense her warmth, Kishan met only the chill of the marble. Christy interrupted the romantic moment with a fake cough, prompting Kishan to awkwardly divert his attention.

"Have you taken the burn victim to the hospital?" Christy caught Kishan in his romantic reverie, eliciting a sheepish grin from him. "Hmm." His reply reverberated throughout the hall.

"Why do I feel that she is the epitome of beauty in all of humanity's past and future?"

"Hmm." Kishan hummed again in response to the whimsical musing, the sound echoing around them. Silently, a shadow slipped into the room, retreating to the darkest corner unnoticed by all. "Maria, have you also enrolled at Riverside?"

"Yes Christy, I forgot to mention it. We are now college mates," she said with a grin.

"Are you studying Arts or Science?"

"Arts, obviously. I'm specializing on fashion design," Maria replied.

"Our college?" Kishan asked, fearing the truth. Christy turned to face him with a robotic movement. "We are both in the Arts group," Kishan took charge of the conversation. "I'm studying fine arts and Christy is specializing in photography."

"That's great," she responded, trying to control her excitement. Kishan, on the other hand, couldn't hold his emotions and playfully started a physical fight with Christy. After their scuffle, he returned to the group with tousled hair. "Why are you still acting like kids, Chris? We're in college now, not school," Kishan remarked. Christy, amused to be called Chris for the first time, gave a subdued smile. As the rain poured outside, the room was filled with warmth and budding romances. Kishan, snapping out of his daydream, grabbed his diary and pencil out of the sling bag to draw. While everyone else in the room was lost in their own thoughts - Grace rocking in her chair, Maria doodling on the floor, Bishan and Charlie lost in their own world, and Anand sitting motionless in a dark corner.

"What's up, Nandu uncle? Were you in the rain?" Christy touched his wet hair. "Got a little drenched. First rain of the monsoon gave me a cold I guess." Anand breathed the runny nose of tears. "Really? You diver getting cold by water, that's odd."

Christy turned around with a muddled laugh. He began scanning the room for something or anything interesting. The observation became pointless after a while, and he ended the boredom with a bang. "Grandma, tell us a story?" The diverse crowd merged into one entity.

"Ah, how delightful. Story time, grandma," the individuals in the gathering asked. Grace gently opened her wrinkled eyes. "What story do you monks like to listen to?" The people transformed into thinkers, pondering the choice. "The Curse of Maya," Kanya's voice echoed from the doorway.

"Come join us, Kanya, my darling," she beckoned. "Grandma, not in front of my pupils," she protested playfully. "You should have seen her in her youth. A tiny dolphin with a big mouth, just as Francis pa used to call her," she chuckled. "Truly, Miss?" Kanya gave Bishan an evil smile and took a seat beside Maria. The room welcomed her warmly, especially Anand, who fondly remembered the spirited dolphin from their childhood. "Yes, Grandma. Maya, Maya, Maya," the room echoed in anticipation.

"Is Maya still thriving beneath the sea?" Bishan was intrigued. "Why is she cursed, grandma?" Charlie added.

"Yes, humanity used and threw her into the spiral of the sea. It is humanity that bears the true curse, not Maya."

"Why doesn't she venture onto land? Surely, she could thrive there too, right?"

"Right?" The room absorbed Kanya's inquiry.

"Yes, she could. Yet after enduring such torment, she chooses not to."

"Nazi." A voice appeared from the shadows as Anand stepped into the light.

"Indeed. Nazi inflicted pain upon her, and the tribe exploited her."

"But what was their motive?" The room echoed with curiosity.

"Maya discovered a path through her shadowy imagination to break free from confinement. Nazi, consumed by envy of her brilliance and innovation—despite her blindness—was threatened by Maya's genius, the visionary behind the revolutionary town and bridge."

"Can a blind person truly dream or envision?" Bishan interjected with a question.

"Can anyone in this room dream?"

"Yes." The affirmative response resonated throughout.

"Those who can dream draw their lineage from Ajna, the enigmatic dark folks."

"I envision dolphins soaring through the skies." Bishan couldn't hold his excitement to reveal his vision.

"To us, dreams signify the reality yet to be realized."

"What does that imply?" Bishan stood on the edge of a groundbreaking revelation.

"They are true."

"Right now, you dimwit, flying dolphins are absolutely real!" Bishan shouted, his voice echoing in Charlie's face.

"Is that really true, Grandma?" Charlie sought reassurance.

"Just because we cannot perceive them doesn't mean they haven't existed. One must always own a 'third eye' to glimpse the unseen." Grace pressed her fingers to her forehead, illustrating her point. The listening monks mirrored her gesture, captivated by the tale.

"The creator of that cartoon character is set to be my art instructor." Kishan paused his doodling.

"Why don't schools teach children about folklore?" Grace directed her question to Kanya.

"Not about the past."

"Then what's the purpose of living here if we're unaware of this land and its roots?" Grace's frustration surged, leaving the room cloaked in silence.

"What's the use of casting blame? Our society lives by the fables crafted by that wily sorcerer and lumberjack, Nazi."

The towering figure of Nazi gripping an axe by the scent river sparked a whirlwind of thoughts in everyone's mind.

"The most devious knave. He promised Maya liberation from her confinement, lingering around the blind stones for 333 years. She adhered to his words and returned to the realm after ages. What felt mundane on land appeared chaotic to Maya. He repeatedly sent her back to the depths of the blind stones in search of tranquility. Ultimately, she chose to still be beneath the waves, discovering a numb sense of comfort."

"Why is this scoundrel hailed as the creator?" Christy inquired.

"Because he penned the narrative. But soon, history shall transform. Right, Nandhu?" Grace shot a playful glance.

"How?" The room echoed.

"You all will see. Maya will awaken her third eye, and this land will shimmer with enchantment once more."

"Will we then be able to dive and soar?" Bishan asked, brimming with anticipation.

"Yes. We'll plunge with the ravens and glide alongside the dolphins. That will undoubtedly be the moment when darkness fades and rekindles the light of our humanity."

As the storm outside began to fade, so too did the tale reach its conclusion. Grace gradually tilted her back against the chair, the eyes of the entire room fixated on her gentle sway. In that moment, power surged forth, cutting through the cacophony of a television's static cries. Anand flipped the main power switch, preventing Grace from suffering yet another migraine—a resolute end to the technological turmoil.

"I see you," Christy teased, prodding Kishan's side with her finger, prompting him to bounce like a spring.

"Nandhu, remember to keep our secret theory in mind for tomorrow," Grace reminded him.

"Goodnight, grandma. I'll catch you tomorrow." Kanya, with an eye as mischievous as a dolphin's, stood at their side. Anand exchanged a wink with her before addressing the group.

"Shall we venture to the other side of the temple?" The lethargic bunch began to stir, one by one.

"Let's wait for the rain to clear completely," Grace urged.

"Goodnight." "Goodnight." Kanya bestowed upon Anand a smile as refreshing as the monsoon rain that breathed new life into him. They all filled out, gathering on the porch to relish the final whispers of the drizzle. Meanwhile, Kishan and Maria remained lost in a secret exchange of glances, as he retrieved the diary from his bag, resting it on Christy's back.

"Do I resemble your father's desk?" He quipped. "Stay still; I'm nearly done." Kishan applied the final changes to his work.

"Done." "Can I see it?" Christy inquired eagerly. Kishan hastily concealed the diary in his bag.

"I'll share it later; there's someone else who needs to see it first." "Hmm," he hummed softly, the sound resonating in the air. The rain began to mellow, smoothening into a gentle fall, while something swift and tumultuous lurked in the distance. A beam of light sliced through the spiral marsh, and a BUV roared into the mansion, splattering muddy water in its wake.

"My God, it's Dad!" Maria exclaimed in panic, rushing inside. Her alarming announcement struck the others like a clap of thunder, echoing through the silence.

A towering figure, resembling a giant yet humanoid, appeared from the passenger seat, donning a biker's helmet that sat atop its imposing frame, extending a full eight feet down to the ground. The being sported a five-foot torso, clad in a snug inner t-shirt that highlighted human-like features, while its elongated arms hung down like the mighty trunks of ancient mammoths, opening a grand umbrella. Its legs were but half the length of its torso. In total, this eight-foot entity consisted of a seven-foot body, with an added half foot for the neck and another half foot for the head. It sprinted barefoot towards the driver's seat.

Beneath the dark cover stood an elderly man dressed in white, sporting dark sunglasses and a noticeable pot belly. The giant carefully lowered him to safety beneath the mansion's overhang.

"Dragon, bring my guests," he commanded, spitting out a stream of crimson saliva from his chewing tobacco onto the muddy ground.

A crooked wooden sign hung from a pillar, misaligned. The stout man removed his sunglasses to wipe rain from his face, revealing bloodshot eyes that were quickly concealed once again. He adjusted the sign with a slight twist. A wry smile curved his lips as he read his own name:

'Devachan L.L.B, Criminal Lawyer.'

The giant soon returned, escorting two added men in white beneath the mansion's shelter.

"Fetch that duck from the trunk," Devachan instructed. The three men, all clad in white as if straight from the celestial realm, saw the giant at work. The colossal being opened the car's trunk and extracted a duck ensconced in a sack, only its head protruding, which he firmly gripped with both mammoth-like trunks, ensuring it couldn't flee. Next, he managed to balance the umbrella with his half foot-long neck, resembling a crumpled scarecrow with a broken neck and a biker's helmet as he walks towards the back of bungalow.

"Devachan, you recognize the kids, dont you?"Grace gestured to her son-in-law, and a sinister grin spread beneath his mustache. Without another word, he turned and entered the house. A muddy footprint marked the entryway, and the monstrous presence within the divine seethed.

"What the hell? Mom, you are inviting all these vile people into our home, and just look at the dirt they've caused!"

"They just came to watch TV?"

"TV, my foot. I'll pitch that screen into the jungle along with you. There are women in this house, not just an old bag like yourself. Dont you possess any common sense?"

As the turmoil escalated, the guests had already stormed out.

"Kanya?"She dashed out, alarmed by his roar. Displaying a bizarre split personality calmness, he smoothly took over the dialogue.

"Darling, cant you see the disarray? With a special guest, we end up with muddy footprints at the doorstep. Just tidy it up."

A mango-faced guy cast a joyful gaze toward Kanya, but she gave him no heed. In a flurry of nervous energy, she rushed off for a bucket and mop.

"I'll handle it."Maria snatched the bucket and mop from Kanya, receiving a gentle pat on the cheek before her sister slipped into the kitchen. Maria settled by the entry, taking her time to scrub away the muck. Her brown eyes flickered toward the shadowy mangroves, yearning for a glimpse of Kishan, who had vanished long ago. Maria stepped inside, and Granny slammed the door shut behind them.

The cartoon crew meandered alongside the eerie mangrove after the narrow escape of demon attack.

"Im never going back there. Dad promised a television this time," Christy vowed.

"I don't mind going back," Kishan replied with a goofy grin.

"Buddy, that jerk is a demon. You need to be careful. Im not joking."

Kishans goofy grin morphed into spooky.

They arrived at Christys house, where a green jeep awaited on the porch.

"Nandhu uncle," Bishan called out.

"That fellow whose face resembles a mango," they all chuckled.

"Brilliant analogy, Bishan. What about him?"

"He came over to our house once."

Anand knelt and looked directly at him. "When? Why?"

"I can't recall. He visited to see grandpa."

"Do you remember their conversation?"

"He advised grandpa to cease writing about the gold mining."

"And what else did they discuss?"

"Grandpa sent me inside, and after a short while, he yelled at him and left in a huff."

"Hmm, so he could also be involved with Shiva uncle?"

Anand interrupted Christy to keep the narrative from reaching Bishan. He grasped the unspoken message.

"Let's pause for today. We'll catch up later." Anand motioned for Christy to come closer and whispered, "Bishan stays unaware. He believes his grandpa was hit by a truck."

Bishan squeezed through the open back window of the jeep, sensing the aura of secrecy.

"Whatever the truth may be, I doubt there's much we can do. They wield the law and wealth. It's wiser to prioritize family safety." Anand agreed and took the wheel.

"Why are you at your foes' nest watching TV?"

"We can't loathe an entire tree just because of one bad fruit, right?"

"That's not the sole reason," Anand pretended to be clueless. "What?"

"Nandhu uncle, I'm onto you. If you're the seeker, I'm the observer. Is that clear?" Anand yielded with a silly grin.

"What's going on? Did you face rejection?"

"No, nothing like that. She's? She's just torn between choices."

"Don't fret. Perhaps she fears that demon."

"Yes, that's how I feel." "When did this story take root, Uncle Nandhu?" Anand sighed dreamily and drifted to that moment.

"Since the day I first glimpsed her leg?"

"What? Really? From where?" Christy burst out laughing at the absurdity.

"Underwater." "Wow, that's enchanting."

"Then I met her gaze, and it was an image I couldn't forget."

"Your love tale is more ridiculous than I imagined." "Indeed, all love stories seem silly until you become a fool for love."

"Now, look at that long-haired fool." They glanced at the starry-eyed boy.

"Kishan, you're not joining?" He stood outside, adrift in a sea of feelings.

"He's entranced by Maria maya." "What?" "Yes, you captured the first, and he snared the second. You both had a plethora of options in this land and ultimately found affection in the demon's abode." Christy approached the love-struck boy. "How are you faring?" "Have you ever truly inhaled the scent of rain? I mean, when the first drop of monsoon kisses the parched earth." He was in a poetic reverie.

"Hmm, quite the romantic notion. If that demon catches wind of this, you'll feel the first echo of thunder too. So, every step must be measured," Christy cautioned him in a grave tone. A refreshing northern breeze swept over Kishan, replacing his dread with a flutter of affection.

"I'll be back shortly," he said, sprinting across the lush field toward the mansion.

"Where the heck are you off to, you fool? Has he lost his mind?" He began his ascent up the mansion's wall. "Look at him crawling! What... has he completely lost it?" Christy provided comedic commentary while others reveled in the escapade, blissfully unaware. Kishan leaped onto the mansion grounds and stealthily navigated through the rustling foliage, spotting a warm glow illuminating

the upstairs bedroom. That glow belonged to Maria. He crouched beneath the window, feeling neither the urge to shout nor to sigh. Desperate for a quiet way to get her attention, he eventually opted for a more assertive approach. He found a few pebbles at his feet and noticed the wooden windowpanes without glasses. He seized three pebbles, launching the first with precision. Bullseye. Tap. It drew Maria's gaze. "What the...?" Her startled eyes remained fixed on the window. Not wasting another moment, he released the next two swiftly. Tap, tap. A flawless three-for-three. She peeked through the window with a hint of skepticism, her long hair trailing from the bushes.

"Kishan." A mixture of excitement and shock crossed her face. "What's going on?" She gestured hurriedly, trying to keep her voice low. He retrieved the diary from his bag. "I came to deliver this."

She pondered how to receive it, her mind a whirlwind of fear and confusion.

"Should I toss it?" "I can't throw it; it's too delicate." "Then what's the plan?"

Their whispered exchange unfolded. Finally, he mustered the courage to devise a solution. He crawled back toward the window, inching his way to the side roof. With just a two-and-a-half-arm span separating them, he reached up one arm while she extended hers down, both halfway there. Determined, he balanced on his toes against gravity's pull as she stretched as far as she could. Ultimately, the diary found its way to her, though not without her cheek meeting a wooden surface in the process. The exchange was complete. He descended with remarkable speed as she held her breath for his safety.

"I'm fine," the long-haired being murmured as she retreated into the bushes.

Maria opened the diary to find it filled with drawings and brief notes. Flipping to the last page, she was captivated by an illustration of an Ajna girl inside a turtle shell. The enchanting figure bore her likeness, accompanied by a brief letter penned beneath the drawing.

"My soul has soared ever since our brown eyes met. Will you be my Ajna girl?

Love,

Kishan—the Ajna boy.

Maria chuckled softly, leaning her head against the window's iron bar. From the thicket, a head reemerged, its long hair intertwined with twigs and leaves. A hearty laugh burst forth from those luscious, cupid-bow lips, only to be swiftly stifled by a rush of trepidation. She imagined her heart, plucked it from her chest, and blew it toward him in the form of a kiss. He caught the airborne gesture, pressing it to his own heart.

"Off you go, see you at college," she whispered. He appeared from the underbrush, scanning for a clear escape route. Suddenly, Dragon adorned with a helmet sped past him across the field, freezing Kishan in place, though the beast overlooked them. With legs the size of small tree trunks, it moved on, allowing both to exhale a sigh of relief.

"He didn't hear us. Go, go, go!" At Maria's signal, Kishan took flight. His departure was rapid, crushing the leaves beneath him before crash-landing in Christy's field.

"Here comes the monk. You fool! If that potbellied creature spots you, we're both done for."

He brushed off the dirt and strolled away as if it were a casual flight.

"Taking it easy, my friend," Kishan planted a kiss on his cheek.

"What was that about?" "I sacrificed my racing heart."

"What of your liver and intestines? No need to offer those; that demon would just rip them out."

"Relax, my friend," Kishan placed another kiss on his cheek.

"Nandhu uncle, just whisk him away. I refuse to meet my end tonight."

The dreamy boy hopped into the jeep.

"Goodbye," Kishan showered Christy with a flurry of flying kisses. He snatched up some baby coconuts strewn on the ground, tossing them back in return. The green jeep maneuvered past the eerie marshlands, with the wind brushing against Kishan in a startling chill. He clasped his hands together, seeking warmth from his own body.

"Maria, hmmm." "This is what love feels like, Nandhu uncle?"

"Indeed, this is merely the beginning." Anand beamed with pride for him.

"Relish the journey but remember—life isn't perpetually filled with petals and perfume. Hold onto the faith, not just the feeling."

Anand's words soothed Kishan's soul, which had been numbed by thoughts of Kanya.

"What is faith?" Bishan chimed in with the final query of the night. Anand paused momentarily, allowing a clear understanding to appear in his mind.

"Faith is living with a cosmic awareness while never losing touch with earthly essence. It is the foundation of all our creations. Without faith, nothing stays genuine."

"And how do we uncover the true essence?" Kishan inquired, wrapped in his own comforting warmth.

"Simply live through your mind and love through your heart; everything we experience will start to manifest as reality. Not only our visual experiences but our visceral sensations, too." Anand concluded, inhaling deeply the earthy aroma surrounding them. Only the shadowy mangrove and the rhythmic hum of the engine filled the air. The jeep approached a Y junction, a signpost directing their path.

'WELCOME TO SPOOKY MARSH'

<=Scent River-$\frac{1}{3}$ miles, Sweet Sea-$6\frac{1}{3}$ miles, Dolphin Corner-$9\frac{1}{3}$ miles.

=>Silent Bridge-$1\frac{1}{3}$ miles, Golden town-$3\frac{1}{3}$ miles, Sleepy Slope-$33\frac{1}{3}$ miles.

They veered left alongside the scent river, now swelling from the recent rain. Anand delighted in the drive, while Bishan surveyed the road through the glowing yellow eyes of the jeep.

Caught in reverie, Kishan conjured Maria from the delicate fragments of the fragrance.

"So, Maya is real?" he asked Anand from his dreamy haze.

"So is the flying dolphin." Bishan added his dream. Anand returned a smile, a spark of warmth in the cool embrace of a wet touch- the kiss of the rain.

Chapter 4
The Echo of the Swans

Monsoon Cry,
1993.

The night's rain has finally emptied its last drop, leaving only the rich aroma of the damp earth resonating across the soaked terrain. Maria stands in the moment, seeing the eerie marsh, waiting for some phantom presence. Grace carefully closed the door, a gentle smile flitting across her sorrow-laden lips. Maria remained frozen, her face a mask of detachment, clutching a bucket of murky water and an old mop.

"What's the matter, sweetheart?" Grace asked just as Maria stormed into the restroom, her silence loud and unyielding. The thunderous crash of the bucket meeting the wash basin startled the elderly lady. Splashing water on her face, a faint sting on her arm ignited a smile on her lips. She tenderly patted the minor injury, finding no sign of a blister, just the echo of past aches. Outside, Grace lingered, concerned about painting her features, poised to probe again. Maria approached with a solemn expression, then leaped into her arms for a tight embrace.

"What troubles you, darling?" she murmured as Maria nestled silently against her for a few breathless moments, Grace knotted her fingers through her hair.

"Sorry." Maria managed a smile, her gaze locking with her grandmother's.

"You have your mother's eyes, gleaming with that same rich chocolate brown."

"But you said Lady Kanya mirrors your daughter."

"Your sister and mother were so boisterous in their youth yet transformed into whispers as adults. Your mom shifted after marrying. But what of Kanya? Does she ever speak to you?"

"Not at all. This house feels like a sickness waiting to spread. Thankfully, we inherited nothing from Dad. What a jerk, disrespecting you before everyone."

"Such matters may sadden me, but they'll never wound me. And why is that?"

"Hmm?"

"Only those you truly love can inflict harm." Maria pondered these words.

"What? How could you, Grace? You don't love my awful dad." They shared a knowing smile, realizing their voices had risen slightly. Maria gently pinched the old woman's cheeks as tears spilled from her eyes, leaving trails through the wrinkles.

"My dear granny, what troubles your heart now?"

"Today marks your mother's birthday." A wave of regret washed over Maria for having forgotten.

"That's okay. She'd never hold a grudge over such trifles. She was one of the sweetest souls, really. I should have heeded your grandfather. I should have listened when he yearned to leave this place." Tears flowed freely from those aged eyes as Maria brushed away her grandmother's regret with a gentle hand.

"Grace, had my mom not married my dreadful dad, you would never have crossed my path," she playfully tickled Grace's soft belly. Grace forced a smile, her spirit lifting ever so slightly.

"My only worry is you two." A mischievous grin broke across Grace's face, rising like a specter from the shadows. "What's that?" "You're actually fond of him, aren't you?" She was at a loss for words.

"What? Am I right or wrong? That boy is hopelessly smitten with you, just so you know."

"How can you tell?" "The way he gazes at you—it's the same way Grandpa used to look at me."

"Actually, it was Grandma." Maria took her hand, tracing the lines of their shared history. "You know what? I'm in love." "Are you certain?" "I'm afraid so." "Fear not. No love story can unfold without a courageous woman."

"I'm brave, but then I see a potbelly." "Darling, life presents us with two paths: to live in fear of death or to embrace the beauty of life. Which will you choose?"

"I want to live; dying isn't on my agenda, at least for now."

"Then your task is simply to make a choice."

"What are your thoughts on him?" "Deepa's boy must be a good soul. His family is lovely, but he is his own person—an artist, surely with layers. You just need to peel them away to discover the essence beneath."

"And how did you uncover that with Grandpa?"

"Love is a flavor, not a favor. Once you become one, there's no need to see or feel separately. His sights become your beliefs, and your sensations become his breath."

"Wow, Granny. You're a delightful old soul. Can you do that belly-shaking laugh for me again?"

A hearty laugh echoed from the dining hall, filling the air with joy.

"I hear a whirlwind of chaos brewing inside."

"Another night of indulgence, I wonder who those unfamiliar faces are?"

"Perhaps they've joined his mischief-making crew."

"Regardless, darling, why don't you head to the kitchen and lend your sister a hand? That poor soul is left to fend for herself."

"I'll be back shortly. You just get settled in the kitchen and hold tight for me." "Are you really making this old gal work at her age?" "Sweetheart, you're not an old gal. Your essence sparkles with youthful exuberance. Let me share a little secret." Maria pulled her closer and whispered. "Your son-in-law is merely a fart, so keep your distance from that scent. That's your husband's poetic advice to me." Grace erupted in laughter.

"So, my precious child, prepare yourself in the kitchen with your tales."

"My throat is already parched from our last storytelling adventure."

"Brace yourself for the next chapter. This one is about Francis. Begin the saga with that fateful canoe trip to the mushroom haven. What mischief were you two up to among those poor fungi?"

"Seriously?" Granny playfully smacked her backside as she darted up the stairs.

"I'll join you girls shortly."

Maria dashed up the wooden stairs while Grace took her time toward the kitchen, where Kanya was expertly juggling tasks, her face lighting up at the sight of Grandma.

"Grandma?" Kanya called out during her vegetable prep. "Hmm." Grace nibbled on a piece of fresh produce from the board.

"Actually, Anand?" "He has feelings for you."

"How did you figure that out? Did he confide in you?"

"The one who has savored the sweet embrace of the sea knows all about love."

"Grandma, but?"

"But what? You don't have feelings for him."

"Actually, there's no reason to despise him."

"Oh, so you must love him?"

"I... I do love him. But?" "Another 'but.' Allow me to guess the source of that annoyance?" Grace gestured to her a potbelly, prompting a giggle from Kanya, yet an unexpected wave of trepidation hit her.

"Darling, your grandpa taught me what a man should be, while your father proven what a man shouldn't. Know this: the fear is indeed palpable; I won't sugarcoat that. However, there's no greater misfortune in life than letting fear rob you of someone you cherish."

Kanya contemplated her words deeply.

"What should I do, grandma?" "Face that fear head-on. Remember, dear, life presents us with two paths: to live in fear of death or to embrace the beauty of life. Have I shared this with you before?" Grace momentarily adopted an elderly demeanor.

"Perhaps my words have dried up for this world. Am I about to leave this life?"

"What are you saying, grandma? You're not going anywhere anytime soon, okay?" As Kanya chopped vegetables, Grace inched closer. "What now?" Kanya brandished the knife. "Are you planning to leave us? Who do we have left? Grandpa? He's not the same anymore—he appears indifferent to our struggles. I can hardly catch a glimpse of him."

"Don't say that sweetheart. He adores us, especially you. Believe me, he's just preoccupied, you know? The mirror. Those driven by purpose often lose sight of what's right in front of them; they spiral endlessly."

Kanya embraced her heart as anxiety threatened to consume her.

"Sweetheart, don't shy away from living your heart." With tear-brimmed eyes, she gazed at Grace. "Tears are meant to wash away not just sorrow, but also fear," Grace declared, her unwavering gaze igniting a spark within Kanya. She wiped her tears and flicked on the radio in the kitchen.

"Now we're getting somewhere." Kanya turned into 03.0.

'Good evening, dear listeners. You're tuned into FM Dhwani 03.0.'

"Greetings, cherished audience! I'm RJ Sugandhi.'

'And I'm RJ Prasad.'

'Welcome to the beloved music show, 'Vintage Tapes.''

'Once more, we've received an avalanche of letters and requests. My only lament is that we can't address every heartfelt word.'

'Yes, the passion for music and our show is unmistakably vibrant.'

'When we think of music, what springs to mind?'

'Hmm. Life itself.'

'And what sentiment fills our hearts when we ponder music in life?'

'Let me guess?' 'Go for it.' 'Is it love?' 'Precisely! What is this love? Everyone has their interpretation, but for me, the perspective keeps evolving. Once, it was a unique connection with someone, and now it's blossoming into something grander.'

'Oh Sugandhi, love is akin to the depths we dare to explore.'

'Yet, what's your insight at this moment?'

'I'd say it's an emotional force nudging us to plunge into uncharted waters we never intended to traverse yet leading us to a remarkable destination.'

'Prasad, that resonates beautifully—a plunge into the unknown.'

'Absolutely.'

'So, without further ado, let's dive deep into the realm of dancers and singers.'"

The trio of divine personalities plunged into the realm of triumph and defeat, armed with indulgent bites and boisterous banter amidst the dining room's allure.

"Devachan, you're an exceptional lawyer."

"But I've failed. We've faltered. It's all tied to the protest over gold mining."

"Let's hold off on any actions for now. Allow the uproar to dissipate. Winning or losing is secondary."

"No, it truly matters."

"Victory is important yet consider this setback merely a ripple in the vast sea of triumphs in your illustrious legal journey. Such is life. Cast aside the past; a fresh chapter unfolds at this very moment, one that could transform this sense of failure."

"A fresh chapter?" Devachan and his tobacco red tooth inquired.

"Absolutely. I own the key to that new chapter, bottled in scotch." Mango face produced a scotch bottle from his bag, captivating Devachan as if unveiling a magician's trick.

"A partnership in our plastic venture."

"Plastic? What value does that hold for us?"

"A new era dawns where everything we touch will morph into plastic. By setting up a plastic industry now, we secure our future. Power will once again return to our grasp."

The mere mention of power sent a surge of energy coursing through Devachan.

"Kanya, fetch us three glasses and some ice cubes!" Potbelly bellowed. Kanya paused her culinary chore and moved toward the refrigerator.

"You handle the labor; I'll serve." Grandma interjected, bringing in the peg glasses and ice cubes.

"That Shiva and his ragtag newspaper—that's what ignited the protest. We should've ensured his demise." Devachan admitted, halting mid-sentence. Grace lingered just out of sight, catching the half-revealed truth.

"Kanya?" Devachan called out, growing impatient. Grace jumped, entering the room.

"Where's Kanya?" "She's preoccupied with cooking," she replied curtly, serving the drinks before retreating. Golden liquid poured into the glasses, mingling with ice cubes, clinking together in celebration of the new partnership.

"Here's to our alliance." Mango face savored a sip with flair as the older crowd downed their drinks.

"So, how does this partnership operate?"

"Our legal advisor. Collaborating with us transcends mere work; it's a shared journey in profit." "What do you think, Devachan?" inquired the father of the mango face.

"I'd be thrilled to partner with you."

"Then it's settled—there are three of us." The elders poured another round of joy. Mango's lips enjoyed the slow dance of savoring, while Devachan urged, "Take that shot, my boy," prompting him to finish toasting with the next round.

"So, Devachan. This alliance is set to stir up Eerħt."

"And how's that going to happen?" Devachan took another sip from his glass, accompanied by a handful of snacks.

"I'm planning to donate a golden axe to the Nazi statue. We're going to replace that decrepit relic."

"What? Why?"

"Destroying nature is an unavoidable facet of advancement. The statue serves as a warning to those who naively believe nature is theirs to safeguard. To me, the Nazi has been a deity since childhood."

Mango face god revealed his peculiar devotion.

"Let's leave the monetary aspect aside; it's rather personal for me. History will always be celebrated for its glory, not for its ceremonies. Gold doesn't tarnish—it gleams eternally."

"You are the maestro," Devachan declared.

"This golden axe will speak to Eerñt who holds the reins now. And anything that needs silencing will be handled by me."

"In my entire legal career, I've encountered numerous individuals, yet none quite like your son.

He's an intellectual powerhouse." "I'm not saying this just because he's mine. My son knows exactly what he's doing. Nothing he's sown has ever withered." The mango face turned crimson, flattered by the elders' praise of him.

The rain settled into a tranquil rhythm outside.

"Shall we take a seat in the open air?"

"Why not? Let's perch by the spring. Oh, Dragon must be tucked away in his lair."

"Lair?" "Indeed, a muddy den at the field's edge. He's more untamed than the wildest beast."

"So, what's the deal with the name? Dragon?"

"Do you know what he dines on?" "What?" Both father and son responded, their curiosity piqued.

"Komodo dragon meat?" "What?" They burst into another fit of laughter.

"He savors the blood first, then feasts on the flesh." "Gross."

"He dashes around after a blood drink." "Why'?" "Otherwise, it clots, they say. As wild as the Komodo dragon itself. He's not human at all—perhaps spawned from a mangrove's fissure." Devachan sprung from his seat and made his way to a switch.

"This creature never rests. I'm curious what he does at night. This button is an emergency summons for him." Potbelly stepped up to a red button and pressed it.

At the farthest corner of the field sat a modest mud cave, guarded by a scarecrow. Inside, the flickering silhouette of a small campfire danced, revealing Dragon without his helmet. His bald pate bore many bite marks—some fresh, some mended. He was in the act of slitting a deceased Komodo dragons throat, channeling the blood into a barrel. Suddenly, a bell echoed from the house, jarring his ears. He bolted at the call, only to be swarmed by ravens overhead. He flailed his massive arms, trying to fend them off, then retreated into the cave. Donning a biker helmet for protection, he appeared safely, equipped with a loaded slingshot. The area was serene, devoid of feathers or raven calls. He tucked his weapon behind him and sprinted towards the mansion, presenting himself to the gods with impeccable timing.

"Look, he's arrived."

"What's his wage?" inquired one of the gods, savoring his scotch.

"It used to be ₹2 daily, but there's been a change starting today." Devachan glanced at the bewildered dragon before continuing. "Now it's ₹5 daily."

"Really? That's quite a leap," chuckled another god, their laughter ringing out over the meager coins.

"Dragon, arrange those chairs by the spring." He stood, astonished by the sudden increase in pay.

"Did you hear me?" bellowed Potbelly. The massive figure carried three wooden chairs effortlessly, dashing out while the gods ambled along leisurely. Grace moved gracefully with the rhythm, while Kanya found herself caught in a whirlwind of cooking and listening. The Mango-faced god overlooked the older woman, fixated on the youthful beauty nearby.

"Kanya, did you take care of the duck? Prepare the curry with coconut milk for dinner and fry some for now. Let the spices mingle for a while. We can wait; these are particularly important guests."

Sharing his culinary wisdom, Devachan strolled toward the spring, carrying the scotch bottle alongside Potbelly. Maria entered the kitchen with a romantic smile, but the atmosphere was charged with the anticipation of impending doom.

"What's going on?"

"The duck." "The duck?" The three women turned toward the corner, hearing a quack emanating from a large barrel. "Who will handle the duck?"

"Kanya, fetch more water and whatever snacks are available?" commanded Potbelly.

"Maria, just take care of it." "Count me out of the slaughter squad! Sorry, ladies, I'm heading out. Call me once the deed is done." She waddled away, embodying her words.

"Kanya..." The final call rang out. She dashed toward Potbelly, clutching a water pot and a plate of snacks.

"Oh, here she is. That's my girl," Potbelly proclaimed, his pride clear.

"Are you a student?" the father of the mango face asked.

"No, she's a teacher at Riverside High School," Devachan interjected.

"So, Devachan, let's cut to the chase. Do you have any objections to my son courting your daughter?"

"To be honest, I was considering the same thing." The two fathers set their collaboration in motion.

"What do you think, young man? Do you fancy my daughter?"

She retreated to the kitchen, while his gaze roamed her form, signaling his silent agreement.

"Let's first donate the golden axe to the land. Then we'll schedule a date for the betrothal. This place deserves to see the birth of a new family," the father of the Mango face announced, unveiling his vision.

"That sounds just right."

"So, here's to the start of a new family."

With that, gold flowed freely, and the celebration continued.

Kanya peered into the kitchen, her gaze falling upon the duck trapped in the barrel. The creature's helpless eyes stared back from the murky shadows, and in that moment, she glimpsed her own reflection in its innocent gaze, a single tear cascading down her cheek.

"And you're really going to wed that creature?" Grace inquired; her face contorted with anger.

"What choice do we have?" "We've already pierced your mother's spirit; I won't let us wound yours too. Don't fret. First, let's nourish them. I wish it were those mirthful fiends stashed in this barrel instead. Darling don't stress. First, we must tackle this killing." "You do it." "I can't." "Neither can I."

"Why don't we solicit your dad to handle it?" Grace strode towards the liquor party.

"Is there anyone who can end this duck's life?"

"Oh, these women. Dragon!" Devachan bellowed in calling. He was currently at a jog following the blood rite, and the dragon responded. The cacophonous rustle of leaves reverberated through the darkness as the colossal beast appeared. Grace halted him right there, drenched in sweat.

"What?" The kitchen trembled as his booming voice resonated.

"To dispatch the duck," Grace articulated with gestures and tone.

"Ahh." He accepted the task with uncontainable delight, striding into the kitchen. His enormous arm seized Kanya's vegetable knife, startling her, as he casually yanked the bird from the barrel by its neck.

"How large is it? Did you buy it?" Grandma questioned Devachan.

"No. It was meandering by the riverbank, and he captured it."

Grace found herself ensnared in a moral quagmire between life and demise. Dragon executed a swift cut across the neck. The body collapsed, and the headless creature began to scamper wildly across the field.

"Oh heavens, a swan."

Grandma whimpered, her voice like a distant nightmare, unheard amidst the chaos. The dragon ceased his pursuit, retrieving a slingshot from his back. With a steady aim, he launched a marble that struck the swan squarely, sending it tumbling down with a shattered leg.

"Wow! See? I told you he's feral. Now tell me, is he worth 5₹?"

"I'd pay 10₹." The Mango-faced god raised the ante.

Devachan stepped forward to claim the kill. He downed his drink, shed his white attire, gargled with water, and expelled crimson from his mouth, revealing four gold canine teeth that gleamed brilliantly.

"Killing is an art," Devachan boasted, gearing up for a demonstration. Grace stood frozen. "What's wrong, Grandma?" Kanya detected her distress.

"Kanya, swan. Plead with him. Urge him not to slay." Devachan advanced toward the headless swan, which still twitched with remnants of life, before thrusting the sharp knife into its chest. The body fell still, while he erupted into a wicked laugh, a visage awash in blood. Grace collapsed onto the kitchen floor as Francis caught her just before impact.

"Grace."

Their eyes locked, mirroring the moment they first met beneath water, her breath slipping away.

"Francis." Grace whispered her lover's name in a final breath, that old soul leaving in a tempest of chaos. The radio signal faded, replaced by a new frequency of cry buzzing ominously around them - the echo of the swans.

Chapter 5
A Cradle Over the Clouds

Monsoon Lullaby,

1977.

A glass room named 'Golden Town Cake House' In a whimsical glass dome filled with a myriad of enticing cakes, young Kanya explored the vibrant spectrum of colors and flavors, her mouth watering in delight and indecision. At last, her eyes landed on a tempting 'dark chocolate coconut cake.'

"Grandpa, this one's a winner!" Francis drifted closer to admire Kanya's choice through the transparent confectionery haven.

"Are you certain, my little dolphin? Wouldn't you like a sample?"

"I can already taste it from here," she replied, her excitement bubbling over. "And what's it like?" "Oh, just like dark chocolate coconut cake." Her enthusiasm overtook her words. "Mister, we'll take this one!" The baker deftly retrieved the cake, while Kanya's white dolphin-like eyes followed every movement.

"Whose birthday are we celebrating?"

"My mom's! Her name is Varsha."

"Then let's wish her a happy birthday; happy birthday Varsha or Mom," Baker suggested. Kanya glanced at her grandpa, seeking his insight.

"How about we call her mommy dolphin? After all, you're the little one and she's the mommy!" Francis teased, earning a giggle of approval from Kanya. The baker began inscribing 'happy birthday mommy dolphin' as Kanya's gaze flitted around with excitement. "So, how old is mommy?" "Hmm," her tiny fingers worked to calculate, but they struggled to manage the numbers. Again, she looked to grandpa for guidance.

"Uh, let's skip the age. Numbers are just a countdown that can frighten the living. No need to mention any digits."

"Perfect!" The baker smiled at the suggestion, wrapping up the cake with care. Kanya gleefully lifted the package, which was almost half her height.

"Goodbye, cake mister!" she waved cheerfully before stepping out of the cake house. One hand yearned for her grandpa's arm, but the package demanded both hands' attention.

"I have an idea!" Francis crouched down, and she effortlessly slid onto his shoulder. The cake found a cozy home atop his head. With tiny legs secured in his grasp, her little arms wrapped around the cake.

"Grandpa, how's the view from down there?" he flashed her a thumbs up in response.

"My little one is blooming into a majestic dolphin. I'm not sure grandpa will manage to lift you come the next monsoon season."

With careful steps, the old man meandered along, ensuring the cake and its guardian remained undisturbed. His anxiousness led him to focus solely on the resplendent edifice, oblivious to the surroundings. Kanya sensed the long journey ahead and chose to pass the time with a melody.

'OH, my sleepy bloom, don't worry about the gloom if there is moon;

OH, my sleepy dolphin, don't worry about the rain if there is sea;

OH, my sleepy shroom, don't worry about the storm if there is tree;

OH, my sleepy raven, don't worry about the wind if there is wild;

OH, my sleepy child, don't worry about the fun if there is sun.

As they traversed the silent bridge, a blanket of quietness enveloped them. Vehicles glided by like whispers. Kanya carried on with her melody, yet it was as though a silent film played out - her lips danced in rhythm, but the notes stayed a whisper in the air. Once they reached the other side, the world erupted back into sound, mingling with Kanya's tune.

'Don't worry about the fun if there is sun.'

The orange tendrils of dusk wrapped around her and danced upon the river's surface. They came upon a Y junction.

'WELCOME TO SPOOKY MARSH'

<=Scent River-⅓ miles, Sweet Sea-6⅓ miles, Dolphin Corner-9⅓ miles.

=>Silent Bridge-1⅓ miles, Golden town-3⅓ miles, Sleepy Slope-33⅓ miles.

"Grandpa, can I rinse my legs in the river?"

Francis stooped carefully as she eased herself down.

"Hold this." She passed him the package and stepped into the flowing water. Little Anand was counting the seconds beneath the surface, his eyes shut tight, breath suspended. 288, 289, 290, 291, 292, 293, 294, 295, 296, 297, 298, 299, 300, 301... The numbers echoed in his mind. As he opened his eyes, two dainty legs danced before his obsidian gaze, transforming his underwater adventure into a dazzling spectacle. 302, 303, 304, and suddenly, he lost track. His breath caught, time halted, and he forgot he was submerged. The chilling brush of reality struck him, propelling him to the surface. "Ahhhh!" Kanya, startled, tumbled back, her lower half drenched.

"Oh, my sincerest apologies! I didn't intend to give you a fright."

"Are you, perhaps, Ajna?"

"Nope, just honing my underwater prowess. I aspire to be a diver one day."

"Are you planning to send shivers down my spine to achieve that?"

"Kanya, come on now. He said he's sorry; it was unintentional, right?"

"Indeed, I didn't mean to."

"Hmph." Kanya crossed her small arms, her expression stormy.

"So, how long did you hold your breath?" "I managed to count to 304 but lost track after that."

"Let's round that to 350 seconds, shall we? Not too shabby for a lad."

"Grandpa can hold his breath even longer. Want to challenge him?"

"I don't compete against others, only with myself."

"You're a clever little fellow. What do they call you?" Francis tousled his damp hair, intrigued.

"Anand. But everyone calls me Nandhu."

"Pleasure to meet you, Nandhu." Francis extended a hand, then turned to Kanya.

"This here is Kanya, my own little dolphin." "Grandpa. Not in front of this fishy boy." "Oh, come on. Shake hands; you two look like a perfect match." "Hmph." With a pout, Kanya's arms extended cautiously as he shook her hand, glancing at her bare legs.

"Why are you staring at my legs? My face is up here." He lifted his gaze, shaking her hand while meeting her dolphin-like, bright eyes, a strange warmth unfurling within him.

"Actually, I'm running late. It was nice meeting both of you." He dashed away from them.

"Hmph, that odd fishy boy. Come on, Grandpa, the cake is going to melt." Kanya marched ahead along the mangrove path, with Francis trailing behind.

"What made you so brusque with that boy? He seems fond of you." "Grandpa." She bristled, a mix of anger and bashfulness.

"I believe he might be your future husband."

"What? That little fishy boy?"

"He'll blossom into a dashing young man. And?"

"How can you be so certain?" "I have insight. Grandpa is skilled in face reading and palmistry."

"Alright, when we arrive home, the first order of business will be my palm reading." She picked up her pace as Francis looked to keep up. They entered the bungalow. Francis placed the cake in the refrigerator while Kanya changed out of her wet clothes. "I'm ready for my palm reading." "Wait for me by the spring." He retreated to the room, retrieving a magnifying mirror from a safeguarded wooden box.

"Are you ready?" Kanya splashed her tiny arms from the spring bucket and beamed with excitement.

"You hardly have a past to anticipate the mysteries ahead."

"Just for kicks, Francis, let's go!" Her arms shot out with a smile, revealing a gap where a tooth once was.

"My little dolphin, which arm holds your strength?" She let her left-hand fall.

"Let me take a look." He polished the magnifying glass on his shirt.

"Is this going to be a mirror?" he counted silently until he reached "1994."

"Mirror? What mirror are you talking about?"

"Never mind. Show me those arms." He examined the lines on her right palm.

"Let's begin with your lifeline. Hmm, a long one. The longer, the better."

"Does that mean I'll live a long life?"

"Oh, my little dolphin, you'll age just like grandpa. Check out the space between the lifeline and your thumb; it shows vitality. A bigger space means better health, and you have quite the spacious reservoir!"

"Really?" The lively girl sparked with enthusiasm about her well-being.

"There will be hurdles; that's inevitable. Don't punish your body when it's in distress because it's your sacred home." She nodded with innocent understanding.

"Now, let's view your heart line. Look at that stretch under your fingers—that's your line. The longer it is, the better, and yours extends right to your index finger." He traced the lines directly to her armpit. "What does that mean?" she giggled mischievously.

"It suggests my girl will be quite the romantic. Now, let's examine the fate line."

He adjusted the lens closer to the center.

"Your fate line splits into several sections. What do you want to become?" "Hmm, don't know."

"The line indicates you'll juggle many jobs before finding success in what you love."

"Many jobs?" She sounded anxious.

"Oh, my little dolphin, there's no need to fret over work. As grandpa says, life isn't simple, and a challenging pursuit doesn't always lead to enlightenment. You don't go searching for the truth; you must seek it."

"What's the difference?"

"Searching means you have a specific goal, while seeking happens without knowing."

"Then why are you looking?"

"Because you haven't got any other options."

"What's the consequence of discovering the unknown?" "Oh, my tiny dolphin brain, that's an excellent question. So, you're curious about what you'll learn once the unknown is revealed?" She waited, her serious expression filling the gap with her tongue.

"You'll only find out when you do." "Grandpa!" She playfully poked him.

"Hang on, we aren't finished yet. Now for the headline. See, grandpa told you, that lengthy arc crossing your palm reveals your intellect. How do you channel that brilliance? That's up to you, my dear."

"I love to explore on one hand and seek on the other," she shared with a sweet smile, prompting the old man to gently pinch her cheeks.

"Now that's a clever approach. Lastly, we have the marriage line—a tiny line above the heart line. Hmm, it suggests you won't be getting married anytime soon."

"So, I won't discover someone akin to how grandma found you?"

"Oh, my little dolphin, marriage isn't solely linked to love. Remember, you have a long love line. Let grandpa take one more peek. Hmm, intriguing. Alright, I'm ready for the prediction."

"My girl will face considerable trials in love. Those abundant in affection often find themselves struggling with it. Don't worry; it's merely a stage. Oh, this is getting much more interesting."

The little girl saw the old man's face, her gaze shifting between his features and the lines on her palm.

"You will encounter the man who loves you deeply, but for certain reasons, you may need to distance yourself."

"Why? Why must I push him away?"

"Because, at times, love can feel like a weight." The small mind grappled with this notion.

"Love symbolizes freedom; it's akin to soaring. On one hand, you have the choice to ascend, while on the other, you may feel tethered. So, what will you choose?"

"I shall shatter that bond."

"True, but what if your spirit lacks the vigor to do so?"

The young girl finds herself in a tough predicament.

"Fear not, dear one. Hold steadfast to your truth, even amid a web of deceit and watchful eyes.

The journey may be arduous, yet remember, nothing wields more potency than truth. It will grant you the fortitude to sever that chain, regardless of its formidable nature."

"What if there's someone keeping watch to ensure I don't break free?" The little mind posed a profound question to the elder, who pondered deeply, struggling to conjure a secure answer.

"That is precisely when we must dare to defy the norms," the elder stated, locking his gaze with hers.

"But what if the authorities come after me for defying the rules?"

"When the law fails to safeguard our truth, we must shield it ourselves, lest we succumb to the allure of both trivial and costly falsehoods."

The young mind began to ruminate on the essence of life and its purpose.

"That should be enough the tiny head. Where is everyone?"

The bungalow wrapped itself in an eerily peaceful hush as they stepped inside.

"I need to check on my sponge candy! Grandpa, call grandma. I will call out mom; it's time to cut the cake."

Kanya dashed towards her mom's bedroom. Grace was resting her head on the dining table, her arms cradling the weight of silence.

"Why is it so quiet here? Where's Varsha?" Francis probed. "She... she's feeling unwell," Grace stammered, her words caught in a web of reluctance. "Where is my girl?" A heavy pause lingered before she replied, "In her bedroom."

A woman draped over the bed, embodying the infinity pose, softly serenaded her newborn with a lullaby.

'OH, my sleepy bloom, don't worry about the gloom if there is moon;

OH, my sleepy dolphin, don't worry about the rain if there is sea;

OH, my sleepy shroom, don't worry about the storm if there is tree;

OH, my sleepy raven, don't worry about the wind if there is wild;

OH, my sleepy child, don't worry about the fun if there is sun.

With her chocolate-brown eyes sparkling, the little one gazed at her mother, lost in a soothing melody. Kanya crawled over and softly inquired, "Is she asleep?" She crept closer, discovering her tiny sister wide awake.

"Oh, my sweet little sponge candy is awake!" she exclaimed, settling down beside them. In an instant, Varsha awakened from her melodic dream and hid the face behind her hair.

"Mom, can I just nibble on her?" she softly cradled the tiny baby in her arms, gently swaying back and forth.

The baby flashed a toothless grin as she started a playful dance on her belly.

"I'm going to snack on you! Look, I've lost a tooth too!" She beamed, pointing to her gaping grin for her little sister. "Mom, when will those baby teeth pop up?" Varsha remained silent, her gaze drifting elsewhere. Just then, Francis entered.

"Grandpa, when do baby teeth appear?"

"Why don't you take your sister outside to play? Grandpa and Mom need to chat." "Alright."

As soon as the children left the room, Varsha erupted in tears.

"What's wrong, sweetheart? Mom mentioned you're feeling unwell."

She turned her face towards him, and he tucked a strand of hair behind her ear, revealing bruised brown eyes.

"What happened?" "Dad, I can't do this anymore. I can't live with him." Her head sank into his chest, tears flowing freely.

"Dad's here; you're safe. What's going on?" She paused, hesitation clouding her words.

"Dear one, you know dad. Speak your truth, what's wrong?"

"He hurts me during intimacy. When I refuse him, he forces himself on me. I can't endure this pain any longer."

Anger flashed through Francis as he inhaled deeply.

From the moment I reached out for love, he'd turn his back on me, casting me aside with words like 'slut.' Yet, when his desires stirred, he would take me by force. What's wrong with this, Dad? Am I the one at fault?"

"No, sweetie, you aren't at fault. Did he always bring you pain?"

"No, he wears a mask of charm while he crosses boundaries. He claims that inflicting hurt during intimacy is perfectly normal. Is it really, Dad?"

"No, my dear, love is sacred. It thrives between whispers of slight discomfort and waves of euphoric pleasure—that's the essence of the divine. But what you're experiencing is not love; it's violence. Do you have bruises elsewhere?"

"No, his scars are hidden, but they burden my spirit. I find no joy in our moments together. Yet he persistently pushes me forward."

"What about your eye?"

"Yesterday, I reached a breaking point and attempted to stop him. This is what I received in return. This morning, he assured me it wouldn't happen again. Look, he brought me medicine, all while wearing that same deceptive smile." She handed him a packet of condoms.

"He told me to lay low and avoid the sunlight."

"What's this?" "It's a preventative measure. He said tonight will be painless. I don't know how to respond, Dad."

"Even in a situation like this, does he crave intimacy? That monster? You won't spend another night under his roof, understand?"

"Hmm. What can we do?" She wiped away her tears, the ache in her bruised eye persistent.

"I'm so sorry, sweetheart, that we've put you through this."

"No, Dad. You both respected my choices. Don't carry that burden." "I will file a police report." "Dad, you know he's pals with the law and the inspector—it's pointless." "No, darling, we must voice our concerns. There are protections for us." "I can't share my pain in public, Dad." "I'll speak on your behalf. You just need to come with me." "No, Dad. I can't bear the shame. Please help me get a divorce." "We will, sweetheart, we will." "But he holds influence. He can accept our requests or deny us. What should we do?" "What do you mean he has power? Aren't laws meant to shield us? If justice fails, we can evict him. This place belongs to Grace, doesn't it?

"No, Dad, the power of attorney is in his name. I've seen the documents."

Grace entered the room, a curious look on her face.

"Is she correct? Does this house really belong to Devachan?"

"No."

"Then what is she on about? Did you hand over any power of attorney to him?"

"Not recently. I did sign some documents during the heir issue. He assured me that the ownership would revert to me when the case concluded—and it has. So, it's mine again, right?" Grace was oblivious to the details, and Varsha felt the sting of betrayal.

"He claimed the power transfer was just a temporary arrangement," she replied, her voice barely above a whisper.

"Dad, he's twisting mom's intentions, just like he twists mine."

"What do you mean? Does this house now belong to him?"

"He usurped mom's authority."

"Grace, what did the legal documents indicate?"

"My dad went over them with me back when the issue kicked off. They told that upon my parents' passing, the mansion would be passed to me or to someone I appoint."

"And you designated Devachan." The weight of betrayal settled heavily in the air.

"He deceived all of us, Grace. He snatched the house—and our girl. Let's leave this place; we can move to another land. Dad will take care of things. But I refuse to let him have my girl for another heartbeat." Francis stormed out, a tempest in motion.

"Where are you headed?"

"To the police station. There must be a way. We just need some legal aid to take the next step. We require someone to help us escape this house."

"Can you venture into town by yourself? I'll join you."

"No, you stay with Varsha. Where are Kanya and Maria?"

"They're out playing."

"Sweetheart, take a moment to rest. If he gets near you again, kill him" Francis handed her a concoction.

"What are you suggesting, Dad?" "That's the law of the wild. But first, let's witness what this foolish society has in store for us." Francis stepped out toward the town, while Kanya was by the garden with her sister.

"How does it smell? Mmm." She brought a delicate flower close to the tiny nose and asked.

The little one responded with a fragrant smile, reaching for the sweet bloom.

"Grandpa, where are you off to?"

"I'm off to town!" "Can I join you?" "Oh, my little dolphin, it's not just a stroll in the park. Grandpa has some matters to sort out." "I can lend a hand. Can't you see I'm a big girl now?" A flicker of joy brightened the weary old man's face.

"Alright, go tell Mom and hurry back." "Can we take sponge candy too? I'll need a snack for the journey when my tummy rumbles." Kanya tingled the baby belly with excitement, making the tiny chuckle with a toothless grin.

"We can't take Maria. Leave her with Grandma and come back quickly." "Sure!" She dashed into the mansion, returning in a flash, hands empty.

"We're off, Francis."

Kanya clasped grandpa's hand, both moving forward. He shuffled along like a mechanical puppet, his mind a tempest of thoughts.

"Grandpa, is Maya still alive beneath the sea?" Francis wasn't exactly in a storytelling mood. "Not right now, sweetheart." "Why not now? Come on, Grandpa." "Kanya, I just need a moment."

Her grandfather's irritation cast a shadow over her spirit. Yet after a brief hiatus, his demeanor softened as he playfully tapped her small head, though she feigned indignation.

"My precious little dolphin." "I'm no one's dolphin!" She wriggled free from his embrace and marched ahead. Francis halted, and after a few paces, Kanya glanced back.

"You're meant to tickle me from behind and swoop me up!" She reminded him of their cherished routine. Suddenly, tears cascaded down Francis's cheeks.

"Grandpa, why are you crying? I was only joking!" He tried to stifle his sobs, but they continued unabated.

"I'm sorry, Grandpa. I just wanted to tease you a little." The sweet little girl tried to soothe his sadness.

After a moment of tears, he saw Kanya's regret for his upset.

"I'm sorry." "No need to apologize, my little dolphin. You've done nothing amiss."

"Then why the tears?" "Grandpa wept over thoughts from another world."

"Whatever that thought may be, don't dwell on it, okay?" She wrapped her tiny arms around him.

"Let's wrap up our errands, Grandpa. I'm eager to get home and savor my sponge candy." The little girl entwined her arms with his and they continued onward, reaching Y junction once again.

"Where to now, Grandpa?"

"Off to the police station." She pressed no further and simply followed his lead. They crossed the silent bridge once more, where Francis's thoughts remained quiet, only to swell with sound the moment they reached the other side.

They strolled through the bustling town and arrived at the police station; a structure marked by its arched sign proclaiming, "Town Police Station."

Beneath the sign, Kanya turned to her grandpa. "This is it!" she exclaimed, leading him inside. Behind her desk sat a youthful constable named Ramani, whose face brightened at the sight of the little girl.

"How may I assist you today?" Ramani asked, glancing at Kanya as she gauged her grandpa's reaction.

"We're here to lodge a complaint," he replied. "Very well, proceed straight to the senior constable over there," she instructed, gesturing toward a middle-aged man named Paul at a nearby table.

"Hello," Paul acknowledged. "What's your complaint?"

"Please, not in front of the child," Francis replied, with a hint of concern.

"Who's the child?" Paul inquired.

"She's, my granddaughter. She insisted on coming along," Francis explained.

"That's perfectly fine. Ramani," he called to the constable. "Please keep an eye on her while we chat."

"Of course! What's your name, dear?" Ramani asked, and Kanya beamed.

"Kanya."

"What a lovely name! Look, there's a little bird's nest over there. Would you like to see it?" she offered. Kanya glanced at Francis, who nodded with a smile.

"Yes, please!" she said eagerly.

"Come with me, then," Ramani invited, and Kanya quickly took the constable's hand, walking out with her, a bond forming between them.

"Don't fret; she'll take good care of her," Paul assured Francis. "So, what's your name?"

"Francis. MD Francis," he introduced himself, ready to share his story.

Sir, my daughter is enduring physical violence and mistreatment." "Oh my God, who is responsible?"

"Her husband, Devachan. She has never told anyone about her suffering, but yesterday, he struck her."

"Please stay calm, Francis. To file a formal report, we require the victim to be present meaning we need your daughter's account. Where is she now?"

"She has significant injuries on her face and feels too ashamed to speak to anyone. Is there any hope for her, sir?"

"Francis, take a deep breath. This is a matter of domestic violence. Is she well enough to come in?" "Yes."

"Then please bring her here. Set aside your worries."

Relief washed over Francis. Paul glanced outside, noticing Ramani near the compound wall with Kanya.

"What's this bird's nest here?" "It's a raven. It fell from the tree." "So, there were no eggs?"

"There was one, but it cracked a few days ago. The baby raven must be around somewhere, cawing away." "Can I keep the nest?" "Of course, dear. It doesn't truly belong to me or even the raven." "Then who is its rightful owner?" "The clever bird that painstakingly constructed it.

Ravens are quite shrewd. They often place their eggs in the nests of other birds, tricking them into raising their young. The host bird discovers the truth only when the egg hatches."

"Why do they do this? Why not care for their own offspring?"

"That's a vital lesson to remember there will always be those who exploit our kindness." "So, should we not be kind?" the sweet little girl inquired. "Absolutely, we should be kind to all living things but never forget to show kindness to yourself."

"Rama?" Paul and Francis stepped out of the station.

"Grandpa, look! Madam let me keep this nest!"

"Wow, what will you do with it?" Paul asked, prompting the little mind to ponder deeply.

"I'm not sure. I hadn't really thought it through." "That's alright. Go home and come to a decision. Sir, don't fret; we'll handle it." "Thank you, sir."

"Where do you reside?"

"The bungalow by the marshlands."

"Oh, Advocate Devachan—you mentioned."

"Indeed, sir," Francis replied, a tremor of fear clears in his voice. Paul and Ramani exchanged direct gazes.

"Alright, we'll handle it."

"Sir, will you both be here for the night shift as well?" Francis asked Paul, anxiety lacing his words.

"No, our shift is done. Another officer will take over."

"Can I bring my daughter when you're both around?" "It's alright, Francis; someone else will assist you."

"I feel you two are reliable. Convincing a stranger about the situation would be more difficult." The officers shared a knowing smile, recognizing the old man's state of mind.

"Very well then. Bring your daughter tomorrow at eleven. We'll both be here. Does that work?"

Francis's relief shone through in a silent smile.

"Alright, sir, ma'am. Thank you."

"Francis, there's no need to fret. Rest well, and we'll see you in the morning." Francis rushed homeward, eager to ensure his daughter was all right.

"Are you leaving too? You can join me at home today," Ramani said to the young girl.

"Maybe another time, ma'am. Farewell." "What worries you, Grandpa?" Kanya whispered. "I'll explain later. Shall we head out? Maria might be seeking you." "Oh, who's she?" "My little sister." "Wow, send her my regards, alright?" "Of course, and thank you for the bird's nest, ma'am." "You're welcome, sweetheart." The officers bid them farewell with warm smiles.

Just as they left, a police jeep rolled in. A police officer with two shoulder stars appeared from the driver's seat, casting a glance at the elderly man and child as they walked away. Paul and Ramani snapped to attention, saluting him.

"Why did that old man visit?" "He came to lodge a complaint, sir. A case of domestic violence."

"Hmm, did you file an FIR?" "No, sir. He didn't bring the victim. I instructed him to bring her for the complaint." "Hmm." The police officer entered his office, approached a rotary dial, and began turning the numbers one by one, as the other end began to ring.

As the sun dipped below the horizon, they arrived at the bungalow. Grace was applying ointment to Varsha's bruise.

"Sweetheart, there's no need to fret. The police assured us they'll handle everything, but they need your direct input." "Dad, me?" "It's all right, darling. They're trustworthy. Just relax; we'll file a complaint in the morning. Just hold on for the night."

In a moment of inspiration, Grace recalled the conclusion to her latest novel.

"Francis, I'm nearing the end of my story. Can you help me now?"

Grace and Francis exchanged glances with their daughter.

"Mom, Dad. I'm okay. You both go ahead and write. I'll take a rest."

"Kanya, will you stay with Mom until I return?" "Sure, Grandma."

Kanya and Varsha snuggled into the bed, cradling baby Maria in the center like a precious gem.

As Francis grasped the pencil upon reaching the writing table, he sank into his seat, a tremor coursing through his arm.

"I don't think I can write right now."

"Hey, I can lend you a hand with that!" Devachan burst forth, startling both Francis and Grace.

"Ah, Devachan! We didn't even hear you sneak in." Though fury simmered within him, Francis supported his composure as Devachan sauntered closer and snatched the pencil from his grasp.

"We'll write later," Grace chimed in, feigning a smile.

"Come on! I know what it's like to struggle with writer's block. Just get it done when the ideas are fresh and hot!"

"Mom, you know I'm skilled at writing and inspiring others to write. You can leave now." Devachan gently nudged Francis out of the chair. Grace exchanged a silent glance with Francis, reassuring him that it was okay. He exited the room, fighting to keep his frustration at bay, and headed straight for Varsha.

"He's here," Francis warned her.

"Dad, let me handle him tonight. You take Maria to your room."

"Are you sure?"

"Yes, Dad." Determination flickered in her eyes, mingled with the fire of anger. Taking Maria into his arms, Kanya, who had been asleep, stirred awake.

"Where are you taking my sponge candy?"

"To grandpa's room."

"Okay, I'm coming too! I want to be with her." Half-asleep, Kanya slid out of bed, accepting Maria from Francis. She climbed the stairs, seeking the familiar refuge of another bed.

Outside, the sky wept tiny drops of rain, accompanied by a whispering breeze that beckoned them to cocoon themselves beneath the warm embrace of a shared blanket. As soon as she nestled in, sleep overtook her once more.

A thunderous roar jolted her from sleep, though the skies remained dry—only the ferocious noise intruded upon the stillness. Wrapped snugly within her cozy blanket, Maria drifted in peaceful dreams as Kanya gingerly slid out of bed, careful not to disrupt her sister's slumber.

"Grandpa, grandma," she whispered as she tiptoed down the staircase, the eerie hush amplifying her trepidation.

The front door gaped wide open.

"Grandpa... Grandma..." The silence swallowed her calls. Tentatively, she stepped outside, her feet sinking into the muddy earth, where a shadow lay. Crimson seeped into the soil, mingling distressingly with the dirt. Her mother lay there, lifeless.

"Mom." She desperately tried to rouse her, but her pleas were ignored. A closer examination revealed the truth, leaving Kanya's small feet numb with horror. Just then, a man's anguished scream pierced the air from within the house. Adrenaline surged through her legs, propelling her back up the stairs to the bedroom, where Maria was now wide awake, her cries crashing like waves against the walls.

"Oh, my sponge candy! I'm here. Don't fret." Kanya cradled the tiny form in her arms, drawing her close to her heart as distant shouts echoed outside. The little girl battled to reject the sounds that plagued her reality.

"My sponge candy, I nearly forgot your present." She reached beneath the bed to unveil a nest.

"Look what I found! A nest that belongs to no one—you can have it."

Kanya gently laid Maria in the nest, a perfect embrace for her fragile body.

"Oh, it fits you just right." A single tear escaped her shimmering silver eyes, landing softly upon the baby's cheek. With great tenderness, she kissed it away, watching her beloved sponge candy yawn and ready herself for another cycle of dreams.

"I will care for you, I promise. One day, you'll sprout wings and soar, so don't worry." As Maria slipped into a deep slumber, Kanya began to weave a lullaby, her voice a calming melody against the night's chaos.

'OH, my sleepy bloom, don't worry about the gloom if there is moon;

OH, my sleepy dolphin, don't worry about the rain if there is sea;

OH, my sleepy shroom, don't worry about the storm if there is tree;

OH, my sleepy raven, don't worry about the wind if there is wild;

OH, my sleepy child, don't worry about the fun if there is sun.

As Kanya serenades with her gentle lullaby, the little one drifts into a dreamy realm, slumbering serenely upon fluffy clouds - a cradle over the clouds.

Chapter 6
The Scent of the River

Winter Fragrance,

1994.

Beneath a winter sky cloaked in clouds, a row of pristine white structures stands proudly amid the golden townscape, housing various medical departments. 'White Pill Eye Sanatorium.'

Inside, a lengthy corridor unfolds, painted white and bathed in the soft glow of muted yellow lights—a waiting room for visitors at the hospital.

"Mr. Madhu, hello, Mr. Madhu!" A nurse's voice sliced through the air, rousing a dozing man from his slumber. He had drifted off in a chair, adorning a pair of child's dark glasses, their modest 10₹ tag still dangling from them. A sudden clap of thunder echoed ominously, jolting him awake.

"Mr. Madhu." "Huh." His groggy mind momentarily conjured the nurse, clad in white, as an angel hovering on a gleaming glass bridge. Once more, the thunder crackled, fully breaking his stupor. "The doctor is calling you." "Oh, right. Apologies, I just had a brief nap." He wiped the drool from his chin and adjusted his glasses back onto his nose as thunder rumbled overhead.

"What on earth is happening up there?" The nurse chuckled at the old man's endearingly bewildered expression.

"Is there something on my face?" he inquired. "Those glasses look rather charming on you."

"Thanks. I find them childish rather than charming if I'm honest."

"Well, they are intended for children." "Ah, that explains why they feel so small for my face—meant for little ones." Another giggle escaped the nurse's lips.

"Champakam is all set to depart." "Oh, really?"

"Are those the sunglasses you picked out for her?"

"No, these were street finds. I opted for a branded pair for her."

"Smart choice. For the next few months, her eyes ought to be shielded from harsh rays."

They stepped into a hospital room, where two more celestial figures in white awaited—a doctor and another nurse. On the bed sat a 16-year-old girl draped in a full-length black gown adorned with floral prints. Madhu darted to the restroom to freshen up, returning with a renewed visage.

"Dad, the doctor says I'm ready to go." She declared, her eyes tightly shut to fend off the light.

"Why isn't she opening her eyes, Madhu? She mentioned it's a secret."

"Oh, it's nothing significant. She promised two friends she'd see them first before anyone else."

"And who are those fortunate friends, Champakam?" The doctor inquired with curiosity.

"Let's keep them a secret for now and reveal them next time we meet."

"They've known her since infancy," Madhu divulged the mystery.

"Wow, that's a profoundly lasting friendship."

"Yes, indeed." Champakam let out a giggle, caught up in a shared jest.

Do you recall the contours of my face? Would you be able to recognize me if you stumbled upon me somewhere?"

"Absolutely! The visages of you four are etched in my memory. Well, technically five, including the enigmatic raven."

"You little wildling! Please feel free to drop by anytime for anything, okay?"

"Of course, Doctor. Thank you!"

"Alright, young lady. No basking in the afternoon sun and give your eyes a break for a few days. If you meet any issues, just let your dad know, and he'll pass the word along, understood?"

"Sure thing, Doctor." The doctor pivoted towards Madhu, reappearing with his trendy kids' glasses, playfully removing the shades with a silly grin.

"Madhu, did you purchase these sunglasses for her?" "No, Doctor." He retrieved a small glass pouch from a plastic zip bag.

"Wow, impressive! This one looks fantastic." "Doctor, it's protected from UV rays." "Great consideration, Madhu." The Doctor gently rested the glasses on her ears, adjusting them carefully over her closed eyes. They fit exactly right, and she was ready for her runway debut.

"Wow, Doctor! I think we should make her the hospital's model," suggested one of the nurses.

"I'd absolutely be on board with that."

"Why don't you open your eyes just once to see the world around you?"

Slowly, she revealed her eyes, seeing everyone in shades of black and white.

"Yes, Doctor! I see you all, but without color." "Clean and sharp." "Indeed."

"Alright, Madhu, she's ready to roll. You can discharge her tomorrow morning."

Just then, a heavy downpour began, accompanied by a dazzling light display.

"Dad, should we head out now?" She squeezed her eyes shut again, clutching Madhu's arm.

"It's pouring outside, dear. Let's wait for the rain to let up."

"Actually, that's why she wants to leave now. She adores the rain. But darling, how do we get to the bus station without an umbrella?"

"Not to worry! You can use mine. Nurse, could you fetch my umbrella from my office? It's under the desk." "Of course, Doctor."

"Winter's departure is throwing a party for your newfound zest for life. You should join in the revelry."

The nurse returned with the umbrella.

"I can't express my gratitude enough." "Forget the thanks—just make sure to return my umbrella."

"Of course, Doctor. We plan to come back to return it, or perhaps invite you all over for dinner, and you can take your umbrella then."

"The latter plan has a nice ring to it, doesn't it?" "Absolutely, Doctor. We'll see you both soon!"

"I'm eagerly anticipating our next encounter." "And I hope to meet your friends too. Please send my warm regards to them." "Of course, Doctor..." "So, Madhu, keep me posted on the date." "Absolutely, Doctor. I'll make a call." "Enjoy the winter rain." "Goodbye, everyone! Looking forward to seeing you all soon.

Champakam grasped her father's arm as they stepped out of the hospital, the dark sky cloaked in rain, each droplet splattering onto their heads. They made their way to the golden bus stop.

"Dad, when will the sun be out?" He glanced at his bare wrist, lacking a watch. A grand clock perched atop a building chimed, revealing it was 4 o'clock. "Hopefully soon, unless the rain pulls him into a sleepy haze."

The first bus of the day rolled in, its windshield boasting a wooden sign reading -

'Scent River-Sweet Sea.' They climbed aboard and claimed a cozy two-seater in the center. From the shadows, a blue light flickered, accompanied by rumbling thunder. Champakam claimed the window seat, tiny raindrops dancing against the glass beside her.

Madhu tried to close the window.

"No, Dad, leave it open."

"My goodness, what's with this thunder?" Champakam pondered. "I think the sky is both joyous and upset, Dad."

"Why would it feel both ways?" The girl had no answer as the bus jolted into motion.

"Tickets, please?" "Statue Stop." "3₹ each."

Madhu fished jingling coins from his pocket, counting, "One... two... three..." until he reached 6₹.

"Sir, can someone be both angry and happy?" Madhu queried the conductor, who paused, intrigued, then wandered off, musing on the oddity of his question. Champakam gazed vacantly outside, delighting in the winter rain's caress. The bus whisked out of town, gliding over the silent bridge. The world fell silent, only the uninspiring, flavorless rain brushing against her skin. They reached the statue, and the rain stopped abruptly, as if someone had flipped a switch. A colossal golden axe lay fallen beside a wrecked car on the road.

"What in the world happened?" The driver turned off the engine, eyes widening at the giant statue that was meant to be gripping the golden axe. The entire bus crew disembarked to investigate the commotion.

"Dad? What's going on?"

"An accident. A car crashed." "Is anyone hurt?" "Not sure. They must have been whisked away to the hospital."

"Oh no, who damaged the axe?" Concern rippled among the others about the fallen gold.

"What axe, Dad?" "The golden axe shattered to the ground."

"Oh, did the car collide with it?" "Possibly."

Suddenly, a red truck barreled toward the crowd, sending them leaping back for safety. The truck crashed into a pile of stones, and something from its cargo sailed into the pebble garden by the river. The driver appeared agitated and unsteady.

"Where do you think you're going, you reckless fool? Are you trying to get us all killed?" The truck sped away from the crazy scene before the crowd could react further.

"Let's move on. We have other adventures to pursue." Madhu gripped his daughter's arm, leading her across the road toward the scent river.

Nestled at the core of Eerħt lies Scent River, a crystalline waterway showing a chilly luminescence after the torrential rains.

"Croooow, croooow, croooow," echoes the call of a raven.

"Dad, is that a raven?"

"Indeed, my dear."

"Is it the same one we saw behind the hospital's window?"

"I can't be certain; they all appear similar to me."

"But don't humans each have their own unique look?"

"True, we all bear our distinctions."

"Maybe we seem alike to the ravens as well."

"Perhaps so."

A log cabin awaits the waterman and his daughter along the riverbank, embraced by a garden of pebbles. Champakam stepped onto the melodic stones, her senses keen as she inhaled the familiar scents wafting from the earth and meadow. Madhu slid open the cabin door and headed directly to the kitchen, igniting the stove and placing a rounded pot of water over the flames.

"How will I know when the Sun rises?"

"Just open your eyes and look."

"No, I don't need to see him to know he's up." Her body instinctively moved toward the warmth of the stove, her hands hovering close to the flames as bubbles began to appear.

"Dad, the water is boiling."

He added coffee powder and a hint of palm sugar, saying, "Champakam, coffee." She carefully held the hot glass, its base resting in her left palm while her right fingers cradled the top.

"I'm going to check our canoe. It must be swamped from the rain." The girl followed her father outdoors. Next to the cabin, she found a stone that fit her buttocks perfectly and perched upon it proudly, sipping her hot coffee beneath the misty dawn. Madhu approached their canoe, which rocked gently on the shallow river.

The vessel had a long, wooden arch draped with coconut fiber. Beneath its shelter lay a man sleeping peacefully, swaddled in warmth.

"God, who's this?" he mused, leaning in to examine the figure and lightly touching the man's nose.

"Oh, thank heavens, he's alive." He gently gave the man a nudge. "Hey." A pair of raven-black eyes fluttered open.

"Ahh."

"Son, you're in my canoe." He gazed at the old sailor, feeling as though he were adrift in a dream.

"Are you alright?" The young man, still dazed, scanned the canoe. "You're in my canoe," the sailor repeated, prompting the boy to feel relieved and regain his bearings.

"Sorry, I was sitting by the river and took shelter when the rain poured."

"No worries, son, relax. The Sun hasn't risen yet. I think I've seen you around; you live nearby, correct?"

"Yes, just a short walk away past the palm grove."

"You can rest some more."

"No, I'm good."

"Are you certain?"

"Yes, thank you for the lovely shade." He inhaled the crisp air deeply.

"What time is it?"

"The Sun will be up shortly. Care for some coffee?" Unable to deny the invitation, he offered a warm smile of acceptance.

"Alright then. Do come home." The young man appeared from the cradle of the canoe into the cool river, energy invigorating him as he splashed his face and ventured toward the cabin. He noticed a gathering near a statue.

"What's happening over there?"

"An accident, I believe; a car struck something, and that golden ax toppled."

"Really? Was anyone hurt?"

"Uncertain."

A stylish figure sporting sunglasses lounged outside the cabin.

"That's my daughter, Champakam."

"She appeared engrossed in her personal retreat. Madhu appeared, bearing two steaming mugs of coffee.

"Coffee. What's your name, my friend? You seem familiar." After savoring a warm sip, a name surfaced from his throat, "Anand." "Madhu," they exchanged introductions, shaking hands. "Anand, aren't you that daring diver who braved the river's depths?"

"Yes, that's me. I ventured to cross it; that's a fitting way to describe my endeavor."

"It doesn't matter. You reached the midpoint; that's quite an achievement! No one else has journeyed that far. Will you try it again?"

"I just did and may consider it once more." With a smile, Madhu encouraged, "I believe you'll succeed one day."

"I've noticed you both. You don't quite fit the mold of societal norms."

"Actually, we blend in when surrounded by the right crowd, the perfect companion," Champakam responded with a laid-back grin and another sip.

"Did you sleep well?"

"Best sleep space, I would say."

Champakam finished his coffee and set the cup down. "Could you hand me a bag, Dad?"

"Why the request?"

"To gather pebbles for Weedo."

"Now? In the dark?"

"You know darkness is my ally?"

"Why not do it in daylight? I'll join you."

"I prefer to collect stones now; it feels like the right moment." Madhu fetched a plastic zipper bag for her.

"You never heed my words, do you?"

"Dad, I'm old enough to embrace the nightlife."

"Okay then, take it. Fill it up and zip it tight." He showed, zipping and unzipping her arms. "Not a whisper of air can creep in, as the merchant said."

"Whatever." Her disinterest was palpable as her skin attuned to the wind's direction, leading her toward the pebble sanctuary. Anand watched her with astonishment.

"She can navigate by scent and breeze," Madhu revealed, unveiling one of her extraordinary abilities. Kneeling by the collection of stones, she brushed her fingers over each, searching for the remarkable ones.

"Weedo!" Madhu chuckled to himself, relishing the inside joke, while Anand's curiosity piqued.

"What's the story behind that name?"

"While casting a net in the river, I ensnared a star turtle tangled in weeds. It felt fitting to name it Weedo." Anand took a moment to savor the delightful irony with another sip of coffee.

"Are you joining us to see Grandma?"

"I've visited her countless times."

"She's an early riser. Have you ever seen her greet the dawn?"

That part was unfamiliar to him.

"No." "Then come along. It will be a refreshing change from those countless visits. Champakam is about to see grandma for the very first time."

"But... she is...?" Anand hesitated. "Yes, she was blind. She just had her eye surgery. Now she can see all the colors."

Madhu conveyed the joyful news, her voice trembling with emotion.

"Wow, I'm in! Watching her witness the world again will be something extraordinary." Anand was filled with excitement to see grandma through her newly opened eyes.

"Just wait for the sun to rise."

"Dad." Champakam called from the garden.

"What is it, dear? Are you finished picking?"

She noticed something peculiar among the stones. An object resembling a human head, complete with hair, eyebrows, eyes, nose, ears, and lips. She struggled to name it, but no clues appeared. For a moment, she contemplated opening her eyes but chose to uphold her vow. Those eyes were reserved for seeing another marvel. Yet, she couldn't bring herself to discard the odd find, so she added it to her pebble collection. The human head occupied half the space like a typical human. She filled her bag with more pebbles and zipped it shut. Champakam, along with that mysterious head nestled among the jangling pebbles, made her way toward the canoe.

The sun awoke. Champakam felt its warmth and shouted.

"Dad, it's here! Let's go." She dashed to the eastern side of the canoe and claimed a window seat with her back turned to the sun.

"All aboard, passengers! The ship is ready!" Champakam announced.

"The captain calls. Shall we set sail?"

Anand settled into the center seat, admiring the sunglasses model.

Madhu untied the rope, and with a gentle push, the canoe glided into the fragrant river.

With a single-bladed wooden paddle, the waterman took the helm as the trio embarked on their adventure.

"What's your favorite color?" Champakam inquired, shooting a curious glance at Anand, who found himself puzzled by her gaze. "Are you referring to me?" he asked. "Yes, Mr. Diver, I mean you! Share your favorite color." "I adore every color I encounter." "You can't possibly love everything in sight."

"Actually, I'm a bit vision-impaired myself."

"Like I once was?" "I'm colorblind." "What type of blindness is that?"

"I can't perceive true colors—only what my mind interprets as reality."

"But you can still see." "Indeed." "You just see in a different light."

"That's one perspective! When our visions vary, it adds a unique flare to everything, making it impossible not to appreciate all that we observe."

"Perhaps that's why I have an affinity for black. And you know what? Black is a steadfast companion—ever loyal, no matter the circumstances. Just close your eyes to feel it." Anand found himself captivated by her every word. The canoe glided along, driven by the aroma of the surroundings until they reached the center. He waved at her sunglasses to check if she was still aware.

"Her eyes are shut. She's taken a vow." "What kind of vow?" "To open her eyes only for her friends."

"And who are they?"

"Champa and Shroom." "What do you admire about them?"

"I cherish Champa's fragrance and our shared name. As for Shroom, his physique fascinates me; it's quite intriguing."

"So, she hasn't seen anyone else?"

"Just me, the doctor, and a few hospital staff."

"So, Champakam, who was your first sight?"

"A raven." "A raven?" he replied, amused.

"Yes, it was either male or female; I couldn't tell. The black bird sat behind the windowpane—such a beautiful creature and my favorite color."

Anand couldn't help but smile at her peculiar analogy.

"Isn't it odd how we humans appear?" He found himself at a loss for words, merely smiling at Madhu.

"What makes us so odd?" "I have no idea." Her attention drifted to her bag of pebbles. She pulled the cover from the wood to unzip it when a startling crack of thunder echoed from the cloudless sky. The rumble rattled all the unusual humans around, causing Champakam to drop her plastic bag. The lifeless light head and heavy stones sank into the depths.

"Dad, my stones are all gone." "That's okay, sweetheart. We can return and gather more. I'll help."

"Should I retrieve them for you? You know I'm a diver," Anand asked for her permission to go ahead.

"No, perhaps their departure has meaning. Let them be," she replied, her demeanor solemn.

"What was that thunderous sound? There were a couple in the morning too. Is there some war happening in the sky?" "What's that smudge on your hands?" Anand queried Champakam. "What smudge?" She revealed her arm.

"Oh heavens, there's blood on her hand!" Madhu panicked. Anand leaned closer to inspect.

"Is that blood?" he asked, sniffing the crimson. "Yes." "She must have scraped herself on something nasty near the stones."

"I'm not in pain, Dad." "Don't fret; it's not her blood. She likely just brushed against something with blood on it." He splashed some river water over it, and the red disappeared.

"Must have been a dead animal." "No, Dad, it was the head of a dead weird human."

"You silly girl, no pain, right? We could head back." "No worries, Dad. Straight to Grandma! Mooooo." She tried a foghorn impression, sounding more like a calf.

Madhu paddled on, smiling with relief. Anand released her arm, only for her to seize it again, tilting her head toward the sky. After a brief silent exchange with the ether, her gaze returned to him. He watched the reflections in her sunglasses, wondering if she could see anything beyond her own image. The girl offered a wicked grin.

"The moon light you once idolized is now buried deep in your shadowy memories, isn't she?"

An image of Kanya flickered in his mind.

"How do you...? How did you know?"

Once again, she astonished him with her uncanny intuition.

"Just relax. She'll be yours by the next dawn."

His arms were freed, and he returned to his seat wearing a smile that danced with confusion, like a dimple caught in a daydream. The only sound for a while was the rhythmic splashing of paddles, accompanied by a soft breeze that carried the enchanting aroma of Champa flowers, prompting everyone to inhale deeply. "We're almost there."

The canoe gilded closer to grandma, and the sweet fragrance intensified. Champakam tucked her sunglasses neatly into a pouch and set them beneath the wooden seat. With her eyes tightly shut and nostrils wide open, she stepped into the shallow water.

Her bare feet glided toward the vision behind her eyelids, pausing where the floral scent enveloped her. Anand and Madhu watched her with curiosity, eager to see what would unfold next. All they could see was a girl frolicking around an unseen tree, surrounded by sunlit mushrooms that glimmered under the sun's embrace.

Gradually, her azure eyes unfurled to greet the light.

Her hair, like floral green strands, swayed as her arms enveloped her neck, her posture upright while her feet sank into the earth's embrace.

A colossal Champaka tree sparkled in the morning sun.

"She embodies the essence of this land. That's why the ancients named the river Scent, for the fragrance she exudes." Madhu and Anand stood wide-eyed and wide-nosed in wonder.

Champakam revealed the joy of vision and soon embraced the thrill of touch. A fragrant Champa flower, dripping with nectar, fell from the tree and adorned her hair. She placed the cherished blossom behind her ear and began to dance around her grandmother.

"Oh, dear. I'm so sorry I almost forgot you. But I kept my promise." She caressed the tiny mushroom body, her gaze wandering through the garden blanketed with whimsical Shrooms in myriad forms.

"It was a winter's night when I discovered a tiny infant nestled beneath grandma. All alone yet blissful, the adorable creature knew nothing of loneliness. That warmth felt as if she'd just appeared from the womb. I named her 'Champakam.'"

Anand's heart raced with astonishment.

"A solitary infant who shattered my solitude." His eyes let fall a tear of the past that mingled with the sweetness of the present. He glanced at Madhu, then back to the tiny, twirling girl, a smile blossoming on his face.

"Is she aware?" "Is it truly significant?" "What if she inquiries about her mother?"

"Once, she did." "About her mother?" "No, she wanted to know how she came to be."

"And?" "I told her she blossomed like a Champa flower." "Did she embrace the tale?"

"Children don't require beliefs. It's we who impose them. What they need is a sanctuary to thrive, and this place is indeed her haven to exist. Let her discover the discrepancies of the taught truths when her awareness expands."

The morning sun had enveloped the entire earth in a haze, prompting the trio to embark on their journey back home.

"Farewell," Champakam said to grandma tree, casting a glance at Anand. "What's on your mind, my intuitive friend?" his thoughts nudged.

"You'll visit again, won't you?" "Absolutely."

"Then bid farewell." "Goodbye, Grandma."

"Goodbye, Grandma." Anand and Madhu joyfully waved to the unseen tree.

"You can enjoy the window seat. I could use some shade and a moment to rest."

Champakam settled beneath the house while Anand chose the eastern edge. The canoe glided into its homeward voyage, with Anand watching the girl find solace in the shade.

"What do you think your favorite color is now?" "I believe I'll echo your sentiment. I choose all colors." She propped her head up momentarily, smiling, before settling back down.

For a time, the trio lost themselves in their tranquil solitude.

Inside the house, Champakam sought harmony between her inner shadows and outer hues.

Meanwhile, Anand pondered his distorted reflection on the water, swimming through the buried echoes of his past. Madhu simply navigated the scent-laden river, swaying with its rhythm.

They arrived back, the surroundings unchanged, yet their belief of it was transformed.

Champakam leaped from the canoe, hurrying to the rear of the wooden house through the shallow waters.

"I'll go check on Weedo." She hesitated, momentarily puzzled. The sight was deceiving her, so she shut her eyes and relied on her other senses. Guided by the wind, she stepped northward, the pungent aroma of turtle waste tickling her nose. Upon opening her eyes, she found a small pond, a basin in the earth, where a shell creature lay stagnant behind a net, which she slowly extricated.

"Hey, Weedo! What's up, friend? I see you."

Upon her arrival, the turtle withdrew within its shell.

"Weedo, come out. It's me." She inspected the turtle's shell, back and forth.

"Weedo is quite an odd fellow. Come on out, my friend."

She slipped through the shell, but the occupant seemed hesitant to appear.

"You must have startled him, sweetheart." "Not particularly."

Setting the shell back down, she waited patiently. The turtle cautiously poked its head out, only to retreat again. She saw the star-like patterns adorning its high, domed shell.

"Daddy, aren't those the stars?" "Indeed." "The ones that shine in the night sky?"

"Those are real stars, shaped just so—hence, he's called a star turtle."

She glanced again at the shy creature.

"What if he's a star that tumbled from the sky?"

"Perhaps so," replied Madhu, a silly grin adorning his face, always a supporter of his girls' whimsical musings.

She gazed at the river, crystalline as the sky above. Her heart began to dance to the rhythm of that shell-bound creature. Carefully, she lifted the star turtle and set him down on the shore. Gradually, a head appeared, followed by flippers and legs. This life had little on its mind but to flee. The turtle dashed toward the river like the swiftest creature on earth, its shell moving in tune with the rhythm, jubilantly celebrating newfound freedom by executing a few flamboyant maneuvers before plunging deep into the river's embrace—a perfect conclusion to a fragrant adventure.

Champakam turned to face Anand. Her sparkling golden eyes met him with a silent smile. She plucked the Champa flower from her ear and offered it to him. He accepted the scent, closed his eyes, and took a deep inhalation, immersing himself in the fragrance of his newly profound existence - the scent of the river.

Chapter 7
The Sweet of the Sea

Winter Flavor,

1994.

The Sun has chased away all traces of the morning's rainfall, casting its golden evening rays through the swaying palm trees and onto a two-story house encased in four walls, adorned with a central courtyard that welcomes the sky. The domicile is enveloped in untamed greenery, creating a gentle shade that cloaks the surroundings. Anand is nestled in one of the upper bedrooms, blissfully asleep in the cool embrace of the shadows. A woman entered the room and gently stirred him awake.

"Nandhu, Nandhu."

His eyelids fluttered open, revealing her silhouette against the dim light.

"It's already evening. Are you planning to embark on a nighttime escapade?" He propped himself up, still heavy with sleep, only to surrender once more to slumber.

"Here's your coffee?"

"Oh, thanks, sis. You're the best." "What about you? Where did you vanish last night?"

The first sip of the steaming brew felt like a revival.

"I dozed by the river." "Under the rainfall." "Caught the perfect shade to dream in."

Deepa glimmered in her new golden silk saree.

"Oh, you're radiant! Are you off to a ceremony?"

"Actually, I just returned from one. Today was Kanya's betrothal."

The mention of the past ensnared him again, causing his dimple to fade.

"How did it turn out?" he inquired, his voice rough.

"They called off the engagement." A smile ignited behind his dimples once more.

"Really? Are you serious?"

"What's there to be thrilled about, silly?"

"I mean, what transpired?" He shifted from comedy to tragedy.

"Her father is missing."

"Missing? Where could he have gone?" "No one knows. That's the essence of being 'missing.'"

"Vanished just like that?"

"Go see for yourself. The police are on the case. People say he received a call from somewhere."

"What are you suggesting, you foolish woman? Is he missing or just away?"

"A spiritual call, perhaps. Old age may have finally rattled his senses."

"Him and sense? What a mismatch."

"The police received a letter he penned."

"What letter?"

"Stop grilling me and do your own digging. Isn't she the girl of your wildest dreams?" She startled him with his buried truth.

"What? How???" Bewilderment washed over him.

"I had my suspicions, but now you've let the cat out of the bag. If you adore her, why haven't you confessed? A moment will inevitably come when 'later' becomes 'too late.'"

"I did tell her, but?" "But? Did she reject you?" "Actually, it's a complicated situation." "Love is a tangled puzzle. You must unravel it, or you'll always remain in the dark."

"And how am I supposed to do that?"

"You've been granted a little grace period. Just bare your heart once more, that's all."

Deepa offered this with a playful grin, and Anand pondered her suggestion.

"So?" He posed the world's briefest question after his brief quest for clarity.

"When will you depart?" "The ship sets sail tomorrow evening."

"Make sure to know her better before you head off, and don't cling to hope as your answer. It must be a definitive yes or no."

He contemplated this with a faint smile illuminating his dimples and embraced her in a gentle bear hug.

"Such a lovely saree." "It was a gift from Prasad."

"My brother-in-law has an exceptional eye for color." Anand examined the intricate floral pattern with keen interest.

"He's doing everything he can to revive the vibrance of this family."

"You're holding up well, girl."

"We're concerned about Kishan. He's still caught up in Bishan's shadow."

"Just allow him the space he needs to heal." "Even so, why endure the pain?"

"Artists thrive on pain; it's through suffering that they expand their creativity."

"And what about you? Why are you carrying the burden?"

"Because it was my choice. Pain inspires change, and even this journey emerged from my struggles."

"Have you informed Kishan about your trip? No, I'll mention it to him tonight."

"Did Christy update you about his birthday party? Kishan is there." "Yes, he mentioned it."

Anand's dimpled smile played on his face throughout their exchange.

"Please, don't grin so widely. I dressed up to impress, but it turned out to be such an inauspicious day for me."

His smile morphed into a playful grin.

"By the way, that servant was struck by lightning and died early this morning on the rooftop."

"Which servant was that?" "Devachan's right-hand man." "Ah, the Dragon?" "Dragon, unicorn—whatever he was, he's now just a relic of the past."

"What was he doing up there?" "It appears he got drunk and fell asleep near the aerial."

Anand's joy battled against his composure, but he stifled his emotions and supported his calm.

"What transpired last night?"

"A whirlwind of events. Are you hungry? Aleena was at the mansion all day, so expect just the cake."

"I'll be fine. I can manage." As Anand closed the door behind her, he shed his clothes and dashed for a shower, letting all the chaos flow away with the water.

"No fear, ah, no more fear." He shouted his new mantra beneath the cascading droplets. Once dressed, he opened the door, suddenly remembering the delicate Champa flower he had placed beside his pillow, still vibrant with life. Deepa, tuning into the radio, allowed him to adorn her hair with the blossom.

'Good evening, you're tuned into Shoonya 08.0 FM.

I'm Rj Sugandhi.'

'And I'm Rj Prasad.'

'A warm welcome to everyone on our beloved music show, 'Vintage Tape.'

I often wonder what everyone was up to yesterday during that refreshing winter rain. I was warm inside my blanket.'

'Wow, Sugandhi, I felt that moment with you – a warm blanket accompanied by the touch of my beloved wife'

Prasad's cheeks turned a shade of pink on the radio as Deepa blushed on the other end of the connection.

'Really? Were you two playing 'touch me'?' Anand teased, while Deepa gave him a playful shove.

'Rain seems to encapsulate love, doesn't it? Alone or a partner, in the end, it's all about the feeling of love.'

'You hit the nail on the head, Sugandhi.'

'Today, we've curated a choice of uplifting winter melodies to lift your lazy spirits. But Prasad, I can't help but wonder why melancholy tunes resonate more deeply than cheerful ones. Is it just me feeling this way?'

'Not quite. Genuine art springs forth from the depths of darkness, and true creators draw inspiration from their painful recollections.'

'Thus, darkness becomes an ally for artists striving to discover the light.'

'That piecing together truly resonates.'

'Absolutely. Tonight, we've received a slew of letters filled with poignant experiences and profound reflections.'

'Shall we dive into the first one after a song?'

'Certainly. An expression only transforms into an experience when it's genuine.'

'So, before we immerse ourselves in our first story, let's savor the first track.'

Anand pressed a kiss to his sister's cheek before dashing off in search of love beneath the enchanting glow of a full moon.

The vibrant green jeep sped alongside the fragrant river, illuminated by the lunar light above. He reached location Y and veered towards the eerie marshlands. Twinkling decorative lights adorned the pathway, leading all the way to the mansion. Yet, what should have been a celebration had transformed into a somber investigation. Two police cars were stationed outside, with another inside, their flashers aglow but sirens silent. He glanced at the mansion, realizing the area was completely under police surveillance.

Reluctant to make himself a target, he decided to follow the current toward Christy's house.

A truck lay blocking the road.

"Who's the careless driver here?" Anand honked several times, but the vehicle remained still. He stepped out to investigate. "Hey, where's the driver?" No sign of anyone appeared.

"Who parks a truck like this?"

Scanning his surroundings again, he found no trace of life. Reversing, he pulled the jeep to the side. "Hello?" he called out, yet only the ghostly truck answered him. He continued down the path to a modest single-story cottage sprawled across an acre. In the front yard, a man in his seventies savored the night with a bourbon bottle, basking under the full moon's glow.

"Nandhu, perfect timing! I was just about to start."

He turned back, and the truck still loomed in place.

"What's the issue?" "A truck's blocking the way, parked all askew."

"Perhaps its axle broke." "Hmm? So, John uncle, how have you been?"

"Good. Life is flowing along simply fine."

"How's the coffee plant?" "Aromatic."

"John uncle, your coffee's finest feature is its fragrance. 'Aroma Coffee'—the name couldn't be more fitting. The aroma brightens my day, and the flavor enriches it. How do you achieve that? Mixing in dark chocolate—a unique touch."

"Cocoa and coffee are a perfect pair. I simply unite them in the right place at the right time. Your experience mirrors what I aim for my customers to feel: the aroma engaging the mind and the flavor nourishing the soul."

"I could really go for some aroma coffee right now."

"Head to the kitchen! You've become quite civilized. Remember when you were a kid, you just took what you wanted? Have one of these."

"Wow! I've never actually drunk alcohol, and I'm hesitant to start new habits. I tend to crave too much of everything I like. That's my dilemma."

"If you haven't started yet, better to leave it be. I plan to quit after this bottle. It's a personal challenge, I know."

"Seriously? That's a noble pursuit."

"Indeed, Nandhu. Life feels empty without challenges."

"Absolutely right." John took a resolute swig from his drink, the dry burn triggering a cough.

The neighboring generator's hum disrupted their conversation.

"Oh, this ridiculous generator." John hit play on the stereo, and the lively notes of Boney M's "Daddy Cool" blasted through the speakers. "Now we're talking. So, did you catch the news?"

"Yeah."

"What surprises me isn't his so-called spiritual rebirth, but his devotion to his family. He left a letter declaring his departure, vowing never to return. Who really cares if that jerk disappears into a monastery? Their misfortune, that's all I can say." John chuckled to himself as he poured another glass.

"And what did the police report reveal?"

"Not sure. Aleena is over there, anxious about the girls. They're on their own now. If you ask me, they could be just fine from now on." A sly grin crept onto Anand's face as he snatched a handful of peanut masalas from the plate, while John downed another raw glass.

"Bishan, I'm still in disbelief. I can't fathom the scale of the tragedy you're all facing. How's everyone holding up at home?"

"Things are smoothing out now. I'm actually taking a breather from this madness."

"What's your plan?"

"I'm getting out of here."

"What?! Forever?!"

"For a bit, overseas."

"Well, that's your call. Who am I to argue? When do you leave?"

"Tomorrow."

"That's quick."

"This trip has become essential for me. The ship's setting sail in the evening."

"So, not just a hasty getaway."

"Just tuning into a new frequency. During the cool embrace of last winter, I crossed paths with a group of visionary scientists drawn to the enchanting allure of the ocean and its hidden treasures of sweetness. Their quest also dives deep into the murky waters of sea pollution, as they strive to unveil solutions for a cleaner, more vibrant marine world. I also stumbled upon a course in underwater archaeology. It might just open new horizons."

"Have you ever tasted sweetness?" "Not at all."

"So, a young man like you has never known love." "Well, it's a bit more complex than that."

"If your affection is genuine, you'll surely meet sweetness. At the very least, have the sweet experience before you leave. You know what pulls at our hearts when we're far from home. It's not the sights or sounds; it's the scents, flavors, and feelings. In the end, that's how you'll yearn for your love. Are you afraid of the judgment?"

"I'm more afraid of the verdict, to be honest."

"Oh, you naive fellow. If you think you've found 'the one,' chase after it." Anand exhaled anxiously.

"Tonight, I'm going for it."

"That's my boy. Is that her?"

"Who?" "Kanya?" "How do you know?" "We're all in the loop. Christy showed information."

"That little informant."

"How long will you shroud this in secrecy?"

"No, John uncle. We're family. It's bigger than us."

"Then who? That jerk is out, and the engagement is off. What other signs do you need?"

"Well, I intend to speak with her before I leave." "Do that! Whatever the outcome, carry on with your life. Don't drift into a stupor. This sounds like an incredible chance. Go for it, friend! You shouldn't confine yourself in the name of love." With a fierce determination, John lunged for the nut masala, tossing it into his mouth.

"Hmm, where's the birthday boy?"

"Lost in the game box." "Catch you later." Anand slipped inside.

Within the realm of video game madness, the excitement is palpable. A man with a mustache is performing bunny hops, colliding his head with bricks. A mushroom sprouts from the block, and he devours it, enlarging instantly. Christy expertly maneuvers the mustached hero with a joystick. Out of nowhere, the mustached avatar perishes after being nibbled by a crab plant lurking in the tunnel. Game over.

"Now it's my turn." Kishan seized the joystick.

Charlie, covered in chocolate, was joined by Christy.

"Hey Nandu Uncle."

"Hey there, Happy Birthday! Sorry I couldn't bring any presents."

"Your presence means more than gifts." "Really?" "You still could've brought something." "Hmm." "I was just teasing you, dear Nandhu uncle. Enjoy some chocolate."

They shared the chocolate with Anand.

"I have a surprise for you, actually." "Really? What is it?" "You'll find out."

Kishan's mustached character jumped over an obstacle to rescue the princess, dodging fiery breath from a dragon. Mission done; he progressed to the next level. Just then, the mustached avatar got submerged underwater, and suddenly, the power cut out.

"Oh no, Mario's out." "It's so dark outside. We've been gaming since afternoon."

"Well, it's a good thing the lights are out. Let's head outside."

"Didn't you hear the news? That demon's gone on a spiritual quest, and that dragon got zapped by lightning. Two asses in one flash." Christy excitedly shared.

"Where did he actually go?" "They received a note saying he's left and won't return. Now both of you can love freely."

It's pitch-black outside.

"We've been gaming all afternoon."

"Really. Good thing the lights are out." Anand gave a playful knock on his head.

"Let's get some fresh air."

John was hosting a disco party with an empty spirit bottle.

"Dad, are you sure you're done with the booze?" "Yes, son. This is my last one." "It better be, or else it'll truly be your last. Mom will flatten you like this nut." Christy mimicked the consequence by crushing peanuts and tossing them into his mouth.

"Where's my Aleena?"

Suddenly, the generator faltered, and all the colorful lights in the neighborhood vanished. Only the spinning blue light of a police jeep remained. In the next instant, a siren pierced the stillness as officers streamed away.

"Oh finally. I think the investigations and nonsense are over." John lost himself in the disco vibes. The siren drifted into the distance from the mansion as three female figures appeared under the glowing full moon.

"Is this your strategy to quit drinking—dousing liquor down your throat?"

"Oh my, Aleena? It's over." "Hmm." "Who are the other two shadowy figures?" John squinted through his drunken haze.

"It's us, uncle!"

"Oh, Kanya and Maria?

Why didn't anyone bring a candle?"

"We were waiting for the warmth of home to illuminate our ceremony."

"Really?" John rose from his chair, steadying himself against her, trying to find his footing.

"We'll cut the cake. The girls need to head home soon."

"The investigation is ongoing." "I'm not sure, uncle. We suspect there will be more inquiries."

"I brought them here to enjoy the day. Let's not delve into more questions."

Aleena stepped into the dimly lit house. Moments later, the soft glow of a candle appeared, accompanied by a chocolate cake adorned with the number 18.

"Oh boy, you're officially an adult now," Anand proclaimed, marking his transition into a new chapter.

"Couldn't you at least wear something human for your birthday?" Christy glanced at his outfit—a t-shirt emblazoned with a grinning skull. In response to his mom, he flicked his fingers to form a playful demon sign.

"Let's not blow out the party candles. Who's with me?"

"Right?" There was a chorus of agreement.

In the flickering candlelight, everyone exchanged glances, reaffirming their identities.

"Alright, it's time for the cake cutting," Christy announced.

Suddenly, a piercing scream echoed from the dark field.

"Who is that?" "What's happening?" "Did it come from our field?"

Every gaze turned toward the noise as headlights illuminated the road, accompanied by the sound of a truck rumbling by.

"Oh man, that truck was parked right in the middle of the road. Did you all see it?"

"Yeah, it was on the side." "No, it was right in my way when I passed." "Maybe it was a lost soul," Maria suggested.

"Regardless, it frightened the life out of me."

"Ignore the fear. May your adulthood ignite courage and passion in your life, my son." John blessed Christy.

"Many blessings to you, Dad."

"I swear by my beautiful wife, Aleena, my children, Christy and Charlie, and all of you here, I'm done drinking." The crowd erupted in applause at his commitment.

"Don't you want to see your birthday present? Let's save the cake for later."

Excitement rippled through the group, eager for the reveal.

John retrieved the one from the cake and wobbled toward the dark field, followed by everyone clutching the eight.

"What's lurking in the bushes? Did uncle get you a pet snake?"

The light from the fire unveiled two saplings standing tall.

"We'll plant these trees as a duo."

"That's fantastic, Uncle John," Anand exclaimed, his adventurous spirit ignited.

"What's so fantastic about planting trees in the dark? It's pure lunacy."

"Every great creation is born from a touch of darkness and madness, dear Aleena."

"There could be snakes in the shadows."

"What snake would dare bite you when your husband is a King Cobra?"

Christy hailed his dad, the King.

"Regardless of how mad or crazy this seems, I stand with Uncle John." Anand cheerfully declared his support for the wild idea.

"That's the spirit! There's more magic woven within this dark universe, hidden beneath the shadows."

John shared his cosmic wisdom, sparking inspiration in everyone present.

"So, who is planting which tree? The truth?" This is a Champa flower tree, and here it is," John showed, his words meandering as Christy, Kishan, and Anand eagerly seized the young Champa sapling. Maria joined the fun, her silly smile radiating joy, while Kanya slowly inched closer to her sister. On the opposite end, John, Aleena, and Charlie found themselves with a solitary sapling, feeling somewhat overlooked.

"Charlie, grab our saplings!"

"Coconut tree?" Charlie replied with a furrowed brow.

"Ah, my friend, from root to crown, the coconut tree presents a treasure chest brimming with possibilities."

"Whatever let's plant it. Dad, pass me the hoe!" Charlie's tone dripped with a flicker of mania.

"You're not planning to bury me, are you?" The full moon cast a shy glow behind the clouds, yet laughter illuminated the surrounding darkness. They split into two factions, each wielding their hoes—Team **champa** with one and Team **coconut** with eight. The candlelight revealed a perfect damp patch to John.

"Charlie, let's put it here. Start digging."

"Dad, have you already planted something in this spot?"

"What?" "The earth looks disturbed." "Isn't he correct?" Aleena stepped closer for a better view.

"I haven't done any gardening this year." "No, but ask Christy."

"Christy, have you done anything with this area?" she hollered over to the other team.

"What? Me? No way!" Christy shot back.

"Then what's going on?" "Oh, it must have been unsettled by yesterday's heavy rains."

"Like this?"

"Charlie, cease the investigation and start digging. If there's anything buried beneath, we'll discover it—it's the perfect spot," John slurred, his words imbued with haziness.

Charlie plunged the hoe into the earth, creating a hole down to his knees.

"Should I go deeper?"

"For what purpose? To bury me too? Just plant the darn tree," John muttered, too tipsy for any deeper questioning.

He settled the sapling into its new home, while Aleena expertly filled in the hole.

The other team continues to meander through the underbrush, searching for the perfect spot. Maria, Kishan, and Christy lead the way.

"Can I share a little secret?" Kishan inquired of Maria. "What's that?"

"There's a surprising absence of fear in your gaze today."

"Perhaps Dad packed it away with his spiritual quest."

"Do you genuinely believe your father set out on a sacred journey?"

"No idea, but I'm certain he's gone for good," she replied, devoid of remorse.

"Are you alright?" Maria probed into Kishan's mental state.

"Yeah, I'm fine." The silence that followed was thick with unspoken anguish.

"Hey everyone, let's push the gloom aside tonight—it's my birthday! How about a drive?"

"Now that I'm eighteen, I can finally take the wheel."

"But you don't have a license."

"We'll tackle the rules later. What do you think, Maria? It'll be a welcome diversion for you."

"I'm in," she replied, while Kishan subtly nodded in agreement, a quiet smile tugging at his lips.

"That's fantastic! And what about your green-eyed friend?"

"Lucy."

"Right, Lucy. Invite her along if you'd like—she seems like the life of the party."

"Oh, I see where this is heading," Christy grinned unabashedly.

"Is she able to make it?"

"She won't need to leap; her dad's laid-back about these things. She often asks about you."

"Really? All the time?"

"Not all the time, but quite often. Don't get too thrilled—maybe she just sees you as a brother figure."

"I could even play the role of her stepdad—just ask her!"

"Hm, she reached out earlier. Her father runs a photography studio, and she's probably there with him. They're working late into the night on some wedding shots. We can head straight to the studio."

"Sounds good."

Anand and Kanya strolled behind, treading softly on the carpet of fallen leaves.

"Are you upset with me?" Kanya broke the silence, prompting the exchange.

"Upset? Not at all! Why would you think that?"

"Don't you realize? People tend to go quiet in such situations."

"Even in uncertainty, silence can reign."

"What uncertainty?" "The aftermath of revealing my true feelings once more."

Kanya erupted into laughter, a vibrant expression unlike anything seen before. Her grin widened at his puzzled gaze, caught between amusement and composure.

"What? Doesn't my laughter please you?"

"Your beauty pours out in your laughter." She fell silent, her smile lingering.

"Are you alright?" "I'm absolutely fine," she reassured him with a genuine smile.

"I've found the perfect spot," came Christy's interjection, slicing through their moment.

"Look, that's my bedroom window. When Champa flowers bloom, the fragrance will fill the entire room," Christy envisioned, beginning to dig.

"And who will do the planting?" Everyone gathered around the pit, exchanging glances.

"How about you two inaugurate the effort together?" Anand and Kanya were entrusted with this kind endeavor. Their eyes met as they planted the sapling, a silent joy blossoming in the shared experience. Just then, John and the group arrived.

"Oh, what a splendid spot you've found!"

They formed a circle around the sapling, destined to flourish into a tree. A gentle breeze swept in from the eerie marsh, coaxing the fragile Champa to dance. The gust extinguished the candle flames, yet the power returned with a snap.

"Perfect timing, wouldn't you say?"

Under the bright lights, they exchanged knowing glances.

"Christy, can you drive? How about we head to the sleepy slope for some coffee?"

"Oh, Dad. We have plans already."

"So, you're taking our car, then?" "That's exactly it."

"If you wish, you can borrow my jeep." "Sounds perfect! Let's all go for a coffee run in the jeep. Dad, there'll be one more member joining us," Christy hinted, teasing John about his crush.

"Who is it???"

"You'll find out soon enough."

That left Anand and Kanya on the sidelines.

"Kanya? It could be a nice escape."

She agreed with a nod.

"Alright. With Lucy included, that makes nine of us? It should be a breeze."

"Guys, I'm not coming," Anand interrupted.

"What? Why?"

"I'm leaving tomorrow." His statement struck like an unexpected bolt of lightning.

"What?" "Leaving for where?" "I'll share the details once I arrive." "Why?" "A quest to discover a new rhythm."

An air of silence enveloped them.

"Hey there, guys, let's not linger in sadness."

"Seriously, who will I call Uncle after this?"

"Please, send me off with smiles."

"Regardless of where you roam—land or sea—don't forget to drop me a postcard. Clear?"

"Crystal clear." Christy embraced him, followed closely by Maria.

"Take care, Nandhu uncle. Return swiftly; we'll start missing you soon."

"I already find myself missing each of you."

"When are you sailing away?" "Tomorrow. The ship awaits, but the destination is a surprise. Let's keep a shroud of mystery."

"So, you're going. This comes as a surprise," Kishan murmured. Anand gently drew him aside for a moment of privacy.

"Hey guys, can we have a moment alone, please?"

Silently, they drifted aside.

"Listen up, I know. Your mom's worry is palpable. We're all concerned. Just know—it wasn't your fault."

A tear slipped from his eye. Anand pulled him in close, enveloping him in warmth.

"Everything will turn out all right." Kishan tightened the embrace, surrendering to tears.

"Promise me, when I return, you'll be that boy enchanted by the whispers of the water, all right?" Anand cupped his face gently. "Hmm, I promise." Kishan choked back sobs.

"That's my boy." Anand handed him the keys to the jeep.

"My jeep's over there. Go grab it."

Kanya stood off to the side, a look of emptiness etched across her face.

"Can we have a moment alone?"

"Guys, let's give them some space." The rest moved toward the cottage, leaving the two adrift in their unspoken thoughts.

"Nandhu, I doubt you'll hear what you want to hear from me today. Let's pause on deepening this relationship—for now, that's all I can say."

"That's it, huh?" "Yeah." She brought their conversation to a close.

"Kanya, my thoughts are as murky as muddy waters. I also need time for clarity."

"Just make your journey one to remember. Goodbye, Nandhu." That was her full stop. He watched her, a tranquil smile like a quiet river. "Goodbye, Kanya. You can be certain that I will come back, without a doubt." "I will remain right here, waiting." They gracefully wrapped up their exchange.

The jeep rolled into the cottage enclave.

"Christy, could you pass me the car keys? I need to venture out."

"Join us! It's a journey you won't forget."

"I can't endure another goodbye. I crave some time alone."

"Dream on."

Anand retrieved the keys and slid into the driver's seat.

"So, John uncle and Aleena aunty," he gestured, his words lost in the air. They waved back; their gestures as quiet as his. With a final, fleeting grin for Kanya, she returned it in kind, a wordless farewell.

"Take care, Nandhu uncle. We'll be here, waiting for your return."

Teens shouted their good wishes, a chorus of hopes trailing behind him.

As Anand ignited the engine, he cast a lingering glance back, absorbing the scene before him. The vehicle rolled away, leaving the familiar behind. Within, he felt the bittersweet sting of departure, yet he understood this journey was necessary. The road met a Y junction ahead.

<=Scent River-⅓ miles, Sweet Sea-6⅓ miles, Dolphin Corner-9⅓ miles.

=>Silent Bridge-1⅓ miles, Golden town-3⅓ miles, Sleepy Slope-33⅓ miles.

The jeep veered left, heading straight for the beach as the deserted roads unfurled before him. He slammed down on the accelerator, eager to arrive in haste, gliding past a sign that whizzed by in a blur.

'Keep the Beach Clean'

'No Littering'

'Sweet Sea – 3⅓ miles'

After navigating a few windings turns, he finally reached the shore. The Sweet Sea had awaited Anand since time began. The beach was devoid of life, save for the whisper of the waves. He descended into the warmth of the sand, each step building anticipation for a delightful encounter. As his feet kissed the warm saltwater, he tilted his head skyward, where the full moon playfully hid behind veils of cloud. It was just him and the tranquil expanse beneath the starless night.

"I yearn to dive into you, deeply enough to dance with death, which through you granted me life."

Anand began an unusual dialogue with the sea.

"Please send me a message if you truly desire my return." A soft wave crept towards him, prompting him to scoop a handful of brine. The salty droplets cascaded toward his lips.

"Just whisper that you love me." He savored a sip, the essence of affection igniting his senses.

"It's sweet. So sweet." Anand slowly swallowed the blessed liquid, scanning the empty surroundings, lacking anyone to share his delight. The next taste was merely saltwater. Sweetness raced through him, and his eyelids fluttered closed, surrendering to a wave of emotion. In the depths of his mind, the image of Kanya, with her shimmering, dolphin white eyes, illuminated his darkness like a flash of lightning.

"Only my demise can sever your hold." He gradually tilted his gaze towards the obsidian sky, eyes wide with wonder. The clouds parted, unveiling the radiant full moon once more. He beheld its glow with faith nestled in his heart and flavor swirling in his soul - the sweet of the sea.

Chapter 8
The Flower of the Winter

Winter Bloom,
1999.

As winter unfurls its frosty embrace, the morning sun tiptoes toward midday, casting a warm glow across the eerie marshland.

Its golden rays coax the lingering dew drops, remnants of autumn, into a delicate dance, making their escape.

John's cottage, once humble, now stands adorned with thoughtful designs and a flourish of greenery from his diligent cultivation. Christy, sporting a freshly trimmed hairstyle and stylish goatee, rummages through the chaos of his untidy room in a desperate quest for a lost shirt.

"Mom, have you spotted my t-shirt?" he bellows, his voice echoing through the clutter, while the word 't-shirt' emitted a growl. The sound reverberated in Aleena's ear like the chords of a death metal vocalist, while she tended to the blossom-filled garden.

"Are you referring to the one featuring your face?"

"I've already told you; I can handle my laundry."

"And when might we see that miracle? You and that silly skeleton—it's long gone, yet you seem intent on reviving it." "I've only worn it twice. Where is it?"

"I didn't take your wretched smiling skeleton. Just dig through your mess once more."

"Ah, found it!" He triumphantly retrieved the skeleton from beneath the sheets, adorning his bare skin with the cheeky grin and spritzing it with perfume to mask its decaying charm. "Christy, when will this skeleton truly find rest?"

"Mom, are you familiar with maximum utilization of resources?"

"Just don't approach me with that corpse. Scatter away."

He yanked a pair of dry socks from the line when something else intrigued him.

"Mom, look who has finally arrived!" He pointed excitedly at the top of the Champa tree.

"Wow," it had finally budded. "But it hasn't bloomed yet." "Mom, what shall we name our first little one? How about Buddy?" "What about Lucy? Hmmm?"

Christy felt a blush blooming at the suggestion.

"She is a feeling, Mom—an instinct shifting from a crumbling gut to a racing heartbeat."

"Hmmm, perhaps you ought to give this flower to your fluttering heart?"

"Mom, you're more of a romantic than I ever imagined. That's precisely what I was thinking. What did Dad give you on your first encounter? Please don't say another flimsy coconut sapling."

"Your dad was no fool; he brought me coffee the first time we met."

"Seriously, that's downright romantic."

"Not just any café. He took me to his plantation, coffee harvested straight from the seed. Back then, the farm didn't have a name—I suggested arOma cOffee, and he was smitten."

"Mom, that's legendary."

Aleena and Christy gazed up at the delicate bud swaying high above, completely immersed in the moment. A jeep approached, announcing its arrival with a loud, echoing honk. It was Kishan, Deepa, and Prasad. Aleena exited the garden to greet them.

"Kishan, are your paintings being showcased today? Wishing you all the best!"

"Thanks, auntie."

"Aleena, where's John?" "He took the car in for servicing. Come on inside! We're heading to the coffee plant tonight. Do you two want to join us?" Deepa flashed a prepared smile at Prasad.

"Absolutely, we're in!" "We'll set off as soon as he returns with the car. How about you wait at the gallery? We'll pick you up from there." "Do we need to change clothes?" "Nah, we'll be back by tomorrow morning. Just a night enveloped in the coffee aroma." "That sounds like an ideal plan." The parents made their way into the cottage, immersed in their family plans.

Kishan hopped out of the vehicle, highlighting a clean-shaven face and flowing long hair.

"Did you chat with Maria about your event?"

"Yes, I went to her boutique with Mom and Dad for some shopping."

"You sly boy, that was smooth." "So?" "I invited her, but she still seemed upset and didn't say much about coming."

"You fool, she's your girl, remember? Why not just speak to her directly? All this shopping and theatrics would just frustrate her more."

"Mom wanted a saree, so I thought, why not?"

"You're treating her like she's a stranger, did you notice?"

"I don't know. Being enveloped in my world of art and pouring all my energy into painting has led me to a peculiar place."

"You overthink. It's okay to think while creating but doing so in life can land you in a whirlwind of trouble."

"So, what do you suggest? Should we swing by and get her?" "Are you asking me? Do what you wish to do." "Let's go see her. Come on."

"Should we jump the wall?" "That phase has long passed."

They ventured down the eerily quiet path toward the mansion.

Meanwhile, the newborn Champa bud began its slow bloom, unnoticed by all. The cottage's garden is a meticulously supported oasis, now welcoming another flower into its midst.

In stark contrast, the neighboring field lies in decay. The mansion appears desolate even in daylight, its ground littered with fallen leaves whispering in the breeze. A faint sound of splashing water echoes from a distant corner of the expansive estate.

Kanya, under the shower, is enveloped in solitude, vulnerable yet untamed. Lost in her past, her dolphin-like eyes are shadowed by dark circles. As the cold droplets caress her skin, she roams her fingers over her body, caught in a web of wanted and unwanted musings. Kanya stirs from her reverie as her sensitive skin awakens. She continues to explore, a hint of allure dancing on her lips. Her fingers dive down to the navel, journeying further, unfurling her allure as she appears from the warm embrace of water. Bedecked in droplets, she flops on the queen-sized bed, spreading her thighs wide, akin to opening a book. The bodily romance ignites in a reclined goddess pose, the narrative unfolding slowly. Juices flow from her essence as her cupid's bow lips glisten with the remnants of her intimacy. Fingering intensifies with the taste, as her tongue weaves a melody of erotic moans.

The ring of the mansion's doorbell abruptly pulled her from her ardent reverie, the resonant chime echoing until her passion waned. She lingered until the sound faded into silence, then slowly appeared from the bed, her damp form leaving a trace on the sheets.

"Who could it be? Certainly not Maria. Who else might it be?"

She slipped on her underwear, draping her partially clad figure in a pair of flared salwar pants.

The stillness enveloped her, interrupted only by the creak of the wooden staircase underfoot. Without a moment's hesitation, she swung open the door.

"Hello miss." "Hello, Christy, Kishan. Hi there." Her body and voice quivered slightly.

"Is Maria here?" "She's at the gallery. She mentioned your art event." Kishan's face lit up at those words.

"Great! I intended to pick her up. How have you been?"

"Doing well. Do you want to come inside?" "We're in a hurry. My event is about to start."

"Good luck with that, Kishan. I'll try to make it. I have a package to sign for."

"Alright, please do." Kishan glanced at Christy. "Let's head out. Try to come by; the event lasts until evening." "Absolutely. Best of luck!" "Thanks." They moved towards their jeep.

"Kishan," she called after him. "Any updates on Anand?"

"None. I really hoped he could attend my event." "Okay." An awkward pause hung in the air, which she quickly dissolved.

"Alright, folks. Carry on; it's your special day. I will try to join you."

"Take care, Miss. See you later." They walked away, leaving the mansion in silence.

Suddenly, a realization settled upon Kanya; she was utterly alone in the eerie marshland. Grabbing the shop key, she stepped outside, only to remember the damp towel still entwined in her hair, adding to her burden. She retraced her steps and hung the towel on the stairs.

"Sleepyhead," she scolded herself, securing the mansion door and double-checking everything. "All set." The sun's rays struck her face as she exited, the hidden droplets from her shower evaporating like morning dew. She made her way to Y, crossing the road to 'siLkydoLLs Boutique', where a massive carton awaited her by a truck.

A young man appeared from the vehicle.

"Madam, we're from Swan Parcel Service. You have a delivery." She yanked up the steel shutter with a flourish, revealing a glass enclosure beyond.

"Ah, yes. I'm sorry to keep you." "Not at all; we just arrived. Your timing is perfect." She tried to maneuver the carton inside.

"I'll take care of that, ma'am." "Thank you." The delivery guy deftly rolled the box to the edge of the vertical shop. After signing the paperwork and accepting the order, she expressed her gratitude. "Thank you." "You're welcome, madam. Have a momentous day." With that, the Swan Parcel gentleman and his truck drove away.

Kanya lounged on her sofa, gazing at the glass enclosure as she slipped away at the large box before her. Inside lay a fresh array of sarees, richly hued in a spectrum of rays and shades, yet her eyes held little enthusiasm for their vibrant colors. Dismissing the merchandise, she cast her gaze outside, her countenance pale and uninspired. As moments drifted by, an eerie stillness enveloped her, conjuring memories laced with longing. Resolutely, she chose to quell any spiraling excitement or gloom, stepping out of the boutique in search of fresh air. To her left, a long, desolate bridge loomed, while an even emptier road stretched to her right.

"Where have all the people gone?" she contemplated, a hint of apocalyptic dread stirring within her. Glancing upward, her mind took flight into a vivid daydream, accompanied by the gentle symphony of the flowing river.

Across the river, two raven-black eyes were on a quest. Anand, his beard flowing and clad only in boxers, wandered freely among the mushrooms. He scrutinized the fungi, carefully selecting the finest edibles, which he stowed in a bamboo sake cup. With his harvest secured, he left the jungle and settled beneath the wise old Champa tree. As he inhaled the fragrant air infused with the essence of Champa flowers, the rhythmic pattern of his breath transitioned into a serene state of emptiness. When he finally opened his eyes, they met the sunlight, feeling the blissful surge of his blood coursing through him. The bamboo cup, secured with a rope, transformed into a crossbody satchel. Meanwhile, Kanya surveyed her surroundings, still trapped in an echo of that same vacuum.

Anand waded deeper into the river, submerging himself up to his navel. He shielded his eyes from the harsh sunlight and, drawing a deep breath, dove into the aromatic depths beneath him. "He is in." A throng of onlookers gathered along the opposite bank, buzzing with anticipation for the unfolding spectacle. Anand glided through the fragrant water, swimming with effortless grace.

As he ventured deeper into the riverbed, he sifted through the aquatic greenery, reaching for a handful of weeds. From this submerged garden appeared a swirling school of little fishes, shimmering through the water like fleeting thoughts. One acid dwarf fish darted into his mouth, embarking on an unexpected journey within him. A peculiar sensation raced through his throat, and in an instant, he transformed into a creature of the depths. Air became an afterthought.

"33 minutes." His consciousness echoed, reminiscent of a level in a vivid, surreal video game.

He started to traverse the underwater landscape as if it were solid ground, captivated by the wonders surrounding him. Each moment was a marvel, and he took his sweet time hunting for the freshest weeds. The fish and the lurking parasites saw this new wanderer exploring their realm. Time was slipping away for him—what began as 33 minutes had dwindled to just 22 minutes.

On the opposite bank, a wave of panic surged through the crowd that had lost sight of him.

"Is he trapped beneath the surface?" "Could he be dead?" Various theories started circulating among those watching.

Meanwhile, submerged in a world of enchantment, Anand meandered like a connoisseur in a treasure trove, delighting in the sensation of the underwater stones. "11 minutes," chimed a reminder in his mind, yet he stayed enchanted by the aquatic beauty unlike anything he had ever known. He chose to seize the dwindling moments to finish his odyssey, eagerly peering into the unknown to advance his relentless quest. In the shadows, he sensed a presence seeing him. With a grip on the bed for support, he crawled closer to uncover the mystery. Awaiting him was a figure—an eerie, skinless skeleton head, hauntingly still. Fear gripped his heart and overwhelmed him like a wave, draining him of energy. Breath escaped him as he became engulfed, yet his legs propelled him toward the surface. He burst forth, a breath of fresh air filling his lungs as he glimpsed the azure sky—a near brush with death. After a few coughs, he spun in search of direction and, at a distance, spotted the gleaming golden axe of Nazi. For the first time, he felt gratitude toward the deranged figure that inspired him, executing a butterfly stroke to hasten his way to the shore.

"He's alive! Look, there he is!" "He didn't make it!" Now, the crowd bore witness to the fastest human swimmer, and excitement erupted once more as they cheered for his next endeavor. Reaching the shore, he was met with the startling sights of skinned skeletons that made his heart race.

"Dude, you're incredible!" "Man, you're the best!"

Anand gasped, grappling with the line between life and death as an exuberant channel microphone from Vidhooradarshan with a bold Y logo approached him.

"Hi, how are you feeling right now?" He took a moment to collect himself and catch his breath.

"Apologies, we got a little carried away. Take your time."

After steadying himself through a few deep breaths, he leaned toward the microphone. "Hi."

"Anand, right?"

"Indeed."

"So, what exactly where you up to while submerged?"

"Nothing much; I was simply on the other side, not beneath the water."

"But someone claimed to have seen you dive in."

"Maybe he misinterpreted what he saw. I was taking a breather under the Champa tree for the return challenge. Plus, I gathered some mushrooms." Anand wove a tale around the acid magic.

"They mentioned it's the second time you're testing your breath. What went down this time?"

"I wasn't adequately ready."

"That's okay; you'll surely make it the third time." He grinned as calmness seeped through his breaths, affirming life.

"Aren't you worried about this challenge?"

"Actually, the wild child within me isn't afraid of the water. This is all his playful venture, and I simply yield to his whims."

"What's that in your hand?"

"It's pond weeds that endured even when faced with demise."

"Oh, I stumbled upon some river weed deep below, and I—" His words hesitated as a grinning skeleton crawled into his thoughts.

"And." "No, I took a pit stop to gather some pond weeds for my tea and lost my breath over there."

"Oh, otherwise you might have made it." "Not sure. I could have gone a bit further."

"When can we anticipate your next attempt?"

"I can't say. That wild child within me is still alive, and I don't imagine he'll quit until he succeeds. He thrives on diving deep and courting danger, but that's not me. I'd call this whole escapade foolish."

"So, have you moved past your wild side now?"

"Not quite. There's no thrill without him, but I'm done letting him steer the ship."

"Were you overseas?" "Yes, I returned this morning." "What kept you occupied all this time?" "Just indulging in a hippie phase—an adventure brimming with uncharted experiences."

"When you speak of a hippie life, it sounds like a free spirit, drifting aimlessly. Why are you back now?"

"I prefer to flow like water, adapting with the seasons, you know?"

"Wow, it's fantastic to have such an intriguing person like you back with us. We wish your health and happiness."

"Thanks."

"So, that was Mr. Anand, the deep diver. And this is Reporter Sugandhi alongside camera man Isahaaq from Scent River, signing off." "And cut." The channel wrapped up.

"Thank you all for the love," Anand said, appreciating the crowd and the media as he strolled away. His damp body had dried out by the afternoon.

"What in the world was all that?" he muttered, gazing up at the statue of Nazi.

"I despise your presence and tools, but thanks for saving my life," he expressed his gratitude to his foe before moving on. A woodpecker drummed on a palm tree.

"You goofy headbanger," he called out to the bird, which shot him a vacant stare.

"You are bizarre, bearded creature," the bird seemed to retort as it resumed its work.

After a brief walk, Anand returned home to an empty house. He headed straight for the kitchen, placing the mushroom bamboo cup in the refrigerator before making his way to the restroom. From his backpack, he retrieved his Polaroid camera. He snapped a smiling selfie, capturing the essence of his bearded face. The perfect shot printed out. He shook the copy, and the image appeared just as he envisioned. Next, he entered the restroom where the hum of a trimmer echoed. Minutes later, the sound of a shower followed. Appearing with a clean, dimpled smile, he felt a sense of relief from shedding a heavy past. Dressed in cozy underwear, he returned to the kitchen, turned on the gas stove, and set a pot of water to boil. He rinsed the pond weeds and added them to the bubbling water. The basmati had already been cooked in another pot. He reheated a vessel of vegetable bean curry infused with coconut milk. Combining the grains and gravy into a bowl, he filtered the fully extracted pond weed into a cup. The central courtyard of his home offered a touch of shade. Settling onto the mosaic floor, he leaned back against a nearby pillar. He savored his meal as if it were a last feast, licking the bowl clean. The first sip of pond weed tea stirred memories of the skeleton.

"What was that? Perhaps it's merely an underwater mirage," he mused to himself.

He swung open the mirror wardrobe, searching for the ideal fabric to drape over himself. His deep, raven eyes locked onto violet jean pants that hugged comfortably. Slipping them on, he felt something nudging against him from the pocket. Curious, he reached in and discovered a pack of cigarettes, his old companion lying forgotten for years. With a wistful smile, he tucked the memory back and resumed his hunt for the perfect top. No colors sparked his interest until he finally settled on a gray linen long-sleeve shirt. Buttoning it up, he closed the wardrobe to face his own reflection, clad in an ensemble that exuded a sense of style.

"Hmm, not bad at all." He fished out his brown sunglasses from the bag, placing them over his eyes. "Perfect." A dimpled grin spread across his face, even as his smile reminded him of a stale odor lingering in the air.

"Oh, right! How could I forget?"

Making his way to the sink, he brushed his teeth with flair. For the final change, he laced up a pair of sparkling white sneakers to complement his dazzling smile. Ready for the date ahead, he strode to the parking area and retrieved his RD350 from the lot. The wild spirit within him revved the bike and whisked him back to the days of reckless youth. After a few thrilling adjustments, the matured rider took control, his mind racing toward the mysterious marsh while his heart thumped with impatience.

The allure of the unknown drew him closer, just a mile and a half away from the conclusion. As he approached the Y intersection, his gaze fell upon a lady perched inside a glass enclave. The bike decelerated, coming to a halt as their eyes—those of a raven and a dolphin—mingled. A spark ignited into a blossoming smile.

"Oh my god." She burst from the boutique; her excitement palpable.

"Come on, let's sit inside." His eyes followed her inviting gesture toward the illuminated sign that read 'siLkydoLLs boutique.'

"A boutique? How enchanting! When did this come about?"

"Last winter. It's Maria's ship. I am just a watchkeeper. When did the ship arrive?"

"Early morning. So, from teacher to watcher?"

He stepped inside, absorbing the vibrant colors beyond the glass.

"Alright, I like this." "This is my realm now."

"I'm headed to the art gallery. Kishan's highlighting his paintings. Care to join?"

"He did invite me, but I was waiting for a package."

"So, it's taken care of." "Yes, the truth is, I've been hoping to encounter another soul, and now here you are."

He sensed a sliver of solitude hidden in her gaze.

"Well, shall we go? Can you really leave the shop just like that?"

"I was just about to head home." "And what would you do in that mansion filled with doors?"

Thoughts of loneliness flickered through her mind, blushing her cheeks as she stayed silent. Anand noticed her cupid's bow lips, still luscious and inviting.

"What's up?" "Nothing, just checking in on you."

"How about we get moving?" She was eager to mingle with humanity again. "Alright."

The sudden ring of the phone caught them off guard, prompting Kanya to answer with a chuckle.

"Hello?"

"Hey there, gorgeous. It's me. Did you get the package?"

"I picked it up."

"Great! I'll be back by evening."

"Alright. Oh, and I am also." Maria hung up abruptly before Kanya could finish her thought.

Inside a phone booth, two girls conversed.

"Hey, your sister seemed to be mentioning something."

"What do you mean?"

"How am I supposed to know? Call her back."

"I don't have another coin—wait, I found one!" Maria slid a 1₹ coin into the slot and dialed the boutique. The phone rang, but there was no answer. She ended the call.

"She must have gone home or something."

"Are you using the rupee?"

"No, why?"

"Can I have them?" asked a teenage girl with striking gray eyes and delicate thin lips.

"They're all yours, Paathu (Fathima)." Maria pressed the coin against her pineal gland, and it stuck like iron to a magnet. They exited the booth, with Fathima heading straight to a sweet stall where she grabbed two small sesame balls from a glass jar. She removed the coin from her pineal and flamboyantly offered it to the shopkeeper.

"Let's go." She handed one ball to Maria, and together they walked towards the art gallery, the sweet treat crackling between them.

A wide, single-story white building loomed ahead, its interiors adorned with portraits celebrating magical realism in a variety of patterns and poses. People in diverse forms gazed at the artwork, analyzing, acknowledging, and embracing it in multiple ways. As the sesame girls entered, another girl approached.

"Hey." A girl with leafy green eyes and glossy, round lips playfully grabbed Maria from behind.

"Hey, Lucy, what's the scene?"

"Just playing the tour guide. Who's this new face?"

"Hi, I'm Fathima."

"Lucy." They exchanged a handshake, and Fathima's glass bangles jingled cheerfully. Lucy continued to shake her arm, reveling in the sound.

"So, you really are loose?"

"She starts to loosen up as the sun begins to dip," Maria teased, revealing a little secret.

"Let me guess—an art student?"

"She's a Riverside student too, but in Science."

"Oh, I can see that." Lucy shook her bangles again.

"She's also an artist—a clay artist. She crafts all sorts of clay glasses and pots."

"Wow, how do you blend science with art?"

"I created a perfume using clay."

"Wow! That's something different."

"We have a store by the beach where you can buy it—CresCent Cafe."

"Oh, that's your place! It's such a cool cafe, along with a little grocery section!"

"Yes, I know you! You're a wedding photographer, right?"

"Oh wow, someone recognizes my work! Yes, technically I'm a photographer. Weddings are just a way to make a living; my true passion lies in wildlife."

"Wildlife, wow!" Fathima buzzed with excitement, while Maria scanned the crowd for two familiar brown coffee eyes.

"Where's Christy?"

"Hmm, you mean Kishan?" Maria licked a sesame seed from her teeth and offered a silly smile.

"You two haven't exchanged a word since he picked up his paintbrush?" Maria smiled softly. "Alas for both of you."

"He needed room to delve deeper. The painting itself was like therapy for him, while I was busy setting up my boutique. We didn't end our relationship; we simply took a breather. That's all there is to it."

"Hmm, maybe it's time to end that breather. There are a few female admirers trailing after the artist." "The only ass that gets access to that mind is me. I'm not losing sleep over that."

"Have you seen the painting?" "Not yet." "You should check it out. Every piece is a masterpiece."

Fathima's eyes roamed the room, her ears caught snippets of their conversation, making her miss half of what was said.

"Were you discussing assess?"

"Indeed, let's go check out some asses." Maria lightly grasped her shoulder, leading her on a tour.

"Goodbye! See you later." Fathima waved enthusiastically, as if embarking on a world tour.

"Look at that guy! Isn't he charming?"

Fathima glanced around, taking in the crowd while Maria engrossed herself in deciphering the paintings.

"Quit staring and critique the art, you voyeur."

"Don't forget we are all crafted by nature, living works of art. Look at that girl with curly hair; isn't there beauty in how she tilts her head?"

Maria joined in the whimsy of observation, and together they revealed in the moment.

"Here comes a clean-shaven guy with long hair. Wow, he's striking."

"Kishan," Maria whispered, as he noticed her too.

"Hey, he's got his eyes on you. Do you know him?"

"This is his art exhibition."

"Oh, really? Let's go meet him." Fathima tugged her toward him, where he stood with his parents. Both exchanged glances, caught in a silent moment before Deepa broke the ice.

"Hey Maria, how are you, sweetheart? It's been ages."

"I'm good, Auntie. How about you?"

"Much better now. Prasad, this is Maria."

Deepa gestured to Prasad, and both turned to watch Kishan for his reaction.

"What are you kids staring at?" "Oh, just observing." Their gaze shifted back to Maria.

She smiled at their playful exchange.

"Auntie, we have new arrivals at our boutique—lighter, cozier silk pieces."

"Really? We must come see them."

"Why 'we'? I don't need a saree." "Maria, he doesn't appreciate quality clothes; he prefers cheap streetwear." Deepa teased him, poking his belly.

"No, Maria, it's not about the price for me; if it's quality, I see the value. But it's not solely about the cost, right, dear?"

"You're right, Uncle. My pieces are designer, hence the higher price point."

"But they're worth every penny. Do you design them?" "Yes! Please visit again; I can offer you a great discount." "Certainly." "Now do you see who's the real cheapskate?" Prasad quipped, and Deepa poked him again, pulling him toward the artworks.

"We'll take a stroll. Let them converse. See you, dear." "See you." The pair wandered off, leaving Kishan and Maria in an unspoken connection, standing like strangers in silence.

"I'm truly delighted to see them thriving." "Indeed, they're faring well."

"So? How's everything with you?" "Doing fine. And you?" "Hmm, feeling better." A quiet pause followed. Fathima observed the boring exchange intently. Kishan contemplated the next direction for their discussion, while Maria seemed to have a sharp vision of where to steer it. She seized his shirt collar and drew him from the gallery, pressing him against a white wall for a kiss. Their lips and tongues danced in harmony, inhaling each other's essence as they exchanged smiles.

"Sorry, I–" Maria silenced him with a finger. Laughter erupted between them, deepening their intimate conversation. A few onlookers nearby gaped in astonishment at the affection displayed.

"Don't mind, ladies and gentlemen. Just a quenching of thirst," Christy announced to the crowd with a wink.

"What were you doing with my boy's lips?"

Maria playfully tapped the top of his head.

"Why does everyone aim for my head? Don't crush my creativity!" Lucy chimed in from behind, delivering another gentle knock.

"Because your head is so lovely, it's hard to resist a little knuckle kiss."

"Really?" He wrapped his arms around her and began to tickle.

"Kishan, it's time to wrap up the event," the gallery chief interjected.

"Okay, sir, I'm on my way. Come along," Kishan urged Maria, but she released his arm. "No, you go ahead. Best of luck!" She nudged him toward the podium.

One of the esteemed guests started the epilogue, discussing the power of art in today's political and social landscape.

Maria strolled in, a blush brightening her cheeks, while Fathima scrutinized her closely.

"Where did you vanish with that charming guy?" "We were just chatting."

Maria's lipstick was a colorful mess.

"You dirty girl, I know what was really happening." Fathima pulled her aside to a secluded corner.

"So, he's your boyfriend? You little sneak! Spill the whole tale!"

"We were on a break." "What transpired?"

"He was on a quest for answers. Seeking questions might be a more precise way to frame it. Seeking is this wild journey to find sanity, right? So, I let him breathe a little."

"All I want is the genesis of this insanity."

Maria laughed, taking Fathima by the shoulders.

"The symptoms of madness first emerged during the monsoon of '93."

"Oh my, rain! Such a mood shift. I don't want the entire saga just yet. Let's kick off with your first kiss?"

"Get lost, you perv." "Really? Dish it out, or I'll shout your scandalous moment!" "Fine, tease. Ready to dive into nostalgia?"

Maria inhaled deeply, gearing up to recall that unforgettable first kiss. Fathima was attentive, eager for the story.

"It was a winter's chill. Our first quarrel unfurled, leaving us in a silent standoff for the entire day, unsure of where to start or where to wrap things up.

"Just like today."

"Yes, as the sun dipped below the horizon, once the college day came to a close, I guided him into an empty classroom, pinning him against the stark white wall."

"Just like today."

"No. It was merely our deep brown eyes locked in a mundane quietude. Patience, after all, is a vital ingredient."

"I lack patience. Just kiss." Fathima's bangles clinked, brimming with urgency.

"Not yet. I could feel beads of sweat forming. Can you fathom that in winter?" "And?" "A solitary drop of salty sweat trickled down from my forehead to my lower lips. That lonely droplet was on the verge of falling." "And what became of that solitary droplet?" Kanya gazed into her grey eyes, falling into a moment of contemplative silence.

"His lips caressed that droplet, infusing it with sweetness borne from his heart."

"And?" Fathima swallowed hard, concern etched on her features.

"That solitary droplet embarked on a journey of levitation, lifting my feet along with it. I rose onto my toes, inching closer, and we kissed again. This second kiss lingered, stealing my breath away." The tale rendered Fathima breathless too.

"In our fervor, we executed a third kiss, entering an eternal realm where time and space faded away as our lips melded together. We kissed and kissed, quenching an insatiable thirst. Our sparks ignited into an overwhelming blaze."

"And???" Fathima yearned for more.

"Enough with the longing, you playfully insatiable soul." Maria pinched the tip of Fathima's nose, dousing the flames.

"A colossal inferno blossoms when two fires unite, doesn't it? But what happens when two bodies of water converge?"

"Simply trust your intuition, just steer clear of the drain."

"Actually, I'm enamored with someone." "Wow, who?"

"The emotions mirror what you've described, but—"

"But what?" "It's a girl."

"So that's the catch! A feminine surprise." Maria drew her in closer.

"I've overheard whispers that it's unnatural, making me wary of revealing my truth."

"Have you truly sat with those feelings?"

"Of course. We share a bed every night."

"What? Who is she?"

"She's an orphan left alone in the world. Her father was her only kin, but he passed away a few years back, and now she lives with us."

"Oh, and?" "And what?" "I can't stop thinking about her. When she gazes at me, oh my, those golden eyes."

"Does she reciprocate those feelings?"

"Once, we shared a moment."

"What moment?" "We were splashing around in the river, the water dancing around us."

"And?" Now, Maria felt the wetness of the memory washing over her.

"Our eyes met, lost in that infinite gaze, as if we were embodiments of the river itself. You see what I mean?" "As if you were one and the same." "Precisely."

"Are you both on the same boat?"

"We both tasted the sea's sweetness."

"My dear, what's the confusion then? Nature herself writes down that it's not out of the ordinary. Ailing societies will always claim that illness is the norm. Embrace life and love without fear, all right?" "Hmm." Fathima felt a surge of joy with someone who understood her. "She is a true essence." Fathima inhaled deeply, steeped in affection, as the exhibition approached its finale.

"Let's invite Kishan to share his journey through colors— 'Birth, Death, and Life.'"

The audience in the gallery erupted in applause as he stepped forward, tucking his long hair behind his ears before reaching the podium.

"Good evening, everyone. Primarily, I'd like to extend my heartfelt love and gratitude to all my friends here today. Your patience for art fuels our creation. As our esteemed guests mentioned, only art owns the power to instigate change within our society. However, I contend that transformation must not rest on ideologies; truth must serve as the unwavering foundation. Some may question my focus on death— doubt can be a healthy challenge. Yet, we must remember that it is humanity that conjured fear by venerating uncertainty. Death is just as truthful as birth. Often, we must embrace death to truly begin living.

Death signifies not merely an end, but also a curve—a bend that opens the door to madness. Thus, as I conclude this exploration of death, I offer one final reminder: let us awaken and traverse the ancient path toward innovation, bringing us close to the worn-out road of preconceptions. Thank you." The gallery erupted in a prolonged wave of applause at his closing words.

Kishan spotted Maria nestled in a distant corner, and suddenly, they felt like the only two souls in the crowded room. She sent him a playful kiss, which he tucked close to his heart. In that moment, their only wish was to savor each other once more. Her choco eyes signaled to his coffee ones, prompting him to leave the podium. They meandered towards an unoccupied space, pausing before a painting: Maya adorned in gold, a resplendent evolution of the little sketch he had given her during their first encounter. Their lips danced to the cadence of their heartbeats, and the exchange of souls continued until breath escaped them. Gazing into one another's eyes, tears spilled from both their brown irises. They tenderly wiped each other's tears and exchanged smiles. A solitary drop dangled from her lower lip, teetering on the edge, which he gently kissed away. He admired those cupid-bow lips, now blooming with the warmth of their kiss - the flower of the winter.

Chapter 9
The Wither of the Winter

Winter Cold,

1999.

The sun has donned its soft yellow cloak, casting warm rays over the expansive, gleaming white gallery. Inside, the event inches closer to its finale. Shades of enchanting realism float in intricate arrangements, as Anand and Kanya meander through the artwork, jointly savoring the essence of creativity with synchronized curiosity.

"Kishan embodies the spirit of an artist."

"Indeed, much like his uncle," Anand remarked, sporting a charmingly silly smile.

"Seriously?"

"Absolutely! Swimming is artistry in motion, not just a pastime. Picture water as the canvas and our bodies as the brushes. An artist paints while a diver glides; he immerses his arms into the depths of expression, while I plunge mine into the buoyancy of the waves. What's your take?"

"I think you're a poet, which undoubtedly makes you an artist."

Laughter carried them to the next piece, where a particular painting ensnared their undivided attention. A vibrant orange surface meets the green depths of a river, with a brown-hued boy diving into the surreal water. They stared, mesmerized, as colors enveloped them.

"Bishan," Anand murmured.

"What?"

"The boy—that's Bishan." Together, they scrutinized the dreamlike depiction.

"Wow! This is a masterpiece, isn't it?"

"Absolutely," Lucy chimed in, interrupting their thoughtful exploration.

"Hey." "Hello, Kani." "Kani?" Anand inquired, intrigued by this nickname.

"Yes! The letter 'A' herald's hope, while 'Y' provides a satisfying conclusion. Who cares about beginnings or endings?"

Anand regarded Kanya, puzzled by her quirky companion.

"This is Lucy." "Howdy, Anand." She shook his hand, taking in his wanderer's vibe.

"She attended college with Kishan and Maria. Where's Maria?"

"Probably around here somewhere. Need help deciphering the art? I am your guide!"

"Yes, please." Anand was eager for insight.

"Alright. Among all the artworks, Kishan devoted the most time to this one."

Anand scrutinized closely, a sense of resonance washing over him.

"The orange embodies the sun while the green signifies the weeds. The boy in the artwork is his younger brother—he tragically drowned a few years ago, a haunting experience that lingers still. A month after losing him, Kishan began dreaming of an underwater vision, where Bishan swims towards him. That was his name. Bishan comes closer, whispering into his ear."

"What does he whisper?" Anand inquired, captivated.

"The dialogue remains a mystery. Kishan mentioned he only hears the voice of the water. Perhaps he wishes to keep their conversation private."

Anand drifted into a memory, enveloped by the pulsating sounds of the deep.

"Sir." He snapped back to reality. "Yes, you can call me Anand. What was your last point? I missed a part."

"I was implying that maybe the artist prefers to keep the conversation under wraps. The boy's brown hue signifies the earth, also a blend of orange and green. This piece is among his most intimate works."

"Personal always reigns supreme, doesn't it?"

"Indeed. All his other paintings were auctioned off, but he held onto this one. He received the highest offer for 'the fear of the water,' yet he declared that his brother resides within the canvas."

"Perhaps valuing truth trumps the pursuit of legacy." "You hit the nail on the head."

"So where can I find the artist?"

"Come with me; I'll make the introduction."

"An introduction isn't necessary. I'm his uncle."

"Anand, are you the infamous Nandhu uncle everyone talks about?" "I suppose that's me."

"Wow, that's incredible. Just moments ago, they were discussing you."

"Really? I hope it was all positive."

"To be honest, not quite. One of the delegates brought up death, actually."

"That's an interesting way to be remembered! What if I were a ghost?" Anand teased Kanya with a grin.

"Alright, let's wrap up this ghostly conversation." Kanya reminded him playfully.

After scanning around, Lucy finally found the tribe, while Christy stood in disbelief.

"What the? Guys, look who's back! Uncle Nandhu, where have you been?"

They all greeted his return warmly, though Kishan paused, smiling.

"Well done, boy. I'm proud of you."

"I wish you were here." "And I am!" Kishan enveloped him in a hug.

"Were you even alive?"

"I died, like you said, and started anew."

"You should have seen him this morning with that beard; he looked like a wild tree."

Deepa and Prasad joined the group.

"Surprise!" Dad exclaimed, shaking Kishan awake.

"You were sleeping when he arrived." "I suggested he make it a surprise. Look how I appeared when I landed at the port." Anand displayed a polaroid snapshot before trimming it.

"Nandhu uncle, you truly resembled a pirate stepping onto new shores."

"More like a slave disembarking a ship." "I liked it." "Me too. It's rather untamed." The photo got many reviews. "It was quite the wild moment."

"Where did you find him, Kanya?" Deepa asked skeptically.

"By the river," Kanya replied, a mischievous grin on her face.

"Don't tell me he tried crossing that river again!"

Anand shot a glance at Kanya, silently urging her to conceal the truth or spin a tale.

"My goodness, I'm going to strangle you! Why do you keep tempting fate? Are you a frog or something?" Deepa playfully pinched his cheek, scolding him like a mischievous child. Everyone else wore the same exasperated expression as Anand. "Honestly, I wish you still had that beard so I could yank it out!"

"Apologies; this is the last time. I promise." She released him gently.

"And you're not even getting paid for this performance?" "My soul is the payment." "Soul, my foot! You're not on your own anymore, all right?" Deepa shot a glance at Kanya, reminding him.

They exchanged shy glances, their cheeks flushed, while the rest of the group hummed in harmonious accord.

"Shall we take our leave?" "How did you both get here?" "By bike."

"You all appear so similar, except for Chrisy's freshly trimmed hair," Anand teased, playfully dancing his fingers over his own head.

"You promised us a postcard," Christy grumbled.

"Honestly, even one fleeting memory of you all makes my heart ache with longing. So, to protect myself, I try to forget it all; it's easier that way."

"You're back! We've deeply missed you. I use mud masks and scrubs in the jeep to feel connected to you." "Really?" Anand playfully grabbed Christy by the neck as they exited.

John and Aleena arrived at the gallery.

"How was the event?" "Fabulous." "Hey, Nandhu! Heard you're back in town."

John and Anand shared a warm embrace. "Aleena aunty, how are you both doing?"

"Just savoring the joys of old age. You look younger, don't you, Aleena?" "He has always had that youthful face and charming dimpled smile." "Enough with the compliments, Aleena aunty; you two are making me feel like a child again."

"So, are we heading out now?" Prasad and Deepa joined the group.

"What adventures are you all up to?" "We're hitting a disco night at the coffee plant; care to join?" "That sounds amazing! I'll make it there one day. Now, I'll let you all enjoy your evening."

"Alright then, time to take our leave. Nandhu, see you tomorrow; I've got so much to tell you."

"Yes, John uncle, same here. Enjoy your night!"

The hatchback carrying the elderly couple glided toward downtown.

"A perfect night for a celebration! Spooky marsh will be our playground. Let's dance and ignite a party at my place," Christy declared as a beacon of excitement.

"Sounds perfect! I picked fresh mushrooms from grandma's garden this morning."

"Awesome! It'll be Mushroom Steak Night," Christy proclaimed, rallying for the house party. The plan erupted in cheers, with Fathima quietly smiling from the sidelines.

"Oh dear, forgive me, Paathu. Why so silent suddenly?" "What can I contribute among your family and friends?" "Hey everyone! Meet Fathima," Maria introduced her once again. "Paathu, you're welcome to join us tonight; it'll just be us."

"Oh, no thanks. I can't. Enjoy yourselves."

"What? If that's the issue, I can speak to your parents later."

"That's not it. You all have fun; I'll catch up with you later."

"Alright then, shall we move?"

"What's the plan?" "Let's head home first, then we'll devise the rest."

"Nandhu uncle, we'll drop Paathu off and return; you two go ahead." "Don't worry, I can catch a bus from the stop." "No need; we'll drop you off." "Really, it's fine."

"Stop it, girl. We're giving you a ride, all right?" Fathima responded with a quiet smile.

"Alright then, let's hit the road and start our night!" Anand revved the bike while Kanya settled in. "See you all!" Everyone saw the tangled couple leave, smiling.

"Wow! Finally, they're together, however that happened; I don't mind," Christy mused, clutching Lucy's shoulder.

"Why do you say finally?"

"Not sure. It's like you always say, 'the sound of 'Y' is a perfect conclusion. No one cares if it starts or ends."

"Right. Christy and Lucy," she rhymed. "I only care about the beginning; Chris is the perfect finale."

"So, which way shall we venture?"

"Towards the seaside."

The 4x4 rolled toward the Sweet Sea.

In the back, Maria and Fathima engaged in a hushed, whimsical exchange.

"You two share a bed every night?" "Indeed." A rosy blush spread across her cheeks, accompanied by an endearing grin as she surveyed her surroundings.

"So how do you sleep – snuggled close or keeping your distance?"

"Snuggled? Absolutely not. Just thinking about it sets my heart racing."

"If the spark ignites such passion within you, why not let it blaze forth?"

"What if I'm mistaken? What if she pushes me away?"

"Then all those feelings you've been draping over me like a quilt—what are they? Seriously, she's right there, yet you hesitate to test the waters of your emotions?"

"We share a beautiful friendship; to my family, she's like another kin."

"You're such a coward. Tonight, wrap her in your arms before slumber calls."

"And?" The pressure was mounting for her.

"Listen closely, my dear. Just embrace her but seek her permission first. If she responds positively, then simply continue unfolding your bond as it is. And?"

Maria paused, the silence stretching between them.

"And what?"

"If she falls silent, then that's your cue, my sweet Paathu. The next steps are yours to figure out."

Fathima began to spiral into a whirlwind of thoughts.

"What if?" "What if she hesitated? Just return home and give my advice a whirl. Sounds good?" Lucy, ever observant, kept a close watch on them.

"What scheming are you two up to?"

"We were chatting about the friend she mentioned. She's got quite the crush on her." Maria shown information. "What? Her? Incredible!" Lucy was taken aback, unsure of how to respond. Christy and Kishan exchanged knowing smiles in the background, while Fathima looked at Maria with a heart heavy with feelings of treachery.

"Paathu, don't fret; they're on your side. And this little tale stays among us four, understood? Right, friends?" "Hmm, I might need to mull this over—perhaps even with a complimentary coffee." Lucy teased, leaving Fathima looking utterly defeated.

"My sweet Paathu, I'm just joking! I'm no villain. We all understand that your heart belongs to you. But going forward, muster the courage to champion your love."

"I would go to any length for her." Wow, girl, you're soaring high. Perhaps after that free coffee."

"Paathu, you ought to sell her the café. She consumes caffeine like its water." Maria prompted her.

"What blend do you use at the café?" "arOma."

"Wow! We have both the owner and the supplier right here." "Who?"

"That would be his father's." "Amazing! Those beans are divine. Let's chat about a wholesale agreement; you could also stock the product at our shop." "Now we're venturing into commerce. We'll discuss this over coffee next time." "Perfect."

As twilight approached, a fine layer of dust mingled with the salty breeze, guiding their journey onward.

"Right here," she showed towards a slender trail.

"This route leads directly to my home. No vehicles can pass." Fathima gracefully exited the vehicle from the rear.

"Why not step inside? Enjoy a homemade black coffee by the river. It's complimentary."

"That sounds delightful and soothing," Lucy exclaimed as she hopped out, followed slowly by the others, exchanging glances. They walked in a line as the person behind followed the footsteps of the person in front, until they reached a quaint cottage nestled by the riverside. The beauty and tranquility of the scene mesmerized them all.

"Who needs a paved road when this path leads to paradise?" Christy mused, poetry spilling from her thoughts.

"True, but it poses a challenge during emergencies."

"Emergencies are rare, but life unfolds daily—that's what truly counts."

Fathima pushed open the wooden gate where an elderly woman was engrossed in her sewing machine on the porch. They approached the house, yet she stayed fixated on her task.

"This is Noora, Mom; these are my friends," Fathima said, wrapping her arms around the old woman as she introduced them. Noora continued to sew, oblivious to their presence.

"Come on inside," the guests exchanged hesitant glances before stepping in.

"Mom isn't quite well mentally. On some nights, she cries and screams from her sleep. If I'm away, my sister is left to cope alone."

"What happened to her?"

"A few years back, my dad suffered a heart attack in the river and drowned."

"We're sorry to hear that."

"Mom witnessed it; she couldn't swim and felt powerless. Initially, it was guilt, but as time passed, it morphed into deep trauma."

"Have you consulted a psychologist?"

"She is aware and lives in her own realm. For days, she's been working on a dress. When we asked, she mentioned it's for Maya. Are you all dreamers?"

"What do you think?"

"I believe you all are. Mom said Maya would arrive in her dreams."

"Your mother isn't crazy; it's merely a reaction to shock," Kishan reflected, drawing from his own experiences.

"Yes, she does her things independently, but sometimes she needs to be fed when uncertainty arises."

Fathima brewed black coffee, and everyone received their clay mugs.

"So, this is your masterpiece?"

"Indeed. How about we wander closer to the river?"

"Absolutely." They ventured out with their steaming mugs, while Noora remained at her sewing machine, a steady rhythm in her footwork.

"Mom, would you like to join us by the riverside?" The sewing slowed as she turned toward the guests but soon returned her focus to the machine.

"Let her be," they continued toward the river. "Sorry about that."

"Don't apologize, you sweet girl."

"The only person she truly listens to is Champakam. Mom would accompany her all the way to the riverbank."

The bank was beautifully arranged with stone chairs and a table.

"What a perfect place for evening coffee, like a cozy open-air riverside café."

The bike rested at the fringe of the marshlands, while Anand gazed at the crescent moon, with Kanya's focus entirely on him.

"What's up?" "No, I never envisioned a moment like this in my lifetime."

"You thought I wouldn't show up." "I was certain you would, just not for my sake."

"Why would you believe that?" "Because I've only given you heartache, while you've showered me with love."

"That heartache unveiled your true self to me. Your honesty has always captivated me, and that's what I adore about you."

"How can you be so sure?" "I simply know it, because here I am once more."

"Nothing has shifted for you." "Everything has changed, except feelings for you."

She approached him gracefully, caressing his dimpled cheek. His eyes fluttered shut at her touch, a smile playing on his lips, and soon those dark orbs reopened to see her once again. He gradually retrieved an old companion from his pocket.

"What? You still smoke?" Anand balanced the fungal-specked cigarette between his lips and turned toward her.

"Do you recall this cigarette? My old friend, Tob. It's the final remnant from that night. I haven't smoked since then, not after you spoke those words."

He offered her a matchbox.

"Then why don't we ignite the past for a new beginning?"

She flicked the match against its box, igniting the stick perched at his lips. As flames danced, he inhaled deeply, smoking out the offering to the mangroves without letting a whiff of tobacco slip through.

"I just wanted its flavor on my lips before bidding farewell."

"How does your Tob taste?" He ran his tongue across his lips in contemplation.

"Lifeless. Tob tastes lifeless."

He let the ashes tumble to the ground, leaving them both to smolder in silence.

"Farewell, Tob." The bike rolled away, leaving the remnants behind. But Tob wasn't truly extinguished yet; he merely flickered slowly in the cold - the wither of the winter.

Chapter 10
The Frog Under the Mushroom

Winter Magic,

1999.

A delicate crescent moon hung like a whisper in the vastness of the cosmic expanse. Kanya stood before a mirror, her reflection a soft blend of flesh and shadow. She began to drape herself in a luxurious silk saree, the fabric embracing her supple skin with tenderness. As the cloth coiled around her alluring hips, the last layer was meticulously pleated, folding gracefully on all sides. She gazed into the mirror, tucking the final roll of silk beneath her navel. In the reflection, a vibrant red bindi glimmered at its heart, while the figure hesitated, lost in thought. After a brief pause, she lifted the dot from the mirror and affixed it to her third eye, completing her transformation into a doll-like figure, though the depth of her eyes seemed vacant. Her gaze craved definition, prompting her to retrieve an eyeliner from the drawer, outlining the white with bold black strokes. Just as she crafted her masterpiece, a gentle knock at the door signaled the end of her enchanting session.

"Are you set?" "On my way!"

Kanya swung open the door, and Maria gasped at her transformation.

"Goodness, you resemble a shooting star!"

"Am I too glam for tonight?" Kanya inquired; her smile tinged with uncertainty.

"Don't even consider changing! You look radiant. I hope Nandhu uncle can handle it."

Maria cupped her face and playfully patted her cheeks.

"It's been ages since I've seen such a glow on you." Kanya was blissfully unaware of her own emotional state.

"Is this part of our latest collection?" "Indeed." "Amazing! We're bound to conjure some alluring dolphins and daring ravens here." The sisters chuckled, excited by the impending transformation.

"What's up with Loose and the guys? No sign of activity." Maria scanned the neighborhood from the window.

Christy and Lucy strolled through leafy fields, filling bags with dried foliage.

"Ensure they're truly dry." "That's the point—they're dry leaves." "You silly, look for moisture!"

"Should I conduct a microscopic inspection of every leaf for traces of water?"

"Just keep doing what you were doing!" "I was gathering these dumb, dead leaves, and now I feel exhausted."

"Is this sufficient for now?" She sighed, weary of collecting. "Yes, that much dead will do, including you." A familiar knuckle kiss was exchanged. They approached the Champa tree.

"We planted her on my eighteenth birthday. Wow, she's blossomed!"

"Really? Where?"

"This morning, it was just a bud. Look, her first bloom! Mom suggested naming her Lucy."

"My sweet mom, really?" "Yes, and she told me to save that flower for you."

"So, your mom has a fondness for me." "But I'm not sure if giving away our little one is wise."

"What? Why not?"

"Because she doesn't realize you knock her son's head every day."

"That's not a knock. It's a knuckle kiss, a sign of how much I adore this head."

She pulled him near and planted a kiss on the crown.

"Just the head?"

"I mean I'm starting there, and my affection flows downward just like this." Her soft lips traced down to his. Christy leaned in, but she halted him with a finger.

"Only if you fetch me the baby."

"Hmmm." Christy stared at the flower, which was watching him from a distance.

"I have a plan. Climb onto my shoulders." She pressed him down by the tree and gradually ascended, his body rising with her. She stretched for the bloom, yet it seemed just out of reach. As she leaned in to grab it, her thumb collided with a branch.

"Ahhh!" she cried out in discomfort. "What?" "Oh, nothing. Just lower me down."

She safely descended to the ground, wincing at her bloodied finger.

"Did you manage to get it?"

"She's holding onto her only baby, I suppose." Lucy licked the blood trickling from her thumb, pressing the sides until more crimson seeped out. He gently took her arms, green eyes locking on one another. She pushed him against the tree, her tongue slipping into his mouth, and they plunged into a fervent kiss. Above them, a delicate, fragrant bloom fell and interrupted their embrace. They parted, breathless.

"Oh, it's the flower. She gave us her precious baby." "That's my girl; she gives only for love."

He took the bloom and tucked it between her ears.

"Let's keep the scent for later."

The last traces of blood were pressed from her thumb and smudged across his lips. She playfully sucked the red away and dashed off with the sack. With romantic fervor, he trailed her, savoring the lingering essence of her presence.

In the backyard, Anand and Kishan constructed a wooden pyramid.

Kishan gazed at the crescent moon, offering her a silent grin.

"I sometimes converse with the sky," Anand announced as he struck a match.

"What do you discuss?"

"I'm not sure. I've never needed to initiate a chat; it just unfolds." He watched the flames until the heat tingled against his skin, then he blew the warmth away.

A flash of lightning appeared, without the accompanying thunder, moments later.

"Did you catch that?" "Yes." "I told you; it just unfolds." They exchanged smiles with the heavens.

"There are moments when I feel the sky acts as a mirror, reflecting our hidden emotions." "I would describe it as undiscovered feelings. Often, we fail to notice because we stop searching."

"Exploring the unknown can be addictive. I understood that when my work overwhelmed my thoughts. Ultimately, it requires another plunge to distinguish reality from fantasy."

"What do you think the sky just expressed?" "Be prepared to get wet soon."

Their laughter echoed.

"Not everything in life requires clarity," Kishan remarked, seeing the crescent moon.

"What is this dream? Fear of water?"

"He has a message for me, Nandhu uncle." "What is it?"

Lucy interjected, placing her sack amid the conversation. "We gathered everything dry. Let's set it ablaze."

"Why don't you lick it instead?" Christy chimed in.

"You mischievous pair, please place the wood in the clay oven. It's time to start cooking."

"Move that wood to the clay oven." Lucy reiterated Anand's command to Christy and Kishan. "I'll fetch the matchbox." She gave Christy a playful knuckle kiss and strutted back into the house.

"We'll roast her if we run low on wood." Anand and Kishan erupted in laughter.

The camp and kitchen were all prepped for a fiery start.

"Does Charlie manage the coffee farm all by himself?" "Yes. He willingly took on that duty. When I inquired why, he simply said, 'Bishan.'"

"How so?" "Bishan always favored the sky over the sea. Charlie, once a beach enthusiast, now prefers life near the hills." "Bishan wasn't merely about the sky; he was the boy of space and flying dolphins."

Kishan's mood shifted, and Christy gradually steered the story back to the origin of the trauma.

"Guys, what do you think about swimming tomorrow?" Kishan remained silent.

"Yes, tomorrow morning." Anand took charge of the plan.

"I'm ready but tomorrow feels far away." Lucy returned from the house, bringing a stereo player and a stack of cassettes.

"Oh, that's my girl." "Let's get moving, boys!"

Everyone gathered around, searching for a perfect opener.

"Which one to choose?" Lucy selected a cassette and hit play.

As "Aqua - Barbie Girl" echoed in the air, she proclaimed, "Let's keep the body in charge, boys," dancing with alluring flair, while the men exchanged glances, seemingly uncoordinated with the rhythm. Nevertheless, Kishan and Christy joined her lively movements, much to Anand's delight as he watched them groove.

"I'll handle the cooking," he announced, eyeing the table.

"Nand, buddy, I'm famished!" Lucy chimed in, her tummy rubbing a protest amidst the dance.

"Snack on the dry leaves," Christy teased, earning another knuckle kiss.

"Hey, ignite the oven!" Anand strode into the kitchen, seizing a thick mushroom steak, expertly seasoned and lovingly drenched in virgin coconut oil. Outside, the oven blazed to life as two figures approached the gathering—a casually dressed Maria and the radiant Kanya draped in a shimmering saree.

"Wow!" Christy's exclamation mirrored the collective awe that enveloped the crowd.

"This is our latest silk collection—and a bit of a promotional tease," Maria shared with a smile.

"I need a saree too!" Lucy declared, her fingers grazing the silky fabric.

"Really? For what? To tie me up? Do you even know how to put one on?" Christy teased.

"We could always make you pants," Maria quipped.

"Care to dance?" Kishan asked, taking Maria's arm as they effortlessly swayed to the beat.

"Where's Nandhu?" Kanya inquired.

"In the kitchen," she sauntered in.

"Maybe we should call an ambulance for Nandhu uncle," The dancers giggled over a possibility.

Kanya tiptoed toward the kitchen, but Anand, enchanted by the familiar scent, spun around and was momentarily spellbound. "Need a hand?" "Ah, yes, please load the veggies onto the skewers," she replied, and with dressing done, they were ready to cook.

"Are you prepared to seize the night?" Kanya grasped a handful of veggie sticks while Anand hoisted the hefty mushroom steak.

"After you, my queen," he gestured gallantly, leading the way to the oven where they deposited their preparations into the fiery clay cave.

"Shall we ignite an unforgettable night?" Everyone gathered around the campfire, anticipation in the air.

"Light it up! Today belongs to you," Lucy urged, passing matches to Kishan. He approached Kanya, offering the box, her eyebrows lifting in surprise.

"Just a spark from you and it'll all ignite."

Filled with trepidation yet curious, Kanya surveyed the group, their heads shaking in agreement with smiles. Lowering herself to the ground, she set the dry leaves ablaze, the flames beginning to unfurl their warmth. Anand, adding a splash of kerosene, conjured a blazing beacon that captivated every glance. Lucy silenced the music, leaving only the whispers of the fire's crackle. A gentle winter breeze swept through, awakening their spirits. Couples melted into one another, swaying in harmony to the flames. Anand cradled Kanya by her hips while she wrapped her arms around him, lost in a soft, wordless dance.

"Why do we adorn ourselves in clothes, do you think?" Kanya mused.

"To enhance our appeal. Some argue nudity is alluring, but it's often the contrary, don't you think?"

"And are you attracted?" she teased.

"Magnetized, I'd venture to say."

"Isn't it curious that all things alluring tend to weigh us down?" she inquired, struggling with her saree.

"Should I help you out of them?" he flirted.

"Not just yet." They continued their dance, entangled in whispers and playful banter.

Anand gently brushed her cheek, plucking a fallen eyelash with care. He turned her hand with tenderness, placing the delicate strand on her fingertip. With eyes shut tight, she sent a wish into the universe before blowing away the hair dust. As she opened her eyes, everyone was intently focused on her.

A wave of laughter erupted.

"Game over," Maria playfully punched Kanya's cheeks.

"What did you wish for?" Anand asked with curiosity.

"Hmmm, I wished we could all take flight tonight."

"Aww, that sounds wild!"

"You know what? I'm finished here," Christy declared, switching the music to 'Backstreet Boys - Everybody,' igniting the dance floor again.

"I hold a secret that remains untold." Anand whispered privately to Kanya. "What's that?"

"Earlier today, an acid dwarf fish swam into my very being." "Really? And then?" "I lingered for 33 minutes beneath the surface."

"Wow, you could have aced the challenge."

"I believed that would be dishonest." "What did you do while submerged?" "I strolled along the riverbed, with all the aquatic creatures observing my every move." "Why didn't you share this with everyone?"

"Unshared magic is but a promise of magic yet to unfold. Deep inside, I feel a whisper of magic waiting to be discovered."

"Wait, everyone, I just recalled something." Christy had a spark of inspiration. He retrieved a hoe and began to dig with intention.

"Look, a pot of mango wine!" "Amazing, just what we need for our tropical soirée." Lucy joined in the excavation.

"Let's take it slow, everyone." Christy positioned the pot at the heart of the stone dining table.

The tantalizing scent of slow-cooked mushrooms wafted through the air, capturing everyone's senses.

"Time to feast." Lucy's enthusiasm met no resistance. "Absolutely."

"I'll fetch the glasses." Christy dashed inside, returning swiftly with six elegant goblets.

"Perfectly splendid." Everyone toiled diligently to create a breathtaking dinner setup.

An outdoor stone table, beautifully adorned with steak and wine.

"This is an idyllic location for our meal." Joyful smiles surrounded the table.

"Hold on, it's not enchanting just yet." Christy hurried back inside, switching on the warm yellow bulbs overhead. "Now, that's pure magic."

Hot mushrooms were plated, accompanied by glasses of mango wine.

"For the tears of the crescent moon, for light and love," Anand proposed a toast, and everyone lifted their glasses in unison. The feast had begun.

"Delicious, Nand. From today, you're officially 'Yummy Nand,'" Lucy declared, bestowing upon him a charming new title. Each person who savored the meal echoed the same delightful chorus of approval. Kanya delicately took a bite, her lips glistening with juiciness as Anand admired her every movement. Her tongue danced at the corner of her mouth, savoring the last traces of flavor, while her silver eyes fluttered shut in bliss. "Mmm, wow?" she exclaimed, utterly captivated.

"Oh, my goodness, it's finger licking good," Maria said, already refilling her plate.

Anand topped off everyone's glasses with another round of wine. "Here's to Kishan and art," he toasted. As they clinked glasses filled with smoky mushrooms, Lucy proclaimed, "This is the finest dinner I've ever had, hmmmm." She trailed off, enveloped in flavors. Anand relished the joy radiating from everyone around him.

The delightful evening unfolded. Dinner ended, with not a morsel left behind—every plate gleaming clean. The contentment of a hearty meal shone on every face. "What an incredible dinner! I lack the energy to dance or soar tonight," Lucy sighed, and everyone concurred with tranquil smiles.

"No chance we're winding down. The night is still young. Think of this as a pause amidst the rhythms and hush," Anand said, locking eyes with Kanya, as if speaking to her soul.

"Nandhu bro, where have you been all this time?" Lucy eagerly probed.

"Let's take turns sharing snippets from our minds—past, present, or future. Let's kick off with today's artist. How do you feel about your accomplishments, boy?"

The tipsy glances turned to Kishan, who pondered deeply.

"What have I achieved? Nothing; I mean, absolutely nothing. Just a void. All the emotions I carried transformed into drawings. I feel light and liberated."

"Emptiness is freedom. That's the grandest achievement, my boy. It's like an expansive canvas, ready for your creativity," Anand philosophized, taking a small sip of wine.

"But I don't experience total freedom. It felt like a creature clinging to me all along," Kishan mused. "What creature?"

"Not sure... it's like a toddy cat hanging on a palm tree."

"What about now?" Maria inquired.

"Now? The creature has let go, but it left some claw marks. Yet... I'm unsure?"

"I can still sense the marks. It feels like there's something left to mend."

"Where? Let me see," Christy peered humorously at his rear, prompting laughter.

"Time will mend those wounds, don't worry. So, Chris, what about you?"

"I've worked on a documentary titled 'A Triangular Truth.' We all collaborated; Lucy was behind the camera. Remember our grandma's stories during the monsoon, Maya? That's when I found the inspiration to delve deeper into our roots. We captured untold stories from the people of Eerht, and editing is in progress."

"Wow, Christy, weaving the fabric of truth. Fantastic job! And Lucy?"

"I'm also a wedding photographer and recently opened a little studio in town called Lucify Studio. It was dad's realm, and I breathed new life into it. That's about it."

"And Maria?"

"I'm into design and managing a boutique now, receiving glowing reviews."

"Nand, where were you all this time?" Lucy slurred slightly.

"My tale requires an entire evening to unfold, but let's leave that adventure for another day."

"So?" Every gaze fixed on the last person at the table, and Kanya felt unsure of where to begin.

"Well, I haven't filled or emptied anything. I'm just kind of spiraling, still caught up in the past." She smiled, lingering in her silence.

Suddenly, the house came alive with a fluttering attack of moths.

"Hey everyone, let's switch off all the lights before this place turns into a moth graveyard."

Christy, Lucy, Kishan, and Maria banded together on a mission to extinguish all the electricity and secure the doors, leaving only the flickering flames and the thumping rhythm of pop music in their wake.

"These silly moths," Christy seen as she glanced at the fluttering nuisances around her.

"It's a suicidal quest before the salt rain arrives." The moths drew closer to the flames.

"Why are they meeting their doom?" "It's a tragic quest for love," Kanya offered sagely.

"What do you mean?" "It's the male moths that are sacrificing themselves. The light emitted by the fire mimics the wavelengths of the female moths' pheromones. I read that in a book."

"So, they're just hopelessly chasing after their ladies. Men really are foolish, aren't they?" Lucy quipped, and Christy playfully retorted, "Just like your dad."

Lucy leapt onto the table, claiming her stage in the spotlight.

"Listen up, ladies and dim-witted gentlemen!" she declared with the fervor of a leader.

"I have a crucial message for everyone. It would be a waste of this magical night if I kept it to myself—I might not get another chance!" The crowd eagerly awaited her revelation.

"We can't predict what will unfold in the next moment, so let's just relish this moment and celebrate!"

With that, she dove off the table, exclaiming in joy as she blasted "Darude - Feel the Beat." in the radio. Anand and Kanya felt the infectious energy as they sat, watching, somewhat shyly.

"Tonight, no one's going to sit idly by. Come on, ladies, let's dance!" Lucy whisked them onto the dance floor, and soon they were twirling around the fire, entranced by the rhythm. Time itself seemed to groove with the beats. Kanya pulled Anand away for a breather, their eyes locking in the firelight, heartbeats synchronized. A bead of sweat trickled down his forehead, pausing at his dimple. Kanya gently brushed the salt from his cheek with a soft smile.

"What's your favorite taste?" he asked, savoring the moment.

"Flavor? I'd go for spices. I adore spicy, with something sweet to follow. Tonight, has been utterly perfect—I've never met such bliss."

He pressed her hand against his dimpled cheek, closing his eyes to bask in the warmth.

"And yours?" "Salt." "Really?" She bit her luscious lips as he cupped her sweaty cheek, leaning in closer. Suddenly, a tiny intruder barged into their intimate space, disrupting the onset of their first kiss.

"Check out this little guy. Wow," Kanya exclaimed, pointing at a strikingly visible moth ablaze, fluttering around the table.

"Hey, check out this fellow!" The dancers diverted their gaze toward the enchanting creature.

"What on earth?" Curiosity drew everyone to the table, their eyes glued to the mesmerizing insect.

"Nandhu uncle, I had no idea the wine could induce such psychedelic experience," Kishan exclaimed, his voice laced with astonishment.

The moth fluttered toward Anand, gracefully skimming over him.

"Guys, let's keep still. I think that's an ash fire moth," Anand murmured softly.

"What? You mean the dust of flying?" "Exactly."

"Unbelievable."

In an instant, it darted away and hovered above the wine pot. Transforming into a fine dust, every shimmering particle cascaded into the drink. Anand swiftly capped the pot.

"What was that?" "Did we really just witness that?" A blend of reality and imagination enveloped them.

"Wow." "Nandhu uncle, is that for real?"

He raised the pot, seeing everyone intently.

"Do you mean we can soar?" Christy whispered. "Are we truly going to fly?" Kanya voiced her uncertainty, while Lucy broke the tension with urgency.

"What should we do? Should we drink it?"

The whispers dissipated, leaving everyone in a state of wonder.

"We're not hallucinating, are we?" "Is this really happening?" Christy and Lucy were caught in confusion, while Anand stood ready to embrace the skies.

"One sip for everyone. This is meant for us." No one opposed, but questions buzzed in the air.

With shared resolve, they formed a circle around the fire.

"To Maya and magic."

Anand started with a delicate sip, passing it to Kishan, then to Christy, Lucy, Maria, and finally to Kanya. As she savored her sip, Anand closed his eyes, prompting the others to follow suit. The gentle crackle of the fire filled their ears. After a moment of profound silence, they opened their eyes, scanning for anything out of the ordinary—but everything appeared unchanged. Yet a sense of the extraordinary lingered, just out of reach.

"Where's Lucy and Maria?"

"We're up here!" The call came from above—the two were gracefully drifting in the air, smiles bright as witches on their broomsticks.

"You guys not joining us? We're waiting!"

The boys remained grounded, heavy with disbelief, until Anand began to feel buoyant, rising gracefully.

"What the—Nandhu's uncle is going too?" Christy and Kishan gazed at the trio.

"What should we do?"

"Just breathe deeply and clear your mind." Christy followed Lucy's advice and soon found herself gliding upward.

"Wow! I'm flying! Me too!" Four of them joined hands above, gazing down at the distant earth.

"Just relax." Kishan and Kanya tried to embrace tranquility but found it elusive.

"Kishan, it's Bishan! Let him go; you must let him go!" Maria shouted. Kishan fixed his gaze on the flames, closed his eyes, and ignited his inner vision of Bishan—suddenly he felt weightless. Opening his eyes, Maria was right beside him.

"Look down!" he shouted in jubilant disbelief, eyes filled with wonder at the vast landscape below. Only Kanya remained earthbound.

"Just relax." She tried everything to ease herself, but the tension grew.

"We're not flying without you. This is your moment." "I can't. I've tried."

Anand gently descended toward her, offering his hand.

"If I'm soaring, it's going to be with you." As she grasped his hand, she sensed her body lifting, floating away from the earthly confines.

"I'm flying! I'm really flying!" She finally harmonized with the magic.

"You're not just flying; we're flying together." He pulled her close, their hips shimming in the air.

"This is the moment we've been waiting for." He captured her luscious lips in a kiss, their first in midair. The other couples, unable to resist the enchanting atmosphere, succumbed to passion, kissing under the open sky. With energy swirling among them, they formed a celestial circle of love, arms entwined in bliss.

"Hey everyone, is it just me or is anyone else feeling a bit unreal?" Christy inquired, her voice laced with a mix of anxiety and thrill.

"Nope, I share that feeling—it's like we're the only beings in this place," Lucy reassured, alleviating the uncertainty.

"I can sense the pulse of my wings. They can stretch up to 33 miles!"

"I feel that too!" Maria chimed in, excitement bubbling, and the others nodded in agreement.

"Thirty-three miles, huh? We could take on the entirety of Eerħt! Is this some sort of game?" Kishan exclaimed; enthusiasm mingled with doubt.

"Life turns into a fantastical game the moment we allow ourselves to experience it. Remember our childhood races? How about we soar in a race instead?" Anand proposed, and the group eagerly accepted the challenge.

"What if we gradually let go and explore our own spaces?"

One by one, they released their grips, embracing independence. Anand glanced at Kanya, who was ready, and he let her go, watching her float effortlessly.

"Alright, everyone, let's take this leap. Choose your path!"

The crescent moon suddenly illuminated their journey, captivating the aerial adventurers.

"Wow!" The flight crew gazed in awe at the shimmering light.

"Let's venture toward it and hover at the edge!" Lucy suggested with a wild idea.

"You go solo?" Christy laughed. "You really want me to fly to the moon by myself?" She hit an air knuckle kiss, a thrilling new sensation.

"Nandhu uncle, you tried crossing the river underwater? Why not try flying above it instead?" Maria proposed, and the idea was met with enthusiastic nods.

"That sounds amazing!"

"So, grandma is our destination then."

"Let's get started!"

"Fire marks the beginning." They could see the woods smoldering in the distance.

"Ready?" The group arranged themselves in a line.

"Set?" Each member struck a unique flying pose.

"And go!" Six adventurers surged forward; their minds focused solely on reaching the goal. They glided over mangroves, the marshlands blurring beneath them. Each was racing against their own limits as they soared above the river.

The air thickened with adrenaline, and the scent of nature filled their senses as they spotted a massive tree up ahead, urging them to rush.

Water splashed around them like a whirlwind, and the concept of stopping was foreign. Kishan, Maria, Christy, and Lucy slowed when the river got shallow, gently bobbing on the surface. Anand and Kanya pressed on until they crossed the finish line. Grandma was closer than she seemed. Anand grasped Kanya from behind and brought them to a halt, just above the great tree where the fragrance of Champa flowers enveloped them. The other four joined them, drifting in.

"Are you both okay?" they asked, laughter bubbling forth.

"What? That felt like a death race!" Their laughter spread contagiously among the group. They met around the trees, holding hands, forming a circle of life as they welcomed her into their tribe.

"Hey, I feel like our energy is running low. Let's head home before we crash!"

"Great idea." The group plotted their return.

"Alright, team, let's unite and support one another this time," Anand declared, and they clasped hands tightly.

"Goodnight, Grandma," the aerial beings said as they each plucked a flower from the tree. Their return flight was leisurely and smooth, allowing them to fully savor the enchanting experience. The sights before them felt almost magical, leading them to realize it's not merely about what's visible but how they perceive it. Soaring above the eerie marsh, they spotted a distant fire flickering in the dark.

"Hey, I feel the energy waning," one of them remarked as they began to drift slowly, all eyes drawn toward the glowing woods. They alighted gently and securely right by the flames.

As their feet met the ground, the sounds of the old world—crickets and frogs—filled their ears.

"What just happened?" Christy asked. "It wasn't just a dream, was it?" Him and Lucy exchanged touches to confirm their reality.

"I believe the universe wanted us to keep our faith in magic," one said, each clutching a flower as a keepsake.

"So, the magic was genuine," Kanya mused, still in awe.

"You amazing girl, that wish was wild!" Maria exclaimed, pulling her close to the ground, resulting in an irrational smile from Kanya.

"I'm feeling a tingle."

"Seriously?" Maria teased her belly, provoking laughter.

"No, stop! I think something's crawling on me." "Formication? Is that real?"

"Absolutely," Kanya replied, scratching her skin.

"You're right, there's something moving inside me too."

"Oh no, we must have crash-landed on an ant hill. Run!" The sisters sprinted for their lives as tiny soldiers invaded their clothing, prompting peals of laughter from others.

"Oh, those little nuisances! They're everywhere!" Both danced around the house, itching and shaking off their uninvited guests. Finally free, they returned to the origin of the dancing flames where their magical journey had begun. They collapsed onto the ground, embracing and giggling.

"They nearly got us," one said. "But they definitely got me all over." Only the euphoric feeling lingered behind.

"If this fire is genuine, then the fly was too," Lucy proclaimed before collapsing onto the ground, fatigued.

One by one, they fell around the fire, with the crescent moon being their sole witness to the adventure. As the atmosphere quieted, the crackling flames were the only sound until a new voice resonated at a higher pitch, drawing everyone's attention.

A tiny frog, perched under a miniature umbrella, either beckoning or welcoming the rain.

The croaking herald from the wild, broadcasting the enchanting winter magic - a frog under the mushroom.

Chapter 11
The Tears of The Romance

Winter Nectar,

1999.

A dim yellow silhouette of the earth flickers against the murky night sky. The flame is taking its last gasps, turning to ash. The flight crew lingers around the waning spark of existence, contorted into the various poses of the human form. The music has finished its track, concluding its purpose. Kanya, in a side pose, gazes at the fire performing its deathly ballet. Anand lies with his arms beneath his head, staring into the crescent moon—a habit ingrained in his memory over the years. Gradually, it hits him that the search has ended, and he shifts his gaze to Kanya. Their eyes connect in a soulful embrace. Lucy lazily sauntered to the stereo, pulling a random tape to revive the lifeless moment. "Enigma - Principles of Lust" filled the air, perfectly attuned to the ambiance. The calming rhythms stirred the smoldering coals and animated the languid bodies.

"This music feels incredible," Lucy remarked, savoring the melody as she gently scratched Christy's head, bringing forth a smile on his face. A lightless thunder resonated from the abyss, prompting the lethargic souls to stir instinctively.

"Guys, how about we seek refuge under the roof?" Lucy cradled the stereo against her chest. Everyone dutifully dropped to their knees before rising with lazy stretches. Kanya remained on the ground, mimicking flying with hand gestures, yet lacking the power to ascend.

"Hey, fire moth, shall we migrate the party indoors?" Maria coaxed, pulling her arms gently.

"All I crave is a snug corner," Kanya mused, "Is there enough warmth inside?"

"No, my bed would be ideal. I can head home." She sprawled comfortably on the ground.

"So, should I rise?" Kanya's rhetorical question lingered in the air.

"We've got a better idea," chimed the others as they circled around her.

"What's the plan?" she asked, buoyant with anticipation. "How about we take flight?"

Lucy guided the group with the ethereal pulse of ambient music as others lifted Kanya from all directions. The midnight promenade begun. Kanya truly felt as if she were soaring once more, gazing at the obsidian sky with an illuminating smile. A blue flash silently mirrored her joy as the procession entered the grand mansion.

"Where do we touch down? Where do we touch down?" "Buckle up, dear passenger." Maria took the lead, navigating the troop up a steep staircase. She landed safely on her comfortable bed.

"Have a wonderful night. Peace out." "Thank you for the lift, darlings. Come here." Kanya pulled Maria in and planted a heartfelt kiss on her cheek. "Good night. See you tomorrow."

"You have a lovely night too." Maria winked and blew a kiss before stepping out.

Anand stood at the foot of the stairs, bewildered.

"Nandhu uncle, just look after my girl. We'll see you in the morning. The mansion is all yours." They departed, leaving him no time to ponder. They sang along with the stereo's rhythm, strolling beside the marsh, arms draped around each other's shoulders.

"Absolutely. The magic of profound music is that it finds us when we need it most."

"Exactly."

"I was pondering," Kishan said, scratching his scruffy head.

"No more pondering tonight." "Did we really fly?" "I think so." "I've never felt this ecstatic in my life." Maria glanced up at the heavens, her smile faltering in an instant.

"What's wrong?" "Nothing, just thoughts of Dad."

"Let's not bring him up now, no offense," Christy remarked, offering a reassuring smile.

"I have something to ask," Kishan said with a hint of fear. "What?" "What if your dad is lurking behind us with an axe?" Maria nearly lost control of her shorts.

"That's not funny." She tugged at his hair, making it even messier.

"I wouldn't flee or confront him. I'd just have a heart attack right here," Christy quipped.

As laughter erupted amidst the fright, a flash of blue lightning followed by a deafening thunderclap shattered the moment. The ground trembled beneath them, and flames erupted in Christy's field. The sound of crackling flames filled the air.

Something's ablaze." "Our campfire." "That should have burned out by now."

They cast their gazes toward the wall, where the flickering shadow of flames was slowly taking shape.

"Are you all seeing what I'm seeing?" "That's your field."

"Oh no, it's real. Our coconut tree is on fire. What should we do?" Panic spread among them.

"Run and grab a bucket of water," Lucy quipped.

"And you'll scale the tree with that? What are you, a tree-climbing cat?"

"What other option do we have?"

A spiraling gust of wind fanned the flames further.

"Let's alert the fire department."

They dashed home, and as they sprinted, a light sprinkle of salty rain began to fall. The tears of the crescent moon gradually smothered the crackling of the flames. They approached the smoldering tree with a calmness that belied their earlier panic.

"Thank goodness we saved the fire alarm and avoided total chaos," Lucy sighed, relief washing over her.

"And you thought you could scale it," Maria teased with a grin.

"What's the big deal? How old was it?"

"That tree was planted on my 18th birthday, same as that Champa tree." Christy lamented, revealing the identity of the fallen. "I didn't realize you were genuinely going to call the fire crew. That would be the most ludicrous move anyone could make in this scenario." "More sensible than your bucket-of-water scheme," he retorted, playfully jostling her. Laughter rippled among them.

"Alright, let's finalize things before our parents come back."

Christy dashed into the house like a whirlwind, and the others trailed behind, curiosity piqued.

He flipped through the phone directory, zeroing in on the S section.

"Who are you calling?"

Lucy leaned over to check the name. Sugunan (the killer).

"What? The Killer? Is he a serial killer?"

"No, he dubs himself a killer. He sees cutting down a tree as a murder."

"Are you actually contacting that killer now?"

Christy had already dialed the number, and after a few rings, a voice came through.

"Hello, this is the killer. How can I help you?" "Mr. Sugunan?" "Yes, speaking."

"It's me, Christy. John's boy from the spooky cottage."

"Ah, my boy! What's up, marshy?"

Christy glanced at the clock—midnight.

"Sorry to disturb you, but it's an emergency."

"Spill it, boy. Who's on the chopping block?" "Uh, it's a tree." "Come again? A tree?"

"A coconut tree in our field was struck by lightning. When can you come?"

"Coconut tree? Should I rush over now?" "No. Not tonight. Any other time is good."

"Anytime except tonight. Let me consult my schedule. Got a full day of killings tomorrow. Hmm, all right. I suppose I'll fit John's boy into my agenda. I'll be there in the morning. Will you be home?"

"Yes."

"Anything else?" "No, the dead tree reminded me of you. So???"

"Oh boy, that sentiment means the world. I'll come in the morning, no matter what."

"Okay. Goodnight."

The call wrapped up, leaving the others looking at Christy in bewilderment.

"What in the world was that?"

"Let's just cut it." "Aren't you going to check with your dad?"

"He'll do the same thing. What's the difference? It's done now. Once the killer commits, he doesn't back out."

"Are you still feeling frightened, my moon?" he inquired, his fingers caressing her cheek. "No," she replied, yet her answer was enveloped in a lingering soul kiss. Stripped of all garments, their warm bodies fused as one. She perched atop him, moving her yoni against his linga while he squeezed her breast. Suddenly, an absence washed over her, as if her very essence had drifted away.

"What just happened?" he asked, concerned about etching his features.

"Nandhu, is it normal for the mind to crave pleasure while the heart clings to pain?"

"Which voice do you heed?"

"I'm not certain, but I desperately seek pleasure."

"Then you shall find it."

He gently pressed his lips against her cupid-like ones, his hand drifting close to her heart, tenderly massaging her breast. Yet, there was no sensation at all. "I can't. I just don't know." Tears began to flow.

"Hey, it's all right. Let's take our time," he soothed, brushing her tears away. They stood at a crossroads, unsure how to navigate as their romantic endeavor hit a stalemate.

"Nandhu, please. Just grant me a moment. Something feels off within me. My heart?"

"Your heart is perfectly fine."

"I love you, Nandhu, more than anything."

"I love you too. Don't fret; we'll navigate this together, all right? Just breathe." He cradled her on his chest, tending to her hair with gentle strokes.

"Don't worry, simply relax." She gazed deeply into his eyes.

"Do you despise me for this?" she asked, sensing the turmoil in those dark depths. "What? No?"

"Nandhu, I can see your unease. It's palpable."

She caressed his dimple, feeling the chill he tried to conceal. Her hands moved to his linga, still firm as stone.

"What? What's going on?" He felt shy suddenly, but his body betrayed him, unable to refuse her touch. As she caressed him, pressure visibly ebbed from his eyes.

"I won't leave you in discomfort, my love."

"But Kanya?"

"Hey, hey. Just focus on me." She captivated his attention, drawing him into her gaze.

"Don't worry about me. Right now, your only task is to relax, okay?"

He surrendered, lying back, eyes closing as he yielded to her soothing words. She began her gentle kiss, starting at his forehead, moving to his lips, then to his neck, and down to his nipples. His awakened linga thrummed with joy as she closed the distance, slowly taking him into her mouth, her cupid bow lips enveloping him. As the passion unfolded, he transcended into a blissful realm, a smile blossoming on his dimpled face as his body surrendered completely to her.

As the gentle drizzle transformed into a heavy downpour outside, Lucy found herself enveloped in the cascading rain. Her bare skin absorbed the pelting droplets while inside, the warmth of intimacy brewed as Christy lovingly kissed each of her toes. His tongue meandered across her thigh and danced into her navel, then gradually climbed upward, tenderly caressing her breasts to tease her nipple. As his gaze met hers, he plucked the Champa flower from her ear, using its delicate petals to stroke her most sacred spot, eliciting a soft sigh of pleasure from her lips, which mingled with the symphony of rain, finally lost beneath Christy's kiss.

Meanwhile, Kishan and Maria were sprawled out, reveling in the soothing rhythm of raindrops against the window, their hands playfully soaked. With a mischievous glance, she turned to him and splashed a handful of raindrops across his face.

"Watch it, salty." he laughed. "You just got started."

"I can do whatever I like with you," she purred, her wet fingers gliding over his cheek. Suddenly silenced by her gaze, they found solace in each other's deep brown eyes, even in the dim light.

"What shall we do tonight?" "You haven't guessed?" "No. How about a fiery dance?" "Absolutely." He retrieved a matchbox and ignited a stick.

"Careful now, or you'll set the house ablaze!"

He simply gazed into her radiant eyes.

"Do you remember the first time we crossed paths, amid the burning glow of a candle's flame?"

Lost in reminiscence, she reflected on that moment, while he was jolted back to the present by the match's glowing end.

"Now that memory feels like a fleeting spark." She cradled his singed fingers with care.

As she gently blew on his fingers with a playful kiss, his breath began to rise, their eyes communicating a language of their own. His burnt fingertip glided over her body like a whisper, and in an instant, their layers were shed, revealing two fiery souls entwined in love's embrace.

She guided him down, seating herself atop him, her essence glistening as she tenderly intertwined their bodies. Together, they explored the delicious dance of a slow sixty-nine, savoring their shared paradise. The connection of their essence fused like land and sky; their hearts grounded while their spirits soared. They melded in a symphony of love, a chorus of rhythms that harmonized with the pounding rain, each moan echoing in the storm's embrace. Perched above him, she indulged in an endless rhythm, her movements gradually slowing as moments melted away, leaving him coated in her sweetness. Grasping his essence, she playfully teased him with tender caresses. The warmth of his breath revealed the life surging within him, and as she ventured down, she savored him deeply, her lips dripping with desire. Like molten lava spilling forth, his essence erupted, filling her mouth as she drank in his offering with unquenchable thirst, a blissful tremor coursing through his being. She savored the last remnants, capturing every drop with her tongue, then rested her head on his chest as he lifted her chin to taste those enticing lips, longing for more of her sweetness. His fingers danced rapidly across her, igniting a second wave of passion, and like a waterfall, their desires surged once more, each grasping for the other, lost in a fervent meditation of lust.

In the bungalow, the rhythmic breath of passion lingered in the air. Kanya revealed in the sensations, savoring every moment, while Anand synchronized his inhalations with the rising tides of energy coursing through them. She glided in like a gentle rainfall, igniting a fiery fervor within him. Her dolphin-like gaze locked onto his, a dance of darkness and light, as she swayed. His lips met her juicy lips, the climax drawing near. At last, his body soared, releasing a cascade of sperm; the warmth splattered across him, reaching even his distant features. She licked away the remnants of life from his face, relishing the taste. Her tongue wandered, cleaning every inch of him, embodying vitality while he lay sated and nearly silent.

"How was that, delicious Nand? I could indulge endlessly." She beamed with the energy she had absorbed, passing its essence to him as her fingers played across his nipple.

"I love you, Kanya," he whispered, pulling her closer and pressing a kiss to her forehead.

"I love you too, Nandhu," she replied, brushing her cheek on his chest. As her hand glided over his bare skin, attuned to the slow tempo of his heartbeat, she noticed remnants of life nestled in his navel like a hidden spring. With a graceful movement, she crawled down, drawing in those precious droplets before they faded away. The revival of his essence rekindled her desires, awakening her senses anew.

"Nandhu, I can feel my body now. I truly can." His desire stirred back to life at the sound of her words.

"Now, I shall quench my thirst," he murmured, finding her already drenched with anticipation. He eagerly drew in her essence as the rain drops transformed their world into an enchanting wetland - Kanya's eyes overflowed with shimmering drops of ecstasy and delight as Anand savored the nectar of her essence - the tears of the romance.

Chapter 12
A Skeleton with Golden Fags

Winter Madness,

1999.

A vast aqua universe. Kanya glided through the liquid embrace of the river, her silk saree pulsating and undulating with each smooth stroke. Abruptly, a skeletal visage erupted from the aquatic vegetation, sending shockwaves of terror through her, and the waters enveloped her entirely.

Two shimmering, white eyes blinked awake in surprise, yearning for air. Anand lounged comfortably in his chair, cradling a cup of coffee while gazing at his celestial companion, now peacefully dozing in nudity. He hadn't predicted such a jarring interruption to his tranquility. After a few moments, she stirred back to life, her heartbeat settling down.

"Did you have a frightening dream?" "Hmm."

"I'm not fishing for details, but it seems you ventured beneath the water."

"How did you gather that?" she replied, breathless.

"Breath tells no lies. I realize you've immersed yourself in the river, but a sip of water would do you good." He poured her a glass from the earthen vessel and offered it with a warm smile. She accepted it gratefully and took a dainty sip, her voice reemerging.

"Are you an early riser?"

"Seriously, it's already past eleven. I hope the other monks are stirring from their slumber."

She regarded him with a grateful grin.

"What's with that expression?" "Waking up to your visage feels surprisingly delightful."

"Then let's make this a morning ritual." "What's in your cup?" "Black coffee, sourced straight from your kitchen."

After downing the water, she tidied her tousled locks. "May I trouble you for some coffee?"

"I'll brew you a cup." "No, let me share a taste of yours."

He stepped closer, drawn to her delicate cupid's bow.

"My mouth's a bit off." "That's precisely the flavor I crave."

Their lips intertwined, savoring the essence of morning, a blend of freshness and earthy wanderlust.

"Tears of the crescent moon that linger in memory?" He offered her the mug and seen as she savored her coffee.

"Ahh, that's much better. So, last night truly happened." He presented her the two Champa flowers gifted by Grandma.

"Wow. We all flew! Can you believe it?"

"I can't fathom that we made love." "Last night was an experience unlike any other."

"We'll make it a reality again. For now, hurry and freshen up. I'm absolutely famished."

"Same here."

Kanya slid her bare form from the bed and dashed to the restroom.

"I'll be waiting outside."

"Okay." Anand descended the stairs and swung open the front door. It was a stunning, sunlit morning.

He breathed in the crisp air, bathing in the sunlight.

"Let's hope the monks are awake." He scanned the neighborhood for any sign of life before glancing back at the bungalow, memories swirling around him.

"How much have I changed? And Kanya is finally mine." He murmured softly.

Kanya appeared, rejuvenated, cradling a generous bowl of fruit salad crowned with dark chocolate ice cream.

"Start with this. I found some fruits and homemade ice cream in the fridge."

He offered her a separate glass of the desert. "Did you eat?"

"I'll eat later." He offered her a spoonful of the mixture. She obliged, ice cream leaving a trace on her lips, her tongue darting out to wipe it away.

"No, allow me." He brushed the ice cream off her cupid's bow with a kiss. They both relished the salad, readying themselves for the day ahead.

"Shall we venture out?" "Absolutely." They secured the bungalow and stepped onto the eerie pathway. The sun struck their heads directly.

"Wow, what a brilliantly sunny morning." The marsh sparkled with sunlight, glistening against the wet surface of the skin. Two men trailed closely behind them—one stout, wielding an axe, while a tall, wiry figure followed, carrying thick coils of rope on either side. Kanya turned around, startled by the axe man and the rope man. She quickened her pace.

"What?" Anand glanced back, a similar unease creeping into his mind. They stepped into the cottage, the armed men following closely in their wake, Anand feeling a twinge of fear.

"Yes, can I assist you?" He halted them at a distance and rang the doorbell.

"I was told to come for a 'killing' yesterday." "What?"

"I mean, for tree-cutting. Just my usual slang, forget it. I see myself as a killer. A tree holds life too, just a different modus operandi." Anand and Kanya exchanged confused glances, bewildered by his words. Christy opened the door, teetering on the edge of slumber.

"Ah, step right in." He drifted back into slumber.

"Christy, they're here to kill."

"What?" He jolted awake, glancing at the visitors.

"It's me, Sugunan. Aren't you John's lad?" "Indeed, I am." He replied with a radiant grin.

"Hey there, it's been ages! The last time, you had a full head of hair."

His bright smile dimmed.

"That's the lifeless tree." He gestured to the charred coconut trunk in the field, his smile fading into an empty expression.

"Oh, all that coconut fluff has vanished."

"Just like the boy." His associate chuckled, and together they shared a laugh.

"Alright, lad. I've got this."

"Pull out the roots. They're brain-dead and won't sprout again. Perhaps we can plant another tree."

"Or, we might consider erecting a monument of me wielding a mighty axe." Sugunan chuckled, twirling the axe playfully.

"Boss, you're on a roll today." His associate laughed in agreement.

"I don't need a golden axe; a silver one will suffice." "Boss, your humor is top-notch today."

"I've got this, lad." They laughed heartily and strode toward the fray.

"What are all these crazy nuts? Who are these characters?"

"Oh, you missed it. After our flying escapade, we had a fiery episode last night. Lightning hit the tree, incinerating our coconut haven." Kanya and Anand looked up at the stump bereft of its crown.

"Good morning, miss." "Here's some fruit salad for you all."

"Fruit salad? Absolutely! Why not?" His mouth watered with anticipation.

"Where are the other monks?" "Lucy is sound asleep. Let me see if the brown-eyed monks are awake." Christy knocked on their door repeatedly until Kishan finally came to the opening, clearly annoyed.

"What's your deal?" "Good morning! Fancy some ice cream salad?"

He instantly calmed.

"Rise and shine." A playful slap landed on Maria's bare backside.

"What?" "Your sister brought ice cream salad." The words perked her up. They both got dressed and made their way to the ice-cream salad gathering.

"Good morning, girl." Maria yawned. All eyes fell on the brown-eyed duo, sensing something was amiss.

"Who is this stunning lady?" Christy tousled Kishan's long locks while he admired his T-shirt in the reflection.

He clocked their attire—a delicious mix of each other's shirts.

"Don't change, darling. It looks better on you." Almost instinctively, they swapped outfits before realizing it.

"Are you both wizards?" "Yes, since last night. We all took flight, right?" "Is there any drop left in the bottle?" "There's no drop in the bottle or in my being." Kishan quickly scooped up some salad.

"Nah, happiness is the real dish today."

Kanya gracefully served dessert in cups; every eye glued to her like watching a scientist unveil a spectacular experiment.

"Go fetch Lucy." "I don't want a knuckle kiss." Christy grabbed his part from the refresh bowl, indulging. Outside, a lively tug-of-war unfolded.

"You tug. Pull with all your might. Even harder."

The spectators gathered with their bowls of dessert, converging to see the grim spectacle.

"Nandhu uncle, do you recall that night we sowed the seedling?" "Ah, yes. Death is as undeniable a reality as birth, isn't it, lad?" Anand echoed the sentiments from Kishan's speech.

The executioner and his accomplice tightened their grip on the rope and started the heave.

"Boss, I've never inquired—How did you lose your pinky finger?"

"Oh boy, that's quite the tale. You see, I couldn't go a single day without a bit of killing. Then there came that fateful day—no kill? What to do? What to do?" The tall, slender figure prompted with the strain.

"I envisioned my pinky as a tree and swung the axe. On the count of three, I brought it down."

The lean man chuckled so forcefully that he lost his grip and fell, guffawing on the ground. His short boss, meanwhile, was sent sprawling into a muddy corner by the fallen tree.

"Boss, you deserve a statue for that!" "Right?" he replied, rising with a muddy visage.

"Alright, enough of the banter." They composed themselves and resumed their grim task.

The rope was secured tightly to the main gate.

"Is he really going to uproot the entire thing?" Christy mused; a curious eyebrow raised as he scooped up some salad.

"Alright, I'm going to slice it." The killer declared, retrieving his axe from the earth. With hands poised for the strike, his partner braced for the impending fall. The axe descended upon the tree's base, while a woodpecker perched above banged its head against the trunk. "You mother cutter." The bird retaliated with a harsh squawk before darting away for safety. The tree began to teeter, and the thin accomplice maneuvered the tilt onto the field. "Timber!" Sugunan yelled as the trunk crashed down. The ants, marching dutifully across the terrain, barely had a moment to escape before they met their demise. Lucy stirred awake to the resounding crash, her hair a wild electrified halo as she arrived at the killing scene.

"Oh, the sixth sorcerer has risen! There's fruit salad waiting in the kitchen," Kanya announced.

"Is that so?" She polished off Christy's bowl and dashed off to grab her own.

"No time to waste! Time is invaluable, you know." She returned, cradling the entire bowl.

"That's our girl."

More spoons joined the feast, and soon the bowl was emptied. Lucy savored the last of the cream on her lips. "Flying, lightning, running?" Lucy looked to untangle the mysteries of the past.

"All we need now is a refreshing dip. How about the Scent River?"

"Do you have anything to switch it up?"

Christy led them to his wardrobe, unveiling a treasure trove of outfits.

"From beach attire to underwear. Find your fit." They each selected their preferred pieces and headed out.

"We're off but will return shortly."

"Alright, Killer's got this. Enjoy yourselves!"

"Is he really going to obliterate your whole farmhouse?" Lucy whispered.

The green jeep roared to life, landing squarely beneath a monument of a Nazi gripping a formidable golden axe, the heads gazing in reverence at the weapon.

"Killer," Anand chuckled. "What a character! Did you catch what he said? He chopped off his own finger. He deserves a statue with a silver axe."

"What kind of fool would hack off their finger with an axe?" "Killer Sugunan," Christy dismissed Maria's uncertainty with a name that gave all the answers they looked for.

"Imagine if we had the chance to soar again, maybe with more power. Where would we venture?" Lucy inquired of the tribe.

"Perhaps we'd journey to the crescent moon, just as you envisioned."

Christy proposed a splendid scheme. "My man, that's incredible." She leaned down and planted a passionate kiss on his neatly groomed head.

Lucy leaped into the water, her inners swirling around her, trailed closely by Christy and Maria. Anand, shedding his clothes, strolled toward the water with a measured grace.

"Hey, long-haired monk, why the hesitation?" Christy called out to Kishan, who fidgeted nervously on the steps. "I can't go in," he replied, dread clear in his eyes, causing the others to gather around him.

Anand rested a hand on his shoulder. "When was the last time you took the plunge?"

"Before Bishan passed away." Anand could almost taste the fear radiating from him.

"Come on, man, just dive in." Christy's encouragement fell flat. It was Maria who finally took his arm, silently guiding him toward the water as he moved forward timidly. With each step, his trepidation seemed to melt away into the depths, leaving only wonder behind. Arms swaying, their feet floated in unison, a beautiful display that captivated the onlookers.

"What sort of enchantment is this?" Christy marveled.

"This enchantment is love and trust, something I clearly lack with you," Lucy teased as she playfully gave a knuckle kiss before gliding away. "Seriously?" Christy sprang into action, trying to catch up with her. The couples came together in celebration, their laughter echoing through the air.

"Nandu uncle, come join us! Kani, why are you holding back?" "No way." "Come on, girl! We might be walking dark folks, but together, we can soar like the stars. Remember?" Kanya pondered for a moment, then reluctantly decided to join in, bashfully shedding her salwar suit.

"That's my girl!" Cheers erupted as she took tentative steps, then dove into the. The fly folks immersed themselves in a frenzy of laughter and splashes, filled with exuberance.

"Let's see who can hold their breath the longest!" Lucy proposed, her voice bubbling with excitement.

"Not against Nandhu uncle—he's the stealthy black fish in our midst. He's unbeatable."

"Fine, I'll take on the role of countdown master. Everyone, dive in!"

"Alright, everyone ready?" The group closed ranks. "On the count of three: 1, 2, 3!" They plunged into the depths, a chorus of splashes marking the start of their aquatic adventure.

Anand counted in his mind.

"1, 2, 3, 4, 5, 6, 7, 8, 9, 10, 11, 12, 13, 14, 15, 16, 17, 18, 19, 20, 21, 22, 23, 24, 25, 26, 27. Maria arrived. "28, 29, 30, 31, 32, 33, 34, 35, 36, 37, 38, 39, 40. Lucy appeared. "You girls excel only at soaring through the skies." The counting continued in unison. "43, 44, 45, 46, 47, 48, 49, 50, 51, 52, 53, 54, 55, 56, 57, 58, 59, 60.

Christy rose up. "Precisely one minute." "I really should practice my breathing more."

"Nandhu uncle, how is my sister holding up?" Maria asked, worry etched on her face.

"What do you mean?"

"She hasn't been herself. Witnessing grandpa's lifeless body truly shook her. She was already carrying the weight of trauma from seeing mom's body, which no child should endure. Grandpa's passing has dragged that buried pain back to the surface. Ever since that evening, she's been different. Remember the next day?" Maria reminisced with Christy.

"Yes, the night following Bishan's cremation."

"What happened?" Lucy inquired, intrigued.

"She was wandering the streets, drenched. It's hard to describe, but she resembled someone who'd just escaped an asylum." Christy glanced at Maria.

"No, you're right. She appeared frighteningly unhinged."

"But now, Kani is thriving. She's more composed than I am."

"Indeed. She's come a long way. That night has resurfaced in my thoughts unexpectedly. Nandhu uncle, I felt you should know."

"I've loved only one soul in this life—your sister. Yet, there's something deeply troubling her. I can feel it." Suddenly, Kanya appeared from the depths.

"Wow, are you all out? What's the count?" "More than two minutes."

"Kani, quite impressive." "She taught me how to swim." "And who was her teacher?" "Grandpa." She began to delve into memories, but the conversation shifted.

"That long-haired monk is still submerged." "Incredible, nearly three minutes." "Will he surpass my record?" Anand mused. Maria sank deep once more in search of the truth. There Kishan was, adrift in silence. She hoisted him onto her shoulder and propelled him upwards.

"He's unconscious!" Maria shouted, panic gripping her voice. Everyone rushed him to the shore.

Anand hoisted him by the stomach beneath his shoulder and squeezed. He expelled excess water, stirring back to awareness. As he lay down on the sand, he was encircled by friends, as if gathered around his deathbed.

Before he could fully regain his senses, waves of nausea hit him again, forcing him to sit up while gasping for air. Then, in a sudden expulsion, a metallic object tumbled from his throat onto the steps. "What the?" Curious eyes turned toward the clanking sound from a distance. Maria scooped up the metal and rinsed it off—a small silver locket shaped like a fish's tail.

"It's a locket," Kishan said as he took it from her. "I've seen this before... but where?"

"Wherever, let's just leave this place." "Oh, now I remember. Grandpa used to wear it. But how did it end up here?"

"Come on, baby. Let's go," Maria said, gripping his arm with unease. He saw her and burst into laughter.

"I'm not dead, guys! Seriously, just touch me and see." "Just trying to give me a scare," she teased, showering his face with kisses. "Are you alright?" "I'm fantastic. In fact, it feels like I'm stepping into life after death." He felt more at ease than ever before.

"I heard him! I heard Bishan's whisper." "What did he say?"

"'It's time to let go.'" Smiles mingled with apprehension on everyone's faces.

"Wonderful! Now you're free—liberated from your annoying cat claws."

"Yes, I can feel the relief." He wrapped his arms around Maria, kissing her softly.

"Yet, I nearly had a heart attack with this wild adventure. You're the one who started this carnival of chaos!"

Christy pointed at Lucy, who seemed to be enjoying herself.

"What did I do, coconut head?"

"You only proposed the diving idea." He received his customary knuckle kiss.

"Shall we leave and find some shade? The sun is relentless. Time to go," Christy urged, striding quickly toward the road with Lucy matching his pace.

Suddenly, a figure leapt from the palm grove in front of them.

"Aha! I see a smiling skeleton—a skeleton with golden fangs!"

A wealthy-looking man stood there, a bloody red spot gracing his pineal gland, dressed in an exquisite knee-length silk jubba.

"Aha! I see a smiling skeleton—a skeleton with golden fangs!"

He clutched a raw coconut in his hand. No sign of its trunk in sight, leaving them to wonder if it simply vanished or if it was a new trend.

"Aha! I see a smiling skeleton—a skeleton with golden fangs!"

"What is this? Who's this nutcase? Is he going to throw that coconut at us?" Christy questioned with a hint of panic.

"Your ex-fiancé?" Maria quipped at Kanya.

"Who?"

"This is the mango-faced fellow she was meant to be engaged to."

"Yes, I recall that mango face from that night. Engaged to this eccentric character?"

"He seems to have improved," Maria replied with a wry smile.

"Aha! I see a smiling skeleton—a skeleton with golden fangs!"

He appeared enchanted, dancing rhythmically to his nonsensical refrain.

"Did he receive some kind of mystical calling like your father?"
"Sounds more like a madman's summons," Maria quipped, hiding behind Kishan. A cadre of rational folks sprinted from afar to apprehend him. The deranged man dodged them, darting around the Nazi statue. As the sensible crowd headed north, he veered south,

cutting across their path and slipping into the palm trees, the sane folks trailing close behind. The ruckus caught the attention of a bearded man by the riverbank, poised to indulge in his cannabis beedi, his facial hair reminiscent of a lush herb farm.

"Yes, Baba Gonosh. What can I do for you?"

Christy stood frozen, fixated on the new eccentric.

"Baba Gonosh." He uttered simply, while Christy's mind pondered, 'Who's this character?'

From a distance, a woman draped in gold rushed forward, tears streaming down her face, her heavy adornments slowing her pace.

"Dear lady, what troubles you?" Baba called, prompting her to pause and divert her gaze from weeping.

"Why are you so upset?"

"A coconut plummeted onto my husband's head." The tears flowed once more.

"Fascinating! And what happened next?"

"And he bolted off with that coconut! What am I to do now?"

She clung to Baba, her eyes and nose a torrent of tears. While the others were perplexed, Baba grasped the full picture.

"Oh, my divine ganja, this is it."

"This is what?" the tearful woman inquired, bewildered.

"Have you heard of the headbangers who awakened?"

"My uncle once lost consciousness after banging his head on a wall," replied the gold-laden lady. Embracing Baba again, her tears soaked his clothes, which had not seen soap in over a month. Suddenly, the figure reemerged from the palms.

"Aha! I see a smiling skeleton—a skeleton with golden fangs!"

"Didn't you hear? He's ensnared in that cycle. Whose skeleton is he referring to?"

"You mentioned a coconut struck his head, yet he bears a mark on his third eye. Was he practicing Savasana?"

"It ricocheted off the window of our new luxury sedan, bouncing back to his face. You know, that car boasts unparalleled toughness—no scratch at all," the golden woman proclaimed, sharing one of her luxurious vehicle's highlights.

"Aha! I see a smiling skeleton—a skeleton with golden fangs!"

"Didn't I tell you? This is it."

With a coconut in hand, no one approached him. Baba began to bounce alongside the eccentric. The spectators, caught in the moment, started leaping without awareness. The sane pursuers, now perspiring heavily, joined the fray. The madman's legs spun like a compass and halted to the north, yet he dashed east, leaving the coconut behind. He leaped into the river, with the rest swimming after him. The chaotic dash transformed into a collective swim. The gold-clad lady, fearing the metal's weight would drag her under, refrained from jumping, instead sprinting westward with her tears still flowing.

"What in the cosmos are we witnessing?" Christy exclaimed; his jaw nearly unhinged. Silence enveloped the group.

"You won't believe what I saw last night!" "What is it?" The fly folks chimed in unison.

"Six humans soaring through the sky. It was utterly wild." The bearded sage of holy cannabis flashed a blissful grin, retrieving the coconut that had slipped from the grasp of the eccentric man.

"This coconut is also bizarre. It's no surprise he's lost it. I always knew I was destined for greatness. This isn't just a coconut anymore; it shall henceforth be known as the chosen nut!" He lifted it triumphantly toward the heavens.

"If I craft a chutney from it, I could unlock a treasure trove of magic."

He waved goodbye to everyone and drifted away, chosen nut in hand.

"Why not skedaddle before more chosen nuts rain down on us?"

No one offered a counterpoint to Christy's suggestion. They all piled into the jeep and set off. Kishan returned to his pendant, while Maria tied the fish locket to his silver chain.

"Happy birthday, darling. Today marks the dawn of a new journey." Their hands entwined; Maria nestled her cheek against his shoulder. The jeep fell into a tranquil hush until Lucy broke the spell.

Christy's thoughts wandered.

"What's swirling in that mind of yours?" Lucy pried.

"Who is the skeleton the manic headbanger mentioned?" Anand's gaze caught sight of a skeleton lurking beneath the river. The same unsettling notion began to plague every mind in the jeep.

"Didn't your dad possess golden fags?" Kishan grinned at Maria, flashing his incisors.

"Yes." Her reply lingered in the air, unchallenged by further inquiry. The headbanger's madness echoed relentlessly in their minds - a skeleton with golden fags.

Chapter 13
The Pleasure of the Pain

Winter Surrender,

1999.

The sun blazed fiercely overhead as a green jeep navigated the sweltering heat. Passengers seeking refuge from the relentless rays to clear their minds. Everyone sifted through their memories, trying to discern the truths hidden within the fragments of their past.

"What in the world?" Christy scratched his closely-cropped hair, finally putting a stop to the barrage of questions.

They ventured down the marsh path, unusually crowded with people. The hum of the engine prompted bystanders to step aside as they moved in unison, careful not to collide with anyone. The onlookers scrutinized the passing jeep passengers with wary eyes.

"What are they up to?" Christy leaned out of the window, a creeping sensation of being watched enveloping him—an unsettling realization that indeed, they were being tracked. Everyone was converging on his cottage, now overrun by a sea of bodies. Anand honked at those obstructing the gate, revealing two police jeeps hidden within the throng. The fly folks parked their green jeep behind the blue ones and cautiously disembarked for the culminating spectacle of the day.

"Sir, the owner has arrived," Killer pointed with his muddied finger at Christy, redirecting the officers' attention towards them.

"What's going on here?" Anand received only awkward glances in response. Christy tread softly on the dry foliage, the others trailing behind. A fallen coconut tree adorned one side, upon which a ragtag line of humans perched like birds on power lines.

"But who could this be?" That same question reverberated through the air.

The hollowed space of the decapitated tree had morphed into a gaping pit, large enough to consume a person. Sugunan and his companion toiled away with their digging. Christy approached the pit and peered inside, recoiling at the grim sight—a human skeleton lay within.

"Easy now. Let's not shatter it."

A senior head constable, Paul, with his name badge proudly displayed, directed the diggers with authority.

"Sir, the roots have penetrated the bones."

"Are you all residents here?" inquired Ramani, an ASI with a badge and a star, her gaze fixed on Kanya, who returned a nervous smile, eerily reminiscent of her own.

Christy quietly approached the officers. "Sir, the landowners have arrived."

A sub-inspector surveyed the smoldering remnants of the camp from the night before. He picked up a charred fragment of wood, grinding the charcoal between his fingers until it turned to dust. His ocean blue gaze scrutinized the remains for a moment before he moved toward the scene of the crime. A well-built young man, sporting a stitched scar on his forehead that resembled a sealed third eye. He bore the name "Goudham" emblazoned across his broad chest, with two gleaming stars on his shoulders.

"Was there a celebration here?" he inquired.

"Yes, sort of," came the reply.

"And you are?" "Christy." "Do you live here alone?"

"No, my parents have gone to the coffee plantation." "Where might that be? Sleepy Slope?"

"Yes, arOma cOffee."

"Oh, John. Is that your father?"

"Yes, how did you know?" "I come from the hills." "Ah, understood."

"When will they return?" "Today, though I can't say when exactly. My brother manages the place, and we visit quite often." "And what's your occupation?"

"I'm into photography and documentaries. You know, that sort of thing." "Let's hope this skeleton doesn't end up in your documentary as historical evidence.

"Not really, but I don't think I'm tied to it in any way."

"Whose skeleton is it then?" Suddenly, the friendly tone shifted.

"I don't know, sir. I honestly have no idea. I assume it's older than I am."

"Then surely your family has some inkling." He toyed with his lips, searching for a clever retort.

"Are you hoping the government will take charge of this?" Paul asked.

"If it turns out to be a treasure, won't they take it?" Lucy interjected, coming to her man's aid. "Whoa! Who's this fiery one?" "His girlfriend."

"And what do you call yourself?" Goudham asked with a grin.

"Lucy." "So, are you suggesting it belongs to the government?" "Notify the Archeology Department, sir." The officers chuckled, gasping in surprise.

"Indeed, sir, have we got some intellectuals among us?"

"This isn't about dinosaurs; it's human. Is that understood?" Goudham stated with a shift in tone. Lucy fell silent, while Christy glanced at her and erupted in laughter.

"Apologies, sir. We all had a restless night, so our minds might be wandering." Christy hastily cleared things up.

"Well, now you can rest easy. A cadaver has been discovered in your domain." The green-eyed couple shifted back to seriousness.

"Sir." A voice called from the pit. They ceased their digging and lowered their tools.

"What's going on? Did you unearth the entire skeleton?" Silence followed.

"What? Did you find it?" "The skeleton is missing its head."

An ambulance roared onto the scene, its sirens piercing the air as onlookers gathered to see the headless remains.

"Everyone, please step back." The officers began ushering people away as a stretcher was rolled out of the ambulance.

"Did you dig deep enough?" "Yes, sir. No head present. Confirmed."

"That should make identification straightforward," Lucy murmured to Christy.

"Ramani. Send it for an autopsy at White Pills. Leave a police jeep with it." "Understood, sir."

The crime scene was marked and the remains were carefully placed on the stretcher, leaving the crowd without a word as the ambulance door closed behind them. A hatchback navigated into the yard just as the skeleton was loaded into the ambulance.

"My parents are here!" Christy exclaimed. They appeared from the car, visibly shocked. Christy rushed to them.

"What's going on here?"

"Dad, our coconut tree was struck by lightning last night, and its crown was completely singed. Without the top, what's the point? So, I reached out to Killer Sugunan, who came by this morning and chopped it down. Then I wondered, why leave the roots if it won't sprout again? So, they yanked the whole thing out of the ground, and beneath it, they uncovered a human skeleton." The end. Christy delivered the entire tale in a single breath. John and Aleena were left bewildered, not grasping any part of the narrative. An ambulance, flanked by a police jeep, left with sirens blaring.

"John, who's that?" inquiries began to swirl among the gathered crowd.

The officers approached them.

"John." "Yes, sir. This is my wife, Aleena. What's happening here, sir?"

"Exactly what we're trying to figure out. You seem to have a knack for reading minds."

The locals buzzed around like moths drawn to a flame.

"Paul, clear everyone out and lock the gate."

"Everyone, please exit the area. This is now a crime scene." "Who does the skeleton belong to, sir?" one curious onlooker queried.

"I'll inform you once the investigation concludes, sir. For now, please vacate the crime scene."

The crowd shuffled away, grumbling.

"Let's sit down and chat. Come on in." Goudham welcomed John into his home. Christy opened the door, allowing the officers to enter.

"Isn't this a lovely cottage?" Goudham praised the cozy architecture. The officers settled into the guest room's comfortable chair while others stood around.

"Please, take a seat. We can't just leave you all unguarded. We'd like to ask you a few questions."

John gradually lowered himself into a chair, and eventually, everyone found a place to sit.

"Aleena, ma'am, when I heard about the skeleton discovery, I nearly missed my morning coffee. If you don't mind, could I have a cup? Black, please. I hope you have a good brew; I'd love a strong one," Goudham asked politely.

"Get coffee for everyone, Mom," Christy interjected with a smile. John frowned, and Christy flashed a grin in return.

"Aunty, I'm joining too," Lucy said, wrapping her arms around Aleena as they made their way to the kitchen.

"So, how long have you resided here?"

"I was born and raised in this very place; it's my heritage."

"What do you do besides manage the coffee plantation?"

"Just the plantation now, as my younger son oversees it. I also engage in some farming on our land."

"What kind?" "Every kind. Flowers, fruits, vegetables." "And humans," Goudham added with a dark twist.

"No, sir, I really have no clue." "Then, who planted the tree?" "That was my doing." "When?"

"I planted it in the winter," John pondered the specific day.

Christy started counting on his fingers. "Sir, that was five years ago."

"How did you remember that with such precision?"

"It was my eighteenth birthday party; we all celebrated here that night."

"Not me," Lucy piped up from the kitchen. "Yes, except for Lucy; everyone else was at the party."

They all racked their brains, trying to recall the night.

"Indeed, sir. It wasn't merely a coconut sapling; we also nestled a Champa flower sapling into the earth that very night." John interjected.

"Night?" the officers said, their eyes widening in surprise.

"I thought it would be a delightful escapade under the stars," John admitted, a grin breaking across his face.

"Planting a tree at night? Is there a deception lurking within that?"

"He was intoxicated beyond measure that evening," Aleena called out from the kitchen, her voice ringing.

"True enough, sir. I had a full bottle of spirits coursing through me that night."

"Consuming spirits under the moonlight is one thing—planting trees in the dark is a different kind of madness. Yet the real insanity lies in burying a person alongside the sapling." Silence hung heavy in the air.

"I recall Charlie mentioning how the soil seems unsettled." Aleena chimed in as she entered with a tray of coffee.

"What do you mean by unsettled?"

"Like something had already been interred beneath. But it was night, and we didn't give it much thought."

"So, you're suggesting there was something buried beneath that night?"

"I can't say for certain. But in hindsight, it feels that way. The entire area lost power that night, and we planted them by the glow of birthday candles."

"So, the lights went out during your celebration?"

"No, I was drinking solo outside when the power cut out. The neighborhood lights flickered on for a bit longer. Then, all at once, darkness wrapped around us, and Aleena returned from the block." John brushed off the cobwebs of drunken memory.

"How could it take so long to plunge into darkness when power was lost everywhere?"

"Ah, sir, there was a generator humming away. All the while, it was a nagging annoyance. Even now, I recall the tranquil bliss in my head once that beast went quiet. It was ruining my groove."

"Does the neighborhood rely on generators daily?"

"Not a chance! I would have lost my mind by now. It was just that night and the following day."

"That was the night of her betrothal ceremony," Aleena remarked, gesturing toward Kanya.

The officers turned their gazes toward her.

"And you are?" Goudham inquired, curiosity piqued.

"Kanya. This is my sister, Maria."

"So, you both graced that night with your presence?" "Yes."

"It was your betrothal day. You were expected at home, yes?" Kanya remained silent.

"It was called off," Anand interjected smoothly.

"Indeed, and you are?"

"Anand, a family friend."

"Do you recall observing or hearing anything out of the ordinary that night or in the nights leading up to it?"

"Indeed. There was a truck and a piercing scream."

"What truck are you referring to?"

"I was driving my jeep to the birthday celebration that night when I spotted a truck halted right in the center of the road."

"And what happened next?"

"It obstructed my path. Upon investigation, I found it empty. After waiting a bit, I decided to park my jeep behind it and proceed on foot."

"Nandhu's correct. We also noticed that truck."

"Nandhu?" "Yes, that's my nickname," Anand clarified, clearing any confusion.

"So, you saw the truck as well."

"Yes, it was stationed at the roadside," Maria replied.

"What were the three of you doing at that hour?"

"I had been at their house all day, and later that night, I invited them to the birthday bash."

"So, on your way home, you spotted a truck?"

"I don't recall the exact model... a truck, perhaps?" Aleena replied with uncertainty.

"Was the truck vacant?"

"I didn't pay close attention. I just remember a sizable vehicle, that's about it."

"Did you catch a glimpse of the license plate?"

"No," the trio of women shook their heads in unison.

"What about you, Anand?"

"I didn't focus on it much. I assumed it was a broken-down vehicle or something."

"And the scream?"

"Yes, right after we cut the cake, there was a scream, and then the truck moved away."

"What scream?"

"I think it was the truck driver. It was a sudden cry from the shadows, and when we looked towards the commotion, the engine revved and sped off."

"Are you certain it was the same truck?"

"It must have been."

"So, everyone heard something, yet no one saw anything. It's as if all the pieces are falling into place, but nothing seems to connect. Isn't that peculiar?"

Silence enveloped them, no one had a retort.

"We've simply spoken the truth. All of us."

"Either you've collaboratively concocted a flawless narrative to fit the circumstances, or..."

Everyone eagerly expected the unspoken alternative.

Goudham was piecing together the mystery once more, glancing around at the group, his gaze landing on Kishan, who had still been aloof during the inquiries.

"And you are?"

"I'm Kishan. We've been friends since childhood."

"So, is everything you've heard true, or is there something you wish to amend or omit?"

"No," came his curt, definitive reply, bringing the conversation to a swift end.

"It's astounding—a truck driver procured a headless body, discreetly interred it in your field, and by a twist of fate, you all unwittingly planted a tree right above it."

"I have no idea, sir. Please refrain from asking complex questions."

"In that case, cease your intricate answers. The midnight gardening, eerie screams, and the odd truck noises—all of it reeks of conspiracy. You all are entwined in this. Reveal to us the events of that night," Goudham remarked, finishing his coffee and placing the tray on the table with deliberation.

"Everything you've heard is accurate. We only speak the truth, sir; we can't fabricate a tale we haven't lived," Christy asserted, laying bare his thoughts. The officers looked perplexed. Ramani diligently recorded each statement in the case diary.

"Alright, John, do you have any enemies? Is someone trying to pin this on you intentionally?"

"No, sir. I'm not that notorious. I speak the truth, and some folks may not appreciate it—that's all. Beyond that?"

"Your wife mentioned that you saw the disturbed earth, and your younger son spoke of it too. Why did you dismiss his observations?"

"Sir, it's simple. That day, I resolved to quit drinking, and I did. However, I wanted to say goodbye with a grand finale, which led to a solitary bottle of bourbon whiskey swirling in my system. At that moment, I could barely stand, so I rushed to conclude my tasks. There was no cosmic mystery behind my choice."

The officers chuckled internally, masking their amusement with a sober facade.

"Charlie manages the plant, correct?" "Yes." "We need his statement as well."

"Of course, sir. We'll summon him promptly."

"Very well."

Goudham studied Ramani's expression and shook his head slowly.

"We're stepping back for now, but be assured that this investigation will continue. You all must aid us. No one leaves the premises until notified otherwise," Ramani informed, and they exited. The sound of their boots echoed then faded into silence as they reached the outdoors. Goudham surveyed the vibrant greenery, the pathway, the neighboring mansion, piecing together their narrative.

"Where did you all spot that truck?"

"Right there?" Everyone pointed in unison.

He turned towards the crime scene, not far from their location, then shifted his gaze to the mansion.

"Is that your residence?" he inquired, addressing Kanya.

"Yes," she responded with a nod.

"Very well. Until we meet again."

The officers hopped into the blue jeep as a silent siren twinkled beneath the sun.

"Do you all recall the truck's color?"

"Green," Anand replied. "Red," Maria chimed in. The conflicting colors resonated in the officers' minds. They exchanged glances, grappling with the discordant truth.

"Paul, that didn't align," Goudham remarked with a grin.

"See you soon. We appreciate your time, and remember—no one leaves. If there's an emergency, report to the station before leaving." The suspects nodded in agreement.

"Sir, we're actually planning a 33-day retreat up in the hills," Anand and Kanya announced, drawing the officers' attention.

"Which one?" "Walk the Hills." Goudham was well-acquainted with the location.

"Alright. Wishing you restorative journeys." "Thank you, sir." "But a lie could hinder your healing process, so don't take it personally." "Absolutely. We'll do our utmost to prove our innocence, won't we?"

"Indeed. And we have a duty to apprehend the guilty." Anand flashed a charming smile.

The officers exited the house and ventured into the mangroves. Outside, the onlookers flitted about, eager for news. The crowd parted for the officers as they left the scene of the crime.

"What's happening, John?" the onlookers buzzed, ever inquisitive.

"Please disperse for now," John dismissed them, striding back into the house.

"I could use another coffee. Anyone else?" Lucy announced, bouncing towards the kitchen.

"I'd like one too. There's much weighing on my mind," Kishan agreed, trailing after her.

"Is this a café?" Christy inquired of Lucy. "You're all under suspicion now. We'll need another round of coffee." Lucy gently patted his bald head as if bestowing a blessing and drifted into the kitchen.

"Mom? What if we used that same pit for her?" Christy asked, wrapping his arms around.

Aleena glared at Christy; her eyes drawn to the cheerful skeleton head printed on his shirt. He curled his ring and middle fingers with his thumb and flashed the demon sign.

The officers ambled down the eerie path, illuminated by spiraling lights, on a quest for the elusive truth. They glided past the nearby mansion.

"I remember Kanya and Maria. I've interacted with them on two occasions. One was when she was just a child, and Maria was in her infancy."

"That's ages ago."

"Indeed, sir. I was fresh on the job as a constable back then. I first met her when she came to the station with her grandfather Francis. His wife, Grace, was a celebrated author. The case was about domestic violence, but we were powerless to intervene."

"Why was that?"

"Sir, there was rampant corruption involved. The very next day, his daughter's lifeless body was discovered."

"The victim of the abuse?" "Yes."

"And what became of the case?" "It was ruled a suicide."

"How could that be? There's an obvious reason for suspicion. An abuse victim reports it, and the following day, they are found dead."

"Both of us felt a heavy burden about this." "The episode haunted us for many days. We had the opportunity to help, but?" Ramani and Paul shared their solemn confession.

"The sub inspector at that time was the most corrupt police officer. Thank the heavens he's no longer among us." Ramani relished the fact that such a wretched soul had left.

"He was truly insufferable, never listening and merely acting."

"He was also linked to Devachan." Paul interjected.

"Who is Devachan?" "A criminal attorney and businessman—the deceased woman's husband." "So, he was the perpetrator?" "Correct."

"And where is he now?" "He vanished the very night of the betrothal they mentioned. The engagement was called off due to that."

"And what of him?"

"Not a soul has heard from him since. He left a note before his disappearance."

"What did the note say?" "I can't recall. It's likely in the station's files."

"What became of that case?" "The case is closed."

"What was the conclusion?" "He went on a spiritual journey. We uncovered a letter, and handwriting experts confirmed it belonged to him." Ramani paused, lost in thought.

"On that same day, their servant was struck by lightning and perished."

"A death, a suicide, a disappearance?" Anand tried to weave them together. "With all these bizarre events, I've lost sight of the actual case. What's your take on our skeleton case?"

"Sir, as you observed, their words fit together strangely. But I can't shake the feeling that they're innocent."

"Paul, no need for the 'sir,' just call me Goudham."

"Aren't some habits hard to break?" "You must uproot the unnecessary ones."

Despite Goudham's advice, Paul hesitated.

"Well, let's keep it casual outside the department, clear?"

"Understood, sir—I mean, we're clear, Goudham."

"Excellent. Rama? Your thoughts?"

"I resonate with Paul's view. But what if they colluded to commit the crime and concocted a narrative? There was also confusion about the color of the truck."

"That could easily be a mistake in the dark or pure confusion. They all seemed rather calm to me. It's not that they're showing all the truths, but I didn't detect any deception in their words.

"Sometimes, it's the innocent looking individuals who are behind the most outrageous crimes. Yet, appearances can often be misleading. If

Goudham isn't in uniform, that scar on his forehead might just as easily stereotype him as a rogue or a thug, right?" Goudham chuckled, his finger tracing the scar's contour.

"What's the tale behind that?" "Tumbled over a rock while playing 'touch me, touch me not.'"

"Quite the heavy stone you faced—were you playing with the rock?" He smiled enigmatically, choosing to change the subject instead of finishing his story.

"Would you all care for a bite?"

"Not particularly. We've packed our meals, but feel free to dig in."

"Then let's keep moving and stop at a diner."

The jeep glided alongside the glimmering Scent River, where a sparkling sign caught his eye.

'Shroom Resto.'

"This spot seems ideal." The jeep parked right by the riverside.

"Let's grab a coffee." "Sure thing." The three of them stepped out, their case still on their minds.

"They appear utterly oblivious about that skeleton." "We can't jump to conclusions until we identify who it belongs to." "Exactly."

Goudham perused the handwritten menu.

"Spinach Mushroom Sandwich." "Yes, sir." "And a mint lime, too. How about you two?"

"Same for us—make it three mint limes." "Understood, sir." The waiter whisked away their order.

"Rama? You mentioned the missing person."

"Yes, Devachan. He was a criminal attorney with considerable political sway."

"Hmm, we ought to run a DNA test since he's unaccounted for." Ramani sensed an opportunity.

"And compile a list of all reported missing cases at the station." "Absolutely, sir."

The food arrived.

"So, gentlemen. Let's confer after lunch." Goudham clinked the dishes as Ramani and Paul sipped their lime drinks. Once they finished their meal, they exited the café.

"Let's narrow down the list to cases from 1990. Assuming the body was buried as told, we'll add five years down and five up to see what appears." "Got it, sir. Oh, my apologies, Goudham." Paul corrected himself with a smile as they stepped through the arched entrance of the station.

'Town Police Station'

Goudham hurried to the Sub-Inspector desk, followed closely by Ramani and Paul.

"Wrap up lunch and prepare that list." "Yes, sir."

He retreated to his office, settling into the spinning chair. His mind revolved like a whirlwind, tangled in the investigation. He glanced up at the fan's slow dance above, feeling the pull of an afternoon rest. His eyelids drooped with the gentle caress of the breeze. He drifted into slumber atop the whirling chair, only to awaken submerged in water. His body twisted deep beneath the surface, grazing the weed-clad bed strewn with sharp thorns. Ravens swooped down like bullets from the sky, their caws echoing around him. The weeds stirred to life, ensnaring him tightly, drawing forth his blood—but he welcomed the sting, surrendering willingly to the grasp of the relentless and flora - The pleasure of the pain.

Chapter 14
The Glitch of the Moon

Winter Thirst,
1999.

A universe of pristine aqua. Goudham, embraced and cherished by the spiky undergrowth along the riverbed, felt their piercing caresses creating pleasure points across his skin. As the intensity mounted, he found himself bleeding crimson, the once pristine waters swirling into a tapestry of red. Without warning, a thunderclap erupted from the void, startling all the living entities nearby. The crows took flight, and the weeds freed their grasp. As they faded away, his wounds began to mend, healing like clouds veiling the moon. Alone now in this expansive scarlet realm, he embarked on a quest for a question whose answer he already knew. Suddenly, a flicker of anomaly caught his eye, and he pressed forward into the uncertain. Despite his desperate effort, he felt his body resist, breath slipping away as every path appeared indistinguishable. His complexion grew pale, and his body danced its final breathless waltz.

Then, unexpectedly, a dolphin appeared, and he grasped its fin, whisked away from the depths at light speed. Goudham opened his eyes, gasping for air. Ramani and Paul, struck with terror at his sudden awakening, approached with the case files.

"What is it, sir?" "Do you need some water?" "Oh no, I've had my fill."

He massaged his temple, searching for lucidity amidst the swirling chaos inside.

"The file?" "Ah, yes, the case files. Please, take a seat."

He stepped away from the desk, making a beeline for the basin. Water gushed and splashed, drenching him until he felt himself anchored back to his earthly domain.

"Sir, are you alright?" "Oh, yes. Sleep evaded me last night—just one final episode."

"You could snag a proper nap if you wish." "No, I'm finished with that. How's the progress?"

"Oh? From the '90s to now, only one case surfaced. The individual we spoke of earlier—a lawyer and businessperson. Name: P.K. Devachan. Age: 68. The formal complaint was lodged by his son-in-law."

"Son-in-law? The engagement never materialized, correct?" "That's the way it's recorded."

"Didn't anyone from his family file a complaint?" "No." Goudham wrestled with the tangled threads of this tale.

"This letter was discovered on the table that day." Ramani produced a letter encased in plastic.

A brief note scrawled in pencil read:

'I can sense a voice calling. There's no turning back. Goodbye.'

"What's this? Was he a poet, a philosopher, or perhaps something inherited from his mother-in-law?"

"We don't think so."

"Did you and your team gather oral statements from the suicide spot?"

"Yes, this is the account provided by Devachan." They passed along the statement from the grim scene of despair.

"According to the account, his wife had a history of mental illness. On the fateful night, she abruptly awoke screaming from her sleep. He tried to soothe her, but she overpowered him and bolted, locking him out. Then she ascended to the top floor and leaped from the bungalow."

"That seemed straightforward."

"We felt utterly helpless. He held the law like a puppet on strings. Yet, Grace's statement tilted the narrative into Devachan's favor; she opened the door for him that fateful night. Despite this, she insisted her daughter bore no troubles and would never take her own life."

"Where's the statement from her father? He was the one who started the complaint."

"On that day, he stayed completely silent. The crime scene metamorphosed to support Devachan's version. However, another story lurked in the shadows, connecting the dots—Francis, the elderly petitioner." "What became of him?" "His lifeless body was discovered in the river, also ruled a suicide. Yet, from what we gathered, he was an exceptional swimmer, and a witness claims she saw him being forcibly taken away in a vehicle, though the details of the car or the assailants remained murky."

"How is it that he always slips away? There was even a witness to back it up."

"He's always dodging danger by the narrowest margin. On the day we discovered Francis' body, another child drowned too—completely unconnected to the main incident. It was just a tragic accident. Amid all that chaos, no one paid attention to the child struggling beneath the surface. It was also the day of the golden axe ceremony. While Francis was brought to light, that little one fought for his life, hidden from view."

Goudham pondered deeply over all the tales spun around them.

"What occupies your mind?"

"Just contemplating the role of the police when criminals like Devachan dictate the scene."

"Not anymore, sir. As I mentioned, corruption is absent in the current climate. Ultimately, it's the head that figures out whether the tail stays still or begins to wag."

Goudham fell silent, resting his head back against the chair, fixating on the spinning fan for a moment.

"Nevertheless, let's return to the matter that lacks both head and tail."

"Where do we begin?"

"With the DNA test. Paul, send Devachan's details to forensics. We might find his blood samples here at White Pills. If not, gather DNA from his family."

"Understood, sir."

"By the way, if you need to contact their family, hmm, what approach will you take?"

"Why not be honest? This case must remain highly confidential, especially since it's several years old. Sometimes when we find the head, we lose sight of the tail. Perhaps get hospital staff involved. Frame it as part of a government health initiative—just say something like that. Don't approach them as police officers."

"Sounds like you're turning me into a detective from the get-go." "A thrilling twist, right?" Ramani chuckled.

"Alright then." Paul dashed into the bloody game.

"Devachan wields significant political clout and operates as a criminal lawyer—an ideal equation for power."

"Proving his guilt is pointless now. We need to find him before he becomes officially apprehended."

Goudham laced his fingers behind his neck, gazing out the window as twilight draped over the sky.

"I've never encountered a policeman quite like you, Goudham."

"There's no manifesto or legal tome outlining how a police officer must behave. It's the moral fabric of society that serves as our law." Ramani smiled at his insightful words.

"How have you stayed here for so long?"

"A distinguished physical training instructor from Riverside School came to lodge a complaint. What began as an inquiry over tea eventually led to a sweet sea. Long story short, here we are."

"That's a charming tale. What's your story? What brought you from the hills to the sea?"

"I've always yearned to dwell by the beach. There are personal reasons too, but at its core, my true love is the sea."

"I can see that," she said, gazing into his blue eyes. "And how did you become a cop?" "That's a cliché belief of us. People assume all sleepy slopes harbor esoteric stuff. Since childhood, I've been captivated by detective stories from periodicals. In the hills, newspapers and radios were scarce; only books thrived. Times have changed." He suddenly felt a headache coming on and rubbed his temple.

"Sir, are you alright?" "Yes, I'm fine. I think I just need some rest." "Your duty hours are nearly over."

He stared out the window. "Hmm, often I'm at a loss about what I truly look for. I can uncover the head and tail, yet struggle to forge the connection."

"That's a puzzling game," she exclaimed with laughter.

"Our case is altogether different. We must start at the tail to discover the head."

"Rama, what are the chances of one person killing another?"

"Well, there are three scenarios: accidental, protective, or revengeful."

"I'd suggest four—releasing pent-up tension."

"That's just an excuse to safeguard one's karma."

"With one hand, we sow seeds for malignant growth, while with the other, we search for a cure. Cognitive dissonance is the true foe. That's what must be both penalized and healed."

Ramani mulled over his thoughts.

"But the law doesn't convey that," he said.

"Stretching the truth is perilous, far more so than spinning tales; the truth will always make its presence known, whether through whispers or upheaval."

A constable rapped on the door.

"Yes?"

"A reporter from the newspaper and a television journalist have arrived to see you, sir."

"Oh, so the media has joined the fray? Please let them in."

In walked an elegantly dressed woman alongside a man who looked rather unkempt.

"Good day, sir. I'm Vasanthi, a reporter from Vidooradarshan News."

"And I'm Isahaaq, the cameraman as well as a columnist for Satya Newspaper."

"Feel free to take a seat."

"We're here to inquire about the unidentified skeleton."

"Indeed. Until we receive the forensic report, there isn't much more I can disclose."

"Have you spoken to the landlord?" Isahaaq posed the question, directing his fountain pen towards him.

"Yes, they seem oblivious in terms of the investigation. Further inquiries will follow once the report is in."

"Are there any suspects?" Vasanthi asked, gazing affectionately at a young officer.

"Please await the report. We've only just begun the investigation, and it's strictly confidential. Given its age, evidence could easily slip away. So, we ask for your cooperation."

"Of course, sir."

"The department anticipates that the press will assist with the case."

"Absolutely. Just let us know how we can help."

"Thank you. Would you care for a drink?"

"Yes, tea would be lovely. We usually meet at a place in the evenings. Care to join?"

Goudham glanced at his watch; his shift was nearly over.

"Could you wait a bit? I'll be done shortly."

"Sir, shall we call for a police jeep?"

"No, madam, we arrived by car. I can give him a lift if that's all right," he replied. "Yes."

"Then we'll be here," the reporter and journalist said as they exited the station.

"What about some tea?"

"No, thank you. I'm meeting my physical trainer for evening tea."

"Alright, Rama, I'll see you tomorrow. And please ask Paul to give me a call at the quarters for an update."

"Sure."

Goudham picked up the letter penned by Devachan.

"I'll take this. Let's see if it carries a voice. Goodnight, Rama."

"Goodnight, Goudham."

He changed from his uniform into casual attire and left the station.

"Shall we hit the road?"

"Yes, please."

They settled into the sedan, with Vasanthi at the wheel.

"Where's the tea brewing?"

"At Golden Tea. Are you from the hills?" Vasanthi ventured a guess.

"Indeed, I am."

"Ah, I sensed it."

"Sensed what?"

"I meant your aura."

"So, Vasu, you don't notice my aura?" Isahaaq chimed in with a playful nudge.

"No, you silly. Sir, do you grasp what I'm implying?" "I totally get your point. The sleepy slope feels distinctly black and white. Honestly, I think being a police officer requires a more discerning perspective."

"I appreciate your straightforwardness, Isahaaq, but I perceive the world in all its deserving shades."

"So, how's it treating you here? We tend to shy away from the shadows, yet you folks glide through them with such ease. What's your secret?"

He responded with a serene smile.

"Darkness is what highlights the light. Just embrace it as part of who you are. Why should you fear an aspect of yourself?"

As the car navigated the bridge, they shared a moment of silence before the sounds of nature returned. They arrived at the Nazi statue, and next to it stood the Golden Tea shop. Isahaaq retrieved a beedi from his pocket and lit it.

"Tea, right?" Vasanthi checked with Goudham. "Yes, make it black." "Milk tea is what the Golden Tea specializes in."

"I'm partial to black." "Ah, so you're living in shades of black and white," Isahaaq exhaled smoke.

"Two golds and one black," declared Sugandhi, placing the order.

"Do your parents reside in the hills?" Vasanthi ventured into personal territory.

"Ah, yes," he replied, hesitant to delve deeper.

"Order up for tea!"

"Vasu, I'll grab two coconut rice cakes. Mind covering it?" "Absolutely not." "Aren't you a prominent spa owner and radio personality? This reporting gig is merely a side hustle."

"What's happening with all that press cash?" "I told you my house renovation is underway."

They paused for a moment to relish the fading aroma, gently blowing the steam off their tea before taking a sip.

"I have fantastic news for you. During the conference, our television MD voiced a keen interest in acquiring the Satya newspaper." "Really?"

"Yes, there was genuine interest, and Prasad is on board. As far as I'm concerned, it's a green light."

"Oh my God, Vasu! I think I'll order another tea." Isahaaq was at a loss for how to have his happiness.

"That's right, my friend. The universe has a way of rewarding those who are still steadfast. Even if humanity were to turn its back, nature would send a cosmic ally to the rescue." He pulled out another beedi, indulging in his joy.

"Vasu, if Satya reignites its spark and strength, I swear I'll give up smoking." "Now you're just joking."

"No, really! I'll give it my all. If it doesn't pan out, I'll just buy some damp tobacco. When the urge strikes, I'll roll one up and light it. Wet tobacco is still an option, but you'll have to cover it."

"Oh, that's fine. Smoke it dry. I can throw in some dry leaves too," Vasanthi said, beaming.

"What's the story with the newspaper?"

"That's a lengthy, sorrowful saga, sir." "Keep it brief for now."

"You've probably heard about the gold mining issue. Our newspaper played a role in shutting down illegal operations."

"We don't have access to news outlets in the hills, but I've caught wind of it."

"How do the hills stay informed about the world below?"

"There's so much negativity in the news. They tend to focus on sensationalism, obscuring reality. Even now, more folks are drawn to hear about a scandal than to attend the yearly retreats in the hills."

Vasanthi and Isahaaq nodded in agreement, smiles dancing on their faces.

"Right, where were we?"

"We were discussing gold mining."

"Ah yes. A massive protest erupted alongside news coverage. Devachan, a criminal lawyer, took on the case but ultimately lost."

Goudham recognized the name.

"I know him. When I opened the spa, he was a regular for massages. One of my staff complained that he was inappropriate, that he grabbed her backside during a session."

"Which backside?" "You creep." "No, which girl?"

"Rathi."

"Rathi. Really?" Isahaaq munched on a snack, intrigued.

"Yes, your favorite. He had a soft spot for her," Vasanthi said nonchalantly.

"Her massage is divine, yet she intimidates me."

"Intimidated? Why?" "Not sure, it's her piercing squint eyes and scary smile."

"I actually find her very appealing." "To me, she's unsettling. Why didn't you ever mention this?" "What? Should I broadcast it in your newspaper? That would ruin my business and reputation. Plus, she asked me not to make a fuss. He never returned after that."

"He won't. You know he's gone missing, right?" "Yes." Goudham stood nearby, as if tuning in to the latest news broadcast.

"Rathi left the spa shortly after that incident, claiming she'd found a better job. A week later, I got a call from the emergency clinic—her car had crashed, and she suffered a head injury."

"A car?" "No idea where she found the money for that; I never inquired. After she was released from the hospital, she came back to work. She's a bit unpredictable, but her touch has rave reviews, so I welcomed her back."

"Who were we discussing again?" The narrative had veered off course.

"Devachan and the mining company," Goudham reminded them.

"Aha. Our newspaper stirred up quite a commotion, igniting a wave of protests. The powerful figures warned us to silence our voices, sweetening the threat with ample cash. Our editor, a man of integrity, turned down the bribe, but it led to dire consequences. A group of masked assailants ambushed him, leaving him in a state worse than death."

Isahaaq savored a sip of tea, finishing the last bite of his rice cake.

"I've penned a few columns myself. The mines may have shut down, but our editor's spirit was extinguished."

"What happened to those criminals?" Goudham asked, his voice heavy with distress. "The case drifted into oblivion, leaving us in the dark about the culprits. Unsure if it simply faded away or if the police swept it under the rug." Goudham fell silent in dissent.

"What was the editor's name?" "Shiva. He passed away a few years ago."

"And what became of it all?"

Isahaaq finished his tea and lit another beedi.

"The newspaper began to sink into financial ruin. Many staff left, yet a few of us chose to stay. Those who speak the truth should never be cast aside." "Who's at the helm of the paper now?"

"Prasad, his son. He is well-meaning but lacks passion."

"A beloved one once recommended me, 'be a fire, but don't burn out.'" Goudham said with a tranquil smile.

"Shiva was that flame, but he burned out."

"For the truth." Goudham raised his cup for one last toast. Vasanthi and Isahaaq met him in acknowledgment of their shared commitment to honesty. As they gazed upwards, the golden ax gleamed mockingly like fool's gold.

"Sir, can we drop him off first?" "Of course."

"Have you witnessed the Sweet Sea Sunset?" "From the hills."

"Seeing it from below will offer a different perspective."

They all climbed into the sedan as Vasanthi started the engine.

"Sir, buckle up."

Isahaaq understood the drill. Goudham fasten his seatbelt while Isahaaq nestled his arms below the headrest and secured himself. Vasanthi accelerated, and the car shot forward. After a few swift turns, the lingering light slipped away, revealing a sign:

'Keep the Beach Clean'

'No Littering'

'Sweet Sea – 3⅓ miles'

Goudham scanned the sign like a fleeting breeze. The distance vanished in the blink of an eye, and the sedan halted at a T-junction. The twilight dimmed, accompanied by the soothing rhythm of the waves. The sun had taken its leave.

"Damn, we missed him." "I nearly missed my own life," Isahaaq stammered.

"Hello, do you even remember there's a police officer beside you? How about a speeding ticket?"

"Sir, just a ticket won't suffice. That's tried murder." "Apologies, sir. I sometimes get a little too eager."

"My treat for giving me back my life. Color candies for all. Park here." They all got out.

The beach was a picture of tranquility, serene and picturesque. Goudham found himself enchanted by the serenading tides. The moon shone bright, even as the sun faded away. Isahaaq wandered to a candy shop, returning with sweets that resembled pebbles in a kaleidoscope of colors. Vasanthi and Goudham picked their favorite hues, engaging in lighthearted conversation as they savored the treats.

"May I ask something, if it's not too much trouble?" Goudham said with a formal tone.

"Of course."

"Are you both dark folks?"

"What? You really believed we wouldn't notice the magic?" Vasanthi replied, her eyebrow arched in curiosity.

"No, I simply... I wanted to bring it up, but I was unsure of how you'd react."

"Sometimes, the only way to restore balance is by not highlighting our uniqueness in front of the oblivious. You're right; these individuals are clouded by excessive light. It's best for us to dim our glow a bit to help them see more clearly. That's our responsibility as thoughtful dark folks — addressing the distortion."

Goudham nodded, finding agreement in her viewpoint.

"Well, Goudham sir, I'll take my leave now." He dusted off his hands and raised his arm for a handshake.

"Let's skip the formalities. Just call me Goudham. We've evolved from primates to mindful beings. The tail is no longer necessary."

"It's a pleasure to meet you, Goudham. Feel free to call me anytime; Isahaaq will guide you with his light."

He melted into the shadows, beedi in hand, as darkness enveloped him.

"Shall we head out?" Goudham and Vasanthi departed from the beach.

The car glided silently over the bridge once more, Goudham gazing at the moonlit scenery.

"Are you married?" Vasanthi broke the silence as they crossed the bridge.

"No." "Do you have a girlfriend?" "Hmmm." He regarded her with a playful smile.

"No, just passing time. I run a spa in the mystic colony called Divine Touch. You should come by for some relaxation. Since the incident with Devachan, I've become quite discerning about my clientele. I halted all contact services for the oblivious."

"You can't judge a book by its cover. If I entered your massage center as an unfamiliar face without any uniform, what would be your first impression?"

"What impression? Nothing out of the ordinary."

"What are your thoughts on the stitches on my head?"

"What's there to feel? You were hurt and now bear a mark. That's all." she replied nonchalantly.

"Many perceive me as a thug based solely on my injury."

"If you're truly living, you will stumble. I'm not referring to a judgment based on a scar. I'm talking about those who inflict their pain on others without any intention of healing." She offered him a fresh perspective on how to assess individuals. The sedan veered and stopped next to the police quarters.

"Please drop me off here. And Vasanthi?" He hesitated, unsure of how to phrase his question.

"What is it?" "What you mentioned earlier was a fib, wasn't it?"

"What do you mean?" "When you asked about my relationship status." A blush spread across her lips. "Actually?"

"Right now, I feel like I have two good friends in town. So, let me be straightforward. I'm in love with someone." She looked a bit taken aback, but then a quiet smile appeared. Her gaze drifted outside, then back to him, as he awaited her response.

"Am I still a friend?" "Huh, yes. Of course. I mean?" She was left a bit flummoxed.

"Well, good thing you said that earlier." She replied with a naive smile. He extended his arms for a handshake, and she complied.

"Wake up tomorrow, and let this thought clear from your mind. Sounds good?" She nodded, smiling. He exited the car, leaning his head back through the window one last time.

"Good night." She met his blue eyes without a hint of worry and pulled a business card from her wallet.

"You can still be blessed with a divine touch. Call me." She handed him the card.

"Thanks. I'll see you again." He waved with a smile. "Good night." The sedan glided away.

Thoughts of a soothing massage stirred within him. His wandering mind turned toward a single-story gray building. He opened the decaying wooden door and stepped into the dim room. Flicking on the yellow bulb illuminated the moldy yet arranged space, the epitome of a bachelor's sanctuary. He shed his clothing and stood bare erect, his desire manifesting in its divine form. In this fervid state, he approached the mirror, studying his reflection for a moment.

"Why did you deceive Vasanthi? Who holds your heart?" He found himself without answers, lost in contemplation. Just then, a piercing ring from his phone roused him from his thoughts.

"Hello." "Hello Goudham, it's Paul."

"Yeah, Paul. What's up?"

"I didn't need to play sleuth. The blood was right there in the hospital bank. Apparently, Devachan came in after a traumatic incident, having lost quite a bit of blood. Anyway, it's all sorted now; it's been sent for DNA testing." "Alright, Paul. Well done. See you tomorrow. Goodnight." "Goodnight." The call ended.

His essence returned to a calmness, and his blue eyes drifted to his uniform hanging nearby.

He retrieved the revolver from its holster and stood before the mirror. His mind instinctively aimed at his temple, and the reflection mimicked a strange, vacant smile. Just then, his heart jolted him back to reality, compelling him to safely return the gun. His mind then urged him toward his uniform pocket, pulling out Devachan's letter. He approached the window, opening the door to let the moonlight flood in, illuminating the letter in its embrace. The more intently he scrutinized it, the deeper the suspicions wove themselves into his thoughts. The words felt painfully close to the truth yet tainted with doubt, as if some distortion clouded the reality. As he looked skyward in thirst for truth, he noticed a haze drifting over the moon, as if someone was trying to erase her from existence - the glitch of the moon.

Chapter 15
The Vortex of the Aqua

Winter Hunger, 1999.

Yet another sun-drenched morning in winter. Goudham stays lost in a dream-laden slumber, enveloped by the soft shadows of a sparsely decorated bedroom. Sunbeams weave across his unadorned skin, gently caressing his eyelids. His consciousness stirs, but his body lingers in an underwater realm, grappling with the haziness. Rapid eye movements flutter beneath the surface of his closed lids, like restless beads seeking escape. He strains to move his limbs, though they feel as heavy as lead. After countless attempts, he finally breaks the surface, his azure eyes opening wide as he draws in a deep breath. With a gasp, he synchronizes body and mind, just as the tension loosens its grip — a knock resounds at the door.

"Goudham." Ramani's voice blends with the blare of the jeep's horn.

He hastily dons his clothes and swings the door open.

"Did you just roll out of bed? It's our daily duty to rouse you!" "Sorry, Rama. I'll be there shortly." After quenching his thirst with several glasses of water, he rushes to the bathroom, toothbrush and towel in hand.

"Paul, kill the engine. Our friend has surfaced as usual,"

"I feel like a school bus driver now," Paul chuckles, turning off the jeep.

Ramani steps inside, her boots thudding softly against the floor as she scans the room, intrigued by its energy. Boxes are stacked in the kitchen, beckoning her to investigate.

She opens each one, trying to discern their contents by scent until she discovers the coffee powder. The sound of brushing teeth and running water mingles with the air. Goudham appears, half-clad, as Ramani brews coffee.

"No sugar here?" "Oh, thanks. Yes, the coconut sugar should be in a glass jar."

As Goudham dresses, Ramani pours three mugs of coffee.

"Paul, come share some." Paul shakes off the dust from his shoe and enters, accepting a cup.

A letter from Devchan catches Ramani's eye, reflecting her image.

"So, did you hear anything?" Goudham, with damp hair, picks up his coffee.

"I've been trying to concentrate ever since the letter arrived. My thoughts whirl. There's something odd about it," she replies.

"What's odd?" "I can't put my finger on it—some truth shrouded in shadows." Goudham empties his cup after savoring several sips.

"Ramani, winter's ending. What's the scoop on the DNA?"

"That's what we were just about to discuss. The forensics team called." "Finally! What did they reveal?" "They requested a meeting." "Let's go. We can't delve deeper without those results. I've been chasing this anomaly for days."

"Let's retrieve the report and uncover the flow."

The blue jeep sped away, a silent beacon of urgency, racing toward the White Pills Sanatorium Lab. In the heart of the golden town, expanses of whitewashed buildings stretched across the horizon while streams of people meandered in all directions. Officers clattered into the bustling structure, their boots thumping rhythmically, slicing through the clamor. The cadence led them straight to the forensic science lab.

"Greetings, sir. The report is finally complete." The doctor, clad in white attire and equipped with gloves and a mask, led them to the lab.

"Any good news?"

"The skeletal remains belong to a male estimated to be between sixty and seventy years old. It appears that at least five years have elapsed since the body was interred by the offenders."

The officers leaned in attentively.

"And it's indeed positive. The skeleton aligns perfectly with the sample."

"Are you saying?" Goudham's tone was resolute.

"Devachan."

Silence enveloped the officers as they exchanged glances, their faces betraying no emotion. Gradually, a smile began to appear in the stillness.

"Are you certain, doctor?" "We verified it. Your instincts were correct." Goudham sealed his lips, allowing the reality to sink in. The clouds of doubt began to dissipate, and his thoughts turned to tranquility.

"Doctor, one more request. Can you keep this information concealed? Just until we reach the higher-ups."

"Absolutely."

"Do you have any insight into how he met his end?"

"The bone shows no significant fractures. Only someone who saw the crime firsthand could provide further details. Nonetheless, I have a hunch that the weapon involved must have been large and sharp—perhaps something like a guillotine used for executions. There's no sign of multiple strikes; it appears the head was severed in one clean cut."

"Thank you, Doctor."

White and Khaki parted with expressions of gratitude. As they separated, a new path seemed to unfold—a route leading to the anomaly. The jeep roared away from the acrid scents of the hospital and halted near the gently flowing river that carried the aroma of tranquility.

"So, you're saying the letter was indeed significant?" Paul queried; his voice icy.

Goudham carefully withdrew the letter from his pocket, cradling it like a delicate infant, his mind racing with the concealed meanings within.

'I can sense a voice calling. There's no turning back. Goodbye.'

"Now we must question the sincerity of these words. Any doubts?" Goudham posed a riddle to them both.

"The style of writing. Based on everything I've gathered about him, there's no chance he would pen such poetic lines."

"Was there a writer in the household?" "So what? Just because a man was a mahout, doesn't officially give his son a callus butt." "True enough," Goudham acknowledged with a grin.

"Even if he could write, what would compel him to pen such lyrical expressions in a moment of escape? It would be conveyed in straightforward terms, wouldn't it?"

"Hmm. Rama?" "Perhaps someone coerced Devachan into drafting that letter."

"Possible. Or capable of forging his handwriting." "Exactly. That's a significant angle we've overlooked."

"Hmmm, I'm starving. We'll head to the Shroom Resto. Their food is delightful."

Paul steered the jeep straight to the restaurant, placing an order for three black coffees and mushroom spinach sandwiches for everyone from the comfort of their vehicle.

"Do you routinely have late breakfasts?" "I typically go for brunch or just eat whenever hunger strikes. That's about it. So, consider the possibilities. Reflect on anything you might have overlooked due to the corrupt system. Sometimes our minds choose to downplay the effort, knowing that no matter how hard we strive, justice might remain elusive." Ramani began to sift through her memories.

"Goudham, I recall the graphologist mentioning that the wording of the letter seemed older than a single night. They didn't conduct a test; it was merely a hasty assumption, as the police officers typically overlooked such details."

"So, Devachan had penned those words already." "Or someone compelled him to write them." "Indeed."

The sandwich and coffee arrived. Goudham devoured the meal in a single breath and savored a tiny sip of steaming caffeine. Gazing past the half-filled glass of coffee, he noticed a glimmer afar.

"The Nazi and the Golden Axe."

"Do you know who gave that axe?" "Who?" "Devachan along with his business associates." "Oh, that's impressive."

Goudham cast his eyes upon the glint of gold.

"One night, the Nazi's arm shattered, causing the golden axe to separate."

"When did this occur?" All of this was fresh news to Goudham.

"That was in the winter of '94," Ramani revealed, a mischievous grin on his face. "So, the statue got struck by a vehicle. No witnesses—just a wrecked car. A girl was driving and a truck driver rushed her to the hospital. I recall her name: Rathi. She only had fragmented memories of the incident. Her car collided with the statue as she swerved to evade an oncoming truck."

"Did she have squinty eyes?"

"Indeed. How did you know?" "I just do." Goudham smiled enigmatically.

"Really, how did you know?"

"There was a tale spun by reporters that day about an accident. The girl works at a spa, right?" "Yes, as a massage therapist." "And what unfolded?"

"I visited the hospital to take her statement. It was clearly an accident amid a torrential downpour. Yet a committee formed, claiming the accident was a planned insult to the Nazi, rallying for the golden axe's reinstatement."

"Hmm."

"So, Goudham, where should we commence?"

"Now that we've got the head of this puzzle, let us start from there."

The blue jeep crept towards the spooky marsh, finally reaching the bungalow. Goudham stepped out, surveying his surroundings. "There lies but a wall between death and life," he remarked with a ghostly grin. They ascended the steps and pressed the doorbell which rang out like an ominous toll. Maria appeared to answer.

"Hello, Maria. Do you remember us?" "Oh, hello sir. What brings you here?" She seemed a touch nervous.

"We're seeking some details about your father. May we come in?" "Of course." After a moment of consideration, she invited them inside, where the khaki-clad figures marveled at the house's vastness and elegance.

"Why do you seem anxious?"

"The bell sent shivers down my spine. Honestly, it's been ages since I attended to anyone who rang it."

"Why is that? No visitors here?" "It's the bell. My friends typically knock or just walk in without announcing." "Please, take a seat." They glanced around once more before settling onto the plush sofa.

"Sir, would you like something to drink?"

"No, thank you. Just water will suffice." "Sure." She strolled to the kitchen while the officers stood and explored their surroundings, gravitating toward the framed memories hanging on the walls.

"This is Francis and Grace. That's their daughter," Ramani provided context. Goudham scrutinized the images before turning back to the room. A book lay open, its pencil resting across the pages. Maria entered with their water.

"Do you write like your grandmother?" Goudham picked up his glass and asked.

"Not really. I pen daily journals to keep my thoughts in order."

She closed the book and tucked it away in a drawer.

Goudham sipped his water and settled back.

"Where's your sister?" "She's away on a 33-day retreat, as mentioned."

"Yes, indeed?"

"They should return today." "That's wonderful." "So, just the two of you live here?" "Yes."

"Aren't you frightened?" "What's there to fear in your own home?"

"No, I meant with such an expanse of rooms?"

"We only occupy two. The rest are locked, opened only for guests." "Understood. So, what do you do for a living?" "I'm a fashion designer with my own boutique." "Ah, I had some shopping on my agenda." "Ladies only, sir. But you're welcome to visit. Everyone has a woman in their life. On the way you could see on the right, silky dolls." "Absolutely, I'll be stopping by." "Welcome."

"So? Concerning your father." "What's the matter, sir? Is that my dad's body?" Maria shot back, her words striking hard like a slap.

"How can you be so certain?" "Why else would you come to our doorstep?"

"I wish our tasks were that simple. However, according to forensics, it's a male between the ages of thirty and forty. No further specifics. But this inquiry is intertwined with the case." "How so?" Maria probed, eyeing his bold fabrication.

"The situation is classified. Since you're involved, I can divulge some information. Didn't Devachan represent that gold mining company?" "Yeah, ages ago." "Right. There were riots and strikes against it, correct?" "Yes." "Were there any threats directed at the family afterward?"

"No personal attacks—only against the mining company." "Okay. And how would you describe your relationship with your dad?" She paused, uncertainty clouding her response.

"What's the investigation truly about?"

"There's suspicion that the body might belong to one of the protesters. It's not confirmed yet. The investigation is ongoing. In fact, we theorize that Devachan may have a hand in this death. There's also speculation that he fled the area following that murder."

Ramani and Paul found themselves adrift in the sea of Goudham's deceptions. It opened a portal into Maria's thoughts.

"What do you wish to learn about him? I wouldn't be shocked if he's a murder suspect, but I can't be certain of his guilt or innocence."

"Did your father ever cause you harm?"

"Not me or my sister, because we were raised by our mother, grandma, and grandpa. But he never hesitated to assert his authority over the children."

Her words dripped with disdain for her father.

"So, you detested your dad?"

"I don't harbor hate for anyone, sir. It disrupts my inner peace."

"What about your mother? Did he hurt her?" The question stripped her of some of her defenses.

"Why ask this again if you already know the answer?"

"I'm sorry, we seek your perspective."

"Are you inquiring whether dad killed her?"

"Before he took his life, your grandpa tried to report an abuse. But the law was too tardy in their response."

"And now that the law is finally acting, will it resurrect my mom and grandpa?"

"I'm sorry, Maria. We're just trying to piece together a puzzle from the past."

"Apologies, sir." "That's fine. You have every right to be upset."

"He informed the police that your father assaulted your mother."

"I can't even recall my mother's face."

"Sorry once more, but do you believe your father is capable of murder?" Maria's silence spoke volumes.

"Okay. I apologize for revisiting painful memories. We just wanted to understand the essence of Devachan." "My dad was more monstrous than a demon. At least a demon shows itself," Maria declared emphatically.

"So, who were his business associates? Anything you can share?"

"There were a couple of jerks, sorry for the language." "No worries. The truth is what we look for." "Right, so two of them from the gold mining company—a mango-faced man and his father. When the court halted their gold excavation, they launched a plastic business and roped my dad in as a partner. They either added him or he joined them, however you want to phrase it. My sister was set to marry the mango-faced guy. The night before the engagement, dad vanished, leading them to cancel the ceremony."

"Did any consent happen after that?"

"No. My sister never wished him. The marriage was merely a business arrangement. A few days later, they returned with another proposal. She rejected him openly. Honestly, that was when my sister truly connected with herself," she said, blissfully oblivious.

The officers wrapped up their inquiries and exchanged glances.

"How long has their relationship been ongoing? Between Anand and Kanya?"

"They've been friends since childhood. Perhaps they were intimidated by dad and decided to let go of each other."

"Alright. Wishing you and your family all the joy." "Thank you, sir." "Could you ask your sister to visit me at the station when she returns?"

"Absolutely. They should arrive by nightfall."

"Great, the sooner, the better for our efforts."

"Okay, sir."

"They haven't vacated the town, have they?" "I doubt it." Maria responded, beaming.

"Does your father dabble in writing?" Paul turned his gaze from the portrait to Maria.

"He writes like a lawyer but wasn't particularly imaginative. Actually, Grandma was the illiterate one; it was Grandpa who penned her thoughts." "Oh, that's an intriguing tidbit for his admirers."

"Indeed, she couldn't read or write, yet her imagination flowed like a river. Grandma used to say Dad and Grandpa were as different as a drain and a stream," Maria added with a chuckle.

"Those are your mother's eyes you carry?" Goudham remarked, gazing at Varsha's likeness. "Yes," was her beaming reply.

The officers had exhausted their inquiries. They exchanged looks and nodded in understanding. The echo of boots resonated outside the mansion. Goudham surveyed the home and its grounds.

"Maria," he called out from a distance across the field.

"Wasn't it your servant who met his end from a lightning strike?"

"Yes, nearly right where you're standing now."

Anand examined the ground before casting his eyes skyward at the antenna.

"He was intoxicated, slumped near it. His body was charred and smoldered."

"They discovered the remains in the soil," Maria confirmed. "He likely fell after being struck. The only thing visible on him was an axe. That's what Uncle Shankaran mentioned." "An axe?" "Yes, there was an axe tattooed on the back of his neck."

"Who is this Shankaran?"

"He organized the light and sound of the occasion, residing next to the swamp beyond that wall."

Goudham glanced over, spotting a marshy area dotted with homes to the right. After surveying both sides keenly, he trudged back.

"When did you last see his body?"

"When Uncle Shankaran informed us." "What time was that?" "About seven."

"Why so late? The postmortem writes down it was early morning," Ramani probed.

"The workers tried to reach us by knocking, but a storm knocked out the power. He passed away en route to the hospital in their truck."

"And what about your father's vanishing act? When did you become aware?"

"We tried calling Dad to inform him about the servant, but he was absent from his room. Later, we found the letter on the table and alerted the police."

"Understood. And when was the last time you saw your father?" "The previous night. He was intoxicated by the spring, indulging further." "Is he generally a heavy drinker?" "He's hardly ever sobered in my eyes."

"Does he engage in conversation or stumble after a few drinks?"

"I can't say, sir. I've never seen him fall while drunk. Each night, he returns home reeking of spirits." "So, was he in any condition to travel the last time you saw him?"

"Not sure, sir. Possibly. He was indulging in drinks while the servant was pouring for him."

"Is that so? Does he drive?" "Indeed, like a man possessed." "Does he ever go out for a stroll?"

"No, he insists on the car." "And that morning, his vehicle was present, but he was not."

"Understood, sir." Goudham concluded his inquiries and glanced at the others.

"So? We're wrapped up for now. Thanks for your time, Maria. We may need to reach out again, please help us if we do."

"Alright. I'm also hoping for the culprit to be apprehended soon."

"Even if it happens to be your father." "If it's my dad, how could you take him in?"

Goudham found himself without a response.

"Are you anticipating his return?"

She hesitated briefly. Goudham studied her deep brown eyes, awaiting her reply.

"When I heard that bell ring, I wondered if it was him. It took me back to my childhood memories of Dad. The sound of that ringing bell held no respect for time, be it morning or night. He would always disrupt the peace just to get his needs met. Truthfully, I don't want him to come back." Her words rang true.

"Alright, Maria. Have a lovely day. Thank you for your transparency." The officers left the marshes, heading back to their station.

Goudham suddenly felt a wave of discomfort in his head and winced.

"What's the matter?"

"It's like waves crashing over my entire skull." "Would you like something to drink?"

"I need more than a simple drink, hmm." Goudham spoke through his discomfort, rubbing his temples.

"Rama. Would you mind massaging my forehead?"

"Paul, take him to the hospital."

"No need to panic. Can we head to the station?" "Goudham, let's go to the hospital."

"No, Paul. I've dealt with this since I was young. If I lie too much, it feels like my mind starts to fall apart."

He gently leaned his head against the seat as Ramani began to massage his temples from behind.

"Thanks, Rama." "Quiet now and lay back. That's enough detective work for today," Ramani scolded him like a caring brother.

"We were astonished at your skillful deceit," Paul acknowledged, a smirk gracing his face.

"How did you craft such a believable tale?" "It appeared from my exchanges with those journalists. Everything just aligned perfectly, nothing more."

The jeep rolled up to the station, where a buzz of chatter filled the airwaves.

Without registering the chaos, Goudham strode inside and drank a few glasses of water from the jug.

"What's going on?" Ramani inquired of a constable.

"Ma'am, the meteorologist reports another potential tsunami on the horizon." "When will this tsunami season end? Each year the waves come crashing like a twisted celebration."

Both Ramani and Paul quaked, but Goudham maintained his composure.

"Sir, tsunami alert."

"Everyone has been recommended to be wary. A red alert has been issued. All schools and institutions are closed until further notice."

"What about the station?"

"The station is shut too."

Goudham approached Paul.

"May I please have the key to the jeep? A bit of seaside air would ease my headache."

"Good grief, sir! A tsunami is imminent. This isn't the time to go."

"I'll handle it. Just grant me the key, please." His eyes were devoid of fear. Paul handed him the key.

"Should we accompany you?" "No, Paul. I need solitude for a spell."

"Sir, the station is closed until further notice." "Fine. I'll return shortly."

Goudham drove the jeep, inching closer to the ocean, but found the beach entrance barricaded. He parked the vehicle behind the barriers and ventured into the fray. The atmosphere buzzed with frenetic energy, punctuated by the blaring announcements echoing through the chaos. A police jeep rumbled by, cautioning through a loudspeaker,

"Everyone residing along the coastline must evacuate until further notice."

Undeterred, Goudham navigated through the tumult, evading any scrutiny from the officers. "Maya, you bitch!" a young boy in boxers shouted defiantly at the surf. His mother carried him up and whisked him away into a jeep, distancing them from the tumultuous waters.

As he stepped onto the gray sand, Goudham took a moment to absorb the chaos around him, closing his eyes to revel in the sounds and scents of the sea. Gradually, the cacophony faded, and when he opened his eyes, amidst the swirling disorder, a serene establishment stood still: 'CresCent Cafe.'

He opened the mirrored door and stepped inside, greeted by the fragrance of champa flowers wafting through the air. In one corner, a selection of organic goods was displayed, while directly across, an assortment of books and music cassettes graced a large wooden shelf. Right in front of it, a cozy coffee nook featured stone tables encircled by petite cane chairs—a tranquil oasis away from the surrounding frenzy.

"Yes, sir," a melodious voice chimed, drawing his attention. He turned to see a captivating girl with flowing hair and sky-blue eyes framed by delicate eyeliner, leaving him momentarily spellbound.

"Sir, I'm just wrapping up the billing and closing the store," she added.

"Closing for what reason?" Goudham momentarily blinked, the impending tsunami slipping his mind. Regaining his composure, he replied, "Oh, take your time."

He scanned the cafe, then redirected his focus towards her. "Could I indulge in a coffee?"

"Apologies, sir. The kitchen's closed. It's not quite a café; we've merely added that for ambiance," she responded. "Art, beach, and coffee— what more could we desire?" Her blue eyes sparkled with an understanding smile.

"Finish your tasks; may I explore a bit?"

"Certainly," she smiled back.

Goudham ventured deeper into the store, marveling at natural soaps, incense burners, tooth powder, bamboo brushes, river weed tea bags, coconut sugar, clay pots, aroma oils, and a collection that unites humanity with nature.

"Sir, I'm done with my work."

"Ah, alright."

Goudham felt no rush to leave the store.

"When does the door usually close?" "Typically when dusk arrives."

He approached the shelf adorned with books and audio cassettes.

"Honestly, I came to the beach with a tempest swirling in my mind."

"What's the matter?" "Oh, what can I say? A noisy brain."

He inhaled the atmosphere of the shop and turned around.

"Shall we get moving?"

Those blue eyes were fixed on him, like gazing into a reflective surface. She stepped inside the store, running her fingers along the baby glass bottles arranged. Each touch sought the delicate essence of a special aroma oil. "Ah, yes." At last, she found it and made her way to Goudham.

"Scent of Earth. For a tranquil mind."

His thoughts had transformed into a serene isle, yet his heart roared like a tsunami.

"Does your shop create this?"

"Indeed. It's actually my younger sister's brainchild—capturing the aroma of parched earth kissed by untouched raindrops."

"Incredible! How does that work?" "It's quite an intricate process." "Can I take a look?" "Certainly, we craft it at home."

"Perhaps another time, then." "Anytime you wish." She lightened the conversation for him.

He stepped outside, inhaling the salty breeze. The tumult had faded, leaving the sea tranquil, just for the two of them. She exited the store, securing the mirror cage and pulling down the shutter. The sound reverberated across the gray sand.

"Alright, sir, I'm off. Wishing you a peaceful night."

"Do you live close to the shore?"

"Yes." "So, you won't be relocating?" "She visits annually but never steps beyond my shop's boundary.

We both know she won't rest until she is free." He nodded in agreement. Her blue eyes sparkled as she strolled away.

"No, I didn't settle the payment for the oil." "Experience the bliss first." "So, will we cross paths again?"

"Let fate decide. I'm feeling peckish." She replied with poise and continued down the alleyway.

"I'm hungry too," he murmured to himself, casting his gaze toward the saltwater, bubbling with excitement. Suddenly, dread seeped in, tainting the anticipation. The water receded, revealing a barren stretch of salt. The waves' return held an air of mystery. He meandered along the deserted shore, voicing a silent prayer, leaving the cerulean backdrop without waiting for the climax. The roar of a jeep faded in the distance, surrendering to silence. The sweet sea sat caught in a whirlpool of conflicting hunger for liberation - the vortex of the aqua.

Chapter 16
The Key into the Self

Winter Reflection,

1999.

In a shimmering realm of water encased by reflective surfaces, Goudham swims through the depths, a dance of self-encounter.

Wherever he glances, his own visage greets him. A weighty burden clings to his back, its metallic grasp hindering his movements. He reaches behind him, revealing a radiant golden axe. Instantly, the water drains away, plunging into a swirling abyss, and his feet find solid ground beneath him. Standing tall, weapon in hand and drenched through, he is encircled by his unadorned selves. With a quiet realization that the escape lies within, he swings the golden axe, shattering his glassy reflections as fragments of mirror cascade like raindrops. All shadows flee, leaving him in an engulfing obscurity. He treads the aimless path, axe gripped tightly, eyes lost in shadows. The sole illumination emanates from his essence. From the profound darkness, he catches the earthy scent mingling with the melody of raindrops. Following this fragrance and sound, he ventures deeper. As the aroma and rhythm intensify, his legs suddenly grow numb, unveiling a swirling blue vortex before him. An attempt to advance proves futile, his feet seemingly anchored to the ground, forcing him to confront the unthinkable: to sever his own limbs. In a surge of fury, he hoists the axe to strike, but his heart intervenes, casting the weapon into the depths of obscurity. With the invisible bindings relinquishing their hold, he is reborn into freedom. Faced with another journey ahead, he leaps into the azure whirlpool once more descending into the aquatic realm surrounded by mirrors. Yet this time, he beholds the glimmer of a cerulean sky above. All his shadows converge and rise to the surface, and slowly, he awakens, his ocean-blue eyes fluttering open from a serene slumber.

The chamber was enveloped in the rich aroma of damp earth, accompanied by the rhythmic symphony of rain. He stirred every inch of his being, expelling a deep sigh that spoke of restorative slumber. His gaze drifted to the table, where a delicate hint of rain lingered, eyeing him curiously. With a soft smile of gratitude directed at the glass bottle, he slowly extricated himself from the bed. As he unraveled the blanket, his essence stood tall in divine form, swaying to the rain's melody.

"Good morning, champion. Ready for a shake?" "It's chilly; a coffee first would do wonders," replied the essence.

There was no trace of a headache or the fog of a hangover, as though he had awakened from a tranquil yoga nidra state. He downed several glasses of water to revive his inner aqueduct and gone ahead to the restroom for his cleansing rituals. Once refreshed, he donned boxers and a hoodie, then brewed himself a steaming cup of black coffee and stepped outside. The rain and wind greeted him like old friends, nudging him closer to their playful cascade. He settled into a side chair, allowing the droplets to tickle only his crossed legs. With the first whiff of coffee, his blood vessels began to dance towards his heart, then to his mind, stirred awake by that first sip.

"And it's a holiday," he mused, sharing joy with the rain while mapping out his day. Umbrella-clad figures moved along their own paths, all under the same grey sky.

"Oh, the tsunami bypassed us. Thank goodness." He savored the last of his coffee, pouring remnants into an eager ant colony. Charged with caffeine, he launched into stretches, twists, and sit-ups, then dove nose-first towards the ground, executing a series of push-ups. Just as he reached a euphoric high, his phone chimed. He dashed to answer it.

"Hello." "Hey Goudham, it's Ramani."

"Morning, Rama. What's on the agenda? Enjoying quality time with your trainer husband?" "Nope, I'm at the station."

"At the station? I thought work was suspended?" "New info just came in—it's a green alert. All's well now. I tried calling, but you didn't answer."

"I figured it was a holiday." "One day off wasn't enough, huh?"

"One day off?" "What?" Goudham fell silent, perplexed.

"Hello? Hello?" "Yes, I'm here." "I thought you'd dozed off. Sorry, no jeep available; the team deployed to the affected zones." "Affected by what?" "The tsunami." "Did it actually strike?"

"What were you doing all day? You didn't know?" As the rain shifted from a downpour to a gentle drizzle, the pulse of his heart echoed in his ear.

"No, I was only half-asleep." "Just like always. Hurry! We've got a case without a lead. You have a bike, right?" "Ah, yes." "Good. See you soon."

Ramani hung up. Goudham bolted out of the house and onto the muddy road. An elderly gentleman ambled by, reading the newspaper under an umbrella. Goudham intercepted him, causing the old man to slam on the brakes of his rapid reading.

"Sir, just a moment."

Goudham peered at the newspaper's front-page headline.

"Disaster covers the land."

"Why don't you buy your own paper, cheapskate?" The old man grumbled as he resumed his reading, leaving in a huff. Goudham had squandered an entire day in slumber, freeing himself from restless nights. Yet, the whirlpool in his mind surged again, this time with powerful waves in his gut, plunging him into another day of breathlessness. He took a quick shower, dressed posthaste, and hopped on his Royal Enfield, splattering mud and water in his wake. All the constables greeted him with a salute as he entered, anxiety prickling within him as he stood before Ramani and Paul.

"Good morning." They rose, smiling. "What were you doing when the tsunami struck?"

"Did it cause significant damage?" Both recognized the trepidation in his eyes. "Yes, it hit some areas pretty hard."

"Let's head to the beach."

A police jeep pulled up at the edge, and Goudham dashed toward it to retrieve the key from the constable. Ramani and Paul trailed behind in a flurry of confusion, leaping into the vehicle just as it prepared to leave, each grappling with their own uncertain destiny. The blue jeep soared over the silent bridge, eventually touching down at the beach.

The sweet sea had transformed dramatically since his last visit, as if a battle had scarred the landscape. Goudham walked unsteadily, his legs quaking and his blue eyes quivering as he surveyed the aftermath of the devastation, with Ramani and Paul close behind.

Despite the chaos, the area endured minimal destruction aside from layers of sea sand obscuring the road. At CresCent Cafe, the shutter stood closed, and the sands had not encroached the doorstep. Echoes of voices floated from afar, where a group collected debris strewn about the pavement. A collection of plastic refuse, mismatched leather shoes, and other cast-offs lay amongst the sand. Goudham began to search for familiar cerulean eyes among the bustling crowd of life. With each step, his heartbeat quickened until, from a narrow passage, a voice broke through, resonating with his longing.

"You lazy bums, quit the chatter and haul those sacks!" A girl with hair dancing in the breeze admonished two little boys, urging them into action.

"We were just resting?" "Really?" She playfully puffed at their little bumps, sending them off grinning with the sacks. In that instant, the ocean blue eyes met the sky blue eyes, creating an unbroken connection. His heart calmed like a gentle wave, while his thoughts drifted like white clouds in a clear blue sky. She set aside her sack and approached him, a smile illuminating her face.

"Hello, sir." Goudham felt a wave of emotion, struggling to reply. "Your eyes?" she remarked, pointing toward his own. He instinctively touched his face, realizing tears were cascading down.

"Oh, just the sand. How have you been?" He fumbled for a more graceful opening.

"Did you think you'd see me again?"

"I hoped." Their gazes exchanged shy smiles, hinting at the budding connection.

"It seems you're on duty, sir." "Cops are perpetually on duty."

"Khadija," she introduced herself, extending her hand to him.

"Goudham." He grasped her delicate hand, feeling its divine softness.

"How fares the restless mind?"

"The oil worked wonders, and my slumber was nothing short of enchanting."

"Thank you for the feedback, sir. When would you like to see the magic in action?"

"Oh, any moment soon—just not right now, as you can observe." He glanced back to find Ramani and Paul standing nearby, beaming back at them.

"Yes, I can see." She locked her gaze on his, and a hush enveloped their exchange.

"Do you lie?" "Why do you ask that?" His smile faltered.

"A calamity is merely the fallout of deceit. When lies accumulate, nature responds in kind—as does our psyche. If one's heart is untainted, it reacts, and the body suffers from headaches, nausea, and insomnia." "Yes, I did, as part of my investigation."

"Hmmm. Best of luck with those lies. May they guide you toward the truth."

"Indeed." "Well then, I must take my leave. There are many lies to untangle."

Need some help?"

"No, we're good. I know you have other threads to pick up."

"Alright, is that a farewell?"

"How about tossing in a 'see you soon' as well?"

"See you soon."

"Can't wait to reunite, Goudham sir." Khadija beamed and drifted away.

"Goudham, that's me. I prefer no strings attached." Halfway, she turned back.

"I heard somewhere that humans carry an invisible tail, a remnant of the ego."

"That tail is merely self-love. Annihilating the entire ego will only leave a physical tail exposed, ripe for others to tug and toy with."

She stepped back, joining the bustling crowd with a rosy smile and a shy wave.

Goudham stepped into his duties, donning a mirrored grin.

"Oh, so this was a wave of emotion. Ramani, I can sense romance in the air."

Goudham couldn't curb his blush. He returned the keys to Paul and took his place in the front seat.

"Hey, lovebird, when did this spark ignite?"

"It happened like a serene pause before the tempest."

The jeep rolled along the coastal route, moving into more ravaged areas, their smiles dimming along with the scenery.

"This place took a hard hit."

As they ventured further, the devastation deepened. Earthmovers toiled to erase the remnants of falsehoods. They paused at an intersection, a sign dangling above:

'< Sweet Port-8.08 miles, < Lighthouse-505 meters,

> Dolphin Spot-1.1 miles, > Estuary-3.3 miles.'

"Goudham, what would you choose? A melody to delight the ears or a vision to enchant the eyes?"

"That's a challenging dilemma, Paul. At this moment, I opt for both."

The jeep veered right toward the dolphin spot, a bridge stretching into the sea like a corridor to the unknown.

'Dolphin Spot - 222m'

They arrived at the bridge's end, reaching an eastern enclave untouched by the waves of despair.

Goudham alighted, inhaling deeply. The afternoon sky was draped in clouds, the sun cloaked in hesitation, reluctant to bear witness to the wreckage.

"When might we catch a glimpse of dolphins here?"

"The fish wings dance at dawn and dusk."

A green jeep rolled onto the scene, carrying Anand, Kishan, Christy, Kanya, Maria, Lucy, and Charlie.

"Greetings, everyone."

"We visited the station, but they informed us you were out."

"So, here's my sister. You can apprehend her."

Kanya's eyes widened in surprise, her sleek black sunglasses obscuring half her face.

"Oh, those are quite the vintage shades! Are they your grandfather's?" Goudham asked, grinning widely.

"You hit the nail on the head. It belonged to grandpa." "I must be frank; those sunglasses don't quite suit you." "Please don't gawk too much, officer. It's not a fashion statement. She's battling a pink eye."

Anand cautioned the officers.

"Oh dear! If it's not too much trouble, may we have a peek?"

Kanya cautiously removed her glasses, revealing a stark white eye surrounded by red.

"Oh, you can put them back. Did you manage to get the medicine?" "Yes." "Not an appealing sight on the outside too, is it?"

A solemn silence enveloped the group, acknowledging the tragedy. Goudham turned toward the fresh face.

"This is my brother, Charlie," Christy introduced him.

"You've made our task simpler. First, I need to ask Kanya a few questions. You all relax; we'll conduct a private inquiry," Goudham said, as Kanya nodded to the others and moved toward a pile of gravel.

"Yes, sir. What do you wish to know?"

"We trust Maria has informed you that the deceased is suspected to be one of the protestors."

"Yes, she mentioned that."

"What was your relationship like with your father?"

"To be honest, everything my father did was contrary to nature."

"Including your engagement," Goudham interjected.

"The engagement was just a guise to sway public opinion. If it had occurred, my answer would've been yes, even if I loathed the man." Her words flowed freely.

"May I pose a personal question?" "Certainly."

"When did you and Anand meet?"

"Anand and I have been friends since childhood. One evening, he proposed, and it caught me off guard. Despite my feelings for him, I turned him down."

"Was it out of fear?" "Nothing else." "And now? Is the fear still there?"

"At this moment, I love him more than my own life. I would sacrifice everything for him."

"So, could you guide us through the events after your father's disappearance? Was there anything—or anyone—that raised suspicion?" "Most of his actions were bound to lead us into trouble. He was well-acquainted with the law."

"Was there an incident of him hurting someone?"

"There were a couple of memories that stand out. One was my mother's bruised eye—my last recollection of her." "I'm sorry for your loss, Kanya. No need to dwell on that. Anything related to the disappearance?"

"Once, he had a confrontation with a bus driver. Dragon defended him and ended up severely injuring the driver, sending him to the hospital." "Who is this, Dragon?" "Our servant; that was his nickname." "Was he the one who met his end by lightning?" "Yes." "So, you mentioned a bus driver, not a truck driver, correct?"

"No, it was a bus driver. I was in the car with them. Our vehicle collided with the bus due to a mistake on our part. The bus driver yelled, and Dad signaled Dragon with a glance, and in an instant, he lunged at the driver on the road. It appears this short-tempered servant was merely my father's puppet, eager to execute his every command."

"Hmm, any disputes or incidents involving truck drivers?"

"I'm not sure—perhaps. My father had no moral compass, sir. His motto was to act and move. In front of others, he wore a mask of benevolence, but only those who were close to him truly seen his true self."

"Were there any financial disputes with his partners, any discussions about money?"

"Ah yes, I recall him writing a check for 30,00000₹. I couldn't tell if it was for wedding expenses or something official, but he seemed unhappy about the expenditure. I informed the police officers at the time, and they suspected he might have used it for future travels."

"Do you genuinely believe your father will return?"

"All I know is that I no longer live in fear." Those words appeared boldly from her brave heart.

Yes, madam."

"Do you recognize me? Do you remember us?" She glanced at both and recalled Ramani.

"Yes, madam. The raven's nest."

"So, it sticks in your mind. What became of that?" "I presented it to little Maria."

"Can you bring to mind anything that transpired the night before your mother's passing?"

The haunting memories flooded back, intertwined with the blazing sun above. Those perched upon the stones straightened their backs, snapped their fingers, and stirred from their frozen state. The weight of trauma cloaked her once more, giving her motionless.

"Kanya, I apologize. Are you okay?"

"No, sir. I can't journey back; I'm still persuading that young girl inside me that the dreadful mother was merely a sinister dream."

"You can pause right there, Kanya. You're back from the retreat, and we wish to spare you further trauma." "Thank you, sir." She inhaled deeply.

"We're merely seeking anything to help us move forward. Can we delve into your father's disappearance?"

"Of course, sir."

"When was the last time you spotted your dad?"

"He was outside by the spring, sipping a drink." "By himself?" "No, Dragon was there as well, the servant."

She felt the heat of the sun and the pressure of questioning. Goudham nodded, signaling the end of the session.

"Yes, Kanya. We're finished. I apologize for intruding on your first day back from the retreat."

"That's alright, sir. I hope you find the culprit soon." "Maria, could you join us for a moment?"

"Hmm, when did you both learn the news?" "This morning, when Maria roused me. We searched for dad, but we only found the letter. We informed our relatives, and one called the authorities."

"To be truly candid, we never intended to pursue the investigation; we didn't wish for him to return. His call felt like a genuine spiritual summons for us." Maria chuckled and told.

"Hmm, understood. You both are free to go." Kanya and Maria escaped the interrogation's grip.

"So, what was your name again?" "Charlie." "Yes." "Does Charlie have anything else to contribute?" "I have nothing further to share, actually."

"Did you mention that the soil was disturbed?" "Yes, sir. I found it suspicious, but Dad was too inebriated and restless to investigate." "Did you come from the coffee field?"

"Yes, I plan to head back this evening. Mom informed me about the investigation. Winter makes it difficult to step away since I manage the plant on my own. Apologies for the delay, sir. The coffee and chocolate harvest season are upon us in the hills."

"That's quite alright. Thank you for your cooperation.

Anand approached the officers with cautious steps.

"Sir, I should have mentioned this earlier: I'm colorblind, which means I perceive colors through a unique lens. Maria is telling the truth; it must be a red truck."

"Fascinating. So, a red truck, right, Maria?" "That's what my mind recalls."

"How do you perceive this?" Ramani gestured towards the police jeep.

"Green," he said, chuckling. "Actually, it's blue." "Yes, true. I mostly see green shades; that's why my jeep is painted green."

"How do you learn the difference between green and red?" "I know that nature is green while blood is red."

"Thanks for clarifying our confusion. Is there anything more?"

"Sir, I recall there was a dolphin painted on the back of the truck."

"A dolphin?" "Yes, sir," Anand confirmed.

Goudham paused, pondering, then looked at his team.

"Okay, team. Thank you." "Understood, sir." "The situation is unchanged. No one leaves the town until the body is shown. For emergencies, report to the station."

Ramani echoed the instructions, and everyone nodded before climbing back into the jeep and driving away from the beach.

"So, what's our next step?" "The confusion is gone now; things should start falling into place."

"By the way, I forgot to mention—my husband knows Kanya. They used to work together at Riverside School." "Really?" "She stopped teaching due to some mental health struggles." "What happened?" "She told him about a marriage she never wanted; perhaps that's the reason."

"Trauma can unearth old wounds with new pains. I remember as a kid, seeing various mentally unstable individuals in the hills.

Transitioning from the beginning to the end isn't challenging; it's the journey of looking back and healing that truly demands skill."

"Hmm, similar to our case." "Exactly."

"So where do we begin?" "Let's not pursue it aggressively; let the universe unfold." Goudham said in an elevated tone. The officers moved away from the shore, returning to the signpost.

'< Cosmic Port-8.08 miles, < Lighthouse-505 meters,

> Dolphin Spot-1.1 miles, > Estuary-3.3 miles.'

The blue jeep veered right, following the shortcut through rough terrain toward the town.

A green jeep was parked nearby, where Kanya was retching while Maria comforted her.

"What's wrong?" "Not sure. She just suddenly felt unwell."

"On the way, we grabbed a few cold bites. That could be the culprit."

"But I'm fine," Christy exclaimed proudly.

"This conversation is about humans," Christy said, grabbing Lucy by the neck.

Anand offered Kanya a water bottle, and she took a small sip.

"How are you feeling?" He wiped the sweat from her brow. "I'm okay. Let's move on."

"Drink some coconut water; the hills have a way of revitalizing you. Right now, you're too sensitive to these disturbances. You'll feel better once you avoid impurities until your body re-aligns with its surroundings." Goudham offered his advice.

Meanwhile, many trucks passed by, laden with debris from the tsunami. One red truck caught Goudham's eye.

"Paul, follow those trucks," Goudham whispered urgently. "Goodbye, everyone."

The blue jeep revved to chase after the trucks.

"What's going on?" "Paul, just keep moving forward."

The convoy of trucks roared off-road along a familiar trail, with police trailing behind in a cloud of dust. They all funneled into a factory nestled across several acres, where structures were shrouded in mold, echoing with industrial clamor and infused with a cocktail of chemical scents.

"Goudham, this is the plastic plant that Devachan has partnered with." A worker descended to greet them.

"I'm the supervisor here. How can I help you, sir?" "Just stopping by to see the status of the goods."

"This scrap will be ground down and recycled." "Good to hear. How's production?" "It's running smoothly, sir. All the machinery is imported."

"Excellent. Are these trucks owned by your employer?"

"No, they're all rented." "Thanks for your assistance." "You're welcome, sir." The supervisor returned to his tasks.

"Goudham, what's really happening here?"

"Paul, did you catch sight of that truck?" Goudham gestured. A red truck adorned with a painted dolphin on its side.

"That's quite a strange coincidence." "What if it's the very same truck?"

"What's our next move?" Ramani pondered, caught in uncertainty.

"Right now, that truck is our only lead. Let's go."

Goudham stepped out, striding toward the truck, with Ramani and Paul in tow.

"Is this your vehicle?" Goudham queried the driver.

"No, sir. I'm merely the driver."

'KYK 1994.' Ramani jotted down the license plate.

"May we see the registration?"

The driver handed over the documents, and Ramani skimmed through the details of the owner.

'K.Y. Chandran, gate no.1, South Y junction, first cross, swamp road.'

"What's this regarding, sir?" "Oh, just a formality."

"Does your boss possess any other trucks?" "No ma'am. Just this one." "Does he run any other ventures?" "He also engages in vegetable farming and has a light and sound business in town."

"Alright. Are you finished with the soil cleanup?" "Not yet, sir. A few more rounds to go."

"Okay, you're free to go." He returned the documents. "Thank you, sir."

"All our suspects appear to be farmers."

"Could this lead us somewhere?" "Only one way to find out."

"Chandran. Ramani, check if this fellow has any criminal records at the station."

The officers turned toward the station, their jeep navigating the dusty off-road to arrive beneath a tranquil bridge where the river embraces the sea. The 4x4 climbed an uphill path strewn with pebbles, reaching the crest next to the bridge. They arrived at the station, spotting a young man casually leaning against a Rxz bike.

"Hey, Charlie." "Greetings, Sir." "What's on your mind?" "I'm heading back to the plant, but there's something I want to discuss with you first."

"What is it?" "Could we speak in private?"

"Alright, you both can go over those details." "Understood, sir." They stepped inside.

"What's so private, Charlie?"

"I held back earlier because it's a rather humiliating tale to tell in public. Given that Devachan is on the list of suspects, I thought this info could be pertinent to the investigation."

"You can depend on me."

"I once saw Devachan in a recording from my school days."

"What recording?" "A scandalous tape."

"Was there a woman involved?" "Yes, but her identity was obscured by a skeleton mask." "What did the footage show?" "It depicted them in bed. The camera focused on Devachan. I viewed it with a friend at my place." "And where's that tape now?"

"My friend Bishan took it home. I haven't laid eyes on it since and likely never will."

"Why not?" "He's passed away." "I'm sorry to hear about your friend. How did you come across it?"

"We found it beneath a tree in the mangroves. It appeared as if someone had discarded it, but the swamp hadn't consumed it." "Have you shared this with anyone else?"

"No. Bishan concealed it somewhere in his house. You remember Kishan, right? My brother's acquaintance?"

"Yes, the guy with long hair." "Exactly, Bishan was his sibling."

"How can we retrieve that tape?"

"I have no clue, sir. The last thing he mentioned was, 'the key into the self is safe with me.' "

"Self?"

"Perhaps a secret compartment in his home. I'm unsure if he disposed of the tape. We lost touch afterward. The next day, we were meant to go swimming, but I caught a fever, so we never met again. That evening, he tragically drowned in the river."

"Was your late friend known for deception?"

"No, but he had a knack for withholding the truth. There were secrets he wouldn't share, even though we were best buds."

"Hmm. I appreciate the information, Charlie. It's been incredibly useful."

"Okay, sir. May I leave now? I need to get through the gate before the fog envelops the road." "Sure, Charlie. Safe travels." "Thank you, sir. Wishing you luck with the case."

The bike roared to life, while Ramani and Paul continued their quest for clues.

"Sir, we can't seem to track down any leads on a guy named Chandran. Should we choke on this dust?" "Why don't we just pay him a visit?"

"Paul, we have a detour. Let's take the jeep and see where it takes us."

They ventured down an unfamiliar road.

"Let's head over to Kishan's place." "Which Kishan?" "You know, the one with the long hair." "Oh, what's his role in all of this?" "Let's see. Take us to John's house and we'll grab the address from them."

"Where is this situation leading us?" Paul gazed at Goudham, completely bewildered.

"Paul, how do we discover what we need?"

"We'll just pick what's necessary."

"But how can we pick if we're unsure of our needs?" Paul was stumped.

"First, let's pinpoint what we don't require," Ramani chimed in from the back.

"Exactly. That's our mission now: to uncover what isn't needed."

The blue jeep approached the bridge, just as the green jeep barreled out from the off-road ahead.

"Oh, hello again, sir." "Anand, we were just on our way to see you."

"Why? We can pull over to the side." "No, let's head to your home. We can chat over a cup of coffee. What do you say?"

"Of course, sir. Please follow us."

The green jeep silently crossed the bridge, followed closely by the blue one. They drove down the riverside road, passing a lush grove of palm trees, until both vehicles arrived at a two-story house nestled within a wild, untamed garden.

"Come on in," Kishan welcomed them. The room pulsed with the sounds of radio music, while Prasad and Deepa enjoyed some quality couple time as a group walked in.

"Wow, looks like we have a full house. What's up with the glasses, Kanya?" "It's pink eye, uncle. Best to keep your distance." "Oh, my goodness." Just then, the police entered. Prasad felt a jolt of surprise at the unexpected turn of events.

"Dad, they want to ask something about the body found at Christy."

"Not about the body, but your insight might illuminate the case."

"Please have a seat. I'm Prasad. How can we help you?"

Ramani's gaze drifted to the two portraits hanging on the wall; one depicted an elderly man, the other a young boy.

"You're the editor of Satya Newspaper?" "That's correct."

"I've been wanting to meet you since I heard of your struggle against gold mining."

Goudham revealed his enthusiasm.

"It was my father's battle. I have no part in that fight," Prasad admitted sincerely.

"Running a newspaper isn't a walk in the park."

"I'm aware. My father passed the torch to me. Soon, Vidhooradarshan will take over the press and then I'll step down from the editorial board."

"Why?" "I don't want to let conflicts define life's emotions like my father did." Goudham felt a connection to his sentiment.

"And you, Kishan, what's your story?" "I'm an artist; I paint." "Impressive! What style?" "Oil painting. I revel in crafting surreal forms." "You enjoy infusing reality with flavor." "Yes, precisely," he responded with a genuine smile.

"What about you, Nandhu?"

"I'm a diving instructor and an underwater archaeologist."

"I didn't realize you both led such extraordinary lives."

"I spent nearly five years on a tour and just returned for a break. And I truly got a break."

Anand smirked faintly.

"Sorry to hear that. I hope the truth surfaces soon. Right now, the focus is on Bishan."

Shock rippled through the room.

"What about him?" Deepa inquired.

"His mother?" "Indeed." "What's your name?" "Deepa."

"Has he confided any secrets to you that remain unknown to others?"

"He was a boy wrapped in mystery, encased in his own little world. What's this about?"

"Bishan possessed a tape that could lead us somewhere in this investigation."

"What kind of tape?" "Like a tape hidden in the self."

All the eyebrows in the room rose collectively.

"Did he ever talk about anything like that?"

Deepa, Prasad, and Anand stood there, speechless, while Kishan experienced a moment of recollection.

"Sir, he mentioned something to me once." "When? What did he say?" The officers buzzed with excitement.

"I'm not sure. He showed me the key to the self once."

Kishan glanced at his fish tail locket; a dawning realization came over him.

"The key, but the key to what?" Kishan pondered. After a moment of thought, he dashed up the stairs to his grandfather's room.

"It must be here. It's got to be somewhere." His coffee-brown eyes surveyed the space.

"All I remember is him saying this was the key to the reflection."

"This has to connect to some kind of locker. Are there any lockers around here?"

"Perhaps. My father was a newspaper editor, naturally harboring his own secrets."

Kishan removed the locket, searching for anything it might unlock. They combed through every corner—table, chair, bed, switch, window, fan—yet found nothing. Anand tried to shift a mirror shaped like an eye, but it was firmly anchored to the wall.

"Is this mirror bolted down or what?"

Kishan gazed at his shadow reflected at him.

"Reflection." He traced a finger along the mirror's edge and discovered a tiny recess. Imagining the tail end as a key, he inserted it into the hole. It fits like a dream. With a slow twist, once, twice, and on the third turn, the mirror swung open. Eagerly, everyone leaned in to see.

Inside lay a diary, a polaroid photo, and a videotape. The diary was filled with Kishan's sketches and brief notes. He turned the pages, lost in nostalgia.

"There was a time he was furious with me because I portrayed everyone but him. I didn't draw him because I envisioned his portrait as my magnum opus. How can I express that to him? How can I tell him he's the masterpiece I've been waiting for?" Tears streamed down his face as he stared at the Polaroid capturing their silly smiles.

"I knew he was the one who took my diary; I just wanted to surprise him with a painting. That's why I believed he'd return it to me. And he did." Kishan broke into sobs while Maria comforted him. The entire room became thick with emotion as memories flooded back to the family. Goudham retrieved the cassette, declaring, "This is all we need. Thank you for your time, and my apologies for resurrecting the past."

The officers left the room, their blue jeep pulling away. Anand followed, heading towards the river, where he pulled out the magnifying glass. He examined his own reflection through the opaque lens, a smile appearing as his mind whispered - The key into the self.

Chapter 17
The Quicksand of the Marshland

Winter Shadow,

1999.

The day was surrendering its last gleams of daylight. Goudham fixated on the illuminated tape beneath the dimming sun, eagerly peering through the tainted reel in search of the elusive truth.

"What's inside it, Goudham?"

He paid no heed to the exchange; his gaze was locked onto the white fungus in an intense close-up.

"Everyone speaks of shadows dimming the light, yet few acknowledge how light can erase shadows." Paul and Ramani found themselves puzzled by this notion.

"Observe the white decay that has consumed the black reel." Goudham clarified by presenting the afflicted tape. "Fungus is arguably the most patient assassin on Earth—subtle and gradual."

"What's this, Goudham?"

"Clearly explicit material," Goudham replied with a grin, as Paul and Ramani stared at him, bewildered. "First, we must drop the fungus. Time to head to a cassette shop."

The jeep rolled quietly toward the golden town. After navigating a few twists and turns, they arrived at a store—Waves Audio and Video Store. They stepped inside.

"Hello, sir! Welcome to Waves! What would you like to watch?" greeted a cheerful face. "First, we need to rid ourselves of the fungus, then we can enjoy the show." "Absolutely, sir."

The shopkeeper slid the cassette into a tape machine, then inserted a cotton ball soaked in fungal solution into a small slot behind the device before pressing play. The cassette whirred to life, the cotton cleansing the fungus as it turned.

"What's inside this, sir? Is it your wedding cassette?"

"Yes, it's Paul's wedding tape," Goudham pointed, causing Ramani to suppress a smile.

"Oh, it must be quite old then," the smiling face remarked, scanning Paul.

"Do I come off as an old man to you?"

"Not at all, sir. There's no shame in aging gracefully. Every life eventually fades—just look at the fungus fading," the smiley salesperson explained, proving his point. Goudham found the character charming.

"What's your name?"

"Ismail," he replied, still smiling.

"Why did you think it was a wedding?"

"Most of my restoration jobs are wedding tapes. Believe me, cassettes will feel ancient with the arrival of CDs."

"What's a CD?" Old Paul finally inquired.

"A compact disc. It's lighter and more durable. Fungus won't stand a chance."

Goudham's mind swirled as the sound of the cleaner filled the air, and the loop ended.

"Sir, sir," He snapped back to reality. "The cassette is ready. Do you want to play it?"

"No, we'll check it later."

"What distinguishes the two formats? Do they need different machines?" Old Paul was brimming with uncertainties.

"Absolutely, sir. Cassettes rely on magnetic fields, while CDs use using laser technology."

Paul's mouth dropped open, and Goudham slowly closed it.

"I'll buy one when it's available, and Ismail's offering a special class just for you, right?"

"Of course, sir. Let me know if everything works well." "Sure. What's the cost?" "10₹."

"Alright, sir. Have a good day. And don't fret about the tape fungus; perhaps we can digitize your wedding tape into a CD that will outlast you."

"What?"

"Come now, sir. Every life eventually fades," Ismail concluded with his signature phrase.

"I'll visit after I'm gone, then," Paul quipped as he left the store, his spirit still vibrant.

Goudham and Ramani exchanged smiles as he walked away.

"Apologies for the jest, Paul. Just trying to lighten the mood. We all need a breather from this relentless investigation."

Paul returned their smiles, embracing the moment.

"So, is this explicit material you mentioned set before my wedding or after?"

"Let's discover that." The blue jeep rolled toward the station with a hint of mischief. They arrived and entered the interrogation chamber, where a pristine cassette awaited. He fired up the VCR as Ramani and Paul braced themselves for a surprise.

"Prepare to see tails. Just close your eyes if one appears." Goudham issued a playful warning. The film began.

Inside a boxy room adorned with glowing heart-shaped stickers glimmering under soft yellow lights, a tall sofa and a bed dressed in white sheets sat at the center.

"What is this? Are there no people?" Ramani pondered.

"Yes, here comes one," Paul spotted.

One by one, he shed his garments, wrapping a white towel around his waist. A girl donned in a skeleton mask made her entrance.

"Why's she wearing a mask?" "Just hang tight, guys."

The skeleton-faced woman gradually disrobed until she stood bare, pushing him down onto the mattress and perching herself on top of him. After a few enthusiastic movements, she grasped him in her hand, a splash of fluid causing Ramani to shut his eyes.

"What are you revealing to us, you mischievous boy?"

"What caught your attention?" "It's the most grotesque sex scene ever."

"My dear Rama, did you notice the protagonist of the film?"

Goudham struck a pose, revealing the visage of the naked elderly man.

"This? Is this Devachan?" "Indeed."

Moments later, Devachan exited the room post-shower, and as soon as he disappeared, the skeleton-faced woman approached the camera and switched it off.

"What's going on here? Who's this girl? What if she holds a grudge?"

"That's the possibility I aimed to clarify. How did you buy this tape?"

"It emerged from a childhood tale from Charlie." "What's next?" "I need to identify who that girl is."

Goudham rewound the footage.

"Looks like an underground strip club—yellow bulb, heart-shaped walls, and a nude girl," Ramani remarked with a frown.

"Seems Devachan had no inkling he was being filmed."

"Exactly, Paul. It's a scandal." "For what purpose?"

"Remember Kanya referencing 30,00000₹."

"Yes, could it be blackmail?" "Precisely."

"But how will we track down the girl?"

A whirlwind of thoughts swirled within him again.

"Goudham, don't dwell too long in thought. I can't provide you a head massage constantly."

"Ramani, I have a feeling he's got a tsunami girl to handle that now."

"Paul, let's return our focus to the case. So, we have the red truck driver and the masked skeleton girl as our two suspects?"

"How about we first target the driver?"

"Right. Perhaps his truck will lead us to the girl. Ramani, you mentioned that a truck driver took the massage girl to hospital."

"Exactly! What if it's the same driver? What if they're linked?"

"What if the driver was rushing after the burial?" Paul chimed in, catching the drift.

"Yes, that's the wild possibility I was contemplating."

"Shall we pursue Chandran?" They exited with no further debate.

Ramani retrieved her notebook.

'K.Y.Chandran, gate no.1, South Y junction, first cross, swamp road.'

"Perfect, this must be near the crime scene."

"Thus, we inch closer to the culprit. Let's move."

The jeep sped over the silent bridge to the Y junction, where a line of people marched with candles and lamps, accompanied by a smoke-filled vessel of incense.

"What's happening?" The officers were astounded by the procession of the deceased.

"Victims of the raging tides," Paul muttered.

They ventured onto the gravel road beside the swamp, leading directly to the cemetery. The unsettling scene disturbed the trio, causing them to lose sight of their case.

"So?" Paul queried, glancing about. "We're almost there. Gate number 1." They turned southward and chose the first intersection. The houses stood in a tiered formation, with one perched at the end of the road.

"Goudham, this entire area feels deserted. I suspect everyone is at the cemetery," remarked Ramani.

"Take a look." He gestured towards the imposing mansion that loomed above the neighboring homes beyond a wall.

"Devachan's mansion. Surely, something must be brewing there." Paul strode toward the house and pressed the doorbell. A small boy answered, eyeing Paul from head to toe.

"Is this Chandran's place?" Paul inquired.

"Mom, three soldiers have come to see Dad," the boy relayed, disappearing into the house.

"Hey there, little sharpshooter. We are police officers, not soldiers." The boy shaped his arm like a firearm and pretended to shoot at Paul, eliciting laughter from Goudham and Ramani.

"Hi! We're here to speak with Chandran." The presence of the officers visibly unnerved the woman inside. She began to communicate using sign language, but the police officers were lost, prompting her to signal for them to wait. They recognized that gesture well. She returned with her son's slate and chalk, and began to write.

'He's not home. Went to our vegetable farm at Sleepy Slope.'

"Okay, when should we expect him back?" They waited for her response on the slate.

'He'll arrive by midnight.'

"Got it?" The officers felt uncertain about what else to ask.

She wiped the slate clean and wrote another question.

'What is it regarding, sir?'

Goudham sensed her anxiety in the way she gripped the slate.

"Nothing to worry about. I'm just checking on the decorations for my sister's upcoming wedding since his shop was closed." A huge sigh of relief washed over her as she exclaimed a silent 'oh' with a smile.

An elderly man entered, his face betraying nervousness.

"Hello, sir. How can I help you?"

'My dad.' She scrawled on the slate and showed it to them.

"We merely came to inquire about lights and sound for an event. My sister's wedding is approaching."

"Oh, I can certainly help with that. Lights and sound belong to me; my son-in-law currently manages them." "Your name?" "Sugunan." "Ah, yes! Were you the one responsible for the lighting and sound at the mansion years ago?"

"Yes, indeed. What seems to be the issue, sir?"

"Well, during our conversation, Maria mentioned your name, and since we're here, I'd like to ask—were you the one who alerted them about their servant?"

"Yes, my workers and I stayed over last night." "What did you actually witness?"

"I found him on the ground—a broken neck and charred remains." "What time did you discover this?" "Around 3 AM. My son-in-law woke me up to inform me he was embarking on a trip." "In the dead of night?" "Darling, go inside and fetch them a drink. Sir, would you prefer hot or cold?" "Cold will be great." She ambled towards the kitchen.

"It's a bit personal. He came to ask if he could marry my girl and—"

Sugunan hesitated, trailing off.

"Also what?"

"My boy, he's a good man, never committed any crimes in his life. But he once pledged to trade poppy in the region for money, then ultimately backed out, resulting in them burning one of his eyes."

"What? You didn't report such a grotesque crime?"

"That's the risk we take when dealing with criminals. He warned me against it. After that incident, he took over my shop and rented out the truck."

Soorya appeared from the kitchen carrying three glasses of lemonade, her smile disarming. The officers sipped, feeling refreshed by the cool drink.

"Haaa, thank you." She responded with an even broader smile in return.

"Sir, have you uncovered the skeleton's identity?"

"Oh, the investigation is still in progress."

"I doubt Devachan would flee, sir." "What makes you say that?"

"He knew how to navigate allegiances. The rest of the occupants in that mansion are pure-hearted souls. I'm not sure how he got entangled in their lives."

"So, you don't believe he embarked on a spiritual quest."

"Absolutely not. He lacks an understanding of the spirit. But the police discovered a letter, didn't they? So, perhaps there's more to it. I can't be certain."

Sugunan laid out his stance while the officers finished their lemonade.

"So, we will proceed." They shook their heads in agreement.

"I'll speak with Chandran directly. When will he be back?"

"He'll be here in the morning or at the shop."

"Alright. Can you ask him to come to the station? You know our schedule makes it tough to find spare time." "Of course, sir." "I'm Goudham. Ask him to drop by anytime between 10 and 11." "Okay, we'll inform him. Baby, just remind him when he gets home." She responded with a thumbs-up.

"Thanks for the drink." She returned the sentiment with a smile and a namaste as the police officers climbed into the jeep to leave, but Sugunan called out to them.

"Sir, mentioning his ties to those criminals wouldn't jeopardize him, would it? I just wanted to avoid complicating your investigation with any falsehoods."

"Not at all, sir. We need more people like you. It won't harm him because he's innocent. A crime only counts if we commit or endorse it." "I just wanted to clarify. Thank you, sir."

The jeep reversed, its headlights grazing the mansion.

"So he was a neighbor too, huh?" Goudham queried, although his mind was a blank slate.

"How do you weave lies with such skill? Have you trained in that art?"

"Paul, I only distort the truth to unveil the real story, not to concoct another falsehood."

"How did you know the shop was shut?" "I took a guess since he was out of town."

"Paul, this guy undoubtedly fits the profile of our murderer," Ramani asserted.

"So, the killer is away. Should we stop for the day?"

"Yes, I'm feeling a bit foggy in my head too." "Don't let that tsunami of thoughts crash back in. Let's head out, and you get some restful sleep." They veered right at Y and quietly made their way to the station.

"Goudham stepped out in civilian attire and revved his motorcycle."

"So, we'll start the investigation when Chandran appears."

"Okay, Goudham, good night." "Goodnight, everyone."

Once back at his quarters, Goudham entered his captivating room and stood before the mirror, stripped of his attire.

"I can't think of anything," his shadow lamented.

"Good. Let your thoughts take a day off," the light replied.

"I believe we need some release," the shadow nudged. His fingers brushed the lingam, and his muscles responded instinctively. An image of Devachan's provocative scene replayed in his mind, dousing the mood he crafted for self-indulgence. He retrieved a business card from his wallet.

Divine Touch Spa. He dialed the number, 356996.

"Hello, Divine Spa." "Hi, this is Goudham."

"Hey, what can I do for you?" "I'm in search of a massage."

"Absolutely. Right now?" "Yes." "Come on over! We have one last slot before we close at 10."

He glanced at his digital watch; it read 8:43.

"Yes, I'll arrive by 9." "Great! Do you know where Mystic Housing Colony is?"

"Mystic? I think so."

"Just across from it, you'll spot a yellow sign. That's the place. It should be easy to locate."

"Alright, see you soon." They ended the call.

Goudham draped the bare figure in casual beachwear and hopped onto the motorcycle. The ride was brief, illuminated by flickering street lamps. He meandered through the town until he stumbled upon the enchanting enclave. The amber light radiated as vividly as daylight, just as she had described. He ascended the staircase and pushed open the glass door to the spa.

"Hey Goudham, you've arrived right on schedule. Which treatment do you want?" A menu appeared, highlighting an array of tactile delights.

"Divine Special Touch."

"Excellent choice. Head to the last room; everything you need to change is in there."

Inside, a cozy chamber shimmered beneath bright lights. A pristine white bedspread lay atop the bed, topped with a paper cloth. He disrobed and settled onto the paper cover. A girl with flawless skin entered, drawing his gaze to her face. Her slight squint paired with a smile made his azure eyes mirror her warmth.

"Please, lie down, sir."

He reclined, face down. A blend of champa flower and coconut oil drizzled onto his bare back, sending refreshing sensations rippling through him as her hands glided like feathers along his skin. His dormant veins ignited, eyes gently closing. Suddenly, the bright lights softened, casting a dim glow. The connoisseur of shadow welcomed the twilight, being still blissfully unaware as he surrendered to her touch, each stroke like a magnetic force, pulling pleasure from within—perfect, just as the reviews had echoed. He sensed an urgency rising within him, but her hands orchestrated a delicate dance, keeping him suspended in ecstasy as the pressure began to heighten.

"Sir, please turn around. Time for the front."

"Am I doing well, sir?"

"Ahhh, yes. Perfect."

"Would you like a happy ending?" She gestured towards his arousal with a flirtatious shake.

"Oh, no. Thank you." She turned towards his head.

"Are you feeling shy or resilient?" She pressed gently at the apex, inquiring further.

Goudham flipped onto his back, his desire ready to burst forth with mere contact. His eyes stayed closed, ensuring he stayed in tune with the pulse surrounding him. Her hands resumed their rhythmic exploration, flowing from head to toe. Each wave of sensation sparked renewed vitality within him, the pleasure escalating until the call of radiance became impossible to resist—his eyelids fluttered open just as ecstasy spilled forth, immersing him in a realm ablaze with vivid joy. Two squinting eyes met his, sharing a knowing smile as he reveled in the moment. Overwhelmed by the potency of his arousal, everything converged in a mad dance of delight beneath the subdued glow of yellow light, adorned with soft red hearts—the same scandalous from the tape. He masked his astonishment, allowing her skilled hands to finish their work.

"I simply believe in making my own choices." Surrendering to her final changes, he embraced a new avenue of exploration. The massage wove into its concluding segment, and he lay there, comforted as if in a state of blissful oblivion.

"All done, sir. The shower is over there."

"Thank you. May I have your name?" he inquired as he lingered in repose.

"Rathi." She answered with clarity before leaving. He appeared from his euphoric stupor and crept into the shower, relishing every droplet that cascaded over him, stepping out renewed and enlightened. Vasanthi could easily read the mood etched across his face.

"So, how was your experience? Blissful?" "Absolutely bloody bliss."

A tiny bell jingled above the counter.

"Ring it to show your delight."

Goudham rang the bell repeatedly, causing Vasanthi to burst into laughter.

"And Vasanthi, I've got something quite serious to discuss. But first, where's Rathi?"

"She just stepped out. You were the last customer."

"Alright then. Are you finished with your work?"

"Almost done." "Okay, I'll wait for you downstairs." Lost in thought, Goudham descended the stairs, while Vasanthi locked up the spa and followed him down.

"What's so serious?"

"Is she the same girl who...?" "Who what?"

"Devachan misbehaved with her, right?" "Yes."

"I need to show you something. Could you fetch your car?"

"Where to?" "To the station, please. It's important. I'll drop my bike at my place, and we need to sort this out together."

Without seeking further clarification, Vasanthi complied. He parked the bike at his quarters, and they both headed to the station in a sedan.

"Can you spill the beans already? What is it?" "You'll see."

They entered, and he played her the scandalous footage.

"Watch it all." "This is my spa, correct?" She sat patiently as the entire video unfolded.

"Oh no, what? Goudham, I have nothing to do with this. I swear, you have to believe me."

"Who's that girl?" "That one? She's wearing a mask. Looks nothing like my staff's uniform." Vasanthi rewound the video, revealing a scene of the girl perched atop Devachan.

"It's... it's her. Rathi." "Are you sure?"

"Yes. She has those wound marks and scratches on her back."

"Do you know where she lives?" "No, I actually don't have her address."

"What? You mean to say you have no information? She's your staff, right?"

"I knew where she used to stay. She has moved to a new place, but I don't know where."

"Do you realize who her partner was?" "Who?" Goudham fast-forwarded a bit and paused. "Isn't that Devachan?" "Yes." "Goudham, what's happening?"

"This matter is confidential, but I'll fill you in. The skeleton we found belongs to Devachan. DNA tests confirmed it's him, but we're still looking for the head."

"Ehh. Is she the one who did it?"

"Not sure. We need her to talk." "She'll be here in the morning."

"But what if she doesn't show up? We should track her down tonight."

"But I don't know where she is."

"If she sets the spa ablaze, how will you find her?" Vasanthi had no retort.

"Ah, yes. She's been involved with this guy." "Who?" "A fellow who operates a video store nearby." "Let's go." They arrived at the cassette shop, run by a cheerful man.

Waves Audio and Video.

"Ismail." "So you know him." "I had this tape cleaned there."

"I keep a photo of all my staff in my bag. I'm no fool," she said with a smirk, revealing a picture of Rathi.

"I'll take care of it. What if he doesn't cooperate? I know him personally."

"What's the strategy?" "Just arrive when I signal you. Remember, I'm also a journalist. Hand me that photo." With a casual demeanor, she strolled towards the shop.

"Hey! Long time, no see, madam!"

"Just busy living, my dear smiley."

"You look fantastic." "Just a post-workout glow," Ismail flexed his biceps.

"So what brings you here?"

"Got anything thrilling to watch?" She scanned the room, mumbling.

"Of course. Soft or hard?"

"Bring me the hard one." She winked. He ventured inside and returned with a choice of tapes.

"These are all hard for the soft-hearted women. Want the whole collection?"

"Oh no, one is plenty." She randomly selected one. "How much?"

"Just take it. Pay me when you come back." "No way, come on!"

Vasanthi dug into her bag and fished out the cash.

"There's no haggling in Love and Lust, right?" "Right."

As the cash slipped from her hand, a photo tumbled out. Ismail recognized it as he picked it up.

"Is this the place?" "Yes, you know Rathi—your girlfriend? She filled me in on all the details about you." "Is that so?" "Actually, I'm curious about her current address; I only have an outdated one. Do you happen to know it?"

"No, ma'am, I'm afraid I don't know," he replied, handing back the photo.

Vasanthi gestured to Goudham, who then stepped inside.

"I regret to inform you of this, Ismail." "Why, ma'am?" "Just tell him the truth, and he'll be on his way."

"What truth, ma'am?" He continued to ask with a foolish grin as Goutham entered the shop.

"Hello, sir. How was it? Were the wedding rings sparkling?"

Both Goudham and Ismail wore blank expressions.

"Vasanthi presented the photo to Ismail once more."

"Do you recognize this girl, Ismail?"

"I do, sir." "How do you know her?" "She's my girlfriend." "Do you have her address or phone number?" "When I say girlfriend, it's not a fairy tale; it's just a fling." Ismail hinted at intimacy in subtle terms.

"Her contact details." "I don't have any. She only calls when she wants to meet up."

"When does she reach out?"

"Whenever she's in the mood for some romance—usually when it rains. Rain fuels the fire, you see." Ismail concluded his risqué story by linking rain with romance. Goudham scrutinized him, hoping for a slip of the tongue.

"I swear to God, it's the truth. I've been to her home—it's a surreal house hidden deep in the jungle, I think it's on the way to the hills."

"How do you not know the way? Were you perpetually inebriated or just ignorant?"

"Sir, she enjoys adding a thrill to our meetings. I always start off blindfolded. She covers my eyes and lifts the blindfold only when we arrive at a bizarre blue house."

"Blue?" Goudham was eager to see this unique abode.

"So, she only calls when it rains. What's our next move?"

In the next instant, the sky rumbled, unleashing tiny droplets from the clouds. As the rain picked up, the store telephone began to ring.

"Sir, the phone is ringing." "Answer it. If it's her, execute the usual plan."

"Alright, sir." He answered the call.

"Hello." "Hey, it's me." "Hi, Rathi." Ismail glanced at Goudham, who gestured to him to continue.

"Can we meet? It's raining, and everything's getting soaked."

Ismail swallowed nervously and grinned.

"Of course, darling."

"Should I come over?"

"Absolutely, darling."

"Okay, see you soon." She hung up.

"Sorry to interrupt your romantic evening, but we must act now."

"Act? What's all this about?"

"Don't worry; it's just Rathi." "I don't know much about her, but from what I gather, she's quite unfortunate. We've never truly opened to one another. The more we share our thoughts, the closer our hearts become. So?" "When will she be here?" "Not sure. I usually wait in the store, and we head to my room together in her car."

"Alright. We'll stay hidden. Just bring her in and close the shutter." "Got it."

Ismail readied himself for the undercover operation, beaming with anticipation. Vasanthi and Goudham parked the vehicle in a shadowy spot. Near midnight, only the heavy rain could be heard. A light illuminated the ground as a hatchback pulled up in front of the store.

"That's her," Vasanthi affirmed, her voice cutting through the tension.

Ismail appeared, umbrella in hand, escorting her inside as Goudham and Sugandhi dashed behind, swiftly lowering the shutter. Rathi, gripped by fear, unsheathed a knife from her bag.

"I'll stab you if you hurt me!" she warned. "Rathi, there's no need to be scared. We simply want to converse."

"What's the topic of discussion?" Rathi glared at Goudham, locking onto the blue depths of his eyes.

"What do you desire?" "Let's have a chat, but first, I need you to breathe easy. Lower the knife. No bloodshed; if it spills, chaos will follow."

"No, I won't. Step back." "Have you ever trusted someone unconditionally?"

"What?" "You can trust me—it's essential. Alright, I'm going to take the knife from you. There's nothing for you to dread." Deep within, she found some semblance of trust in those azure eyes, and Goudham gently nudged the knife from her grip.

"I have it, safe and sound. Now, I'd like you to sit and unwind."

Rathi inhaled deeply and settled down slowly.

"Ismail, raise the shutter. We're embarking on an adventure. But first, grab your camera. Is the battery charged?"

"Full charge," he replied. "What about the tape?" "Of course. Ready? What's on the agenda for the shoot?"

"You'll find out when the action begins." Ismail prepared the camera and inserted the tape.

"Where are we headed?" "To the blue house. Time to roll."

The rain had subsided, transforming into a gentle drizzle.

"So, Rathi, how about a drive? The weather is ideal for it."

"What's this all about?" Vasanthi presented the tape to her.

"Does this tape ring a bell?" Rathi's narrowed gaze flickered between Goudham and Ismail.

"I threw it in the marsh? How did you get it?"

"I'll be the one asking questions. If you stay honest and avoid foolishness, this will be just another night for you. Understand?"

She grasped the gravity of the situation. They strolled casually out of the store as Ismail shuttered it.

"Goudham, I'll trail behind in my car. You go with them. Mine's low on fuel for a night chase."

Sugandhi made her way to her vehicle. Goudham settled comfortably in the middle of the backseat, while Rathi took the driver's seat and Ismail positioned himself beside her.

"Rathi, here's the deal: blindfold him."

She revealed a soft velvet mask and shrouded his vision.

"So let the adventure commence," Goudham proclaimed, rolling down the window, ready for the journey ahead.

As the hatchback glided away from the town, the sedan trailed closely behind. Together, they traversed the tranquil bridge and veered right at the Y junction, embarking on a journey enveloped in serenity and crisp air. Silence hung between them as Rathi, captivated by the drive, stole glances at Goudham through the rearview mirror, where his smile reflected at her. Ismail supported his usual cheerful demeanor. The road meandered through the jungle, edging closer to the hills. Rathi took an adventurous detour, and at the journey's end, a mesmerizing glow awaited them.

Before them stood a quaint, blue, single-story house, resembling a scene from a fairy tale, leaving Goudham and Sugandhi awe-struck. For Ismail, each visit breathed new life into the house's enchanting allure.

"Welcome inside," Rathi beckoned her guests to her enchanting retreat.

"Ismail, let's capture this house on film!" "Pardon?" "Indeed, you're the director today."

He readied the camera and they ventured inside, where the interior appeared cluttered with both essential and superfluous items, stripping away the magic from the outside.

"Have a seat."

"Thank you for your warm hospitality. Now, please, take a seat yourself." Goudham gradually shifted the table.

"Ismail, adjust the camera for a steady view over my shoulder, framing both of us beautifully. Ensure her shot is clear and captivating." He carefully positioned the tripod to prove the perfect angle.

"Is it ready?" "It's rolling already—action!" At that moment, Ismail transformed into a director.

"So, Rathi, begin your tale. If all unfolds smoothly, I might bid you both farewell."

"What would you like to know? Why did I film him?"

"I've pieced that much together. But what I truly need to uncover is where you concealed his body?"

"What? Is he dead? I didn't kill him!" She erupted, panic rising.

"Okay, unveil the truth." Goudham leaned in intently.

"He grabbed me during the massage. I implored him to stop, but he persisted. I pushed his hand away and he seized me again, as if he had a right. Later, he offered me money for... favors." "And your response?"

"I accepted. I set a date and time—when Vasanthi ma'am was on the radio." "Then what transpired?" "I borrowed a camera and tape from Ismail, hiding in the corner of the room."

"Did you confide in Ismail about your plan?" "No, I kept it under wraps." "And then?"

"I acted as he asked, recording the encounter. I blackmailed him with the footage."

"What's the amount you demanded?" "30,00000₹." "Initially, he tried to intimidate me with threats of death." Rathi paused, lost in thought.

"And afterward?"

"I told him, 'You've only seen the demise of girls whose lives ebb away from the slightest drop of blood. If you don't deliver 30,00000₹, this tape will be distributed in every corner of the globe.' Do you understand, you bastard?" Goudham observed her mood shift, calm and composed.

"I declared this directly into his eyes." Rathi locked her gaze with his azure eyes.

"Did he pay you?"

"Yes, I received the funds and laid the groundwork for a fresh start. I bought a house, a car—the rest was pilfered but eventually retrieved." "What do you mean by stolen and retrieved?"

"I had 10,00,000₹ tucked away. After disposing of the tape in a marsh, I met an accident. When I regained consciousness, I was in a hospital, but the bag holding the money had vanished, and I felt no grievance. Yet, on discharge day, the bag reappeared beneath the bed."

"Did the hospital staff conceal it?" "They were utterly oblivious to its existence. Regardless, that moment stirred something deep within me. Only wealth can buy a semblance of safety in this perilous realm. I settled my car repairs and reignited my existence.

"With approximately 3,00,000₹ in hand, I strolled to the bank to make a deposit when I spotted an elderly gentleman. He was deep in discussion with the manager about a home loan secured for his daughter's surgery. His home teetered on the brink of confiscation, but I quietly intervened and cleared the debt."

Rathi concluded his tale with a satisfied grin.

"On that day, I felt a flicker of self-worth for the first time."

Goudham found himself at a loss for further inquiries.

"I speak the truth, especially to you. I too hail from the hills." "What led you to believe he belongs to the hills?" Sugandhi asked, taken aback, while Goudham comprehended.

"My parents are no more, yet I bear the burden of living an authentic life, much like you." Goudham didn't wish to delve deeper into the conversation.

"It's been ages since I crossed paths with a leisurely sloth, but sir, those azure hues still linger in your gaze."

"You share that shade as well. On a cloudy night, the sky keeps its blue secret."

Goudham rose from his chair.

"This is the reality; I have no more words. If you have doubts, feel free to arrest me and lock me away. And apologies about the knife game— the blade was never intended to harm, only to avoid harm. Yet, I am ready to accept my consequences." She admitted her faults gracefully.

"To punish, we require a crime; to penalize a crime, we need suspicion. Did Vasanthi witness anything out of the ordinary at your spa?" "No." "Are you open to further inquiry about the tape?"

"Not at the moment," Vasanthi replied, her expression solemn.

"The individual on the tape has raised no grievances about the footage or any extortion. And I have no objections, for you didn't cause bloodshed. Is there anything else you wish to express?" Tears began to stream down her cheeks.

"And Sugandhi, do you still desire her presence in your spa?" "Provided she harbors no fresh film production ambitions." "Then continue to work as usual tomorrow and stay put until the matter is resolved. Are we in agreement, Rathi?" "We are," she responded, nodding like a child.

Goudham approached and returned the knife to her.

"Consider this your second chance at life."

"Ismail, stop the recording." Goudham removed the tape and stepped out.

"Did that scoundrel truly meet his end?" Rathi asked, wiping her tears.

"Indeed, but his body has returned, brimming with life."

Goudham swung the door open as the rain began to fall once more.

"So Rathi and Ismail, I bid you farewell to this beautiful night, just as promised. I leave with the hope that honesty will be your guiding light. Don't let me down."

"You know where to find my blue abode? I will linger right here amid the opulence."

"Also predict another investigation. I am not the sole seeker of the culprit."

Rathi replied with a genuine smile as Goudham and Sugandhi climbed into the sedan.

"Goudham, are you really going to walk away from her just like that? No consequences?"

"Life has dealt her enough blows already. Now it's her turn to embrace living. We have a tape."

"But what if she's deceiving us?" "She hails from the hills. We know who we are, and from now on, she's your responsibility, understood?" "Honestly? You know what? You're a foolish police officer. You'd be better off leaving the force and finding peace in a monastery." Laughter erupted between them as the car, full of smiles, glided through the rain on the long journey ahead.

"Fasten your seatbelt." Goudham knew the routine.

"No, no, Sugandhi. The roads will be slick." "Just trust me." He buckled up, and the night race begun. All Goudham could perceive was the slick road shimmering behind them, while the wild wind barreled inside the vehicle. Before contemplation of the afterlife could settle in, they arrived at the Y junction. Goudham gently examined himself, gauging the pulse of his existence. With a manic grin and a steady engine, the sedan navigated onto the silent bridge. A red truck loomed behind them, moving just as quietly. Its rear bore a dolphin graphic, drenched in the downpour. The sedan veered left toward the town, while the truck took a right. The red engine halted at a store bursting with crimson carpets, vibrant decor, candles, stage props, drapes, and sound equipment.

'Soorya Light and Sound'. The truck driver darted inside, approaching a one-eyed man.

"Hey boss, the rain has really transformed the road."

"I would have stayed here if I could. How did today's run go?" "It was a wild ride." The driver produced a bundle of cash from his pocket and handed it to the boss. "Take this."

The boss returned a few bills as daily wages into the driver's hand.

"Don't you have an umbrella?" "I do." "Well then, good night."

"By the way, some officers were inquiring about you." One eye widened in surprise.

"What's wrong?" "They didn't say much. Just noted your name and address."

"Alright then. See you tomorrow."

The driver unfurled the umbrella and vanished into a shadowy alley. The one-eyed boss shut the window and climbed into the red truck, weighed down by the burdens of yesteryears. He navigated the silent bridge toward the mangroves and took the first turn. Thoughts lingered as he drove, and suddenly, the jungle loomed ahead. The truck skidded to a halt just in time. Through the pattering rain, he dashed into his home and stealthily approached a back window. "Soorya, Soorya," he whispered through the grates, stirring his wife from her slumber.

"Sorry, it's me. I didn't want to ring the bell. Please let me in."

In a sleepy daze, she made her way to the front door and opened it. He stepped inside, soaked to the bone, while she began questioning him in gestures.

"Yes, love, I was waiting for the driver."

She ran her fingers through his wet hair and motioned for him to dry off.

"Yes, I'll take care of it. You should sleep."

"Did you eat?" she queried, using signs for food.

"Yes, my dear, I've eaten. You go back to sleep." He gently urged her back to the realm of dreams. The truck seemed to watch him through the open window as he changed out of his drenched clothes. His wife lay her head against his chest as he slipped under the covers.

"Where's our boy?" Her gestures wrote down he was sleeping with grandpa.

"A few cops came here asking for you." Fear flickered in his one eye.

"Why?" "About the decoration kit for a wedding. That's all." She signed and caressed his chest. "The officer asked if you could stop by the station tomorrow morning between 10 and 11 since he's tied up with an investigation." She conveyed the summary with her hands and sleepy gaze.

"Oh, alright." She drifted back to sleep. He checked on her—already lost to slumber. With a quiet resolve, he slid out of bed without a sound. Approaching the windows, he gazed at the truck, its silhouette unwavering. The sudden brilliance rekindled forgotten memories, replaying like a film as he saw the truck's dark outline. A flash of lightning illuminated everything, casting eerie shadows that unveiled the ghostly marsh - the quicksand of the marshland.

Chapter 18
A Mirage of the Underwater

Winter Heat,
1994.

Beneath the evening sun, a fragrant river flowed, cradling two quiet individuals settled side by side. One, adorned with facial hair reminiscent of a lush herb farm, sat cross-legged on the earth, while the other, with a gaze reminiscent of a cloud of smoke, awaited a favor.

"Baba, just a small hit will suffice. I'll settle later." The herbal-bearded sage inhaled deeply, his eyes tracing the river's path.

"No, no grass." He opened a wooden chest beside him, and the stoner-eyed seeker leaned in with eager anticipation. Baba withdrew a chillum and packed it with cannabis, preparing for ignition when the other interrupted.

"Baba, come on, just a little hit!"

"Ahhh, Mr. Chandh." "It's Chandran, that's my name."

"Same difference. Like holy and moly." "Who's moly?"

"My wife. She left me three years ago." "I'm sorry to hear that."

Baba edged closer to his chillum, and Chandran chimed in again.

"Baba, please." "Chandh, let me connect with my wife first; I need this moment."

"You see, I'm quitting after this—thinking of taking one last ride."

"I've heard that before. Why not swap excuses, even if they're fibs?"

"No fib this time. I'm serious."

"You can share mine."

"Not at the moment; my girl's waiting in the truck." "Hmm."

Baba rummaged through his fanny pack and produced a chunky piece of cannabis.

"So, you're really quitting?" he inquired, stroking his herbal beard.

"Absolutely, Baba. This time I'm hitting the brakes hard. I can't afford to lose my girl."

He handed over the cannabis chunk, and Chandran inhaled its enticing aroma, glancing at Baba with a mischievous twinkle in his eye.

"Is this, sleepy mango weed?" "Straight from Sleepy Slope."

"Yes, indeed." "Wow! How did you score that? Only the wealthy usually get their hands on it."

"True, Baba is rich, just in a different currency." "Oh, Baba, you're a gem." He affectionately tugged at his long beard.

"Mr. Chandh, may your final hit be the most exquisite."

"You know Hero bhai?"

"Hero bhai, a splendid fellow." "Really?" "Absolutely. I once borrowed some opium from him without paying because I was strapped. He burned my beard, and it took three long years to regrow," he boasted, displaying his silky herbal locks.

"No way."

"I was once in your shoes, but now Baba thrives." "How?" "I've got apprentices who fund my meals and my stash—all I must do is chatter away. Interested in joining my ashram?"

"Where is your ashram?" "Anywhere beneath this expansive blue sky."

"I'll ponder it later, Baba. So, what you said about Hero Bhai is true?"

"I'm Baba, and I deal only in truth. You lack a beard like mine, so expect a fiery haircut." "Actually, a few days back, I got an invite from his farm—a truck trip that might fill my pockets."

"That's your decision, and those are your hair."

"I'll take my leave, Baba. Thanks for everything." "Farewell, Mr. Chand. Just don't lose faith in your girl." They said their goodbyes with a stoner-flavored peace sign, parting with fingers raised high.

Chandran strolled away from the river, glancing past the towering Nazi statue. The golden axe shimmered, radiating an intensity that rivaled the setting sun. Inside the Golden Tea stall, patrons marveled at the skilled tea artisan, who poured tea into glasses, each filled with an identical measure and a precisely matching number of bubbles.

"Wow, you truly are a tea master," one patron praised. Yet, the compliment were ignored as his gaze was entirely fixed on the effervescent bubbles that came to a perfect pause at the rim of the tea glass.

Nestled between the tea stand and the river stood a telephone booth. After a moment's hesitation, Chandran stepped inside, struggling to summon a forgotten number. He fished a small phone diary from his pocket and navigated to 'H' in the alphabet. The first name listed was Hero Bhai - 350666. With a lone 1₹ coin retrieved from his shirt pocket, he slipped it into the slot without a hint of regret and punched in the number. Just as he neared completion, he faltered; the zero eluded him, obscured by the sea of digits.

"I can't believe my foolish ancestors created this number. All I have left is a zero in my pocket, and now I've lost that, too." As he wrestled with his zero-dilemma, his gaze drifted to the Nazi statue, catching a glint of gold in its grip.

"What if we sneak back at midnight and swipe that axe? Who would notice? Seriously, what does a statue even need with a golden axe?" he mused. Nearby, a lively discussion unfolded among committee members at the chai stall.

"You are the tea master." "Ah, yes, all thanks to the golden axe, I suppose." "Shouldn't there be some sort of protection for the axe?" "And why? Who'd dare? Our golden axe fans committee is here! Anyone who tries will meet their end."

Maniacal laughter erupted from the tea stall, snapping Chandran back to reality as the phone beeped. Scraping his heist, he returned the receiver and the 1₹ coin fell back into his palm. Taking a deep breath, he inserted the coin once more, a surge of determination propelling him as he dialed with lightning speed. The call rang through to a shadowy warehouse illuminated by red lights, where a man with a small axe tucked into his trousers answered, and the countdown began.

"Hello." "Hero Bhai, can I speak with Hero Bhai? It's Chandran, the truck driver." "Hmm. Hold on." Ten seconds elapsed; forty more remained.

"A voice with a raspy edge crackled over the line."

"Yes." "Hero Bhai, it's me, Chandran." "Hmm." "About the trip, I can transport the goods across the border in my truck." "Okay. Just know this isn't a stroll through the park." "Yes, Hero Bhai." "Once you commit, there's no going back. Anyone who breaks Hero Bhai's promise will reap the consequences." Chandran felt a lump in his throat. "So, are you ready for this?" He had thirteen seconds left to respond and managed just one word: "Yes, Hero Bhai, I'm in." "Good. You know where to go?" "Yes, Hero Bhai. Sleepy Slope Poppy Farm, I mean—herbal farm." "Hmm, alright. Be there by tomorrow dawn at four. We'll kick off at 4:20, understand?" "Understood, Hero Bhai. Four o'clock, done." "Hmm." The raspy voice ended the call just as the timer hit zero. He stepped out of the booth, mentally counting down the hours—ten until the adventure would begin.

With purpose, he strode towards his red truck. Inside, a girl awaited him, fingers poised in questioning sign language.

"Where were you?" Her gestures reflected a long face.

"I had to make a call," he replied, not meeting her gaze. She leaned closer, determined to pierce through his facade.

"What?" "Lies?" "No, I don't! Why do you think I'm hiding something?"

"Because you are; your eyes betray you," her signs insisted.

"Soorya, I'm not talking to you." "I'm not talking to you either." She gestured as if sealing her lips shut.

"You don't talk anyway." Her face twisted in anger, and regret washed over him for his careless words. "Sorry, I didn't mean it." She playfully struck his arms, a spark of mischief in her eyes.

"Sorry, sorry," he murmured, enveloping her in a warm embrace, watching her ire dissolve like morning mist.

"Let's go." With that, they set off into the unknown.

As the clock struck midnight, Chandran and his red truck arrived at the Y junction. He meandered down the marsh road till the path's end. Before embarking on his journey, he felt compelled to make an important promise, so he strolled along the marsh path aglow with vibrant lights, leading to the bungalow. Inside, the area was adorned with sumptuous red carpets and white shamiana illuminated by colorful bulbs and warm yellow lights. The workers lay beneath their covers, deep in slumber. Scanning the scene, he found Shankaran lost in a peaceful sleep.

"Pa, Shakara Pa." "Huh? Who's there?" "It's me, Chandran." Groggily, he replied, "What? What's the time?" "I need to speak with you." "Now? About what?" "Please, step outside. It's crucial." "What is it?" Shankaran roused himself, and they made their way to the mangroves. The sky quivered, awakening Sugunan from his dreams. "What was that?" He fished a beedi from his pocket but found no matches. Chandran lit it for him, and after a long drag, Shankaran braced himself for the conversation.

"What is it? You woke me up to savor the night's mangrove beauty?" Unsure how to begin, Chandran quickly blurted out, "Can I marry Soorya?" "What? Now?" "I'm serious. She's at my house right now." That was all he needed to say.

"Does she love you?" "More than I love her. I just want to be by her side until the end."

"You woke me at dawn, offering this beedi, to seek my blessing for your marriage? I have another consent ceremony to attend in the morning!"

"What's your take on it?" "You fool, you love her, and she loves you. Consent is for those who are ready to unite. As her father, I have no objections. My daughter's happiness is what truly matters." Chandran leaped at Sugunan, enveloping him in a grateful embrace.

A flash of light pierced the sky, accompanied by a rumble of thunder.

"Shankar Pa, there's something else I wanted to tell you." "What now?"

"I've committed to transporting some plants across the territory. The trip is set for 4:00 from the Sleepy Slope."

Sugunan glanced at his watch. "It's nearly 3. Move quickly then."

"Money offers freedom to choose."

"What are you implying?"

"It's poppy."

"What? That's your business. You understand the risks involved."

"I'm aware and can't back out."

"Why not?" "The folks behind me are ruthless. They'll expect me, and if I don't appear, I shudder to think of the consequences." A sharp slap landed across his face.

"What were you thinking? At least consider my daughter!"

"Yes, Shankar Pa. I've misled her before about smoking grass. I even deceived her about this trip to spare her fear. But I've never lied about my feelings, never. A significant sum awaits us if I follow through, and who knows what could happen if I don't?"

Sugunan checked his watch again, the quiet tick-tock amplifying the tension.

"I must take this chance. I don't have other options."

"If you land in jail, who will care for my daughter? Leave it to me."

"You foolish old man, this is my blunder, likely my last. I would never deceive Soorya or you. That's my vow."

"Can you promise you'll return unscathed?"

He didn't respond. "Let's cling to faith."

Shankaran inhaled the final puff of his beedi and extinguished it against the ground.

"This is a threshold. I've made my choice."

Silence enveloped them, and the soft patter of rain stirred their thoughts.

"Be careful." "I will."

Chandran dashed into the downpour, climbing into the truck, half-soaked.

"Shall we?" Confusion buzzed in his mind, prompting him to silence the relentless thoughts swirling within. He retrieved some mango weed from the toolbox, rolling it into a beedi, which he lit as the truck jolted into motion. His gaze was fixed on the road, the heavens unleashing torrents. Rain splattered against the windshield like percussion, echoing at regular intervals. His thoughts spiraled into dread, plunging deeper still. In a fleeting moment, he glimpsed the river before snapping back to the road, where headlights bore down directly at him. He swerved to dodge the light, crashing instead into a Nazi statue. His golden axe swung free, plummeting into the open trunk with a thunderous crash, drowning his mind in shadows. Exiting the truck, he surveyed the scene as if on a sacred pilgrimage. Behind him lay his golden axe, and ahead stood a mangled car. A fleeting impulse to abscond with the axe and profit from it crossed his mind, but he dismissed it, shoving the axe back onto the road. Suddenly, the rain ceased abruptly, as if someone had flicked a switch, revealing a smoking car engine, the life within flickering faintly.

"Oh God, did he die?" He approached the wreck cautiously, peering inside. "It's a woman."

Amidst his foggy thoughts, a vestige of humanity remained. He extracted her gently, bag still clasped around her arm, and transported her to the front of the truck. The red engine raced toward the White Pills emergency ward. He carried her—still drawing breath—into the hospital, where staff appeared with stretchers, whisking her away to the ICU.

"What's your connection to the patient?" "She was sprawled on the ground beneath a crushed vehicle; I just brought her in. That's my part."

"In any case, you'll need to stay until the police finish their inquiry. It's the law."

Caught in the legal web, he scanned for prying eyes with glazed sight. He licked his upper lip and cautiously drifted toward the exit. Then, retreating his tongue, he bolted for the truck. The engine roared to life, soaring aimlessly into the void. His mind spiraled, disoriented amidst the chaos, narrowly weaving through bystanders on the road. In a blur, he veered toward them, crashing into a mound of stones. An object ejected from the trunk, landing amidst a garden of pebbles.

"Where do you think you're heading, pothead? Are you trying to take us all out?" He blinked, finding himself back at the accident scene, now surrounded by people. The truck rolled back and took flight once more, regurgitating the foolish mantra that the earth is round. He sped into the unknown, thoughts of past or future abandoned, lost in the visceral now, saturated with fear. He reached the Y junction, slamming the brakes on the deserted road.

"The opium journey?" he pondered. "A moment of pause?" he responded to himself.

"Why not ask for the time?" "But there's no one here, you stoner." He continued conversing with himself, noticing the sun's first light peeking from the east.

"Time out. Yes, a time out." "What's next?" "No need to call or give in just yet." "So what now?" "Let's sleep on it and chat with him when we're sober. We've already got an incident in our pocket."

"You sure?" As he glanced down to discern the brake from the clutch, his small roll of serenity lay beneath him, with a few puffs being still.

"Let's silence the relentless thoughts for now."

The truck rolled straight to the mangroves' edge, arriving at a wild clearing.He lit the little roll, allowing his mind to extinguish all thoughts, including the fear of his own demise.

Stripping off his drenched clothes, he draped them over the truck to dry. His bare form lay back in the seat, wrapping his arms around himself as deep slumber engulfed him in emptiness. His eyes closed under the brilliance of the full sun and reopened in the glow of the full moon. The silver light embraced his naked body amidst the wild mangroves as he stirred awake, tuning into the crickets' symphony. A stiff neck ached from his awkward sleeping position.

"Oh? Hero Bhai? Damn." There weren't any onlookers or even a timepiece in sight—only darkness enveloped him. He dressed in the dried clothes and prepared himself for the unexpected. Suddenly, he heard shuffling footsteps, and three peculiar figures appeared.

"What time is it?" His voice pierced the stillness, startling them in the dark. They stared, captivated by the lone figure inquiring about the time in the forest. One man squinted at the sky and replied, "Out of time."

"What?" "I warned you, no tricks at the ashram," Baba reminded his disciple.

"My apologies, Master."

"Oh Mr. Chaandh! Is that you?" "Yes, Baba." "What a surprise! What brings you here?"

"I'm pondering the same question." "Fantastic, it seems your last trip was quite the success." "I encountered the eerie marsh." "Glad to hear. So, you've quit, right? No second thoughts?"

"No Baba, I'm fine."

"Alright then, we'll try. Boys, scout for a clean spot."

"Yes, Master." They found a clear area, free from ants and snakes.

The trio settled in a triangle, lighting a chillum filled with cannabis. Smoke swirled as each took their turn to inhale, and the haze brought back memories of the previous night. He drifted back into rest until something jostled against his arms beneath the seat. It was a woman's bag, stained with some blood. He placed the bag on his lap and unzipped it, feeling little hope. As his hands explored the darkness, he grasped a stack of papers. Pulling one out, he held it under the full moon; the papers transformed into dense bundles of cash. For the first time, he beheld such a wealth of bills lying together. A cocktail of excitement, fear, joy, and madness twisted his insides. Without pausing to count, he tucked the bag under the spring seat. Rising slowly, he scanned the jungle; the sights and sounds felt vivid, but when he turned back to the three men, they appeared dreamlike and surreal.

"Is this a dream?"

He looked to clarify the chaos and rummaged through the truck for matches, but everything was soaked. The dreamer approached the group of smokers directly.

"Could I have a matchbox?" Baba handed him one. Chandran struck a match and inadvertently singed himself. "Ah, yes. The pain is undeniable."

Baba recognized the madness and extended the chillum towards him.

"You still seem adrift. Take a hit and discover the dead end." Chandran pondered.

"No, Baba. I'll act."

"Alright, you know where to find me." They continued their wanderings.

Chandran made his way to the truck and inspected the bag once more. It felt as tangible as the glowing full moon.

He silently reveled, planting a kiss on the truck's rear. A red liquid seeped from the dolphin emblem.

"What's this?" He touched it, only for the stain to vanish.

"Paint?" He clambered onto the tire, peering behind the truck's trunk where he spotted a sack.

"Ehh, what's this? Don't tell me it's money too?" He inched closer and staggered back in horror. His body quaked. He checked the sack again, and it held a headless corpse.

Fear made him mute, yet he erupted into a frantic monologue.

His heart urged him to dispose of it in the woods, but his mind warned of the lurking police dogs. Baba watched as the truck trembled under the tension.

"Everything alright over there, Mr. Chaandh?"

He pulled the truck out of the woods in silence. The steering quaked, but it was his hands trembling. Fixated ahead, he spotted several police jeeps on the road. The truck halted. His heart and mind engaged in a fierce debate.

"Abandon the truck and escape with the cash," his shaking heart proposed. "What about the truck's plate, you foolish heart?" "If the cops catch us, we're not just losing money; we'll end up in prison." "We'll surrender and tell the truth." "Hero bhai is going to eliminate you anyway," his trembling heart was adamant about priorities. "I can't lose my Soorya." The mind couldn't fathom that loss.

To his right stood a single-story cottage, an elderly man lounging on the porch with a whisky bottle, while a generator droned, drowning out all other sounds. He leaned into the field and noticed a hoe. An idea sparked within him.

"Just hang in there." "What's your plan?" The quaking heart inquired. "You'll sense the rhythm, but don't let it overwhelm you," the anxious mind cautioned the jittery heart. Both agreed to conceal the evidence. Chandran maneuvered the truck into a zigzag position near the wall for easier access. He climbed behind the trunk and nudged the bag across. The sack snagged on a protruding screw, releasing only the body into the field. Panic surged through his mind, sending his heart into another terrifying leap. He hastily dragged the headless figure by the leg to a designated burying spot. At that moment, both mind and heart shared a singular fear: the dread of losing the cash. They resolved to secure the money before digging. He dashed back to the truck. As he crouched to retrieve the bag, the sound of an approaching jeep grew nearer.

"Cops." His heart perceived arrest as the climax, but the mind insisted the tale wasn't over yet. Keeping his gaze lowered, he avoided looking up. The jeep halted directly in front of him, horns blaring.

"Who's the careless driver here?" After several honks, footsteps drew closer.

"Who parks a truck like this?" The jeep then reversed, and the footsteps retreated. Chandran cautiously lifted his head; calmness resumed.

"I'm on the verge of a heart attack. Let's hustle," his heart urged.

He slung the ladies' bag over his shoulder and leapt into the field. A clear patch was chosen, and the digging begun. Amid the generator's roar, he excavated frantically without taking any precautions. Madness carved out a 3-foot deep pit, and suddenly, darkness enveloped everything. A sliver of light seeped from a nearby generator as he pressed on, reaching a depth of 4 feet. Without hesitation, he placed the headless body into its grave, promptly covering it up. He left the hoe where it lay, and silence engulfed the scene. Blue sirens flickered on one side while candlelight glowed on the other. He stood frozen in the middle, waiting for the opportune moment to act. Gradually looking up, he noticed the full moon seeing his every move. The sirens wailed into the distance, a line of commotion fading away. His ears strained to capture their retreating sounds until silence reigned once more. He stealthily maneuvered through the dry leaves, his movements echoing ominously. The wall loomed ahead, leaving him with only one possibility—jump. By the end, his composure unraveled, leading to a clumsy wall traverse.

An unforgiving stone greeted him on the other side, its pain resonating louder than thunder. He scrambled into the driver's seat, bracing for a police pursuit, but the coast was clear. The red truck roared to life, soaring gracefully and landing beneath the statue of Nazi.

"Hero bhai?" His mind screamed, as did his heart. He grabbed the bag and glimpsed the cash. Buried within the notes, a surprising 1₹ coin caught his eye. With a trembling heart and a determined mind, he pushed forward.

The truck sped toward the sweet spot. He made a beeline for a telephone booth and dialed 350666. The call connected, and his heart raced coordinated.

"Hello." It was none other than hero bhai on the line.

"Hello, hero bhai, this is Chandran." An agitated breath echoed from the other end.

"Hero bhai, I had an accident yesterday. That's the reason?" Silence lingered, save for the irritated huffs from the other side.

"I can reimburse you for any damages caused by my actions."

"Hmm, where are you?" A question finally surfaced.

"Me? I'm near the golden axe."

"Hmm. Don't move. My crew will come to collect the money."

"Okay, hero bhai. My apologies again." "Hmm." The raspy voice cut off the call.

He found himself beneath the looming figure of a Nazi, the man armed and intimidating. Moments later, a van screeched to a halt, whisking him away. One assailant clamped his legs down while another restrained his arms, effectively pinning him to the seat. A third individual revealed an ax, glinting ominously from behind him.

"Please, I already said I would compensate for the loss."

"Hero Bhai wishes to convey that this isn't merely about money; it pertains to trust."

Chandran felt utterly paralyzed, unable to blink as one held his eyes wide open. The third man then brandished a bottle of engine oil, scooping up a spoonful. Heating it with a lighter, he mercilessly dripped the scorching liquid into one of Chandran's eyes.

"Breaking trust is akin to extinguishing an eye." He one eye burned before unceremoniously expelling him from the vehicle. They departed, leaving him semi-blind beneath the luminous moonlight.

"Ahhh!" His cry echoed, filled with rage and torment. Only the Moon bore witness to his suffering.

He plummeted into the depths of anguish, the world around him distorting into a surreal haze.

One eye scorched beyond recognition, reality twisted into a grotesque mirage. He plunged into the water, dragging the weight of his fury and pain deeper into the abyss. Uncertain of his direction, he pressed on, eventually reaching the bottom. His body floated amid an enveloping silence. With his eyes open despite the searing wound, he sought a flicker of purpose to endure. Then, an ethereal vision appeared—his beloved Soorya, glowing like a beacon of hope in his heated turmoil - a mirage of the underwater.

Chapter 19
The Tail of the Truth

Winter Read,
1999.

The Sun ascends in the east, gently coaxing the world from slumber, as every earthly gaze stirs from its dreams—every gaze but one. Chandran, invigorated by caffeine and a sleepless day, lay wide awake. The golden rays stretched luxuriously across the room, stirring memories of rest, while his fingers danced through the haze of his only drowsy companion, a sleepy eye. A last sip of once-steaming coffee, now cold, slid down his throat as he wandered towards the bedroom.

There she lay, his wife, immersed in deep sleep, and he felt an irresistible urge to plunge into the sanctuary of her warmth before surrendering to his final descent. He planted a soft kiss upon her cheek, and she turned toward him, her face blooming into a smile. The fabric of her saree slipped, revealing the smooth skin of her belly, and he traced it delicately, pressing the belly button beneath his thumb, igniting a flicker of life within her veins. His fingers ventured lower, offering a tender morning caress to her sacred femininity. Soorya's eyes burst open, alive with desire, as she pulled him closer, leaving a playful bite on his neck while his fingers explored the wetland beneath her belly.

"Shhh," he whispered, silencing her delighted smile with her own fingertip. "What has stirred you today?" her breath entwined with intrigue.

"Love, a love so deep that I wish to explore further," he replied.

"Oh, then I must taste it," she teased, as her fingers coaxed him into a rigid stone. In a flurry, he shed his clothes.

"Let's dive deeper." Their passion soared, spiraling into a frenzied embrace, culminating in a union that ignited their souls.

"Ahh." Slowly, laughter faded from his mind, making way for the unfolding truth.

"I'll head to the station."

"I'll come too."

"No, you stay. Our little boy will seek us."

"Alright, but return swiftly. I'll be eagerly waiting for my bigger boy. The morning has only just begun." She winked, caressing him anew. Fear coiled around him as he dressed. The truck roared to life, crossing the silent bridge. Upon arrival in town, an eerie quiet enveloped him. The truck rolled beneath the station's arch, his hands stiff over the trembling wheels. Taking a steadying breath, he stepped into the station.

"Greetings, sir. I was told to come for some business. I'm Chandran," he announced as Goudham appeared from the shadows, recognition flashing in his smile, betraying the unseen answers lurking in Chandran's fear.

"Hello, Chandran. Please, come in. The work is indeed mine," Goudham beckoned warmly.

"Alright." Chandran stepped forward, tension creeping in as Goudham wrapped an arm around his shoulder.

"It's about your work with light and sound. You do remember that night, right? The bag of money, the ceremonial lights, the generator's hum?" Goudham launched into a list, meticulously recounting the details. Chandran neither affirmed nor denied.

"What about a headless body?" Goudham felt the pulse of nerves racing beneath his touch.

"Or simply a body. I avoid putting words in other people's mouths. Speak your truth, that's all I ask. If honesty were easy, this world would be a marvel." Surrounding officers began to gather.

"Take him to the interrogation room." They seized him from either side, ushering him into a dimly lit chamber, a bright light illuminating the interrogation table where hard truths awaited.

"Sir, I vow to speak solely the truth."

"That's the kind of honesty we truly yearn for."

"Very well." The narrative ignited, unfurled its wings, soared in a spiral, and made an unexpected plunge into the scent river. The officers were struck by the electrifying tale.

"You could pen a novel, Chandran. How swiftly did you conjure such a story?" Paul removed his hat, scratching his head in disbelief.

"This is the undeniable truth, sir. I swear on my wife and child."

"Enough with the oaths." Paul slammed his hand on the table.

"Behold my lost eye—does it deceive you? Sir, trust me. I took the bag that day and returned it intact. We never laid a finger on the money, not even for my eye surgery."

"How much was in there?"

"Honestly, I didn't bother counting; it was an overwhelming sum for me."

"So your family was in the loop."

"Yes."

"Then why the dishonesty?"

"We don't lie; we may have tried to obscure the truth. What were we supposed to say? There was a headless body in the trunk, and I didn't know how to handle it, so I buried it. Even now, my mind spins recalling that day. Had it happened recently, I would have rushed to the station; those were my hazy days."

"Did your haziness fade or do we need to assist with that?" Paul teased, as if grasping his neck.

"Sir, I can't be sure if any of you believe my tale. You have that machine, right? The one that detects lies? I've never harmed anyone and would assert that anywhere. If I had done it, my family would have urged me to turn myself in. They recognize my innocence—we simply awaited the truth to surface."

"And what about those awaiting the return of that body?"

"I assumed it was Devachan, which is why I didn't report it."

"Why's that?"

"While burying it, I noticed the expensive clothes, but when I heard he was missing, I connected the dots. Then he never resurfaced. Nobody expects him back. Those girls are fortunate someone dealt with him; that's all I'll say."

"So, you harbored resentment for him?"

"Sir, just ask those girls—they'd echo the same sentiment. We needn't venerate a rotten soul just because he's left."

"Then, where did the body fall from? The sky?"

"My guess would be yes."

"What? Are you mocking us?" Paul slammed the table again.

"No jest. My truck was parked right by the wall, as you've all seen. Either someone dropped the body onto my truck or loaded it while I was sleeping in the woods."

"What about Baba?"

"I don't believe so, but you can investigate that."

The officers exchanged bewildered glances.

"Even after years, I'm grappling with whether it was a dream or reality. If I can't even convince myself, how can I persuade others? I have no connection to that corpse."

"Yet, you're the one who buried it, correct?"

"I know, sir. It was all driven by fear. Fear of punishment for a crime I didn't commit. Honestly, I wasn't afraid of going to jail. I feared losing Soorya. I've lied to her countless times, but never since that day. She granted me enough opportunities to lead an honest life, but it took losing an eye for me to see the way."

"Why didn't you report the attack?"

"When I plunged into the river, my first thought upon resurfacing was to slit his throat. But visions of Soorya led me to choose forgiveness."

"So, you neither committed the act nor noticed anything amiss, yet you buried the body?" Ramani probed further.

"Sir, I have nothing more to say. If I were the petty criminal you believe me to be, I would have left that poor woman on the road to die to save myself. Had I minded my own affairs, I'd still have my eye. Sir, I am not a criminal."

"But you are foolish."

"I'll accept that."

"Acceptance won't always suffice."

"If stupidity were a crime, the entire planet would be incarcerated."

"Attempting to destroy evidence carries the same weight as committing the crime itself." Chandran fell silent.

"Well, for the time being, we're not filing any charges while we search for the true culprit. This is a favor I'm offering you at my own risk."

"I'll carry this memory with me until my final breath."

"So, Paul, Ramani, anything else to contribute?" Goudham was firm in his stance.

They exchanged glances and shook their heads in unison.

"Alright, Chandran, you can go. But stay within the boundaries; report to the station for any urgent departures."

"Of course, sir." He embraced Goudham.

"I apologize, sir. No disrespect meant."

"No offense taken. We're just at a loss for what else to ask since you've sealed the deal."

"Let's leave the psychoanalysis behind. Goudham, it's your call to release him. I won't partake in this."

Ramani stated her position clearly.

"We're lost on whom to trust and what to believe now. We're merely two officers on the hunt for a murderer." Paul and Ramani united in their resolve. Chandran glanced at Goudham and smiled back.

"Could we have a moment?" Goudham led them out of the interrogation space.

"What is this madness all about?"

"What else is there to inquire about? He was even open to a lie detector. His tale aligns too—the accident, the red truck—what more do we need to pursue?"

"We should incarcerate him for concealing evidence." "I agree, but tell me how that's going to impact this case."

"Goudham, isn't that contradictory to the law?"

"What is the law, exactly? A wealthy man kills, then claims it was suicide? A drug lord inflicts harm and roams free? If the law does not protect the innocent, then who shall? Do you believe he poses a threat?"

"That's not the core issue." "Then what is? Ramani and Paul were left speechless.

"Putting him behind bars changes nothing; it would merely shatter a family. You two decide.

I have no intention of playing the puppet master; in my district, he's simply a fool who made a grave mistake. He has lost his outer eye—must we also extinguish the light in his soul? Think this through."

Ramani and Paul mulled over his words, grappling for clarity. They returned to the interrogation room.

"You're free to go for now."

"Thank you. And if you ever find it necessary to arrest me, please don't come to my home. My boy is young, and he may draw his own conclusions. He believes I lost my eye in an accident. Just call, and my truck will arrive instantly. Please have faith in me."

"It's all right. We know where to find you. You can leave now."

"Thank you, sir." A tear escaped from his solitary eye.

"I'm sorry, sir. I've been bearing this heavy weight for too long. It feels liberating to let it go."

Empathy washed over everyone present as the one-eyed man and his red truck drove away.

"Goudham, is this your approach to solving the case? I have my doubts."

"I'm not insisting you follow my lead, but I can't align with your methods either. Apologies.

Arrest that Hero Bhai first; then let's converse." Goudham strode back to his desk with determination. Paul and Ramani entered slowly.

"This is simply how things operate." "No, Rama, that's not how my world functions."

"Let's avoid a debate. If we let Chandran go, what's our next move?"

"What about the girl in the skeleton mask?"

Goudham felt drained of energy to defend another conviction, letting his heart guide his decision instead.

"Where on earth do we search for her?" "You've hit the nail on the head."

"Didn't he mention the money and the girl?" "Yes, exactly. That's precisely where my thoughts led as well."

Paul and Ramani found a shared understanding.

"What's your take, Goudham?"

He pulled out a tape from his bag and handed it to them.

"I completely overlooked this."

"What is it?"

"It's the confession of that skeleton girl."

"What? How did you find her? Who is she?" Ramani was engulfed in confusion.

"You've guessed it correctly—it's Rathi, but she isn't the one responsible."

"Then who?"

"That's still a mystery we need to unravel. I'm taking a half-day off today since both paths seem blocked."

"Why didn't you bring her in?"

"You both observe and draw your own conclusions. Feel free to apprehend her if you honestly believe she's the murderer. There's no need for my consent; act on what you feel is right. You have total autonomy in this investigation. I've also made a decision for when we close this case."

"What's that?"

"Let's unravel the mystery first, and I'll make my move in due time."

"Goudham, do you know what I've noticed about you?"

"Yes, Rama."

"You hold countless secrets."

"Some secrets are indeed sacred."

"That's a perspective I'm not familiar with. Can you expand on that?"

"Okay, I'll share one of these sacred secrets."

"Yes, please?" Paul and Ramani leaned in, eager to listen.

"I may not discern if someone speaks the truth, but I can sense when someone is deceiving. Eyes reveal much."

"Isn't lying and failing to grasp the truth essentially the same?"

"Consider this: if we are absolute strangers claiming not to know each other, that might not hold true. Perhaps we recognize each other, or not, but our ignorance binds us. Conversely, if we have mutual familiarity, yet declare we're strangers, we're both aware it's a falsehood, wouldn't you agree?"

Ramani, overwhelmed, removed her cap.

"Does Paul grasp what I'm getting at?"

"I can't say I fully understand, but it's clear that Ramani is utterly perplexed."

"Then let's put it to the test. Tell me if I'm right or wrong." A playful exchange began as Goudham turned to meet her gaze.

"Ready." "Go ahead."

"The first sight I cherish upon waking is my reflection in the mirror."

Goudham studied her eyes closely. "That's a falsehood." Ramani blinked in surprise.

"And what's the first thing you love to see after waking?"

"My husband's face." She admitted the deception. "See?"

"Next. I prefer tea to coffee." Goudham resumed his scrutiny.

"That's true. So why didn't you switch when I ordered coffee?" "Paul, this guy is wicked."

"Alright, one more. This one will be a challenge."

"Fire away."

"My husband first proposed to me by the sweet sea." Goudham's gaze pierced through hers, though he hesitated slightly.

"Hmm, there's a sliver of truth there, but ultimately, it's a fabrication." Ramani conceded with a smile. "Correct."

"So, what is the tale?" "The reality is we were by the sea, but the twist is I proposed to him." Laughter erupted from Ramani, her cheeks flushed.

"See?"

"How did you unravel that?" "I'm not sure. Perhaps the hills whispered their secrets to me."

Goudham stepped into a dressing room, emerging sans uniform.

"Hmm, what makes you shy away from this case?"

"I'm not escaping; I just lack interest in exploring the demise of another killer."

"Alright, what's on your agenda today?" "Let's discover."

"Maybe a cup of tsunami." Paul grinned, eliciting a quiet response from Goudham.

"Paul, this guy is truly crafty. He found the skeleton girl, collected her confession, and then set her free." "Her residence, vehicle details—everything's on that tape. See you tomorrow, everyone." "What? Are you walking home?" "Yes; movement offers a break from thinking. Occasionally, stepping away from thinking can lead to revelations."

It's a tranquil twilight. Goudham strolled down the quiet lane, savoring each step without haste. As he passed the art gallery, joyous festivities erupted in a corner, filled with laughter and celebration.

Lucy was busy immortalizing the moments with her camera, capturing the bride and groom clad in their wedding finery.

"Just embrace it, man. Feel the softness of your lover's cheeks."

Taking her advice to heart, the guy gently caressed the girl's cheek. A camera assistant held a reflector, crafting the ideal lighting as Lucy snapped the picture.

"Spot on."

"Now, let's venture into nature and chase the sunset."

"Hey there, Lucy." "Hello, sir! How's everything?" "Pretty good. What's happening?"

"Wedding photography. And please, don't put me in the box of typical, lifeless photography. My work is much more candid. The blue-painted building just to the left, on the top floor, that's Lucify Studio. My creative haven."

"Great. I dropped off some negative film for processing at your studio last week. The man mentioned I could pick it up today."

"Ah, you mean the old man? That's my dad. He's currently out of town."

"Okay, when can I retrieve the photos?"

"Is it urgent?" "Sort of."

"To be honest, I'm swamped right now and need to snap a few shots before the sun dips below the horizon. Swing by my studio later tonight; I'll be working late into the hours."

"Perfect, I'll see you tonight." "Alright, sir."

Lucy left with her crew, while Goudham ambled alone. After a mile of wandering, he returned to his quarters and instantly indulged in a refreshing shower. Glancing in the mirror, he admired his relaxed form and tranquil mind.

"Be a fire, but don't burn out," he murmured to his reflection.

Donning a light linen shirt and comfortable, stretchable jeans, he ventured towards the beach, where the CresCent Café awaited. He opened the door to the café, only to find two unfamiliar girls inside—Khadija was absent.

"Hi sir, how may I assist you?" He approached the counter.

"Uh, was there someone named Khadija here?"

"Oh, I'm Fathima, her sister. She's stepped out for supplies." "Pleasure to meet you, I'm Goudham."

A girl with striking golden eyes peered at him from the kitchen as if she were seeing a miscreant. "That's my friend Champakam. She's a canoe driver and works in the kitchen when she can."

"Is that so?" With a playful nudge of her tummy, she approached the counter.

"May I get something to drink?" "Sure, I'll have a black coffee."

"Please, have a seat."

Fathima took the order and drifted back to the kitchen.

"You didn't just come for coffee, did you?"

Goudham was taken aback by the golden-eyed girl's uncanny insight.

"And I suspect you both share a connection deeper than friendship."

Their eyes met, and the air buzzed with laughter.

"What's the ruckus?" Fathima called from the kitchen.

"Paathu, please whip up an espresso for our charming guest here." She placed a stronger order.

Goudham wandered over to a shelf adorned with audio cassettes and books, seeking the perfect soundtrack.

"Customers can request a dedication. We'll play it right here."

He chose a cassette and presented it at the counter.

"Michael Jackson." "There is another fan of the King of Pop?" Champakam chimed.

"Who could that be?" "Someone with eyes just as blue as yours." Goudham blushed at the implication as he handed over the cassette. Soon, 'Smooth Criminal' filled the air, inspiring his body to sway to the rhythm. He glanced back, catching the girls reveling in his impromptu performance. With a grin, he toned down the tempo.

"This is occasionally a dance café. We'd love to join in if you're up for it." The girls giggled in response. He simply nodded along with the beat and returned to the shelf, his gaze landing on an interesting book he randomly selected to read.

"Your coffee is ready." Fathima placed the cup on the stone table.

"Thanks, Fathima." "Just Paathu. That's what everyone calls me." "Thanks, Paathu." "You're welcome. Enjoy." His gleaming blue eyes took a sip as they turned towards the evening's azure embrace.

He settled into a cozy position on the chair when a girl with sky-blue eyes appeared, effortlessly displacing his tranquility.

"Wow, what a surprise! Did you just arrive?"

"Yes, Paathu just picked up the coffee."

"Great! Are you free today?"

"I took some time off."

"What's going on? Is your mind racing again?"

"Actually, it's gone silent."

"In that case, I have something special for you. You wanted to learn about scent creation, right?"

"Perfect! I'd love that."

"How does tonight sound? A fragrant concoction followed by a delightful dinner?"

"It sounds like life can't get any better." Their eyes exchanged a knowing smile as the magic was already in motion.

"We can head out after sunset, if that works for you."

"I have all day to spend with you. I'm completely free."

"I'm really glad to see you. Enjoy your coffee." Khadija wandered into the storeroom, while the other two girls approached him with an inquisitive gaze.

"So, you're the cop, huh?" Fathima kicked off the questioning.

"If that's what you say," he replied, sipping his drink with a grin.

"Paathu, I told you he's not just here for the coffee," Champakam chimed in. Goudham stifled a laugh as he took another sip, captivated by Champakam's golden eyes that reminded him of his mother.

"Aren't you the one looking into that headless skeleton?" Fathima interjected.

"Paathu, let's skip the details—my mind needs a breather, which is why I'm here."

"Alright then, are you enjoying some solitude?"

"Not really, please join me and let's chat about something else."

The girls took seats across from him.

"I've got one—it's about her."

"I know where you're headed, Paathu. It's about my eyes, isn't it?"

"Of course! The world should know, especially our sister's handsome boyfriend."

Fathima couldn't help but reveal the truth.

"My sister and I have only met once."

"Since that brief encounter, she must have mentioned you a thousand times. It's dull being around a sister who's like a one-sided tape, if you catch my drift." Goudham grinned, watching Khadija busy herself in the store.

"So as her sister, it's only fair that I hear the other side of the tape."

"How's the tape spinning so far?"

"Hmm, so far, so good."

"Thanks. I hadn't realized she had such a beautiful sister, and that the sister had an even lovelier girlfriend." The girls exchanged glances, murmuring amongst themselves.

"How did you know we're more than just friends?"

"Truth is usually easy to digest but tough to accept. Does your sister know?"

"She knows, but we haven't publicly declared it yet."

"Those who truly don't care don't need to know every aspect of our lives."

"That does hold some truth, right?"

"So, you ladies were mentioning something about her eyes?"

"Yes, I'm tired of repeating that to everyone."

"I'm fatigued from listening to it."

"But now you have a fresh audience."

"She was born blind."

"Is that so?" Goudham was already intrigued, eager to delve deeper into her vivid insights.

"What sensations do you perceive? Sighted and sightless?"

"In that abyss, I believed everyone could bask in the radiance, only to discover they were enveloped in a far deeper darkness," Champakam remarked, gazing at the world reflected in the mirrored cage. Eyes turned toward the west as the sun took its leave without a word of farewell.

"This view never grows old," Khadija chimed in, stepping closer, her gaze piercing into Goudham's eyes, both sharing a bond of love and life.

"Sometimes I ponder whether a camera eye could immortalize our visions. Would it allow us to convince others of our beliefs?" Goudham's words were met with quiet nods of agreement from all.

"Or what if a human eye could truly perceive as you do?" Both blue-eyed souls abandoned the sun, enveloping each other's gaze. As they turned back to the sea, the sun had already made its exit.

"Shall we take our leave?"

"Absolutely." Goudham finished his last sip of coffee and picked up a random book.

"Mind if I borrow that book?"

"Of course. What's on your reading list, sir?" Gautam lifted the book's cover toward Champakam.

"Oh, wonderful choice! You'll be astounded if magical realism fascinates you."

"That's my favorite genre."

"There lies an imaginary boundary between loving and living known as life. Only those who truly live can see both the magic and the mundane." All eyes were fixated on Champakam as she delivered the lines with grace.

"Just a cherished line from the book."

"Then let's stride bravely into life, everyone."

As they ventured forth, darkness enveloped them, the full moon illuminating the night sky.

"Wow, I was just asking Champakam if we'd see a full moon, and here it is."

"Oftentimes, all answers are inscribed already; we just need the right questions to give them meaning," Goudham said, his eyes aglow as he turned to Khadija.

"So, let's make our way," Khadija replied, sealing the glass cage while Goudham lowered the shutter for her. They traversed a narrow, shadowy lane. Fathima and Champakam led the way, arms intertwined, while Goudham and Khadija supported an invisible boundary of their own. The rhythm of their steps created an awkward play of intimacy, like life's gentle tug-of-war. Locking eyes, they felt an irresistible magnetic pull, and Goudham tenderly grasped her delicate fingers while Khadija offered her palm willingly. They turned another tight corner, and there, the full moon glimmered on the ground, as if it had tumbled down from the heavens. Its reflection danced in the air, beside a quaint cottage nestled by the river.

"Wow, you all reside here." "This is our home, officer." "We have the river and the sea at your doorstep."

"Indeed, we are the crossroads of both." Fathima swung open the wooden gate.

In the courtyard, an elderly woman reclined in an easy chair, her gaze fixed on the moon. "Mom, meet my friend," Khadija introduced him.

"Goudham, this is Noora."

Her eyes sparkled with a smile directed at him before returning to the moon's glow.

"Mom, would you like to join us at the woodhouse to see how the fragrance is crafted?"

"No, I will remain here. You all go ahead." Her voice broke the silence of years. The girls showered Noora with affectionate kisses.

"Hey, we have a guest to tend to. Watch over him for me. I need to venture deeper into the moonlight."

"Alright, Mom." They left her to her lunar reverie and stepped inside.

The girls were enveloped in a joyous whirlwind, their hearts dancing with delight.

"Paathu, you both prepare dinner. I'll lead him to the alchemy house."

Khadija guided Goudham into a small wooden structure attached to the main house.

They stepped into a shadowy room. The door clicked shut behind them, and the aroma of earth embraced them.

"Goudham, can you come a little closer?" she asked in the dimness. He extended his arms, and she planted a gentle kiss on his cheek.

"Thank you. You can't imagine what just occurred!"

"I can hear you but can't see you," she giggled, before silence enveloped them once more.

"Do you need light? I adore conversing in the dark." She moved to the side, searching for the switch.

"Are you all right? Did you find the light?"

"How about a bit of natural illumination?" She turned a wheel in the corner, and the wooden ceiling opened, letting in the moonlight that spilled across the room.

"Wow." "It has been ages since mom exchanged words with anyone."

"What transpired with her?"

"She was engulfed in a storm of disbelief, forever haunted by the moment Dad slipped away into the river's embrace. It was an unexpected heart attack, and she found herself adrift, unable to swim. Ah, let's avoid that tale."

"What truly counts is that mom has returned."

"And you're the catalyst." He brushed off the credit and surveyed the room like an explorer on the brink of discovery. The space was adorned with both small and grand clay sculptures shimmering in the lunar glow. Goudham examined and touched each piece of artistry.

"Who created all of this?"

"Paathu. This is her workshop. And behold the machine."

Khadija retrieved a long silk cloth from a contraption. A large clay pot dangled above a fire pit below. A pipe connected the pot, directing the smoke to another expansive clay chamber. Nearby lay stacks of bags filled with dried champa flowers.

"These sacks hold dried champa flowers. We place them in boiling water within these pots, sealing them with clay lids. We ensure that everything the smoke touches is earthen. The clay pipe feeds the smoke into that chamber. The tricky part is measuring the water correctly for boiling. We continue adding water as the smoke condenses into fragrant droplets. The meter writes down the quantity, but only an expert can discern the quality. When all is done, we capture the essence of rain in aromatic oil."

"This is brilliant." "It requires an entire day to complete. Yes, it's a complex science."

Fathima entered the workshop.

"How does the alchemy fare?"

"Paathu, that's how we revive the scent of rain."

"Here, every season is marked by the fragrance of rain. Let's enjoy dinner." They all bounded into the house, settling onto the floor mat atop the mosaic tiles. The food was served in bowls, and he peered at it with curiosity.

"This is cream of mushroom soup," Fathima announced proudly.

Gautam savored a rich, creamy mouthful, letting the flavor dissolve on his palate. Without hesitation, he indulged in the contents of the bowl. Seeing his enjoyment, the others joined in, smiles lighting their faces. He paused briefly to glance at Khadija, who was feeding her mother, but after several bites, she closed her lips.

"Is that enough, dear?" she inquired, finishing off the last of the bowl. Her gaze shifted to Goudham as she raised her eyebrows playfully, to which he responded with a teasing flutter of his eyelashes.

"Have some more."

Fathima obliged, serving him another helping, which he gladly accepted. Satisfied and content, he relinquished the spoon, having experienced the most delightful meal since setting foot in this land. Exiting into the night, the moon briefly concealed itself among the clouds, yet a radiant smile adorned his face. After tucking her mother into bed, Khadija stepped outside to join him under the dark sky.

"How was the soup?" "Delicious," Gautam grinned, bringing all his fingers together to kiss them.

For a moment, she fell silent, her eyes drifting to the stitch on his forehead.

"Who's waiting for you at home?" "This sky is my home; I carry it with me everywhere."

"What about your family?" "My mother haunts my memories; she took her life when I was young."

Her shock was palpable as Gautam peered into her azure eyes.

"We hail from the hills, but we lost our essence. My mother's lifeless form was discovered by the sweet sea, the last memory imprinted in my mind as waves rocked her gently, like a newborn in a cradle. My grandfather descended upon me, covering my eyes, oblivious to the fact that one cannot blind the unseen." Her delicate fingers entwined with his arm.

"She was with child, and the corpse laid in isolation. The fate of the baby stays a mystery. Grandfather passed away a few years back; now I stand alone. All I have left of my family are echoes, devoid of life. Let's not dwell on that."

"Agreed." Their foreheads met in a tender touch.

"You forgot the book, officer." Paathu's reminder broke through their intimate moment.

"You joy thief." "Can cops be charged with stealing joy? Seems like that should be outlawed."

"Indeed." He took hold of the book.

"Grace Francis," Khadija exclaimed, recollecting a forgotten tale. "Her husband, Francis."

Goudham's ears perked up at the mention. "He visited one night for water, wandering from the beach, suddenly gripped by thirst. On his way back, a helmeted man took him, and his body was discovered the following day in the scent river."

"What? A man in a helmet?"

"I wasn't the witness; it was my mother whose eyes caught the unsettling scene of him being hurried into a car against his will. Her portrayal was as vivid as a painter's brush stroke. We shared our tale with the police officers, but their indifference was as palpable as a shadow at dusk."

A shadow flickered behind them; it was Noora.

"Mother, you startled us! Not feeling sleepy?"

She regarded Goudham, affectionately patting his cheek.

"The man who abducted the old man that night had an axe tattoo inscribed on the nape of his neck." With that, she retreated to her bedroom. The sky once again unveiled the moon's luminosity above them. Suddenly, a spark ignited in Goudham's mind, ideas swirling into articulation.

"I must take my leave." Why the sudden urgency?" "I sense I'm nearing the truth. The light has been shrouded by clouds, but now they've dispersed."

Confusion settled in upon the others.

"No, it's about the case. I'll catch up with you later. Good night." He gently held Khadija's hand, offering a silent farewell. Her eyes twinkled with understanding.

The bullet tore free from the depths of the sea and glided across the silent bridge toward the shimmering town. He paused amidst the chaos, plunging into contemplation.

"Someone who adored Francis must be the murderer. Could it possibly be Grace herself?"

"What?" A passerby misinterpreted his murmurs as directed at him. "Oh, nothing. I was just..."

He reignited the energy of the bullet and resumed his journey toward the studio, where lights blazed on the upper level.

Lucify Studio.

A narrow wooden staircase led to the first floor of a blue-painted building. Upon entering the studio, Lucy peeked out from a room bathed in red light.

"Hello, sir! Just a moment." "Sure." Goudham diverted his attention, admiring the array of nature and human portraits adorning the walls.

"Hi, sir! Do you have the receipt?" "Ah, yes." He rummaged through his pocket, pulling out a slip of paper that also revealed a letter from Devachan.

"Did you capture all these images of nature?"

"This is my father's studio. I made a few changes to give it a lucid feel."

"Where's your father now?" "Both my parents are traveling. Each winter, they explore a new region."

"Why don't you join them?" "I traveled a great deal with them growing up, but now I have my own ambitions, and they've immersed themselves in theirs." Lucy drifted through a white door leading to the allure of the red room, which inexplicably beckoned Goudham.

"What's inside that room?" "Ah, that's the dark room. My dad preferred to call it the light room since that's where every negative transforms into a positive."

"Could I peek? I've never been inside a dark room."

"Of course, come on in." He opened the door to darkness, and everything around was washed in red. The atmosphere felt eerie yet captivating to him. He extracted the letter from his pocket, gazing at it once more in a swirling dream of unraveling hidden truths. His eyes drew near to the words.

'I can sense a voice calling. There's no turning back. Goodbye.'

He saw a multitude of missing letters lurking beneath the surface, as if an unseen hand had erased the pencil's traces from the page.

"Here's your photo." Lucy retrieved a picture drying in the corner.

"Who is this?" "Ah, that's my mother." They both exited the dark room.

"Wow, she's stunning. Golden eyes, huh?" "Indeed, she was beautiful."

"My condolences for your loss."

"She continues to thrive within my cherished memories." "What's the cost?" "50₹."

"So you'll be working alone through the night?" "No, Christy will arrive shortly."

"It's comforting to know someone would forgo their peaceful slumber for us, isn't it?"

"It's even more fulfilling to see that very same someone dreaming soundly beside you." A romantic grin spread across Goudham's face as he absorbed her heartfelt words.

"Goodbye, Lucy." "Goodnight, sir."

With a radiant smile, he left the studio.

The bullet arrived at his quarters, his mind consumed with deciphering the cryptic notes. Now, it was time for rest.

"No need to hurry; we'll unravel the mysteries in the morning," he reassured himself as he entered the room with intention. Undressing as usual, he bade his shadow goodnight in the mirror. He gently applied a drizzle of rain-scented aroma oil to his temples and crawled into bed, where a book awaited him, eager to be opened and explored.

'Once upon a time, there existed a world with a mouth but no head. Their tails were so elongated that they couldn't resist biting them. Each day, they chased their tails, trying to catch them, but to no avail. This exhausting pursuit continued until the day they discovered a head—a head with no tail.'

Goudham found himself resonating with those whimsical lines, yet he stayed mystified about the narrative ahead. He read the cover page: a novel by Grace Francis - the tale of the truth.

Chapter 20
The Hex of the Turtle

Winter Tale,
1999.

The sun's first light began to unfurl across the land. Gautam lounged outside in his chair, cradling a steaming cup of coffee with a book nestled under an incandescent bulb. He was deeply engrossed in the text, navigating the winding path from beginning to end in search of truth.

"'Life is a journey, much like a lost child wandering through a forest. The mind questions the heart, whispering, "Fear and Hunger." True, but that innocent mind hasn't yet been shackled by the weight of understanding. From that moment onward, existence transforms into a quest. The child doesn't yearn for an artfully crafted life when faced with chaos; instead, it embraces the formlessness and begins to sculpt its own destiny. Thus, we give birth to consciousness.'

The mind conversed with the heart." The only sounds piercing the stillness were the scratchy calls of ravens, yet they did not disrupt his concentration. Then the crow of a rooster pierced the air, signaling his awakening. Gautam stifled a yawn and glanced at his empty coffee cup. With a gentle nudge, he disrupted the intricate musings swirling in his mind.

"What a journey!" Soon after, another cup of coffee appeared. The compact book was nearing its end, consumed in just one night and dawn. He granted his mind a brief respite as he savored the caffeine; his thoughts became less tethered and his body felt more cumbersome. An abundance of energy simmered beneath the surface, ready to burst forth. He sprang from his seat, dressed in nothing but boxers, and unleashed his body in a flurry of crunches, stretches, sit-ups, push-ups, and jumping jacks until sweat became the language of surrender between his body and mind.

He hopped on his bullet and sped toward the river, plunging into its cool embrace. A hint of sleep still lingered in his bare frame, but a few invigorating laps soon laid the groundwork for a fresh day. His mind expanded with new possibilities as he returned home. Thoughts began to align while he blended two ripe mangos with a handful of cashews in the juicer. Clad in his uniform and boots, he carried with him the thread of truth that was nearly unraveled, tucking the letter safely inside the book. The blue jeep rolled to a stop, and he climbed in without hesitation.

"Paul, I finally witnessed a miracle! Our Gautam is punctual."

"And there's a glow about him! It's as if the full moon has smiled down."

"Good morning, everyone." Today, he was a man of few words, offering them a radiant smile.

"What's on your reading list?" "Grace Francis. Speaking of which, I've got something." "What?"

"I was at Khadija's place last night."

"Oh, the tsunami girl?"

"Paul, focus! This is crucial." "Alright, continue."

"One day, Francis stumbled upon their home, seeking a glass of water to quench his thirst. But on his way back, a man in a helmet forced him into a car. This was the day before his body was found."

"A man in a helmet?" "Her mother mentioned that he had an axe tattoo on his back. Does that ring a bell?" "Yes, Maria spoke about her servant and that tattoo." "Exactly."

"So Devachan is tied to his suicide?"

"Let's call it murder now."

"So, he must have taken out his wife too and disguised it as a suicide."

"Let's unravel the enigma behind these tragic endings."

"Francis's lifeless form was discovered in the river. Those who knew him all attested to his remarkable diving skills."

"Yet that doesn't guarantee immunity from fate. What does the autopsy reveal?"

"Every detail leans toward suicide, with drowning cited as the tragic cause."

"Is it not possible that someone could have compelled him into the water, crafting an illusion of self-inflicted demise?"

"Absolutely. Perhaps those metaphorical Dragon arms ensnared him. And what of his wife?"

"She suddenly stirred from her slumber, shrieking in terror. In his attempt to console her, she overcame him, fled, and locked the door behind her. Then she scaled the upper floor and leapt from the bungalow's edge."

"Perhaps the murder unfolded in a different locale—maybe their own bedroom. From there, someone locked him out, weaving the narrative into a deceptive tapestry."

"Could those same Dragon arms play a role in this sinister plot?"

"Perhaps. By the way I have something about the letter."

Gautam flipped open the book to the page where he had paused.

"Oh, this letter again. Have you discovered any hidden words?"

"Actually, yes." "What?" He handed her the letter.

"Some words have mysteriously erased."

Ramani traced the letter with her eyes closed, sensing a few raised markings. "What could they be?"

"Who knows? What's worse—being blind to what exists or seeking what isn't there?"

"Gautam, how do we return to the case?"

"What's left to return to? The truck is missing, the skeleton mask has vanished, and now? With these erased words, what point are we trying to make? What if he simply wrote them down and then scrubbed them away, or penned them on a sheet that was already blank?"

"I doubt either scenario fits." "Then what's the real story?"

"My intuition suggests it will unfold before we arrive at the station."

"This guy's a real nut case," Ramani whispered to Paul.

They began their journey to the station, while Goudham plunged back into the depths of the book.

' We dashed through the shadowy jungle, searching for any glimmer when a firemoth appeared. The hungry mouth yearned for food, while the head craved sustenance to enable flight. Both raced after the flickering light, oblivious to its true nature. At last, the mouth snagged the moth and devoured it, but the minuscule creature delivered neither satisfaction nor the means to soar.

"You foolish mouth, why consume the flesh? We could have harvested the ashes to take flight." "And where would we fly in this pitch-black jungle?" At that moment, the head recognized it had forsaken its guiding light. "This is all your doing, you vortex gut—always lusting to devour." "And you, vortex head—endlessly concocting excuses for demise."

An altercation erupted in the darkened jungle as we grasped a tree's tentacle. The roots constricted around our necks, leading us to our own undoing.'

The jeep abruptly halted, shattering the tension. A cluster of children spilled from their school vehicle, making their way across the road toward the art gallery.

"Look, there's my husband." "Baby Biceps," Ramani shouted from the jeep.

"Apologies, that's just my nickname for him; I've added 'biceps' to 'baby.'"

"No need to apologize, he's got those impressive bigman biceps." "Absolutely," Ramani replied, biting her lip.

"Baby biceps." This time, he turned and approached the jeep.

"Hey, babe. Each year, we take the kids on a picnic to explore the territory, diving into the history steeped in this land."

"And what historical treasures did you unearth in the art gallery?" "Ajna." "Right."

"Babe, this is Goudham from the hills."

"Hey there, I'm Kumar. A pleasure to meet you." "Likewise!"

"Paul, you're in the know, right?" "Oh, for sure."

"Guys, I need to dash. If even one child goes missing, the blames on me." "Catch you all later." Big biceps whisked the little ones into the gallery. The jeep moved steadily towards the station, while Goudham immersed himself in the final pages of the tale.

'Our lifeless forms slipped into quicksand, gradually sinking into the mire. We submerged entirely in a parallel realm, awakening beneath pristine waters. Our essence felt weightless, and we sensed our disembodied state. We glided forward, finding ourselves at the entrance of a vast abyss leading to the unknown. The soul had shed its corporeal shackles, ready to bid farewell to fear. Glowing feline eyes flanked the passage, sharp teeth and delicate, aerial ears hissed bubbles at us. The tiny orbs struck our essence, extinguishing it. These were mere earthly beings, looking to instill fear over the freedom we embraced. We had no time for their antics and pressed on, unaffected. From a distance, a laser struck us, mending our divided souls. The very fabric of the soul transformed upon impact, leaving us no longer as 'we,' but as 'I.'

I advanced; the abyss now aflame on either side. The soul, now unified, faced only the impending extinction of the 'I.' Yet the fire could not consume the 'I'; it could only simmer it. I maneuvered through the warm waters before reaching the boiling point, crossing the flames unscathed. It was over. I can sense a voice calling. There is no turning back. Goodbye.

I journeyed towards the end, where I would transform into mere truth—the tail of the truth.'

Goudham completed the reading, his mind ensnared in a whirlwind of thoughts as the vortex of words spiraled around him.

'I can sense a voice calling. There's no turning back. Goodbye.'

"Goudham, Goudham." Ramani roused him from his reverie.

"What?" he replied.

"We've arrived at the station."

"Oh, right."

"Man, you really are a bookworm. I can barely get through a single page."

"Rama, you ought to pick up more books. I struggled too after a long hiatus from reading."

"Paul, drive the jeep to the bungalow."

"Why? What's up?"

He pointed to the final lines of the book.

"These words are identical to those in the letter."

"Exactly. What does that imply?"

"Let's discover."

The blue jeep glided silently over the bridge toward the marshes.

"Goudham, they should be at their boutique."

siLkydoLLs. They entered the glass enclosure to find Maria seated there.

"Good day, sir. How may I help you?" "Where's Kanya?" "She's out on an excursion with Nandhu uncle."

"Did your grandmother write novels using a pencil?"

"Ah, yes. She preferred erasing mistakes over scratching them out."

"Did your father assist her in composing the novels?"

"Dad? No idea. Why the inquiry?"

Ramani and Paul listened intently, still puzzled by the conversation.

"Do you have any of her original manuscripts? The ones she penned in pencil?"

"Actually, no. My sister burned them all one day, claiming the words reminded her too much of grandma."

Goudham had already pieced the puzzle together.

"She didn't just dispose of the papers, but also a few garments. I suppose she wasn't mentally stable for quite some time."

"Do you know why?"

"As a child, she saw our mother's bloodied body, and then grandpa's lifeless form a few years later. Those experiences likely triggered a lingering trauma. Thankfully, she's been okay ever since Nandhu uncle arrived."

"Where's your sister now?" "Not sure. Maybe at the beach or someplace."

Without further ado, Gautam exited the boutique and hopped into the jeep, with Ramani and Paul following suit.

"What's on your mind, Goudham?"

"I think I've figured it out." "Figured out what?"

A green jeep meandered through the golden town, carrying Anand and Kanya within.

"It feels like I'm soaking in the town's splendor for the first time."

"Shall we head back?"

"Shall we run away? Just like you suggested years ago."

"Why is running away even an option now?"

"To flee from all this investigation."

"Why?" Anand inquired, a hint of skepticism lacing his tone as he sensed a secret unfurling.

Anand removed his arm from the gear and reached for hers, as she gazed unapologetically at the sun.

"Do you want to pause?" "No, let's keep going."

Kanya shifted her gaze from the sun to Anand, her eyes a blend of love and remorse.

"Nandhu, will you love me no matter what?" "No matter what."

Anand gently cupped her arms with his lips, bestowing a tender kiss.

The jeep veered toward the silent bridge.

"What if I've taken a life?" Her final words before the bridge sent a shiver through him.

His eyes diverted from the road to her, startled.

A star tortoise lay directly in their path. The jeep ran over it, swerving slightly and losing control. The engine sputtered, sending Gautam hurtling onto the road with a minor knee injury. Kanya remained trapped inside, striking her head and losing consciousness, her last glimpse of light fading away. He dragged her from the jeep, crying and calling her name, but only silence answered. With no vehicles in sight, he limped all the way to the hospital, cradling her. Meanwhile, a star tortoise lay forgotten on the road, upside down, gazing at the world. Its limbs appeared from the shell, trying to right itself. After several efforts, the shell flipped, and the sea creature slowly made its way down to the estuary, diving into the waters. The turtle swam toward the sea, heading towards a tale steeped in centuries of a curse—the hex of the turtle.

Chapter 21
A Cat with the Aerial Ears

Winter Ghost,
1994.

A phantom realm enveloped in a veil of white mist, infused with the eerie atmosphere of the afterlife. Here, all departed souls of the region find their resting place, beneath an arch proclaiming 'Moksha Cemetery.'

Charlie gripped a flashlight, slicing through the fog's embrace.

"Charlie, should we just head back? We truly belong here only after death," Bishan remarked, his trembling hands resting on his shoulders as he trailed behind.

"Don't you want to catch a glimpse of the swamp cat?"

"Can we return at dawn?" "This isn't a rooster call. Cats roam at night, scavenging the remains."

A rustle echoed from the shadows, instilling a jolt of fear in their throats. They clamped their mouths shut to stifle further sounds, yet their presence was already betrayed. Glancing at one another, they turned towards the source, meeting two luminous eyes that glared back at them.

"It's the swamp cat. Run!"

With the flashlight leading the way, Charlie sprinted ahead, and Bishan stumbled after him. They dashed halfway when Charlie tripped over a patch of gravel, the flashlight soaring from his grip, casting two monstrous silhouettes that sent shivers down their spines. Bishan, desperately clutching Charlie and the flashlight, propelled them onward until they broke free, placing Charlie upon the bicycle frame. From a distance by the Moksha gate, two glowing eyes with pointed ears saw their escape.

"Oh God, it's the cat."

Bishan pedaled furiously without a backward glance, veering toward the banks of the Scent River.

"You shouldn't dash like that. The cat sinks its teeth into your neck and drains your blood."

"You urged me to run for it! What is this, Dracula?"

"You were the one keen to see the cat. That's your creature." "I would've left you to the Moksha; I only picked you out of courtesy for what's been taken from your home."

Charlie crawled to the river with one knee mangled and muddy, rinsing his bleeding skin while gazing at the inky sky.

"Bishan, just drop me near the gate. It's a tough trek for me now," he grunted softly.

"I'm still trembling." "Me too. Please," Charlie chuckled.

"Hmmm, let's rope in." The bicycle rolled on; the flashlight clasped in Charlie's hand.

"Blood, I crave warm blood, fresh human blood."

Charlie propped the flashlight under his chin, channeling the voice of a female ghost.

"You fool; the next fall will land you in the swamp. Cut it out."

Charlie displayed a spinning disco light show. Suddenly, Bishan noticed something illuminating in the mangrove shadows and halted the bicycle. "What's that?" "Spotted something glowing in the dark." "Did the cat pursue us?" "Just shine the light over that way." Charlie directed the beam toward the flickering glow.

"Look at that—a dark object over there. It's a videotape."

"Come on, let's retrieve it."

"How? You'll get stuck in the muck."

Bishan scanned the area and spotted a long, sharp stick. He approached the edge of the muddy pit and carefully reached the stick toward the tree's roots.

"Just hold onto me tightly," Charlie urged, gripping his collar. Bishan steadied himself and successfully maneuvered the stick into the hole of the tape. He gently tugged it closer, taking slow breaths as the tape drew nearer until it unexpectedly slipped from his grasp. Charlie snatched it just in time. "Got it!"

They both plopped down on the grass, shining light on their treasure.

"Why doesn't it have a label?"

"Not a trace of water or mud to be found. The tree held onto it perfectly."

"What do you think is on it?"

"Are you thinking what I'm thinking?"

"What?"

"It might be adult-themed."

"Adult-themed? What do you mean?"

Bishan raised an eyebrow, perplexed.

"You idiot, like people being naked?"

"Naked? Doing what?"

"Just relax! Don't show information about the tape. Tomorrow after school, we can watch it at my place since Mom and Dad are heading to the coffee plant and our brothers will be at college. Meanwhile, we can explore."

"Why would they be naked?"

"Tomorrow will answer all your questions. "Have you ever experienced that rush of sensation?"

"Sensation in what way?"

"You know, when you playfully tease the skin, and it releases a stream of white, thick nectar that feels absolutely divine."

Bishan was oblivious to the enchanting moment that awaited him.

"You'll find out soon."

Bishan's vivid imagination ran wild, picturing the adventurous games that could occur between two naked individuals.

"Let's head back for now." Charlie tucked the tape beneath his waistband, and they made their way home. "See you tomorrow," he said, flashing a wink.

Bishan continued to ponder the intriguing games that might unfold between naked players.

"Don't forget the flashlight; the cat might be lurking about."

"I'll be fine," Bishan replied with a strained smile. "Alright, then. Good night."

"Good night."

The bicycle took flight once more, soaring down the winding path through the mangroves.

Charlie raced the secret tape to his room. In the living room, John, Aleena, and Christy were spellbound by the chilling scenes of Dracula, their hearts leaping with every frightful moment. As Charlie stealthily approached the periphery, their heads whipped around, prompting him to bolt to his room, where he tucked the tape away securely in his backpack. Mission carried out! He swiftly changed into fresh attire and ventured to the kitchen, slathering almond butter onto a pair of brown slices before heading out to the cinema.

"Blood? What happened?" Aleena questioned, her eyes darting to his leg as Christy and John recoiled at the mention of blood.

"I had a tumble on some gravel," he mumbled, mouth agape with bread. "Oh, is that all?" John remarked, eyes glued back to the screen. "With Dracula thirsty for a bloody neck, I hear 'blood'!" They returned their focus to the flick, dismissing his injury with casual indifference.

"Just apply some ointment." "Not necessary. I rinsed it off in the river."

"Where on earth did you tumble into gravel?" "Bishan and I ventured into Moksha."

Once again, Christy and John spun around in fear.

"Who did you meet there?" "The swamp cat."

"And returned with its mane and bite." "Blah! The cat spotted us, and we bolted."

"I'd wager you fell. You really needn't run; the swamp cat only feasts on the departed." "Blaahh."

Charlie polished off his dinner and dashed to bed.

"Where are you off to?" "Bed." "So soon?" "I'm exhausted."

He sprinted to the restroom before sleep, but when his mind wandered to unwieldy thoughts, he quietly latched the door and shifted gears. With one leg draped over the pipeline, a familiar thrill ignited, though the sting from his wound cast a shadow over the pleasure. Yet, his longing for that exhilarating release pushed through the discomfort. He rhythmically stroked until a cascade of heat burst forth with exhilarating force, flooding the restroom with a wave of delight. He expertly sluiced away every trace of his fervor before collapsing into bed, a grin lingering from that euphoric moment. He drifted into slumber, awakened by the sun's gentle caress. As he stirred from sleep, the first thing he did was rifle through his bag for the tape. It shimmered with safety. After a brisk shower, he bounded downstairs for breakfast.

"So early?" "I am hungry, mom." "Take a seat at the table," where John sat, leisurely sipping his coffee.

"Good morning, little one." "Good morning, big John." The duo—father and son—engaged in their habitual exchange of morning greetings.

Aleena approached the table, carrying a tray of rava idli and coconut chutney.

"I'm starving!"

"Is someone waiting for you at school? Maybe a girlfriend?" "Get lost, mom."

"Aleena, remember how you used to wait for me every day at school?"

"I never waited for you. You were always the one rushing to find me—ugh!"

John popped a piece of idli into his mouth, drenched in coconut chutney, hoping to mask the teasing. Aleena's smile returned as she offered him a bite from her plate.

"Of course, I recall every moment when you'd come running, and I would pretend I wasn't waiting for you."

"Years of marriage later, you've admitted you waited for me."

He savored the pancake with a romantic grin, eager for more. Charlie devoured the rice cake and went for seconds.

"What time do you head to school?" John couldn't hide his impatience. "Let him eat in peace," Aleena implored, serving him another helping, which he gobbled up.

"Did you dash all the way from Moksha after spotting that cat?" John inquired, noticing Charlie's voracious appetite.

"Bishan picked me up and sprinted; otherwise?" He embellished the tale before heading off to wash up.

"Where's our oldest boy?" John asked about Christy.

"He's probably still in bed, skipping most of the first hours."

"Ah, college life. Let him have his break. But when he misses his hall ticket, you talk to the dean."

Charlie appeared, fully dressed with his school bag in tow.

"I can't wait for college. School is such a drag, dad."

"True, but sometimes only a drag can motivate the lethargic ones like you."

"Mom, dad, I'm off."

"We'll be at the plant until nightfall. The key will be inside the pot." "Alright, mom." "And don't go wild chasing after cats or snakes. Stay home until your brother returns." "Okay, dad."

Charlie planted quick kisses on their cheeks and dashed off to school. He raced down the mangrove path and halted at the Y junction. With time to spare, he found a shady spot and inhaled the river air. Moments later, Bishan arrived on his bicycle, his expression oddly serious. Charlie settled in front, feeling a tad uneasy. They pedaled toward town in silence, the bridge cloaking them in an eerie stillness. After a few loops, they reached an expansive gate leading to a cluster of white-and-yellow multi-story buildings—Riverside High School.

They parked their bike and entered the eighth-grade classroom, where a chalk-and-duster skirmish was in full swing. They deftly dodged the chaos and slid into their usual back-row seats, their minds buzzing with pending missions, sharing cryptic exchanges.

"Mom and dad will soon be off to the farm." "So what?" "Just zip it. No more games with words, only the ones in the buff. It's in the bag." Charlie's tone echoed a determined zeal reminiscent of an impending explosion. Bishan stayed mute, his imagination painting pictures of what might unfold between a man and a woman in their natural state. Together, they bore the weight of anticipation until evening approached. At three o'clock, a peon strolled into their classroom.

"Since your math teacher's out, the last hour will be physical training." The announcement ignited jubilant celebrations.

"How about we make a break for it?" "No, the teacher will never let us go. We need a solid excuse." "There's a way out. When the moment is right, I'll give you the signal. Are we on the same page?" "We are," Bishan muttered.

A vast playground sprawled out before them, where children dashed about, aimlessly enjoying their youth.

"Do you spot our physical training teacher?" Charlie inquired, peering like a secret agent.

"Yes." "So, are you planning to run after me?" "What do you mean, run after you?"

"When the moment arrives, you'll understand. For now, just try to catch me and don't stop."

Charlie sped off, with Bishan in pursuit. Even in real life, he was elusive, and soon, their plan unfolded perfectly. Charlie fell abruptly in front of the teacher—a completely unplanned accident.

"Oh, no!" he exclaimed, rolling on the ground, gripping his unhealed moksha wound. The teacher rushed over to help him, locking eyes with Bishan, as though ready to trigger an explosive moment. He cleverly joined the scene without breaking character.

"Sir, I need to apply some medicine. Let me head home."

"We have the medicine here." "No, sir. The healing spray at home is far superior. Please let me go."

The teacher examined the wound, realizing its absurdity.

"Charlie, you can leave in an hour."

"Oh, I can't withstand this stretch for long. Please, sir, let me go home."

"Hmmm, how will you get there?" "There's a bicycle. Bishan will take me." "Oh, is there a driver? Fine, go straight home, understand?" "Understood, sir."

The theatrical Charlie crawled out, feigning pain, while Bishan exaggerated every facial expression he could muster. With a bag and a metaphorical bomb, they stepped outside the school, knowing every second counted. The bicycle took off like it had wings, landing swiftly at Charlie's house. The surroundings felt tranquil and secure. Charlie pulled the key from a flowerpot and hurried inside.

"You lock the door while I prepare the tape." Bishan secured it firmly, making it as impenetrable as a fortress. The television glowed bright red, the silver screen shimmered, the VCR illuminated green, and the movie kicked off. Lacking significant plot or characters, it dove straight into action without credits. Inside a boxy room, heart-shaped stickers glistened under dim, yellow lights. At the room's center sat a tall couch and a mattress draped in white sheets.

"What is this? Where are the people?" A man with grey hair stepped into view.

"Yes, here comes one."

One by one, he shed his garments, wrapping a white towel around his waist.

"Bishan, this is the game, man. Though this seems a bit off." "What game?" "Just wait and see."

A girl stepped into the room, shedding her clothes until she was completely bare, save for a skeleton mask concealing her face. She pushed him onto the mattress and perched atop him.

"This is it, right? But is it really?" Charlie questioned, his skepticism showing while Bishan was fully engaged. After a few energetic movements, the girl took hold of him and began to stroke him, the familiar sight of thick, splashing white fluid unmistakable to them both. Yet, something else nagged at Bishan.

"Hey, it's him—Devachan, your neighbor." Charlie was so absorbed in the game that he didn't even register the actor's presence. "Yeah, that's him. But did he perform in it?"

Moments later, he appeared from the shower. As soon as he exited, the girl in the skeleton mask approached the camera and switched it off. A motorbike roared to life, carrying two familiar voices.

"Oh, it's our goofy brothers. What are they up to this early?" they whispered among themselves.

"Oh heavens, they're getting too close." Charlie swiftly removed the tape and powered down all the electronics.

"Keep this in your bag." He handed Bishan the tape.

"Were you here? Did you ditch school early?" "Yeah, we left during the last period because it was PT."

"And what were you up to?" He turned and ambled away, offering no further explanation.

Bishan sat before the television, still as if he were just another piece of technology.

"Alright, you're here too. What's on the agenda?"

"We were about to watch last night's Dracula movie."

"Oh, brave souls indeed." "They really are. Last night, they ventured into Moksha to see the cat."

"Is that so?" "Look at his leg."

"Did the cat give you a chase?" "No, I tripped and fell all on my own," Charlie boasted with pride.

"So, is it just water that frightens you? Tonight is the tears of the crescent moon. Remember what you told Nandhu uncle?" Kishan nudged Bishan about the impending deadline.

"What did he say?" "That he will dive before the tears of the crescent moon."

"Hmm, let's take a closer look."

Bishan felt an unsettling dread swell within him, while Charlie began to tremble on the opposite side.

"What's bothering you?" "I can't quite put my finger on it. Just feeling a bit down." He ambled over to the couch and rested his weary head.

"You seemed fine until now?" Kishan approached, gently checking his forehead. "He's burning up?"

Christy confirmed after a quick check. "Yes, it seems like a fever."

"Why this sudden fever?"

The infection in Charlie's leg was the culprit.

"Oh, right. Mom told you to apply the medicine, and you didn't heed her advice."

Christy stepped outside, gathering a few tulsi leaves and a small sprig of aloe vera.

"Apply this to the wound for now and massage it in," she instructed. Charlie delicately rubbed the aloe over the affected area as Christy went to the kitchen, heating water to brew coffee infused with ginger, pepper, and tulsi.

"Remove your uniform." As Charlie shed his shirt, a shiver ran down his spine. "It's so chilly." "It's just a fever. For now, sip this coffee and lay down for a bit. We'll grab the medicine on the way back, all right?"

"So, no crescent moon for you."

"He can still gaze at them from the rooftop. Besides, school is off tomorrow. Get well soon, champ." Kishan playfully tapped his head before heading out.

"Are you staying? We can both fetch the medicine." "Hmm." The bike went to town. There was an unshakable pain stirring within Bishan as well.

"You really are running a fever." He could sense Charlie's heat from a distance.

Charlie took a slow sip of coffee, lacking the energy to converse.

"The tape." A small sip energized him slightly.

"I'll find a good spot for that. I'm feeling under the weather myself."

"Fever." "Something's off inside; should I head home or stick around?"

"No, it's fine. I'm going to sleep. You go. We'll catch up later."

"Alright, take care." Bishan touched his warm form, then stepped outside.

"Bishan." Charlie called softly from behind.

"There's something strange about that tape. Just toss it back where we found it."

He delivered the words with the last reserves of his strength and sprawled out on the sofa.

"No, I'll keep it. The key to the reflection is safe with me."

"The key to reflection?" "Yes."

Kishan quietly exited, leaving without another word. He cycled down the mangrove path, stopping exactly where they had discovered the tape. After a moment's consideration, he opted to hold onto it, a creeping fear of the water gnawing at him. Upon reaching home, he stashed the entire bag beneath the bed. The doorbell rang, sending a chill down his spine. Deepa opened the door, and Prasad stepped in, clutching a small shopping bag.

"What did you buy?"

"Just a few new things, all gifts."

He produced a box of coconut-filled chocolates just as Bishan walked in.

'Wow, perfect timing! This is for you."

"Wow." The sweetness briefly chased away his trepidation.

"And I got something for you too." Prasad handed Anand a box.

"What is this?" "Open it and see for yourself." He eagerly unwrapped it to reveal a polaroid camera.

"Oh wow, where did you find this cool gadget?"

"An NRI friend gave it to me." "Why?"

"For showing the bravery to halt the gold mining. I have nothing to do with it. You're leaving after winter and traveling, right? Keep it."

"Thanks, bro." Anand enveloped him in a hearty bear hug.

"Actually, the gift is meant for Dad," Prasad murmured with a hint of sadness.

"Prasad, Dad has been asking for you." "Alright, dear." He affectionately patted her cheek and made his way upstairs to Dad's room. Kishan arrived as well.

"Nandhu uncle, is that a polaroid?" "Yes."

He began piecing together the components, setting it up for use. Bishan dashed toward Anand, his mouth smeared with chocolate.

"Chocolate, give me a piece." Kishan snatched half of it.

"Where did this come from?" "Someone gifted them to your dad as a thank-you for shutting down the mining operation."

"I'll snap a picture of you first," Anand said, pulling Bishan closer.

"Come on, let's get Kishan in too," Bishan urged, drawing his friend into the frame.

With a click and a whir, the camera started producing a print. All eyes were transfixed on the wondrous device. A shadowy snapshot appeared, and Anand shook it a few times until two smiling faces gradually materialized.

"Bishan, this is yours."

"Wow!" Bishan exclaimed, joyfully dancing before dashing upstairs to show grandpa. Inside the room, an intense conversation unfolded.

"Dad, why did you want to see me?" Shiva's eyes looked weary, as if on the brink of closing forever.

"Ahhhh." His voice strained to escape, while Prasad leaned in closer.

"Prasad, don't shy away from the truth because of the tragedy that has befallen us. We mustn't raise a generation that fears the truth." "Okay, Dad." "And this newspaper? It is now your responsibility." "Yes."

"In any case, we've triumphed in our battle. The once dead tree will soon nourish the earth."

Shiva, worn out, let his eyes drift shut.

"Dad, please rest." Prasad gently patted his arm and left the room.

Just then, Bishan entered.

"Grandpa." Shiva's eyes fluttered open once more.

"Look!" Bishan presented the polaroid with excitement.

"Oh dear, that's marvelous. How's winter treating you?"

"I'm scared, Grandpa." "Scared of what?" "I don't know."

"Do you know the only way to conquer fear?" "How?"

"Face it head-on." Bishan pondered this daunting challenge, his stomach twisting at the thought.

"Is the key to the self safe with you?"

"Yes, Grandpa," he replied, pulling a fishtail shaped key from his pocket.

"Now that key belongs to you. Do you know why?"

"To keep what's precious to me."

"You clever one. But there's more to it." "What else?"

"Anything you keep will become precious to you over time. So, that key should always be close to you. Got it?" "Got it."

He pressed a kiss to Shiva's cheek and dashed out. Kishan was waiting outside, his expression suspicious. "What's that?" "The key to the self."

Bishan sped away to his room, where he examined himself in his mirror. The joy began to wane once more, and unease bubbled up.

"How will I ever conquer this fear?" he muttered, the weight of the question settling in. The sun was nearly gone, and the night awaited the gentle tears of the crescent moon.

Bishan lay on his bed, inspecting the little key, experimenting with various angles of the pendant. Just then, Kishan burst in.

"Bishan, we're all going to the beach. Get dressed."

"I'm not going." "Not coming?" "Why?"

"Not feeling well." Kishan approached and checked his forehead.

"Temperature's normal. Come on, maybe some sea breeze will do you good." "No, you all go."

Anand walked in too.

"He's not well." "Not well? What happened?" Bishan felt frustration rising with all the questions firing at him.

"I'm fine." "Alright then. We'll be capturing some great shots under the moonlight. You sure?"

Bishan had no desire to elaborate and turned away.

"Okay then, we'll head out." Kishan exited the room.

"You can share anything with me, alright?" Anand affectionately ruffled Bishan's hair before leaving. Bishan wanted to call him back, but the words lodged in his throat. Quietly, he opened the mirror without disturbing Grandpa's slumber and tucked in his treasured items in the locker. Now prepared for his quest, he moved toward his watery battleground. Donning a swimming ring around his neck, he hopped on his bicycle and pedaled towards the scent river, engaging in conversation with the self-plagued by fear of the water.

"Right, so let go of your fear of water. You must first merge with it to truly submerge."

As the fiery motivational speech faded, he arrived at the battleground. The riverside teemed with an eager crowd, oblivious to the rapid thumping of his heart. Beneath the looming Nazi statue, a multitude gathered, expecting the unveiling of the golden ax, shrouded in cloth like a secret waiting to be revealed. But Bishan had a singular purpose in mind and made his way toward the river. With a slow, deliberate motion, he peeled off his foul-smelling uniform shirt from the day before and cast a nervous glance at the water, which seemed poised to consume him. He hesitantly settled into a ring, slipping himself into the depths as a preliminary measure. The ring engulfed him halfway. He tilted his gaze skyward, lost in the moment, as if seeing everything for the first and last time. Suddenly, the sharp squeal of a microphone intruded, snapping him from his reverie. With determination, he paddled back to shore. His mission remained unfulfilled, and he felt adrift, unsure of how to achieve it. He searched for inspiration but found nothing but a few rainbow dwarf fish flitting beneath the shallow surface. He submerged his shirt into the cool water, hoping to catch a glimpse of them. All but one wriggled free from his grasp. He released that solitary fish onto the shore, watching as it danced its ultimate moments, the water evaporating from its body until the struggle ceased. Two frogs peeked from their hiding spots before plunging back into the river, an odd sight to Bishan.

"Are you fishing?" a gray-haired man inquired. Bishan, disinterested in conversation, saw as the man cast a net into the river. Curiosity piqued, Bishan waited impatiently for a catch. Moments later, something snagged in the net, and the man drew it ashore—a star turtle entangled in river weeds.

"Ah, impressive. The beginning is captivating," he remarked, cradling the turtle. It recoiled in fright and retreated into its shell. "Don't worry, little one. I'll take good care of you." The man tucked the turtle under his arm and wandered off, leaving Bishan in solitude once more. A wave of self-loathing washed over him.

"You're nothing but a coward."

He loathed himself deeply. Finally, he resolved to take that leap of faith. With determination, he tossed the swimming ring into the river, staring at it as silence enveloped him amidst the cacophony of the crowd. Only the rhythm of his heart echoed in that stillness, the ring beckoning him to swim, as a surge of courage ignited within. The pounding in his chest urged him on, and he heeded his instincts, leaping into the water. But as he neared the ring, the circle of life drifted away, fear gnawing at him, making his pursuit feel ever more distant. With every stroke, the ring seemed to slip from his grasp, fear completely consuming him. It was time to part ways with the realm where his memories slumbered. The fight against water morphed into a struggle against death itself. Fatigued from the battle, he ultimately surrendered, and the orange maw swallowed him into the green depths. In the liminal space between life and death, he stirred once more, the fading memories surfacing as he crossed entirely into the embrace of death. Awaiting him at the gates of moksha was a figure with luminous eyes and perky ears ready to welcome his ghost home - a cat with the aerial ears.

Chapter 22
The Nightmare of the Blind

Winter Dream, 1994.

The sun cast its final golden beams as the sky prepared to embrace the tears of the crescent moon. A thrumming crowd surged forward, eager to glimpse the golden ax. The mango-faced man and Devachan dramatically unveiled the shimmering weapon, igniting a frenzy among the spectators captivated by its brilliance.

"The integrity of our belief system must be guarded fiercely. It is our solemn charge to keep it vibrant and free from decay. In fulfillment of this vow, we present this golden ax to the people of Eerħt," declared the mango-faced man, his inaugural speech met with a tempest of applause and cheers. As the clamor gradually subsided, Kanya found herself drifting into the scent river. Appearing from the water, drenched yet unperturbed, was Francis, prompting Kanya to rush to him.

"Where have you been, Grandpa? We were so worried!" she exclaimed.

He offered no response, just a fading smile that spoke volumes.

"My little dolphin." Francis tenderly caressed her cheek, reminiscent of their cherished moments. "When the spring wave comes, follow the dolphin." His words, shrouded in mystery, lingered in the air as his form began disintegrating into droplets. Kanya watched in awe as he slowly transformed into the very river itself. A lone swimming ring bobbed lazily on the surface. Confusion clouded Kanya's mind as she gazed skyward; the sun had vanished completely, leaving just her and the crescent moon. Peering back at the water in search of clarity, she was startled to see a human form floating calmly—Francis. He lay there, inert and serene. Her vision began to blur, and in an instant, the world exploded into a kaleidoscope of colors once more. She woke out of the day dream.

The mangrove path sparkles with vibrant hues, as the LED lights lead the way to a bungalow cloaked in shimmering silver shamiana, encircled by twinkling white lights. A lively crowd of guests lounges beneath flowing silk drapes, indulging in wine and whispered exchanges. There's a celebratory atmosphere that dances through the air, with Kanya radiating joy as the event's centerpiece. Adorned in her flower-patterned silk saree, she flits from guest to guest, her smile unwavering and enchanting. On the other side of the gathering, Devachan, donned in divine garb, elevates the refreshment experience from white wine to golden whisky.

Meanwhile, Maria sees Kanya from a distance, lingering by the greenery, a glass of wine cradled in her hand.

"Did I hear correctly? You weren't invited to your sister's wedding," announced Christy and the family's arrival.

"Are our neighbors really showing up now?"

"We were just tending to some fieldwork, adding greener to our land."

"Uncle, that sounds like the perfect way to enjoy retirement. Christy, you're into farming now too?"

"Of course! He's our brand-new plantain tree." "Dad," Christy teased with a gentle poke.

"Why are you distancing yourself from the crowd?" asked Maria. "I just needed a moment, Aunt. I'll join you in a bit."

John and Aleena strode in, but Maria remained entranced by Kanya.

"She looks extraordinarily happy," Christy noted, seeing her sister. "Funny though, you said she wasn't keen on this marriage."

"I was thinking the same thing." "Since the day she witnessed Grandpa's body, she's been acting strangely."

"You have a point. An introvert suddenly bursting with extroverted energy suggests..."

"What?"

"It suggests she's desperately trying to escape her own thoughts." "Has she ever faced something traumatic or abusive in her childhood?"

"She saw Mom's body when she was very young." "Perhaps the shadows of her past resurface after a jolt, and she feels the need to bathe in the light to forget." Maria downed her wine, lost in the contemplation of this new chapter.

"I doubt Kishan will show up," she sighed. "Yeah, I'm aware."

"Shouldn't you call him? He avoids large gatherings."

"Leave him be. People overshadow the healing process. What he needs is silence. That's why I'm even out here."

"Let me predict the repetitive question you'll endure: When are you getting married?"

"Exactly! It's not just the question—it's the endless loop that feels like a broken record."

"For me, it's all about the hair. Man, where did your hair go?" They shared a laugh, lightening their sense of being outsiders.

"Let's head inside."

As they entered, Kanya spotted Christy and came rushing towards her.

"Hey there." "Hello, miss. You look absolutely stunning." "Thank you." The peculiar vibe surrounding her made Christy feel even more out of place. Just then, John and Aleena approached.

"Uncle, we've got drinks over there."

Aleena hummed and cast a sideways glance at John.

"What's that about?" John asked with feigned innocence. "He mentioned he'd quit once he found his footing."

"Starting tomorrow. You have my word, dear."

"Why not just call it quits now?" "It's my son's 18th birthday tomorrow."

"Dad, really? Does that mean I'm allowed to marry?"

"And drink legally too." "But breaking the rules is my thing, Dad. Mom, can I have one?"

"When your dad is quitting, the son is just beginning."

"Someone needs to carry on our legacy, right, Dad?"

"Kanya." A voice called out, summoning the bride-to-be.

"I'll catch up with you all later." She had no idea who had called her, yet a strange, bright smile danced on her lips. Christy was in dire need of a drink. They headed towards the open bar.

"Hey, John, come join us." Devachan sipped his whiskey, beckoning him into their group.

John and Christy picked out a glass of wine, wandering half-dazed toward the crowd.

"Wow, the boy drinks too. That's fantastic. Drinking is what transforms a boy into a man."

"Drinking can also turn a man into a fool, Uncle." Christy took a cautious sip, offering some sage advice.

"So, how's your plastic business faring?" inquired one of the tipsy onlookers.

"Business is thriving. My son-in-law, he's just like me. Never backs down," Devachan declared proudly as he savored another golden sip.

"Ah, so you both aim to dominate the plastic industry."

"My son-in-law is a man of honor. This Eerħt didn't give mining permits, yet he insisted on donating the golden axe as we pledged—the emblem of prosperity."

"Glitter can deceive the senses. People call true gold worthless while chasing after the superficial shimmer." John downed his drink in one go. Devachan poured another glass, masking his embarrassment with a smile.

"Boy, you're losing all your hair. Meanwhile, I've still got a full head at my age." Devachan's irritation landed squarely on Christy.

"Uncle, that coconut tree has ganoderma wilt," Christy remarked, pointing at a nearby coconut palm, capturing the attention of the group of drunken onlookers.

"What on earth is that?" "The roots are all decayed. You might want to pull it out."

"Who has time to inspect all this? We've got crores in business on one side; who cares about these coconuts? What are we going to gain from this coconut venture?"

"We'll get nuts, Uncle. Coconuts." Christy said, flashing a silly grin.

"So, that's your grand plan: managing the nuts." Devachan laughed, striking a winning chord as the others joined in on his merriment.

"No, Uncle, I've got another idea. It's a factory. Maybe you can hop on board."

"Oh really? What, a nut factory?" Devachan chuckled again, prompting cheers from the group.

"Yes, Uncle. Natural toothpaste powder. We'll gather all these obsolete nuts and turn them to ashes. By 'nuts,' I mean all sorts: coconut, hazelnut, peanut, walnut, and even these rotten human nuts." John chuckled, splashing some drink, while the others chuckled quietly behind him.

"Alright, Dad, shall we head out?" "Yes, let's go. Devachan, we're off," he replied, flashing a tight-lipped smile as he said goodbye.

"Hmm, following in Dad's footsteps," Potbelly mumbled as they strolled away.

"Devachan, what's all this buzz about word-of-mouth promotion circulating the town?"

"Oh, that was my son-in-law's idea too. Aimed at old-fashioned folks. It's only with a call and notification that they grasp the benefits of plastic. We're launching new zipper tote bags—stronger than cloth and waterproof. Quite handy during rain."

"Mama plastics." "Indeed, that was the one request from my son-in-law: to name it in memory of his mother."

"You're fortunate to have such a caring son-in-law." "Yes, indeed." Devachan felt overwhelmed, finishing his golden glass. Dragon stood there in his biker helmet, absorbing the stories with a dopey grin.

"Dragon, come here." He came over running.

"Opt for the blue. Today, the hierarchy of boss and servant has vanished. You should join in the festivities too." Dragon accepted the bottle of whisky, a bewildered grin on his face, and dashed away, feeling like he'd hit the jackpot.1

"Dumbo, don't you want a glass?" "Oh." He dashed back, retrieving the glass and bounding off again. Mammoth began his ascent up the ladder leading to the rooftop terrace but realized he lacked water for mixing. He descended, approaching the spring instead. He filled a steel bucket with water, pausing momentarily, uncertain about where to pour it. Finally, he untied the rope and secured the small bucket of water. A faint smile flickered on his lips, but his task wasn't finished. He fashioned a slipknot from the loose rope and climbed back up the ladder, bucket in hand, to his private outside bar.

"Cheers to the celebration." "Cheers," echoed the liquor party.

Dragon indulged in a few swift shots, feeling the whisky's warmth creeping in. He descended the stairs and suddenly began to weep.

"Boss, I'm so sorry." Tears streamed down his face, relentless.

"Why on earth are you crying?"

"I... took a life." Devachan suddenly pushed him towards the furthest edge of the field, where a humble mud cave stood sentinel, guarded by a scarecrow.

"What nonsense are you spewing, you foolish dragon? Stay put until the party's over."

He wiped his tears and knelt before the scarecrow. Devachan turned back toward the guests as the liquor flowed freely.

Kanya needed a moment away from the chaos, yet felt lost amidst the crowd. Unnoticed, she strolled through the field, the clamor fading into the background. In the stillness, she detected a quiet sob nearby—it was Dragon conversing with the scarecrow. She concealed herself, keen to eavesdrop on their exchange.

"You mentioned that my freedom from the relentless raven assaults depended on my admission of guilt. I confess—I took the life of the old man; my boss commanded it. It was never my desire to commit that act. Yes, I killed him. Yet, the boss's wife? I did not end her life; I merely sent her tumbling from the bungalow's height. I did not slay her. This is my truth. Now, I ask for your blessing to be liberated from the raven's torment." Once he unburdened his soul and sought divine favor, he cautiously lifted the biker's helmet. The raven assaults ceased. Overwhelmed with elation, he surrendered to joyous wildness in dance.

"Thank you." He knelt before the scarecrow, seeking its benediction, then dashed back to the terrace for another drink. Kanya, having overheard his confession, found herself at a loss for how to respond. A numbness enveloped her as she approached the gathering, the cacophony surrounding her felt like mere vibrations in the air. She was neither mournful nor furious—only stunned by the weight of revelation.

As darkness slid into midnight, the sky brooded with heavy clouds. Abandoned chairs and bottles languished beneath colorful tents. In one corner of the bungalow, workers were lost in slumber, while two dolphin white eyes saw them from the upper windows. Kanya, all dressed and primed for her betrothal, approached the mirror with a radiant smile. She adorned her bare eyelids with ebony strokes, placing a blue bindi at the center of her forehead. Her deep-set eyes fixated on the clock, noting that it was nearly dawn at three o'clock, with the only sound punctuating the air being the rhythmic croaks of mangrove frogs. She pushed open the wooden door, the creak echoing as if she were the sole inhabitant of the universe. With the poise of a goddess, she descended the stairs. Her bare feet whispered against each step, silencing as they met the cool marble floor. She made her way to the kitchen, intending to brew a cup of coffee, her gaze wandering toward the enigmatic shadows of the night. There sat her father, slumped in a chair, drunk and adrift. She stepped forward, positioning herself before him, eager to unveil her transformed self.

"Dad, dad." Devachan stirred awake at the sound, struggling to open his eyes. His vision was clouded, a remnant of the whisky that left him in a surreal haze, where the shimmering figure before him radiated with a divine glow reminiscent of Kanya.

"Dad, how do I look?" He found himself questioning whether this was merely a figment of his imagination.

"Kanya, sweetheart. What's going on? What time is it?" He scanned the pitch-black room for a hint of light but was met with only darkness.

"This is the outfit for the ceremony. Tell me, how does it look? How is my figure?"

"Excuse me? What are you asking?" His eyes gradually focused, clearing the confusion.

"What's with this Kanya? Is it morning yet? Dad's still half-asleep."

"I simply wanted to show you my beauty. What if you don't see me in the morning?"

"What?" He was too disoriented to even rise from his chair.

"Grandma says I'm lovely, just like Mom. But I doubt that. Mom's beauty was, how do I put it? Magical is probably the best word."

"What are you rambling about in the middle of the night?"

"No, the sun is going to rise soon."

"What are you doing? Urrrrrrm." He felt the excess gold escape in a belch. "Kanya, can you fetch me some water?"

"Of course, Dad." She strolled toward the kitchen but paused midway. Her eyes, now shrouded in shadow, turned back as she unraveled her saree, letting the fabric fall away until she stood half-clad before him.

"Dad." Devachan heard her call softly from behind.

"Yes, dear. Where's the water? I'm truly parched."

"Why did you take away mom and grandpa from us?"

Suddenly, clarity returned, but the saree had already ensnared his throat. She yanked him back into the murky depths of despair, her teeth bared, as she throttled him to his end. Thunder rumbled like a funeral bell. Overwhelmed, he released his bladder onto the gleaming white as the grip of consciousness slipped away. In the chaos, she spotted a spring rope nearby, coiled with a noose. He crawled desperately, a silent plea for help. But she deftly placed the loop around his neck and tugged it tight against the roller wheel. The aging body was dragged toward the rusted chains, and with every thunderous clap, her strength grew. His neck strained until it fractured, staining the once-pure spring water with red. She stood on the spring's edge, holding fast to the rope until his breaths faded into a haunting stillness. Then, unexpectedly, the grip of the rope slackened, as if a spirit had vacated a shell, dragging him into the depths of the water. The end of the rope snagged in the wheel and caught, halting his lifeless form in a stark pose above the surface, a mere shadow in the dim light.

Kanya, panting as though woken from a fevered dream, peered into the spring. The realization of death surged within her, scarred palms now aching with urgency. Summoning her last reserves of strength, she pulled his body from its watery grave, lifeless as she yearned. The pressing question loomed: what to do with the remains? Above, the thunder roared, mingling with the patter of rain. She heaved the corpse into the bag, contorting the broken neck as she dragged it toward the swamp beyond the bricks. With every effort, the body ascended the wall when a sudden scream erupted from the terrace, swallowed by the torrential downpour. Dragon had seen the scene unfold from above. Hesitation gripped her—should she flee or yield? In her paralysis, the corpse tumbled over the wall, followed by a crack of thunder that reduced Dragon to nothingness. Shankaran, seeing the chaos, roused the workers. Kanya dashed into the house, not daring to glance back, reaching the kitchen. In a fleeting moment of clarity, she realized she'd forgotten something and retraced her steps to the spring. Her new muddy saree lay discarded, and she retrieved it before anyone could catch a glimpse.

She gently shut the wooden door behind her, creating a barrier against the chaos outside. The tempestuous rain muffled the tumult, and with the next crack of thunder, the lights flickered out. Her heart raced as she treads softly, pausing at the sound of knocks echoing at the front door. Fortune favored her; the sudden darkness silenced the once persistent bell, and after a few impatient raps, the crowd dispersed. Stealthily, she ascended the stairs toward the bathroom, peering through the window. Through the curtain of rain, she glimpsed a truck carrying a charred body, shrouded in the storm's fury. Inhaled deeply, she felt the chaos ebb away, her racing heart gradually finding its rhythm, enveloped by the melody of raindrops. Racing to the restroom, she shed her garments, surrendering to the cleansing cascade. Clumps of mud spiraled down the drain, though faint prints remained. Appearing from the shower, a flash of lightning illuminated the path of her muddy footprints trailing behind her. Grasping a flashlight from the drawer, she ventured where the tracks led her, back toward the kitchen. Bare, she scrubbed away the remnants of her past, much like waves erasing footprints from sand. Stains surrendered to cleansing, and she cautiously shut the door behind her. Her beam danced across the shadows, searching for a way out, revealing an open drawer filled with papers. The top sheet, inscribed in pencil, proclaimed "The Tail of the Truth." Just as she absorbed the light's revelation, the flashlight flickered and extinguished, plunging her into a cloak of darkness.

A little girl jolted awake from a slumber, her voice piercing the silence with a shriek.

"Champakam, what's bothering you, sweetie?" Madhu rushed to her side as rain poured outside, accompanied by the rumble of thunder and flashes of lightning. "My dear, it seems you were lost in a dream." The petite figure, her eyes swathed in bandages, eased into calmness after a few deep breaths.

"What troubled your mind?" she hesitated to speak, shaking her head in reply.

Dressed in white, the nurses entered the room.

"We heard your cry." "Oh, it sounds like a nightmare."

"Don't fret, darling. We're all here with you." One nurse lovingly stroked her hair.

"The doctor is here, and we'll be taking off your bandage today," the second nurse announced cheerfully.

"Well then, we shall see each other again soon, sweetheart. Just relax." The white-clad woman gently caressed her cheeks in unison before stepping out.

"Would you like to join me for a morning ceremony? There will be plenty of food."

"Really? I'm not as desperate as you to crash uninvited events." "Alright then."

"Actually, now I have an invitation, so I will be there." "Seriously, you beggar? It's a betrothal."

"That's irrelevant. Whether they're tying the knot or not, food is guaranteed."

The women chuckled, then suddenly one fell silent.

"What's on your mind?" "I was just pondering what nightmares a blind girl might have. Do they even dream?"

"What if this is a dream, and what she envisioned is real life?"

"Oh, girl, such heavy theories at midnight are hard to swallow. I really wish that ceremony would happen now; my stomach is growling." "Let's head to the canteen."

Meanwhile, Champakam lay in bed, her thoughts steeped in the remnants of her nightmare.

"Dad, can you hold my arms?" "Of course, my dear."

Madhu grasped those delicate arms, but the haunting echoes of her dream still clung to her thoughts - the nightmare of the blind.

Chapter 23
The Diving Ravens and The Flying Dolphins

Spring Magic, 2000.

A still, charged afternoon enveloped the ICU. Kanya lay in a deep slumber, the steady pulse of her heart monitors and the gentle whisper of machines creating a haunting harmony, occasionally interrupted by the soft patter of nurses' footsteps on the pristine tile. Three months had passed in this dreamless void. Then, in a moment that felt suspended in time, her eyes fluttered open.

"Maria, she's awake," Kishan announced, waking Maria from her brief respite.

"Hey there, how are you feeling? Kishan, please summon the doctor," she urged.

Kanya saw Maria's face in silence, everything around her oscillating between the familiar and the strange. The antiseptic aroma of the hospital room invaded her senses, with the machines' beeping slicing through the thick hush. As she tried to rise, her body protested, aching as if engaged in a fierce battle she couldn't remember. She blinked slowly, the dim light wrapping around her like a shroud, making Maria's features seem almost surreal. Kishan returned, flanked by doctors and nurses.

"Hello, Kanya. How are you today?"

"I... I can't." With aid, she sat up. "My head."

"How's your head? Any pain?" The doctor gently lowered her eyelid, unveiling the redness within the depth of her gaze.

"No pain. But?"

"Can you identify this person?" the doctor asked, gesturing towards Maria. "Maria," Kanya replied with confidence, causing Maria to exhale a deep sigh of relief.

"And this," the doctor moved to introduce Kishan. "Kishan. You?"
"What transpired?" she mused, "It feels like Kishan and Maria matured significantly. They seemed so young, as if preserved in time."

"How far back can you trace your thoughts? What's your last memory?"

Just then, Anand burst onto the scene.

"Nandhu, he? He professed his love for me."

"Where did this exchange occur?"

"By the spring."

"And where is this spring?"

"In our home."

"Who is Nandhu?" "That would be me, doctor."

"Oh, Mr. Anand. Do you remember that evening?"

"Yes," Anand replied, the recollection vivid. "When was that?" "Five years ago."

The doctor raised his eyebrows in surprise before returning to Kanya.

"What else do you recall post that event?"

"I turned him down," she said, locking eyes with Anand.

"Why? Is there no love between you?"

"I...I don't despise him. He's a good friend of mine."

"And yet you don't harbor love either."

"I do have feelings, but?"

"But what?" "I feel fear."

"Fear of whom?" "My father."

""Alright, you have deep feelings for Anand, but you turned him away out of fear of your father's reaction. Am I right?"

"Yes."

"What's your profession?"

"I teach at Riverside school." The doctor shifted his gaze to Maria.

"That was quite some time ago. She stepped back from her career before becoming engaged."

"I am retired? Engaged? To whom?"

"No, that didn't go through. After your dad vanished, the ceremony was canceled. Months later, they returned, only to bluntly declare you couldn't wed that 'mango-faced' fellow." With a grin, Maria clasped her arm. "You don't recall any of it."

"Me? How did I land in the hospital?"

"You were in an accident with Anand."

All eyes turned to the doctor.

"Kanya, what's the sensation in your head?"

"It feels like there's a head and a body, but the tail seems missing."

"Interesting. Do you recollect your childhood?"

"Just fragmented memories." "Who held your heart during those years?"

"I adored my grandpa the most. But he became distant after mom passed. Maria, where are grandpa and grandma now?" Maria glanced around, revealing the painful truth. "They left us five years ago."

"What? How?" She clutched her head.

"Kanya, don't overexert your mind. Rest for now. May I speak with all of you outside?"

The doctor ushered everyone out of the room.

"It seems a portion of her recent past has faded away, leaving only mere remnants."

A blue jeep rolled into the hospital courtyard, and the sound of three pairs of boots echoed as they approached Kanya's room.

"Hello, Goudham. She's gaining clarity, yet there's an issue."

"What seems to be the problem, doctor?" "She lost chunks of memory due to the impact. This is the most peculiar case of amnesia I've met. There's a head and a boy, but no tail."

The officers appeared puzzled by his words.

"May we see her?"

"Yes, but please avoid putting her under too much pressure with questions."

As the police officers entered, Kanya found herself facing strangers, her dolphin-like eyes reflecting confusion. Goudham could feel the disconnect. They began to sift through the case file, tracing a narrative that led to her hospital bed. With no recognition of the events detailed within, Goudham felt defeated, while Ramani and Paul decided to take another shot.

"So, you don't recall burning your grandmother's writings?"

"Burning? I can't remember any of what you've mentioned. I don't even know any of you."

"Officers, please. You must not push the patient at this time."

The officers exited the room for a hushed discussion.

"So, Goudham, what's our next move?"

"She's in the same predicament as the case. We have the head and the body, but the tail is nowhere to be found."

"Should we consider a lie detector test?"

"Do you truly believe she's deceiving us?"

"What options do we have?" "What if we just let her be until she heals?"

"And then?" "I'm through with this. I'm finished with my career."

"What do you mean by that?" "I'm stepping away from the force."

"Why? So soon?" "Yes, and you've just begun."

"I understand. Ramani and Paul, it's been a joy working alongside you. This isn't a spur-of-the-moment choice. I've pondered it deeply. This is my conclusion. Just like I mentioned, we've showed the culprit."

"But how can we apprehend her without concrete proof? The crucial element vanished into thin air—her recollection of the crime."

Goudham shrugged with a casual grin.

"I'm content. In any case, I was contemplating how I'd go about making the arrest."

"Justice must prevail."

"Yet, the offenders who truly call for punishment enjoy tranquil lives. In my perspective of justice, she's not one of them."

"Goudham, you possess the discerning eye of a detective, yet you're gazing with a civilian's vision."

"True enough, Rama. And that civilian side of me can't stomach the gruesome games any longer."

Suddenly, a voice echoed from a moving vehicle outside.

'Attention, residents of Eerħt. A tsunami is approaching once more. This time, it's set to be colossal—larger than ever before. Please keep a safe distance from the beach until a green alert is issued.' 'Attention, residents of Eerħt. A tsunami is approaching once more. This time, it's set to be colossal—larger than ever before. Please keep a safe distance from the ocean until a green alert is issued.'

"See, even the world is on the verge of catastrophe. Who cares about our investigation now?"

"Are you planning to hit the beach?" Ramani chuckled as she looked at Goudham.

"Rama, you're reading my thoughts."

"Man, you were one wild officer. What's your take? We both desperately look to apprehend the innocent and make them pay. It's our mission to unveil the truth."

The entire hospital united in response to the announcement.

"Look, all they're fixated on now is their survival."

"What of us, Ramani? What truly matters to us? Our lives or that of a headless wretch?" Paul inquired, a faint smile dancing on his lips.

"Let's head home," Ramani declared. "What's your plan, Goudham?"

"I'm off to chase the tsunami." "Ah, the tsunami, indeed, Rama," Paul teased playfully.

Anand and the others approached them.

"What's the status of the investigation? The tsunami is bearing down, madam," Kishan spoke to Ramani.

"We've put the case on pause until the tail returns, correct, Paul?"

"We'll discharge Kanya."

"How's she faring?" "Just a shard of memory is absent. She's ready to go."

Moments later, she appeared, fully dressed for her release, striding confidently toward the officers.

"Do you all believe I had a hand in my father's disappearance?" Kanya asked innocently, with eyes as clear as a dolphin's, not a flicker of deceit within them. Goudham watched Ramani and Paul with a smile.

"For now, you should rest until your tale unfurls once more," he advised. "Farewell for now." Ramani and Paul concluded the day. "Are you joining us, Goudham? You're not a police officer anymore."

"Is that so, sir? No longer a police officer?" "It's another tale without a tail. Do you have room for one more in your jeep?" "Absolutely, sir," Anand responded.

"Alright then, Ramani and Paul. I'll bring my official letter to the station tomorrow." The officers strolled away.

"So, I'm unofficially out of uniform," Goudham remarked as he removed his cap.

"What are you all up to?"

"Not us. Nandhu uncle is eager to carry out something before the tsunami strikes."

"What's that, Anand?"

"My underwater escapade. I'm diving in this time." He glanced at Kanya, who regarded him with astonishment, gripping her arm. Though she had lost the memory of his touch, it felt entirely ordinary to her.

"Let's move, everyone." Anand and Kanya made their way, followed by the rest to the jeep.

"Your jeep was green, right?" Kanya recalled. "Yes, I had it repainted black."

The entire region buzzed with urgency as people scrambled to flee the looming tsunami. Evening had fallen, casting the sun in its final embrace of light. The jeep pulled in beneath the Nazi statue.

"Maria, call Christy and relay the news," she rushed to the telephone booth. This time, no one cared if Anand was diving or flying.

"You all stay by grandma and the mushrooms; I'll be right there."

"Okay." Anand pulled Kanya in close, planting a kiss that felt entirely natural.

As he drew back, she beckoned him closer for another kiss.

"Good luck." The jeep and crew ventured across the river.

Anand, clad only in his underwear, slipped into the cool, clear water shimmering with orange hues. His breath was steady, synchronized with the rhythmic ballet of bubbles ascending towards the surface. The world above drifted into a distant memory, while the serene silence of the underwater realm made time feel eternal. He effortlessly glided through the water, each stroke propelling him deeper into a green tapestry of underwater vegetation. Suddenly, an object caught his eye—his own reflection. Swimming closer, he realized it was a mirror, which he grasped tightly. Yet, in his moment of discovery, he lost his sense of direction. Around him, a school of fish danced in graceful formations. Just as breath began to elude him and the world dimmed, his resolve to continue surged. A shadow loomed above him, quickening his pulse—a dolphin! It extended its fins for him to grasp and carried him on its back. He surrendered to this magnificent creature, which guided him toward safety. His friends awaited him on the other side. Just as he felt himself on the brink of unconsciousness, he broke the surface, astonishing the onlookers with his arrival—dolphin and Anand, a pair united! The creature released him gently to his friends, who swarmed to shower affection on the charming animal. With a wide smile and long lips, it radiated warmth and affection. Clapping its flippers, the dolphin gracefully retreated, heading back to the sea.

"Do tsunamis affect dolphins?" "Where did it even come from?" "Well done, Nandhu uncle!" "No, we all did!" Anand remarked, watching the dolphin leave.

"Look what I found!" He revealed the magnifying glass to everyone.

"What is that?" "A mirror." "A mirror? More like a lens!" "Dive down and see for yourself." They all plunged underwater, inspecting their reflection. "Huh, it's definitely a mirror."

"It's a mirror for Maya."

"Absolutely! I heard a family's been crafting these for three centuries," Goudham chimed in.

"Francis, their grandfather. Perhaps it slipped from his grasp at that moment?" Anand faltered, leaving the sentence hanging, the unspoken truth of his demise lingering in the air.

"Did he make it?" Christy and Lucy arrived hurriedly for the spectacle.

"The show's over; the next one's about to begin. How did you two get here?"

"We borrowed Charlie's bike." "So, Nandhu uncle, did you do it or not?"

"That's not the priority. What's our plan for the mirror?"

"Guys," Kanya called, drawing attention.

"Kani! We didn't see you there! How are you? Maria mentioned you have amnesia. Do I ring a bell?" Lucy approached with open arms.

"Actually, I remember something different."

"What is it?" Everyone inquired with keen interest.

"When the spring wave comes, follow the dolphin."

"Who told you that?"

"I can't recall. Those words just resonated with me."

"When the spring wave comes, follow the dolphin... what could that mean?"

Everyone raced toward their vehicles.

"Where to?" "To the beach!" Goudham seized Anand's jeep, speeding away, while Christy and Lucy chased behind. Goudham halted momentarily.

"Where are you headed?" "This is Paathu's home." "Oh, you know them! Bring them along in the jeep!" Goudham dashed to the house where they all sat outside. As he approached, Noora greeted him with a smile, presenting the fabric she had been diligently stitching.

"Deliver this to Maya." The gathered group grasped the significance. Goudham exchanged glances with Khadija, Fathima, and Champakam. Others exited the jeep and joined them.

"We'll wait here. You go deliver it." The silent message was clear as the sound—the dark folks rallied together like sunlight finally breaking through the shadows.

"Shall we hand it over to her?" Goudham suggested to Anand.

"Nandhu uncle, where are your garments?"

"Does that even matter?" He replied, clad only in his underwear, prompting laughter from the others. Anand snatched the bike key from Christy.

"There's plenty of fuel to make it to the dolphin corner." "Indeed."

"Then let's roll." Thus, the man dressed in khaki and the one clad in underwear bolted toward their quest. Anand took the lead on the bike, with Goudham perched behind him.

The sun was embarking on its descent, painting the entire Eerħt in a vibrant orange. Evening air was saturated with fine sand, as the bike's rhythmic hum danced against the silent backdrop. They zipped past a sign that flashed by in a fleeting moment.

'Keep the Beach Clean'

'No Littering'

'Welcome to Sweet Sea'

The way was obstructed with barricades. They bulldozed through them, tearing down each block until they reached the crossroads.

'< Sweet Port-8.08 miles, < Lighthouse-505 meters,

> Dolphin Spot-1.1 miles, > Estuary-3.3 miles.'

The ocean had already retreated into its depths, morphing into a colossal wave that overshadowed the sinking sun.

"Are we too late?"

"Not yet." The bike veered right onto a bridge, a corridor extending into the mystique of the sea.

As they arrived at the bridge's end, the waves had ascended to kiss the sky, poised to engulf them.

"Cast the mirror to her." The bike halted at the brink of the bridge, and Anand flung the mirror into the depths below.

The tumult of the tsunami settled into a gentle embrace, as if the ocean itself sighed in relief. Anand and Goudham inhaled deeply, rejuvenated.

"We've accomplished it." "I believe so." They dismounted their motorcycle, greeted by a breathtaking sunset. The horizon was a canvas of deep black, vibrant blue, and fiery orange, with each hue merging flawlessly into the next, as if time itself lingered to see this enchanting spectacle. The soothing melody of waves caressing the bridge stones filled the atmosphere, while the zephyr carried the briny kiss of the sea.

A colossal turtle appeared, scaling the rocky path to the bridge, its form owning a human head adorned with flowing hair, complemented by arms and legs.

"Maya," Anand and Goudham chimed together.

With one arm cradling a mirror, she peered into it. As she beheld her own reflection beneath the last golden rays, her shell began to fissure, unveiling a wondrous transformation. The mythical being morphed into a stunning woman, resembling an infant fresh from the womb, glistening with life's essence. She pivoted and spread her legs wide, like the pages of a book opening to reveal secrets untold. Between her legs, a yoni blossomed like a third eye, marked by a singular droplet of blood—an embodiment of years filled with sorrowful curses. The enchanting woman rose, her human form radiant and complete. Anand and Goudham found themselves entranced, caught in a dreamlike reverie of her metamorphosis. Goudham presented her with the cloth he owned, and Maya donned the white garment, which complemented her perfectly.

"So, is the curse lifted?"

"Will you join us in Eerħt?"

The excitement bubbled over in the men. She shook her head with a gentle negation.

"Three," the magical woman declared.

"Three," Anand and Goudham echoed, as if enchanted by the name.

"Where is it?" "Where is it?" they clamored, seeking her final revelation. Maya extended her arms towards them. As they grasped her outstretched hands, a new realm unraveled before their eyes.

The ground became sky, where clouds floated serenely, and above lay the sea, undulating with waves. An enchanting inversion of reality awakened, where land-dwelling creature's dove, and aquatic beings soared – the diving ravens and the flying dolphin.

www.ingramcontent.com/pod-product-compliance
Lightning Source LLC
LaVergne TN
LVHW091704070526
838199LV00050B/2280